THE RUNNING TIDE

THE RUNNING TIDE

Cynthia S. Roberts

HEADLINE

First published in Great Britain in 1988
by HEADLINE BOOK PUBLISHING PLC

All characters in this publication are fictitious and any resemblance to real persons, living or dead, is purely coincidental.

British Library Cataloguing in Publication Data

Roberts, Cynthia
The running tide.
I. Title
823'.914[F] PR 6068.014/

ISBN 0-7472-0056-4

HEADLINE BOOK PUBLISHING PLC
Headline House
79 Great Titchfield Street
London W1P 7FN

Typeset by Alacrity Phototypesetters,
Banwell Castle, Weston-super-Mare.
Printed & Bound in Great Britain by
Richard Clay Ltd, Bungay, Suffolk

To my parents,
Olwen and Redvers Dicks,
with love.

Chapter One

When the wind came in from the sea, it came smelling of iodine and salt and small stranded things decaying at the water's edge. A smell both clean and corrupt. Of life and of death. And nothing was as dead as the girl trapped, face down, in the ebbing tide, hands raking the wet sand as if she had fought, and failed, to keep a last tenuous hold on the living.

The fisherman who found her was old and used to death. It had long lost its power to move him. Yet there was in the soft vulnerability of the nape of the neck a curious pathos. The innocent milky dampness of a child newly bathed. He threw his sack to the sand, hesitated, then bent low to grasp her feet. Her flesh was cold and bare, the bones beneath fragile as the skeleton of a bird. He had a sudden fear that he would hear the crack of bone beneath his hands, but the only sounds were the blur of flesh on sand and the suck of the retreating tide. He dragged her to the dry sand above the water line. Then, without a backward glance, went to retrieve his sack. He supposed that he should tell someone, but there was work to do, and the needs of the living were more urgent. He began to tramp across the wide sickle of the bay to where a scar of black rock erupted from the sea.

He was aware that he made a strange sight. He had no personal vanity, and there was no one left to make him care. He was a big man, thickly bearded, flesh still firm on a frame barely shrunken by age. Summer and winter saw him in the same clothes, colourless flannel shirt, and stiff moleskin trousers tied with leather thongs, and rasping like the rubbing of dry old bones, above heavy boots. The boots, waxed with dubbin and stained with sea water, had grown deformed to his awkwardness of feet. Over all, even on the hottest day, went a black alpaca overcoat, faded in its creases to brown, like liquorice. And upon his shoulders, as if it grew there, stiff with dried blood and fish scales, a jute sack, its base oozing freshly severed fish heads and gut for the predatory gulls.

They screeched and wheeled overhead as he walked, or circled behind him as in the wake of a ship until, grizzly spoils emptied upon the sand, bloody in beak and claw, they fed, to rise up screaming their triumph. He had a grudging admiration for them, a kinship of independence and spirit. He liked their arrogance. The relentless selfishness that ensured their survival. Once, when he saw them curved white against grey storm clouds, he had been shaken almost to tears by their perfection. But, even in that moment, he had known that they held no affection for him. If he never saw them again, they would not mourn. They would search elsewhere, fighting, killing, tearing at dead flesh, scavengers of the sea. The only difference in him and them was that to him survival scarcely mattered. To them it was all. Aggression was born in their blood, and would die only when every last drop was stilled in their veins. What matter if people called them carrion, feeders upon corrupt flesh? We all feed one upon the other. At least their cruelty was conscious and cleansed even as it destroyed.

He knew, right enough, what people called him. Never his given name, Jeremiah. That had long been forgotten. But from it, and his ever present sack, some alehouse wit had spawned, 'Lamentations Fish'. So Lamentations Fish he had become and would very likely die. No doubt they would carve it upon his tombstone, as if preserving it in stone might give substance to what was gone. Or was it the weak cry of the living, fearful that they too must pass into nothingness?

To be preserved, briefly, in the living should be enough. If, which he doubted, there was eternal, unchanging life after death, he wanted none of it; it was enough to struggle through three score years and ten, let alone for ever.

He began wading through the small ripples, bending to gather his night-lines from the shallows, the early morning sun reddening a pool of blood about his feet. As he snapped them off the hooks, the bodies of the fish glowed in the changing light, iridescent as the inside of a shell. In death, they were obscenely beautiful, save for the slack mouths and the dull filmed emptiness of the eyes.

He had thought himself inured against death. Yet remembrance was an ache in his breastbone, then physical pain so acute that tears burned his eyes. He shook them away roughly, tasting the salt on his lips. 'An old man's weakness,' he said aloud. Thirty years on and pity for the wife who died in childbirth, and the son who died with her, stayed under the skin. Fingers picking at an old scar until it bled. He wondered if, in thirty years, some other man would weep for the girl from the sea.

When the pony and cart breasted the dunes, the early morning sky was slashed with red and gold, turning the wet sand into a pool of flame. Dazzled by light, the sturdy Welsh cob stopped, then carefully picked its way down the steep cobbled ramp that led to the bay. Beneath its slithering hooves the pebbles rang with a force and violence of their own, while at its fat rump, a wooden cart clattered and swayed, throwing sparks from its iron wheel rims. The air was clotted with noise and confusion. Baskets rattled upon the cart floor. Hooves drummed. Wheels clanked. Harness jangled. Over all rose the shrill cries of the gulls and of the tense figure wedded to the brake as pony and cart trembled to a halt on the damp sand. The cob pricked up its ears, and snorted delicately, nostrils wide, pink underlip bared in a snort of triumph.

The occupant steadied the woven frails and leapt down from the cart. Shapeless beaver cap slipped awry, loosing a fall of sloe-coloured hair. The face beneath was fine-boned, but redeemed from delicacy by over-wide cheekbones and mouth. The eyes were deep-set under thick brows and of a clear washed blue that spilled over into the whites, giving them the unnerving luminosity of a child's. The hands that soothed the rough mane were long, but coarsened with work and weather. The nails worn but clean, as were the grotesque garments bunched under a sackcloth apron, and the sea-stained boots crosslaced to the knees.

She was, perhaps, eighteen or nineteen years of age, but, from her eyes, might have been judged older. She had few expectations of life, and less illusions. Surviving was hard, harder for the poor, and hardest of all for a woman alone. True there was a woman upon the throne of England, with her German prince. Victoria, and her beloved Albert, with their pastel-cheeked infants, so dear to the painters. She patted the cob's wet nose. Perhaps it was easier to preach diligence and cleanliness when you lived in a palace. Who would remind you that child prostitutes were sold in those very streets where you rode out in your carriage? That children toiled from dawn to dusk in coal mines and brickyards, or slept in the filth of gutters?

Poverty was an immutable fact of life, like birth and death. The poor envied the rich. The rich despised the poor as thriftless, or purged their own excesses with useless charity. Neither knew the other. What was that rhyme the village children said?

'God bless the squire and his relations,
And keep us all in our proper stations.'

She laughed aloud and the pony, startled, walked on, wheels rutting the wet sand, sniffing the wind, soft breath forming vapour clouds in the cool morning air. The girl felt the joy of its freedom, the salt breeze whipping the skin to rawness, the vast emptiness of sea and sand. So must it have been when God created heaven and earth, with everything untried and new.

The cob, sure of its way, had halted between the tide and the black-scarred rocks, pawing the sand. The girl unlaced her boots and threw them into the cart. Then she hitched her skirts above her bare legs, and tucked them thigh-high into the belt around her waist. From the floor of the cart she took an old rusting sieve, a wooden rake, and one of the loose-woven willow frails. Laying them upon the sand, she began to rake the surface of the cockle beds, until the clusters of fan-shaped shells appeared, and with her bare hands scooped them into the sieve. When it was full enough, she carried it to a sand-pool at the base of the rocks, riddling away the sand in the clear water until the ridged shells showed yellow, brown and cream. She dried them roughly on her sacking apron, and put them carefully into the frail. She worked sedulously and quietly, moving from place to place, taking only so many from each bed. As she walked, the brown cob followed, nuzzling her gently from time to time, to remind her of its presence. The work was monotonous and back-breaking, her thighs ached and grew stiff, but still she worked on, filling basket after basket with her spoils, and replacing them in the cart. She began to sweat with the effort. She felt it beading her upper lip and running from her hairline, misting her lashes. She wiped it away roughly with the heel of her hand, grains of sand abrasive against her skin. Her hair clung damply, and the wet hem of her dress and petticoats flayed her legs, chafing them raw. The sacking apron was no longer of use. She rinsed it carefully in a rock pool, and draped it over the shallow side of the cart to dry, securing it with a pebble. Her hands, sucked white by sea water, were minutely wrinkled, like the hands of an old woman, skin flaccid and dead.

The cob, alerted, raised its head and neighed a warning.

'I am sorry to startle you.' The old man had dropped his sack on the sand and was shifting awkwardly. 'They call me Lamentations . . .'

'And what do you call yourself?'

'Jeremiah Fleet.'

'Jeremiah,' she nodded, 'And I am Rebecca. Rebecca de Breos.' She offered her hand.

He hesitated, then took it in his own. 'A fine name for a fine lady.' Faded grey eyes looked into clear blue. His lips twitched. Mirth bubbled within her, and soon they were laughing, uncontrollably, at the absurdity of it, she, still holding her aching rib cage, he, wiping away tears with his coat sleeve.

'It's a long time since I have laughed like that,' he said. 'I seem to have lost the habit . . .' He picked up his sack. 'I am sorry,' he apologized, awkwardly, 'I mean the old stench . . . and the way I look.'

'In a manner of speaking, we are in the same business.' She motioned towards the cart. 'I had thought to have it painted with "Purveyor of Crustaceans to the Gentry". Only there was not enough room.'

'With a crest of cockles?'

'Aye. Rampant.'

They smiled, companionably.

'You are a kind girl. Would you do a further kindness?'

'That depends upon what you ask.'

'There is a dead girl, over on the far side of the beach, by the dunes.'

'Drowned?'

'I daresay. Could you take her in your cart? To the constable in the village. He'll know what to do. It would be wrong to leave her here, do you see? The tide would take her, or the gulls might ...'

'Yes,' she said, quickly, 'I'll take her.'

'Not afraid of the dead, are you?'

'They do less harm than the living. If you'll wait until I've fastened my boots ... I'd feel tidier.'

She clambered on to the cart, rearranging the baskets, making room. She lay the washed apron on the floor of the cart.

He declined her offer to ride, or to take his sack, and trudged beside her in silence. When they approached the dead girl, the pony held back, stubbornly.

'Walk on!' she commanded, tugging at the reins, but he pawed the sand, and snorted, and refused to budge.

'Leave him be,' Jeremiah advised, 'animals sense things people cannot understand.'

He walked down and lifted the dead girl, turning her over very gently.

'Poor little maid.' He wiped the dried sand from her face, and the pale, sightless eyes. 'Know her, do you?'

'No. I have never seen her before.'

'Much of an age with you, I'd say.'

She shivered, involuntarily.

'Cold, are you?'

'No. Someone walked over my grave ...' She stopped, raw with shame.

'I've never seen her, either,' he said quickly, 'I'm sure of it. Not from around here, would you think?'

'No. Her clothes are too fine ... that little collar is of lace, and all the stitching is beautiful. You can hardly see the thread.' She smoothed the hem of the dress carefully over the bare feet, as if to protect them from the cold. 'Her petticoats, everything, beautiful right down to the skin . . . and look at her hands.'

'No rings.'

'No, but see how soft they are, and pale. She never worked with her hands, I'd lay my life on it.'

'As I'd lay my life that she was not drowned.'

'She must have been. How else . .?'

He shook his head. 'I don't know . . . I've seen too many bodies swollen with drowning. Ugly, discoloured, almost unrecognizable . . . the sea is cruel. It tears the flesh against rocks, and what it doesn't destroy, the gulls and fishes do.'

Rebecca had reached over the dead girl's bodice to where, half hidden in the long damp hair, was a small silver brooch, chased with vine leaves and flowers. The centre was raised, like the lid of a minute box, and hung loosely. She lifted it up. Inside was engraved, '*Ever Thine*'. Suddenly, and shockingly, the dead girl became a real person, someone of warm flesh, who had loved, walked the earth, laughed, wept, as she herself had done. She began to weep now, silently at first, then aloud, helplessly, not knowing if she were crying for the dead girl or herself, or the pathos of the trite, sentimental words that had taken on a new and irrevocable meaning.

'You cry, my girl,' Jeremiah comforted. 'It will do you good. Ease the shock. I shouldn't have asked you.'

'We'd best lift her into the cart,' she said. She hadn't thought that the girl's skin would be so cold, or that the eyes would have such a filmed emptiness, like the eyes of the very old, and sightless, or a new-born animal . . . as if all that had gone before had been wiped away, with the wiping away of life, nothing remaining save the cold flesh, and even that must dissolve into nothingness.

The pony reared as Jeremiah lifted the girl up, its hooves raking the air, a cry breaking deep in its throat.

'Steady!' Rebecca tugged at the bridle. 'Steady, I say!' But the cob trembled uncontrollably, showing the whites of its eyes, ears pulled down, in fear, and still trembled when Jeremiah finally laid her on the sacking on the floor of the cart.

He bent over and stared at the body intently and without speaking for so long that Rebecca grew afraid. Then she heard the sound of his breath being expelled as by a physical blow. She went and stood beside him, still clutching the reins. The girl's hair was spread out on the damp sack-cloth, and on both sides of her throat, dark bruises showed, like the petals of some dismembered flower.

'I could not think what might have happened to her shoes and stockings,' he said, dully, 'for her feet and legs were without a blemish.'

Rebecca knew that she could not bring herself to ride in the cart, and despised herself, and was ashamed. She wondered if it were true that when someone was killed, the face of the killer was trapped for ever deep in the eyes of the victim. 'I will not look at her again,' she thought.

She trudged beside Jeremiah over the rough track that led to the gap in the dunes, its surface silted over with fine sand that the wind sculpted, forming strange, ephemeral shapes. Carved peaks and troughs, their surfaces pocked with rabbit holes, and tufted with spears of marram grass that lacerated the palms if you clutched at them. There were small green plains, with occasional stunted sprigs of pussy-willow, hunched against the wind. And, below, the tangled skeins of dewberries, crimson stems bearing thorns, sharp as little claws, that drew blood. The fruits were like swart blackberries, but sweeter, more succulent, their surfaces misted with bloom.

Rebecca and Jeremiah saw none of this. Only the cob lightened its step on the springing, green turf scented with the creeping thyme and clover it crushed beneath its hooves. They passed the old stone well, its level ruled by the ebb and flow of the tide, the village green, and the Norman church of St John the Baptist, with its crenellated tower. Jeremiah looked instinctively for the sycamore tree, its branches shading the graves that had long since seeded to grass.

'Returned to earth,' he said, and Rebecca nodded, thinking he meant their burden.

It was the sharp clopping of the pony's hooves on the cobbles that the new young constable first heard and then the creak of the cart as it came to rest beneath his window. When he looked out, the white faces of the man they called Lamentations Fish and an unknown girl with streaming black hair were upturned, trustingly, towards him and, on the cluttered floor of the cart, whiter still, the face of a dead girl.

It was a sight so bizarre and unexpected that it stayed with him always. He was to recall it with sorrow, and with gratitude, in the years ahead.

Chapter Two

The constable, Joshua Stradling, struggled out of his nightshirt and hurriedly pulled on his uniform. He ran a hand through his hair, wetting his fingers to rub the crusted sleep from his eyes.

The small whitewashed room flickered with light from an oil lantern hanging over the door outside. It filtered through the window high in the thick stone walls, casting a monstrously deformed shadow at his head. He picked up a chamberstick from the table beside his bed and, igniting a friction match, held it to the wick. Then, his boots striking the bare stone steps, he descended in the fitful light.

The dog in the yard, raked from sleep by the sound of the pony and cart, and its master's footsteps, began to growl deep in its throat, clanking its chain, then giving hard, staccato barks of fear and agitation. The bolt on the thick oak door rasped drily as Joshua pulled it across. Then he doused the candle flame in his fingers, set it down, and went outside. At his command, the dog subsided, whimpering.

Although he was so tall, to Jeremiah the constable seemed like a small boy aroused from sleep, pale hair disarranged, eyelids still heavy and blue-veined over inquisitive eyes. 'For all the world,' he was to say afterwards, 'like a new born, pink-skinned fledgling leaving the nest.'

It was the girl who spoke first. 'This is Mr Jeremiah Fleet,' she said formally. 'He found the body . . . and I am Rebecca de Breos.'

What surprised Joshua more than the loveliness of her eyes was the unexpected beauty of her voice. It held no traces of the soft, local lilt. It was deep, warm, well modulated. He realized that he must have been staring at her fixedly for some time; that she was aware of his discomfiture, and the reason for it.

'Jeremiah found the body,' she repeated, patiently.

'I see. Where was this?'

They answered his questions politely and briefly, volunteering nothing. Yet Joshua was aware, with some irritation, that it was they who were somehow dictating the course of the interview. Despite their bizarre appearance, there was an innate dignity about them. Some quality they shared which he was unable to define; an arrogance, almost.

He apologized for not having invited them in at once, but would they care to come, now? Jeremiah declined on account of his clothing; Rebecca asked simply how she was expected to leave the pony unattended, adding, 'What of the body?' Perversely, Joshua was as aggrieved by their refusal as by the inference that he was neglecting his duties.

'The body?' he echoed.

'What exactly do you want us to do with it?' Rebecca persisted.

Jeremiah knew that the lad was but one and twenty years of age and had been appointed constable by the vestry less than a week. He was rumoured to be the son of a wealthy farmer in the vale of Glamorgan, and well versed in Latin and Greek. A scholar, or so it was said, destined for some great university. God alone knew what circumstance had brought him to this ... well: Latin and Greek were small comfort to him now!

'Should we take her to the carpenter, perhaps?' prompted Jeremiah.

'The carpenter?'

'He makes coffins and tends to the bodies, too. An undertaker.'

'Would he keep the body for me? Until the time of burial? I have to inform the justices and the Home Office doctor ... there will be an inquiry.'

'Best we come with you,' Jeremiah advised. 'For I know well enough how best to deal with Ezra the Box. Close-fisted and mean, he is, to the dead and to the living!'

Rebecca glanced towards the dead girl on the cart. 'Will it have to be a pauper's burial?' she asked bleakly.

The constable shrugged, helplessly. 'Perhaps someone will claim her.'

'And if they don't?'

Nobody answered.

'Come then,' said Jeremiah, briskly, 'it will soon be getting light. People will be about their business. Give the poor maid some quiet and dignity. She will not have it long.'

They walked on, an ill-matched trio, meshed in thought.

Jeremiah tried to lighten the tension. 'Some swear that old Ezra the Box is so mean that if the angel Gabriel himself ordered a coffin, Ezra would make him fly it to the graveyard, then charge him twice for the horses!'

Neither Rebecca nor the constable looked up.

Outside one of the cottages, a lean cat was crouched over a fish-head, its one good eye giving it a raffish, debauched look, as if permanently winking at the idiocies of life. The cat glanced up as they passed, then went on eating, fastidiously, needle teeth exposed. The constable suspected that Jeremiah had provisioned it.

As they neared the carpenter's shop, an old man was extinguishing a cruse oil lamp, and the rancid smell of fish liver oil hung in the air.

'I have heard say that in some towns, like London and such, the streets are lighted by flames of gas, and it is as bright as day, even in the middle of the night,' marvelled Jeremiah. 'A man with a snuffer on a long pole has to come and put them out, else they would burn for ever. Very satisfying to be able to light the world, or plunge it into darkness ... like being God!'

'Pity crime couldn't be snuffed as easily,' the constable observed, drily.

'Ah, but then you would be out of a job.'

'Good morning to you,' called out the old man as the cart drew near, 'it is going to be a beautiful day. You can feel it in the air. The sort of day when you feel glad to be alive.'

Jeremiah and the constable watched as Rebecca drove away in the cart. She had crumpled the sackcloth apron angrily, and bundled it out of sight behind the frails of shellfish. She knew that she would never feel able to use it again.

'I shall need to speak to you again,' the young constable said.

'Then I shall hold myself ready. You will know where to find me.' And she had driven away, glad to be out in the fresh air and clear of the odious Ezra, whose ingratiating unctuousness to the constable, whom he recognized as a gentleman, and scorn for Jeremiah, had made her seethe with fury. Her only reluctance was in leaving the dead girl with him. He was a prurient, slimy, little toad of a creature. Even to touch a woman would be to defile her. She prayed, most earnestly, that someone would come and claïm the girl.

The constable, too, concluded that Ezra the Box was even more detestable than Jeremiah had claimed. With his attenuated features, beady eyes and small pointed teeth, he reminded Joshua irresistibly of a sleek, vicious little ferret, battening, as he did, upon dead flesh.

'Will you return with me to the beach?' Joshua asked Jeremiah, 'to try and show me where she was found... how she was lying, before the tide turns and takes away all traces of her.'

'If that is your wish,' Jeremiah had answered, formally. 'I shall need to go home however, and wash. Make myself tidy.'

'Come back with me,' the constable urged, 'I have to unchain the dog. You can clean up at the well, in the yard.'

Jeremiah nodded assent.

'By the way, Jeremiah, my name is Joshua. Joshua Stradling.'

'So I heard tell from one of the farmers on the vestry.'

'Will you not call me Joshua then?'

'It would not be fitting. I shall call you Constable, or Mr Stradling.'

Rebuked, Joshua turned to hide a smile. They walked in silence for a time.

'Like Boadicea, she was, standing upright there in her chariot. Full of dignity ... but spirited, too. Plenty of spirit.'

Joshua did not need to ask whom he meant.

When they returned to the house, he motioned Jeremiah to follow him outside to the bailey, and persuaded him to drop his sack alongside the privy midden, hoping that the odour of stale dung and fish might cancel each other out. Then, with the old man's help, he dredged up some buckets of water from the well, and they sluiced themselves thoroughly, splashing their faces and bodies, plunging their arms into the bucket up to their elbows, and drying themselves on some old flour sacks, kept for the purpose. He was chastened to see that Jeremiah's flesh and undergarments were scrupulously clean.

The constable left him making friends with the dog, a bull terrier, chained to an iron ring in the corner of the yard. Jeremiah advanced slowly and confidently, holding his palm outstretched before him, all the time talking soothingly and reassuringly.

When Joshua returned carrying a notebook and pencil, Jeremiah had filled the bull terrier's bowl with water from the well, and was squatting down running his hands expertly over the animal's flanks.

'He'll do,' he said, shortly, 'best take him with us.' He unhooked the dog's chain, and bent to look into the animal's slanting eyes. 'Ugly little bugger,' he said. 'We are two of a kind. Not much to look at, but sturdy enough. And once we get our teeth into anything, we never let go.'

Joshua thought it a fair assessment. A loyal friend, but an implacable enemy.

They went out into the street, Jeremiah firmly holding the dog's chain. The constable locked the bailey gate and followed them, pleased, but aggrieved, that they had taken to each other.

'I knew a girl, once,' Jeremiah reminisced, 'with eyes like his: bare-looking around the edges, except that her eyes were pink. Her hair was white, not yellow, pure white, and like fine dandelion fluff. I always said she looked like a white mouse.'

'What happened to her?'

'She died. Cholera. Funny thing to think of her turning black. Perhaps it was as well that she went. No one would have wanted her. People don't if you are different . . .'

There, in essence, Joshua thought, two of life's cruellest fallacies: that only the articulate feel, and only the beautiful deserve to love and be loved.

'Come on,' he ordered, brusquely, 'we ought to be stepping out!'

As they skirted the village green with its small inns, brew-house and low ribbons of stone-faced cottages, Joshua looked up at the church tower, its crenellations as neatly clipped as if some giant hand had wielded a scissor. It always reminded him of a wooden fort he had once owned as a child, with an army of painted soldiers, some with scarlet jackets peeling and dulled, or rubbed featureless, a missing arm or leg marked by a ragged wound. Jeremiah, winding the dog's chain hard round his palm, willed himself not to think of the grass-edged plot behind the high stone wall, sunlight filtering leaves to a dappled shade.

The dog, chain now comfortably loosened again, relieved himself against the rough stone of the wall on the boundary, balancing on three stout bandy legs, releasing a steady golden stream.

'Fine performance,' said the constable, severely, 'polluting the drinking water of half the village!'

'They'll sup on worse before they die.' Jeremiah jerked his head towards the church, 'some of it harder to swallow!'

They had tracked off now, to the edge of the dunes. The old man and the dog were already part way up a sandhill, feet sinking in the fine, white-bleached grains. Joshua watched them struggle to the top, as if their feet were heavily weighted in lead. The dog did not look back. He followed them, pausing only to take off his boots and knot their laces together, hanging them across his neck, like a yoke, and thrust his socks in his pocket. As he climbed, snaking briars of dewberries tore at his bare feet, raking them with globs of blood. He reached the top, shaking his feet so that the drops of blood ran, stranding small barbs on the skin. Then, unexpectedly, he found himself running down the other side, like a child exhilarated by freedom, faster and faster, swift as a wind.

'Stop, man!' Jeremiah cried out. 'Stop, I tell you, for God's sake!'

Joshua, hearing the rawness in his voice, tried to check his speed, and somehow they were both down, in a tangle of arms and legs, curses and flesh, pierced with the dog's barking.

'What in the name of hell?' he exploded.

'Hisht, man! Hold your bloody dog, if you value him.' Jeremiah pushed through the scrub and brambles to a small outcrop of willows, bending one branch in his great hands until it cracked like bone. He thrust it into the undergrowth. A sharp clanging of metal, and the branch lay severed rawly in his hand. Then a massive kick forced the gin trap on to bare sand, to lie exposed.

'Best put your boots on,' he said, drily. 'Here, give me the dog.'

Sickness burned in Joshua's throat, and the chain shook as he handed it over.

'Bloody lunatics!' Jeremiah said, harshly, 'I've seen animals so wild with terror that they'd gnaw off a limb to be free.'

Joshua warily approached the menacing object.

'Leave it,' Jeremiah ordered, 'it will do no harm, now, and it can be seen, but mark you, I shall be coming back, watching and waiting. I have a score to settle.'

'That's the law's work, mine!'

'No! This is a personal score.' He thrust the dog's lead into Joshua's hands, then rolled down his long, woollen stockings. A raised, livid scar disfigured his flesh. 'I have reason to know how it feels.'

'An animal trap?'

'Man trap, but it's all the same. Same blood, same fear. It's the men who set them who are the animals!'

'Do you know who set it?'

'Oh yes, I know. I was a young lad at the time, twelve or thirteen, perhaps. I had gone into the woods to get some kindling for the fire . . . I swear to God now, as I swore then, that I had never stolen a thing in my life. Not poached a rabbit, or a bird. It seemed to me that old, dead wood, rotting on the ground, was of little account, and we had need of a fire.'

'What happened?'

'When my father found me, late into the night, I heard him call out, but there was no strength in me to answer back. He had to leave me in the dark while he went home for an iron bar. He could not leave the lantern for fear the light should be seen . . .

'Well, it was the blacksmith got me out. A huge man he was. I remember him now, levering at the iron jaws until the veins stood out on his neck, and his eyes seemed to start right out of his head. And all the time he was crying like a child, and I was trying to comfort him, saying that I felt no pain. My father was holding the lantern, and his hand shook so that the light danced about like fireflies, and the smith swore at him, and told him to hold it steady.'

'And after they got you out?'

'The teeth of the trap had eaten right through my leather boots, I recall, and I had been there so long I had wet my trousers ... well, to tell you the honest truth, I had dirtied them, too. When my father lifted me up it ran down my legs. I cried then, for shame, and it was the only time I cried ... So we went home. Three miles or more it was, through woods and fields, and track. My father carried me every inch of the way. The blacksmith offered to take me, for my father's hands were raw, where he had torn at the trap, but it was as if he had not heard ... Not a word did he say, not all the way home, except to thank the blacksmith for his trouble. He had wrapped me in an old sheet; white it was at first, but releasing the trap had made the wounds bleed again, and it grew sodden red. I remember thinking that blood was darker than I thought, and being afraid that with so much blood lost, my body would collapse, flat, like air from a pig's bladder ...'

'But the doctor ... did they not take you to his house?'

'He was one of the justices,' Jeremiah said simply. 'A trading justice, you might say ...'

It did not need explanation. Joshua already knew too much of the lower orders, whose sole purpose in seeking election was financial gain.

'Could your father not have approached the Lord of the Manor? Or the chief of the justices?'

Jeremiah marvelled at such innocence. 'Was it not on his own land that it happened?' he demanded. 'No, I grant you he would not have primed the trap, or set a spring-gun in the undergrowth, to kill or maim ...'

'You suppose he knew?' demanded Joshua.

'The one who set it was a poor, witless wreck of a man, with neither the money, nor the stomach, for man traps.'

They walked on in silence.

'You reckon he should not have done it?' said Jeremiah. 'Not acted against one of his own kind? Should have been a man?

How much of a man can you be when your children are sick, or hungry, and you own nothing? Not the stones of your house, nor parcel of land? Neither the food you eat, nor the kindling for your fire . .?'

'What became of him?'

'He was beaten soundly, one dark night, on his way home with a jug of cwrw da. It was rumoured that his backside was branded with the same mark as his master's sheep, although no one had any knowledge of who could have done it. But thereafter, there was never a child, maid, nor man harmed by trap or spring-gun, for there was a map at the forge with all their locations upon it.'

'And his master, the justice?'

'He took his pew at the church, and appointed the vicar, and very often dictated the course of the sermons, and I continued to raise my cap to him, coming and going. That is what happened. Oh, and if he passed by on horseback, or driving out in his carriage, I stood very still, in case he could see I was limping . . .'

Joshua handed him the dog's chain. 'But things have improved?'

'Yes, indeed. By the time my own son was born, there was a more merciful law. Any cottager poaching a rabbit, or found with a net on him, could be transported for seven years. Only, there was no law to protect the cottagers. Our great English judges, in all their wisdom, deliberated long and hard, and came to the conclusion that man traps and spring-guns were legal. But you know all of that. You are a constable and a scholar.'

Joshua kicked at a stone. 'Books are a poor substitute for experience.'

'But at least they don't cripple you . . .'

The dog had wrenched the chain from Jeremiah's hand, and had started to scratch, furiously, at the edge of a rabbit burrow. Jeremiah jerked him back hard, but the animal strained and barked, pulling so much that the links tightened cruelly around his neck, making him wheeze and choke, eyes bulging.

Joshua lay flat upon the sand and peered in, but could see

nothing. Remembering the gin trap, he snapped a twig and pushed it into the hole. When he withdrew it there was some bunched up and folded cloth at the entrance. He shook it out. It was a light cloak, such as ladies wear over thin dresses. More probing revealed a pair of high buttoned shoes and fine woollen stockings.

'She was killed here, then,' Jeremiah said, grimly.

'It would seem so . . .' agreed Joshua.

'It was just over the next dune, along the sea's edge that I found her,' Jeremiah pointed towards the shore.

'He must have dragged or carried her to the beach.'

'He, or she,' corrected Jeremiah, 'she was a small maid, frail almost, even a woman could have killed her.'

'Maybe, but it does not seem to me a woman's crime. A knife, perhaps, or a blow in a fit of passion, but this needed time, deliberation . . .' Joshua bundled the shoes and stockings in the cloak, tied it securely, and placed it under his arm. 'Best show me where you found her.'

'Wait, there is something I want to say,' Jeremiah began. 'You may accept or refuse, as you please . . . It seems to me that you are a young man, new to this place. That you are bright, honest, painstaking, I have no doubt, but you are also a stranger, and worse, a gentleman, and there is no way you can hide it.'

As Joshua started to protest, Jeremiah insisted, 'No. It is a fact. I neither admire you nor condemn you for it, for it is none of your own doing. But I . . . I can go to places where you cannot. Speak to people freely. Observe. I am simply Lamentations Fish, part of the landscape. Not a person, and so, invisible.'

Joshua listened carefully.

Jeremiah continued, 'I offer you my services, for the little they are worth. Freely. Tell me where you wish me to go. School me in what you wish me to say. I will willingly help you if you will have me. I would not have a little maid of mine treated as that poor child, and perhaps there is no one to speak for her . . .'

'I would consider your help, as your friendship, a rare privilege, and I thank you for it. Here is my hand on it.'

They clasped hands, as best they could, Jeremiah burdened as he was with the dog, and Joshua with the dead girl's clothing, and, for both of them, their burdens seemed immeasurably lightened.

Chapter Three

After Jeremiah had returned to the constable's house, and retrieved his sack, he praised the bull terrier lavishly, saw him comfortably fed and watered, and left, smiling.

Joshua was richer by two large and succulent sea bass, making a welcome change from salted herring, which seemed to be the mainstay of the local diet, and a taste Joshua was reluctant to acquire, since the shore was teeming with fish, crabs, lobsters, prawns. Even the rock pools, especially those at the far Port end of the parish, towards Sker, were rimmed with blue-black clusters of mussels, and smaller periwinkles, while the sandy inlets yielded plump, easily gathered cockles.

He supposed the liberal consumption of salted herrings had some bearing on the copious quantities of cwrw da consumed. Joshua had already sampled that heavy intoxicating blend of ale, peculiar to the principality and brewed at the brewhouse overlooking the village green, and could testify to its potency. The smell of the bruised hops and fermenting yeast seemed to permeate air, soil, and even the stones of the surrounding buildings. It hung over the pavements like some ever present miasma. Such was its potency that Joshua was half persuaded that anybody who tarried long enough was in danger of intoxication from the fumes alone. As for the men who brewed it, whose perquisites included unlimited draughts consumed on the premises, the wonder was that they were capable of doing any work at all! One workman, it was claimed, had fallen head first into a great cask of the brew. Unable to swim, he gulped great quantities of it and, upon rescue, had to be forcibly restrained from diving back. This only enhanced the legend of the superiority of the local brew, and even the rumour that Ezra the Box used it as an embalming fluid barely caused a hiccup in sales.

Joshua skirted the brewhouse now, on his way to call upon Rebecca de Breos in her cottage in the lea of the dunes. He glanced up at the chimney of local brick, colours blending through terracotta and pink to the deep, bruised blue of mussel shells. He felt content with his lot. He was at home in this place; at one with the rugged coastline and the people. It was hard to believe that he had been here barely a week.

Rebecca de Breos, forewarned by Jeremiah, awaited the arrival of the constable. The cob, newly groomed, fed and watered, was settled in the stable, and Rebecca's morning's spoils, copiously rinsed and boiled in well-water, had already been taken to the grocer's in the village. From there, some would be transported by horse and trap to the market at Bridgend, and sold from one of the many market stalls dealing in butter and cheese from the farms, eggs and vegetables brought by the villagers, and fish such as Jeremiah's and her own. The rest would be sold over the counter of the village shop, to those cottagers too busy or infirm to gather their own, or who simply rebelled at the prospect of the long boiling.

The great, round oven, made of bricks, was still hot from the cockle-boiling. It was primitively fashioned, but effective and cheap to fuel. In essence, it was a simple ring of bricks, layer upon layer, with a gap for the driftwood collected along the shore. Into the well of the bricks was fitted a large iron bowl, and over all went a cover of scrubbed wood. When the driftwood was fired and the water boiling, the cover was laboriously removed, and the cockles left to boil or simmer for hours, with an occasional infusion of well-water when it grew dangerously dry. The stoking was tiring, for the boiler was greedy, and the heat intense, but, over the years, Rebecca had come to know its moods and vagaries, and they co-existed, if not in harmony, then in a state of armed truce.

The boiler still being warm, Rebecca had placed therein three small loaves, and replaced the cover, and now the crusty aroma of baking bread scented the air. It could not, however, drown the heavy all-pervading smell of shellfish. Rebecca grew herbs and heavily scented cottage flowers, like mignonette and rue, in the sandy borders, but it was of little use. She sometimes thought that, for her, heaven would be simply a place with no boiler, no cockles. No other refinements would be required.

She took a basket from the stone shelf of the larder, and

carried it out into the yard. In the stable, at the far corner, the cob came to the door and whinnied a greeting. He nuzzled her delicately, and she stroked his smooth neck, murmuring endearments, then kissed the flesh-pink edge of his nose.

She was lifting the awkward wooden cover of the boiler when the constable arrived, on foot. She felt hot and ungainly, but he seemed not to notice. He took the cover and made it safe against the wall, while she lifted out the clay flower pots containing the loaves. She loosened the bread by tapping sharply on the edge of the brick, and placed the loaves on a cloth in the basket. This done, she bade him follow her indoors.

'I love the smell of fresh bread,' he confessed. 'It reminds me of my childhood.'

She motioned him to be seated, and took the basket to the larder. When she returned, he stood up to greet her, holding his helmet close to his breast.

'Is this an official visit?' she asked.

'No. A meeting between friends . . . but I confess I have a small favour to beg.' He had been looking round the room appreciatively. It was large, and low-beamed, the walls white-washed. There was none of the usual clutter of bric-a-brac, heavy furniture, or dusty fabrics. It was clean, light, spare to the point of bareness. What furniture there was appeared small and delicate; an elegant table, some shield-back chairs, a small satinwood writing desk with reeded legs, and some hanging bookshelves with fretted sides. There were a number of delicate, enamel boxes upon a side table, and, on the walls, one or two gentle water colours, and a pencil drawing of a man. It was a face of great power and vitality, which seemed centred in the wide, almost hypnotic, eyes. The rest of the features seemed blurred almost to the point of weakness, as if effacing themselves, unable to compete. The mouth, which was full, could have been generous or weak, the nose straight, the bone-structure finely drawn, almost feminine. Yet the overall impression was one of strength.

'Your father?' Joshua asked.

'Yes, I drew it from memory. After his death.'

'It is vivid. Alive.'

'I felt I needed to do it ... an exorcism, perhaps.'

'A way to get rid of the hurt and bewilderment?'

She nodded. 'I was angry with him for going away and leaving me.'

'Do you think you could draw a likeness of the dead girl? It would be a help to take with me when I meet people and question them.'

'If it will help. But that was not the favour you came to beg of me?'

'No. Jeremiah suggested that there were things that he could do better ... mixing with men in the quarries, listening to them talking in the alehouses, off their guard.'

'He is probably right. In rough company, you would stand out like a cock upon a dunghill!'

'I am not sure that the comparison places me very high in your esteem.'

'If you look for flattery, then you must look elsewhere. My help I shall gladly give you.'

'Then I shall be grateful for that.'

She seated herself, and bade him do likewise.

'I believe, like Jeremiah, that there are places where I could go, where I would be less remarked upon: the milliner's and straw bonnetmaker's in the village, the dressmaker's workshop, the haberdasher's ...'

'True, I have not much need of a straw bonnet.' He smiled, and placed his helmet upon the floor.

'Nor yet, of corsets, I fancy.' Her lips curved, irresistibly, at the thought. 'But have no fear, I shall not present you with an extravagant account ...'

'And, if you did, the good vestrymen would choke upon their ale in the "Crown" and the "Ancient Briton", and very likely die of apoplexy.'

'Or levy a rate. For strengthening the foundations!'

They laughed together, and then he grew grave.

'Forgive me. I had not thought that my coming here, alone, might compromise you in the eyes of your neighbours.'

'Such friends as I have would not believe ill of me, and those who would, I have no need of,' she said simply.

'But living alone makes you vulnerable.'

'No ... being lonely makes you vulnerable, and I am not that. Loneliness has nothing to do with people.'

'You think not?'

'I know it. It comes from within oneself.' She motioned to the books on the hanging wall shelves. 'You see, I have friends all about me, to suit every mood of mine. They ask nothing of me, never argue with me, nor condemn, and I do not disappoint them.'

'A poor substitute for flesh and blood friends. If they make demands of you, they also give support, pleasure, kindness.'

'I have seen little enough of it.'

'Perhaps you have not looked in the right places.'

She shrugged.

'Tell me,' he said, standing now, and studying the titles of the books carefully, 'who was it who taught you to read ... Latin, Philosophy, the Classics ..?'

She said wrily, 'You have forgotten, "and a little Greek".'

He felt himself flushing.

'My father believed that, "A mind in its own sphere, and in itself, can make a heaven of hell, and a hell of heaven".' Rebecca smiled, remembering.

'And you, what do you believe?'

'That learning by rote is of little use, but learning to think and reason can make the dullest, most hated, task bearable.'

'You are thinking of your shellfish gathering. Why then do you choose it?'

'I do not choose it, as you say. I do it because I must; simply in order to live! Surprisingly, there is small demand for a kitchen maid with a knowledge of Greek, or washerwomen well versed in *The Iliad*.'

He felt the anger under her scorn. 'Forgive me, it was a foolish question.'

'As foolish as those who patronize me because I am a woman, and work as I do.'

'Agreed.'

'Or those who declare learning, and intelligence, to be wasted upon women.'

'Most certainly.'

She was unsure if he spoke in mockery.

‘Your house is very pleasant,’ he observed. ‘Spare, elegant, plenty of space . . . a good place to relax.’

‘It is spare through necessity. This is all that remains of the furnishings that my father brought with him. Much was sold to pay debts, and more, during my father’s illness . . . But you are right. It suits me well.’

They regarded one another in silence, each waiting for the other to speak.

‘Where would you like me to begin my enquiries,’ she asked, finally, ‘and when?’ But before he could make a reply, she said, quickly, ‘If you would care to discuss it over a meal, you are welcome to eat with me.’

‘I would be greatly pleased.’

‘It will be frugal enough. Some fresh bread, and butter which I bartered at the farm. A conserve of damsons, and some buttermilk.’

‘A feast, Miss de Breos,’ he said, ‘to one who has learnt to survive on salt-herring, and the smell of the brewhouse.’

‘Will you not call me Rebecca?’ she asked, ‘For if we are to be partners in this adventure, there is no call for over-great formality.’

‘Rebecca,’ he said, gravely, ‘I am Joshua. It is a rare privilege to make your acquaintance.’

They shook hands, solemnly.

‘I shall reserve my judgement until I see how hard you are going to work me!’ She had busied herself with setting the cloth upon the table, and bringing out crockery and cutlery.

‘I had hoped,’ he teased, slyly, ‘that there might be fresh cockles.’

‘Wash your mouth out with lye,’ she said, severely, ‘for using such a disgusting word.’

Joshua was still reflecting upon the paradox that was Rebecca de Breos the next day as he made his way past the village green and up the steep incline of Clevis Hill to the doctor’s house.

She was totally unlike the coy, posturing, young gentlewomen of his acquaintance, whose lives, pursuits, and even mode of dress and speech were rigidly circumscribed by social convention. She was direct, without archness. Independent as no other woman he had met. Despite the roughness of her clothes and occupation, she was educated beyond the sphere of many men. She was also unusually beautiful. Joshua could not get the picture of her dark vitality, and the arresting blue of her eyes, out of his thoughts.

He reluctantly turned his attention to his first official meeting with authority. He was sure that Dr Obadiah Mansel would hardly be impressed by a newly-hatched, still bewildered, constable, awkwardly finding his way. Neither could he be bluffed by spurious confidence. Joshua wondered how he should act? Respectful, but not servile; receptive, but not unquestioning; firm, but not aggressive. Well, that would do for a start.

The Home Office physician's house, as with Joshua's, was in the oldest part of the parish, Newton. This was the only similarity. Situation, height and substance faithfully reflected their respective situation in society.

Joshua's cottage was simple, primitive and low lying. Dr Obadiah Mansel's was large, dominant, and set on a commanding hill overlooking the village. Joshua's dwelling abutted the highway, and boasted a privvy midden, a cobbled bailey and a patch of compacted dirt, euphemistically termed 'the garden'. Its sole decorations were the tiny well, and a few wind-scattered marigolds.

Dr Obadiah Mansel's was, predictably, above the church; if not, figuratively speaking, placed on the right hand of God, it could fairly claim precedence on the left side. It was square, solid, and wore an impressive façade, rather like the physician himself. The garden was screened from the rude gaze of the 'hoi polloi' by an extensive shrubbery, set behind iron railings, suitably barbed. Inside, there were lawns, arbours, with neo-classical statuary, modestly fig-leaved and draped, and neatly incised flower beds. These made Joshua wonder if Dr Obadiah Mansel practised his surgery upon the lawn. The beds themselves were filled with geraniums, or petunias, arranged with the utmost precision. In contrast, the large, domed conservatory looked in danger of collapsing from a superabundance of vegetation. Ferns, climbers, greenery sprouted everywhere; riotous, undisciplined. A glass jungle. This strange dichotomy intrigued Joshua, and puzzled him. Then he concluded that it might be the inspiration of two differing characters: perhaps Dr Obadiah Mansel and his wife. One, restrained, precise, circumscribed; the other, free. It would be interesting to discover which was which.

An adenoidal serving girl let him in. She had a nervous, darting walk, and a pinched face, like a timid shrew. She looked underfed and overworked. She led him to what she called 'the libry', and scuttled away, gratefully.

'Enter!' commanded Dr Obadiah Mansel, who was seated at a vast partners' desk, writing sedulously. 'Ah, Constable Stradling, I believe. Come to get the result of my medical investigations, have you? Sit down, man! Sit down!'

Joshua obeyed instinctively. There was an air of command about the man, completely at variance with his appearance. He was a rotund, busy little man, with plump, baby-soft cheeks, which looked as if they had just been polished with a very soft cloth. His scalp, too, showed shining pink, fringed by a corolla of sparse, fly-away hair. It appeared to Joshua as if the missing hair had all been transferred to his eyebrows, which overhung boiled-gooseberry eyes. Despite their dull, opaque quality, they were amazingly shrewd.

'Odious little man, that undertaker, slimy, little reptile! Brought her here on a handcart, if you please! "Pauper" he called her, "I've brought you the pauper's body". Much rather have had him to dissect!'

Joshua smiled involuntarily, then hastily composed his features.

'A bad business,' Dr Mansel continued, drumming his fingers upon the desk. 'Very bad.'

Joshua agreed.

'First case, is it, Stradling? Hmm . . . thought as much. Ever seen a post mortem?'

'No, sir, I haven't!'

'Like to see her now, then?'

'If you think it necessary.'

'If I think it necessary? Of course it is necessary! If you are dealing with a body, deal with it man! Ought to jump at the chance. This way.'

He leapt to his feet, walking with unexpected lightness towards the door. With his frock coat, stiff collared shirt, and thinly striped legs, Joshua thought he looked absurdly like a beetle which has unexpectedly learnt to walk upright. Dr Mansel turned back to Joshua, 'What's the matter? Not squeamish, are you? Not going to faint on me, vomit, or do anything stupid?'

'No.'

'This way, then. Got your notebook ready, have you? Don't want to have to repeat myself.'

Joshua followed him down a brown-dadoed passageway to a small room which was tiled from floor to ceiling in bottle-glass green. The floor was flag-stoned, presumably for easy scrubbing, and there were clay-lined gutters leading to soak-away drains in the corners. There were shelves with bottles and specimens which Joshua forbore from studying too closely, and glass cases with surgical instruments, known and unknown, which would not have been out of place in a mediaeval torture chamber. There was a small slate-topped table with a moderator oil lamp and assorted glass beakers and phials, medical apparatus, a sink, and in the centre of the room, a vast scrubbed table, upon which the dead girl lay, covered by a blood-spattered sheet. Above, a lighted oil lamp was suspended from heavily bracketed wrought iron chains.

Dr Mansel approached the table, seized the cloth and whipped it away like a conjuror reaching the climax of his act, to reveal the badly mutilated corpse. 'Should have put on my overall and boots. Protection.' he grumbled, making no attempt to do so. Joshua noticed a splash of blood on his otherwise immaculate cuff.

'Right. We'll begin now. No water in the lungs.' He indicated the lacerated chest, then tapped the top of the specimen jar with a plump forefinger, peering at the contents, admiringly; the satisfied artist. 'Excellent,' he enthused. 'Excellent. Beautiful, isn't it?'

Joshua made appropriate noises.

'Now, where was I? Oh yes. No water in the lungs . . . ergo . . . not drowned. Surprise you?'

'No. I had thought . . .'

'Good. Death from what, then?'

'Strangulation ..?'

'Manual strangulation? Man, or woman?'

'I don't know.'

'Guess. I have to be exact ... but you go on, hazard a guess, and tell me why.'

'A man.'

'Indeed? How did you come to that conclusion?'

'It does not seem to me to be a woman's crime.'

'No? Gentle creatures, are they? Incapable of it? Think of nature, man! Scarlet in tooth and claw. The female is the most ruthless, vicious, of all predators. Some species eat their mate after impregnation. After, not before. Still stick to your opinion?'

'Yes.'

'Well, you happen to be right. But it's the size of the bruises at the neck. The pressure, angle ... you understand?'

Joshua nodded.

'Notice her hands ... well formed. No dirt engrained, flesh soft. Certainly never done any manual work. Nails well cared for; sand under them, predictably ... Usual detritus. Small piece of fibre, too.' He picked it up with fine tweezers. 'Wool, not cotton or silk. Ochre brown. From an overcoat or jacket, I'd say.' He placed it carefully into a prepared envelope, and sealed it. 'Now, you will want general information to publish locally. You will investigate every house, I suppose?'

'Yes, certainly.'

'Then you will need to write that she was aged about eighteen or nineteen; weight one hundred and eight pounds, that is with her full complement of organs!' he added, with a grim attempt at humour. 'Well-nourished; not suffering from rickets, obvious diseases, or any skin condition; skin, pale; hair, fair; eyes, light blue. Only distinguishing marks a two-inch scar above the left ankle, and a raised birthmark on her left scapula ... shoulder blade ... dark brown pigmentation, shape of a rough oak leaf. That is the best I can do. The clothes you can see for yourself.'

Joshua, who had been writing copiously in his notebook, thanked him. Obadiah Mansel washed his hands fastidiously at the small sink with its overpump, dried them, and carefully put out the hanging oil lamp, leaving only the moderator lamp aglow.

'We'll leave her in peace.'

For a terrible moment Joshua thought he was going to add, 'not in pieces'.

But all he said was, 'It is post mortems upon the young which affect me most, children, young girls like this, the victims of brutality and violence. I imagine how they must have felt. The terror ... the unexpectedness ...' He pulled himself together, swiftly, mask restored.

He is as vulnerable as the rest of us, Joshua thought.

'I knew your mother, Charlotte, you know,' Dr Mansel said, unexpectedly.

'Did you?'

'Yes. Her father was a surgeon in Cardiff. Your grandfather. I worked with him for a time. A fine man, and dedicated ... contracted smallpox.'

'So I believe.'

'Well, is she?'

Joshua nodded.

'Most beautiful girl I ever saw. There is a look of her in your colouring, about the eyes. Did you know that she wanted to become a surgeon?'

'No. I didn't.'

'As much hope of that as flying to the sun. Fine mind. Pity. Lost on a woman. I was deeply in love with her ...'

There was a rustle of skirts in the corridor behind them, and a shrill-pitched voice instructed, 'Obadiah, your luncheon has been set in the dining room. It is a cold collation ... but the servants require to clear it away.' Joshua she ignored.

'My dear, this is Constable Joshua Stradling. His mother was a very old and dear friend of mine.'

'Really?' There was a cool lack of interest in her tone. 'How very strange.'

This then was the creator of the clinically ordered garden, austere, inflexible. Unlike her husband, she was all angles and darkness.

'Will you not share my luncheon?' offered the doctor, pulling at his cuffs.

'Obadiah, there is blood upon your sleeve,' she accused, with a grimace of distaste. 'I am sure that the constable would be happier eating in his own home and going about his duties.'

'Yes, I am sure that I would.' Joshua agreed, pleasantly.

The doctor looked disappointed. 'Perhaps you would join us another day, for dinner, perhaps ..?'

His wife remained silent.

'Madeleine,' the doctor said, quickly, 'has a great love of gardening ... the conservatory is hers. She grows ferns, orchids, all sorts of exotic leaves and plants. It is her great passion.'

Her only one! thought Joshua, acutely aware of his misjudgement.

The doctor walked with him to the door, then out into the garden. 'The body will be returned to the undertaker,' he said, 'immediately after the inquest, for a Christian burial ...'

'Thank you.'

The older man clasped his hand. 'Tell your mother that I was enquiring after her ... that I have not forgotten her.'

'I will, indeed, sir.'

The shrewd, opaque eyes looked into his. 'I expect that you thought the wild conservatory was mine?'

Joshua did not pretend to misunderstand. 'Yes. I did.'

'I am a reasonably intelligent man. My life is spent analysing, dissecting, carrying out post mortems ... but only upon the dead. The more I see of the living, the less I understand them.' His eyes twinkled, 'Never take anything for granted, my boy.'

He turned abruptly, and went indoors.

Chapter Four

As Joshua walked out through the ornate wrought-iron gateway, and heard the gate clanging behind him, he was reflecting on the carefully clipped arbours, with their neo-classical figures; fig leaves added to cover their aggressive manhood. Odd that a man like Obadiah Mansel, who spent his life with the flesh and blood reality of naked bodies, probing them at their most intimate, should be so unexpectedly squeamish.

What a life of contradictions it was: prostitutes selling their bodies in sordid stews and alleys, while gentlewomen prudishly shrouded their piano legs to hide their nakedness. Parsons thundering hell-fire-damnation upon cottagers with scarcely food enough to succour life, then returning home to wine and dine like hogs. Sentimental artists immortalizing their patrons' children as carefree cherubs, while others, less carefree, laboured in factories, brickworks, coalmines, and the blackness of chimneys . . .

Life on the farm had cocooned him from cruel realities. For many, like Jeremiah and Rebecca, the struggle was in just staying alive. The men his father employed were adequately clothed, fed and with a stout roof over their heads. He had mixed with them, considered them friends . . . yet it had never occurred to him to wonder what their lives were like outside the narrowness of stable-yard or field. Now the threads of the cocoon were beginning to stretch and break apart. He welcomed it, and yet it was all too strange and new. For the first time, people were beginning to turn to him, secure in his authority. He wondered if he had the strength of character, or experience, to deal with it; more importantly, to deal with it in the right way.

He had only reached the bottom of the Clevis Hill, deep in thought, when he heard the unique, unmistakable sound of Rebecca's cob and cart.

'Good day to you, Miss de Breos,' he tipped his helmet, extravagantly, 'a fine afternoon.'

'For those who have the leisure to enjoy it.'

He smiled. 'I have another small favour to beg of you.'

'Then I fear it must wait, for the tide will not.' And she drove past, the cob blowing hard through its nostrils, lifting up its tail, and leaving a pile of steaming ordure upon the pathway. A cottager with a wooden pail rushed out, and scooped it on to a shovel, marvelling at her good fortune.

'I shall be returning in two hours,' Rebecca called back at him. 'Look for me then.'

'I will,' he shouted.

He noticed that she was not wearing the rough beaver cap, or the sacking apron. He did not know about the boots, for her feet were hidden by the sides of the cart. But he did remark the scarlet ribbon in her dark hair and the black cotton dress, sprigged with red.

The cottager, a very old woman, grey hair placed in thin coils about her ears, and cheeks like withered russets, paused at her gate, clutching her prize. 'It is a great thing for us to be having a constable,' she said, with dignity. 'We shall be sleeping safer in our beds. May God protect you and go with you.'

'And with you, ma'am.' There was a spring in Joshua's step as he walked, and a straightness in his back, as she watched him go.

'A fine figure of a man,' he heard her mutter, as she unloaded her steaming burden on to the soil.

On the way to the cockle beds that day, the memory of the dead girl refused to leave Rebecca, but once engrossed in the tedious scraping and rinsing of her molluscs, she had little thought, or energy, save for her task.

As she left the crescent of sand and drove past the cicatrix of raised, black rock, she saw, in the distance, the stone walls and stout roof of Weare House, the bathing annexe of the 'Pyle Inn', whose visitors of quality came by coach to enjoy the waters.

Would those guests, perhaps, welcome some of her freshly

gathered sea-food, she wondered? To those from the crowded cities and towns, they would surely be a delicacy to savour, although despised by the cottagers who might gather them freely. She guided the cob to the rear of the house, then leapt down to approach the kitchen door.

As she did so, a flame-haired rider galloped over the dunes, spurring his mount hard, and whipping it furiously on. He dismounted in a cloud of dust and shingle and strode towards her, tapping his whip on the palm of his leather gauntlet.

'You have no business here! This is private land. Be off!'

The little cob pricked up its ears and fidgeted, but Rebecca stood her ground. 'My business is not with you, sir.'

'Business? I do not do business with trash or guttersnipes. You address a gentleman!'

'Then I am glad you told me, sir, for I was not aware of it.'

His face, beneath the scattering of freckles, flamed angrily, and he made as if to strike her, but controlled himself, affecting languour. 'I see that you have a temper, madam, and a sharp tongue . . .'

'I meet like with like, sir.'

'Indeed!' The redness inflamed his neck, and engorged even the small veins of his eyes. 'Do you compare yourself with me?'

'No! That I do not!' The denial was swift and emphatic.

'Your manners, and your clothes, ill become you,' he said, churlishly.

'As do yours, sir, for they are the clothes of a gentleman which you, plainly, are not.'

Stung by her self-possession, he sneered, 'And you are an authority on gentlemen, having met so many?'

'Had I met but one, sir, I would recognize him for his worth, and not from his clothing. I bid you good day.'

Angrily, he moved towards her, but not before Rebecca had picked up a large pebble that lay upon the cart and heaved it above her head with both hands, as if to smash it upon his face. He hesitated, and then mounted his mare, affecting indifference, then cruelly spurred it towards the wide sweep of wet sand at the water's edge, calling, 'Whore! Bitch!' and striking out at her as he rode past.

'And you are an authority, having known so many!' she called out after him, as she mounted her cart and drove away.

Yet, even as she smiled at the absurdity of the scene, she felt her hands trembling upon the reins, and saw the rawness of his face, and the twisted fury of his mouth, and she shivered, involuntarily. The bright crispness seemed to have gone from the day and she felt as ugly and graceless as he for having replied to his rancour. Such humiliation she would keep to herself.

Ossie, the little bow-legged ostler at the 'Crown Inn' was shovelling horse droppings from the cobbles when the red-haired stranger rode under the archway into the yard, his mare's hooves striking sparks from cobblestones. He dismounted with an oath. Ossie quickly dropped his shovel.

'Here, Ostler, take this horse.' His voice was surly. 'Look sharp, I haven't got all day!'

The mare had been over-ridden, and was in a lather. Steam rose from its flanks, and blood streaked the saliva which bubbled at its mouth.

'You have ridden hard, sir.'

'None of your insolence! Keep to your place, or you will feel the weight of my whip about you!' The man slapped it, warningly, against his boot, and the frightened mare retreated, showing the whites of its eyes.

Ossie steadied the animal without taking his gaze from the man's face. As he turned to lead the horse away, he felt the sting of leather upon his cheek, raking it with drops of blood, as the mare reared dangerously, above him, flailing hooves striking the cobbles. Without glancing back Ossie took the beast to the stables, murmuring, soothing, until the trembling ceased.

'Old Ossie will see to you, my beauty, have no fear . . . A gentleman, is it? More by the cut of his breeches than his jib! I've seen stable rats with better manners, that's a fact!' His leathery face grew gentle as the horny hands loosened the bit from the mare's bloodied mouth, and tended the broken skin where the spurs had entered flesh. 'If there is a hell, I hope the devil metes out the punishment we inflict upon others!'

He spent a pleasurable half-hour thinking up tortures, which Beelzebub might have overlooked, for the young gentleman, as he fed and watered his charges.

When the rider returned to claim his mare, his face was flushed with drinking, his eyes bright and unfocussing. He took the reins without a word, and mounted, clumsily. Ossie felt the mare tremble violently beneath the reins. The man reached into his waistcoat pocket for a coin, and with deliberate malice, tossed one into a pile of fresh horse-muck beside his mount.

'Work for it, Ostler!' he jeered, and spurred the mare out through the archway.

'It is not from animal filth I fear pollution.' Ossie said, softly.

He worked off his anger by immersing himself in his tasks at the stables, but memory of the ill-used mare was harder to expunge. She was a docile, gentle creature, quick to respond to kindness, and deserved better. As for that arrogant, drunken sot who owned her, he would be more at home at a pig trough than in the clothes of a gentleman.

Footsteps upon the flag-stoned pathway alerted him, and he straightened above the split door of the stable, setting down his hayfork.

'Will you saddle my mare for me, Ostler,' called out Joshua.

'Willingly, sir.' He set to work at once, and brought the grey into the yard, neatly groomed and saddled.

The horse, recognizing Joshua, gave a whinny of pleasure, nuzzling for the titbit which he invariably carried. He put the carrot piece flat against his palm, and felt the soft wetness of lips upon skin, and then heard the steady chomp of jaws. He ran his hands over the animal's flanks. 'You have looked after her well,' he approved.

'It is a pleasure, sir, to have the care of such a rare beast, and I have never seen so fine a saddle.' There was no envy in Ossie's tone, simply the satisfaction of a man who loves his work.

'I shall be returning directly. Will you be here to unsaddle her, then rub her down, see to her needs?'

The ostler nodded. 'Is it true that Lamentations Fish and the pretty cockle-gatherer found a maiden drowned?'

'They found a body, yes.'

'I ask, for that is what people are saying. It is well to know the truth of it . . . for there is sometimes much harm in lie and rumour.'

'Do you know anything of the matter?'

'That I do not, sir,' Ossie's weathered face puckered with concentration, 'but I have been giving the matter thought. It seems to me that in a parish of less than three hundred souls, we know every woman, maid, and child upon the farms, and in the cottages . . .'

Joshua nodded agreement.

'But there are others . . . those newly come to work upon the tramroads to the docks, the sailors who berth there, and those in the brickyards and quarries. It is only a thought, but might there not be a woman with them?'

'You are right, Ostler. You have a wise head upon your shoulders. I thank you for your help. But for the moment, I must ride out to see the justice.'

Ossie's face split in a gap-toothed smile. 'That is not a task I envy . . . I would sooner be shovelling muck out of the stables, for you are sure then of what you are dealing with.' He touched his forehead and returned to his tasks.

Joshua rode out through the archway, thankful for the strength and familiarity of the grey's haunches beneath his thighs. Jeremiah had come early, and taken the bull terrier to the shore, with a promise to return the animal later. The understanding between man and dog was remarkable, uncanny almost, as if each had been patiently awaiting the other to fulfil a need.

'What do you call him?' Jeremiah had asked.

'Dog,' replied Joshua, smiling, 'for that is what he is.'

'It is not dignified to be calling him that . . . like a stone, or a clod of earth.'

'Call him what you will. It is of little consequence.'

'It is of every consequence. He is a living thing. He should have a given name.'

'Then give him one.'

'Charity,' said Jeremiah, after much thought.

'Charity?'

'Have you not heard the rector preach, "But the greatest of these is Charity"?'

'Indeed I have,' agreed Joshua, gravely, 'and I am sure that the good parson would be glad that his seed did not fall upon barren ground.'

'Maybe so,' said Jeremiah, doubtfully, tightening the leash as the dog threatened a straying cur, then urinated upon the wheel of a cart, aggressively proclaiming his territory. 'Though I fear it will take no little effort to persuade him that "Charity is not puffed up; doth not behave itself unseemly".'

Joshua was still smiling to himself as he rode out. It was a fine day, clear, and the breeze from the sea smelling of ozone and wet sand, with the clean iodine-sting of seaweed.

He turned the grey away from the main track over the Clevis Hill, and followed, instead, the way that skirted the east side of the church and the village green. On, past the yeasty, hop-filled yard of the brewhouse, the cottages, the 'Ancient Briton' alehouse, where the landlord, unloading casks from the brewhouse dray, gave him a cheerful salute. The fine shires, pulling the dray, stamped and coughed as he passed by, breastplates jingling, brasses winking as they moved. Their tails were plaited and tied with bright ribbons, and their burnished harness gleamed like chestnut falls. Beautiful, proud creatures. But, today, the grey was prouder, because she was free. Her mane and tail streamed, and she moved effortlessly, rhythmically, as though under water; animal and rider fused as one.

Over the Warren; acres of fine wind-drifted sand, forming hills and valleys. They were deserted, now, save for the occasional windhover, and the sad, forsaken cry of the curlew. The cottagers believed that it was the cry of drowned sailors, seeking their souls, and even the boldest and least superstitious of men had been known to cross himself, and hurry away. In the gulleys and little plains, between the dunes, the turf was springy and close-cropped by rabbits and gales. The flora grew close to the sandy earth, thyme, heartsease, violets, and the fragile-stemmed harebells, drooping heavy heads and interspersed with clover. The air was alive with scents, and sounds, from flowers, insects and the sea.

Joshua, as the horse breasted a sandhill, looked back and

saw row upon row of dunes, marram grass rippling across them in the wind like silver water. The banks were pitted with rabbit holes, and the sandy entrances to the burrows thick with their sun-dried droppings. Mile after mile he rode, relaxed, unwilling to return to the other world of questioning, justices and the unknown dead.

As the tracks widened, and grew more defined, he knew that he must be coming to the village. The flowers here grew taller, less whipped by the salt-laden gales. Anchusa, borne upon hairy stems, with flower heads as blue as Bristol glass, and, in contrast, the sulphur-yellow flowers of evening primrose. He passed Cwm Bevos, with its stone-built farm, and veered out through the tiny cluster of stone-built cottages, with their hives of beansticks; vegetable gardens set in trim, patterned rows. There was the occasional, cossetted pig, one in a straw-thatched sty, and another looking droll in a protective sun bonnet. A few scattered hens scratched around at the bare earth in a desultory fashion, and a lean cur with one blue eye and one brown half-heartedly snapped at the horse's fetters.

The Ty Mawr, or great house, rose above the exit to the lane, its imposing gateway topped with stone griffons. Joshua halted, then crossed the main way, and rode into the justice's yard. A groom hurried from the stables to take his horse.

Joshua pulled hard at the great bell to signal his arrival. A manservant, more aristocratic than any duke, took his helmet with a flicker of distaste, and placed it upon a liveried-servant's chair, while he showed Joshua the way.

The justice, the Reverend Robert Knight, was a florid, dark-haired man, whose jowls seemed permanently bathed in shadow. His lids were heavy, somnolent even, over tired brown eyes, set in pouches. With his squat, large-bellied figure, he reminded Joshua of a benevolent toad. He half expected the voice to emerge as a harsh croak, but, when he addressed him, the justice's voice was exceptionally fine, and well modulated, as befitted a clergyman.

'Well, Constable Stradling?'

'I have brought the Home Office surgeon's report, sir. His findings about the girl's death.'

The justice produced a pair of gold-rimmed spectacles from

a shagreen case in his pocket, and clipped them over fleshy ears.

'Hmm ... Yes ... I see ... Hm,' he looked up, eyes deceptively soft and unfocussing behind the lenses. 'Death by manual strangulation.'

'Yes, sir.'

'Did Dr Mansel show you the body?'

'Yes, I saw her before and after the post mortem examination.'

'Any observations?'

'Only what Dr Mansel shows in his report.'

'Come now, apart from the medical aspects, you must have formed some opinion. Well?'

'From her appearance, clothing, state of her hands, she did not appear to be a cottager.'

'What, then?'

'A governess, perhaps; daughter of a merchant or prosperous farmer, clergyman, even ...'

'A gentlewoman, you mean?'

'Possibly!'

'No, not possibly! A young woman of that class would be chaperoned, unlikely to be tramping the backs and dunes alone. Besides, her parents would report her disappearance.'

'But, if she were a governess, or a lady's companion, or a housekeeper living away from home?'

'Then her employer would report that she was missing, surely?'

'Unless there was some involvement ...'

'Hmmm ... pretty, was she?'

'Elegant rather than pretty: slender, delicate almost, small-boned, with fair skin, pale hair, blue eyes.'

'From outside the area?'

'I shall be checking the docks, the mail coaches, and the livery stables.'

'Good! Afterwards?'

'The cottages and farms, of course. Inns. Lodging houses. Then the quarries, brickyards, shops, anywhere she might have visited, or been seen.'

'Not forgetting the great houses?' the justice asked, slyly.

'No, sir,' Joshua smiled, involuntarily.

'Then I suggest that you start here. Always begin as you mean to go on, sparing no one, exempting no one. You understand me, Constable?'

'I do, indeed, sir.'

'A bad business, Constable ... but times are changing, and change is not always an improvement. In the past we knew our tenants, the workers, the cottagers. We were a family, ruled by a benevolent paternalism.' He removed his glasses and polished them with a silk handkerchief, and replaced them in the case. 'I fear it has come too quickly ... the growth of the port, the shipping of coal and iron, the tramroad. People, like animals, need time to adapt to a new way of life, a new environment.'

Joshua nodded his agreement.

'These people are new to us, our language, our customs. Our children and young people are educated by the church. No longer illiterate. They will demand more of life.'

'Yes, sir, I believe that they will.'

'As long as they do not sacrifice the old values and simple virtues to achieve it.'

The lord of the manor of Tythegston blurred into the clergyman. Benevolent paternalism, wondered Joshua, or a desire and opportunity to play God?

The justice drummed his fingers upon a folder that lay upon his desk, and paused as though considering whether to speak. Then, having decided, said abruptly, 'I have here a report of the vestry meeting, Stradling, concerning your appointment.'

Joshua waited.

'I see from the minutes that your father owns extensive lands and farms in the vale.'

'Yes, sir.'

'I have a letter from my good friend and colleague, Dr Peate, your tutor. Does that surprise you?'

'Yes, sir. I was not aware ...'

The justice nodded. 'It seems that you attended Cowbridge Grammar School, and were destined for Oxford; Jesus College.'

'That was his hope.'

'And your parents', also?'

'Yes, sir.'

'Do you not consider it perverse, then, to choose an occupation such as constable?'

'No, sir. It has been my aim in life since I first read of Sir Robert Peel's Metropolitan Police Force.'

'Indeed? A child's romantic dreams and ideals do not always survive real life, Stradling!'

'No, sir. Yet it would be a pity if fear of failure dictated our occupations.'

The justice suppressed a smile, and said drily, 'I can only concur, Stradling.' Then he demanded, briskly, 'And your eventual ambition? Come! Come! You cannot intend to vegetate in this backwater all your days?'

'I hope to set down roots, sir, yes, if that is your meaning.'

The justice peered at him keenly from behind his spectacles, but kept silent.

'I should hope, however, to grow, sir; not to remain mute and intractable.'

'I think, Stradling, there is little fear of that!' He pulled upon a highly decorated bell-ribbon, reflecting, 'You know that there is intent of forming a County Police Force?'

'I have heard rumour.'

'Not rumour. Fact. You hope to qualify?' the justice asked abruptly.

'If my work here is well done, sir, and I prove fitted.'

'The future will be the judge of that ...'

'And higher authority, sir?' suggested Joshua, blandly.

'Indeed,' countered the justice, with a glimmer of humour, 'as I find with my own occupations.' As the supercilious manservant appeared, he instructed, 'Constable Stradling will need to question the household, Leyshon. I expect you to assist him in every possible way.'

Joshua thanked him, civilly.

The justice stared after him thoughtfully. His good friend Dr Peate had told him more than young Stradling knew. How, in a battle of wills, Stradling's father had challenged him to labour for five full years upon the farm, when he would reconsider his opposition to Joshua's plans. The boy had agreed, eagerly, gaining the respect of all who worked with him. Dr Peate had continued tutoring him, granting him full use of his catholic library, and revelling in the boy's growing awareness and independence.

When Joshua's father challenged the good priest for encouraging his son's liberal ideas and iconoclasm, Dr Peate had responded, innocently, that surely what he taught was not new? Christ had been teaching it for nigh on two thousand years ...

The justice smiled at the thought of the exchange, and his smile grew broader as he replaced his spectacles and reread his friend's account of Joshua's words as he left the farm to the care of his brother. 'If I cannot go with my father's blessing, Dr Peate, then, at least, I go with his knowledge. As you know, I have never been much moved by the story of Jacob and Esau, although I have always found a certain wayward charm in the prodigal son ...'

Joshua, ensconced in the estate manager's office, meticulously questioned every member of staff, from the kitchen-maid, a small, raw-nosed girl, with red-rimmed eyes and large, chapped hands, to the housekeeper and butler. No one recognized the girl in Rebecca's drawing.

He learned nothing of import, save that they knew of no governess or servant answering the dead girl's description at any of the manors or larger houses. No, they were sure of it. Nurses and governesses stayed with a family for years, transferring loyalty from mother to daughter, father to son. In the close-knit, esoteric hierarchy of the servants' halls, there were few secrets hidden.

The housekeeper, an austere chatelaine with pursed lips, suggested that he might visit the shareholders and administrators of the new horse-drawn tramroad at the docks. They were the newly rich, she announced, with just the right air of amused condescension, and, consequently, their habits were unknown. Or there was the Weare bathhouse upon the sand, where people of quality stayed during the bathing season.

The disdainful footman, Leyshon, was unhelpful, but turned out to be afflicted with a painful spinal complaint, which necessitated the use of a wooden splint under his jacket; in addition, his teeth were so rotted that he kept them concealed behind tight lips, speaking seldom, and only with difficulty.

It will teach me to draw no conclusions without the facts! thought Joshua wrily as, replete with Welsh cakes, the flat, spiced bakestone cakes of the area, and hot, sweet tea, he rode away.

Chapter Five

Joshua had returned too late from the justice's house to catch a glimpse of Rebecca and her cart returning from the cockle beds. Although there had only been a tentative arrangement between them, he felt depressed and oddly cheated at missing her, as he ate his solitary evening meal.

As he rode out on his grey on the morrow to visit the brickyard, he wondered if the sprigged dress and pretty ribbon had been for his benefit, or for one of the many healthy young farmers or fishermen who must find her equally intriguing and enigmatic . . .

If the thought did little to raise his spirits, his reception at the brickyard indubitably lowered them. He met with no hostility. Indeed, the workmen and their master had been scrupulously civil. But it was, he realized, the civility of an inferior to his betters, the spurious, excessive politeness of one who fears to offend. He damned the gulf that lay between them, and his inability to bridge it. His acceptance by Rebecca and Jeremiah had lulled him into believing that he was one of them. He was not! If he wanted their confidence, he would need to earn it.

He wondered how the men could endure the fierce, consuming heat of the furnaces and ovens. It burned their faces raw, and sucked the moisture from bodies and throats thickened with brick dust. He supposed, as Rebecca had said, that they did it because they must, in order to survive.

He had returned the grey to the stables at the 'Crown', and emerged into the street to the unprecedented sight of a curricle drawn up in front of his door. His mother, elegant in a gown of softest dove grey, with a travelling coat to tone, and an absurdly becoming bonnet, was being helped to alight by Watkins, their groom. She flung out her arms in greeting, embraced Joshua, and kissed him soundly on both cheeks, knocking his helmet askew, to the immense delight of a gaggle of curious onlookers.

Not a whit put out, she smiled at them myopically, giving orders to Joshua to unload the carriage, while instructing Watkins to leave the curricle with the ostler at the 'Crown', to refresh himself appropriately, and return to collect her within the hour. As he left she produced three titbits from her reticule, instructing him to give one to each of the carriage horses, and the other to Joshua's grey, with a stern admonition to 'see that the poor beast is well cared for and happy, for she was ever one of my favourites.' Joshua assured her that it was, indeed, stabled in a very Eden for horses, although, he did not doubt, it missed her sadly ... He opened the door, ushered her through, then returned so laden with packages and boxes, that he could scarcely see over them.

'I brought a few victuals,' she announced, spreading them upon the table, 'for I know how shamefully you neglect yourself. See,' she was unwrapping them, anxiously, 'a home-made cheese, butter from the dairy, some ducks' eggs, a flitch of bacon, for we have salted a pig, some oaten cakes, a cut of salmon from the Ewenny ...'

'Stop! Stop!' he cried, laughing. 'You have brought enough for the whole population of Newton, Nottage and Port until Michaelmas. How will I ever eat it all?'

'You must throw a party. Invite your friends. Are there no attractive young ladies in the area?'

He sought to distract her. 'I met an old friend of yours recently.'

'Oh?' she paused in taking off her bonnet, 'and who was that, pray? The Griffins of South Farm, or Candleston?'

'No. A gentleman.'

'A gentleman? Come, Joshua, you tease me.'

'A gentleman who sends you his fond remembrance and bids me tell you that he has not forgotten you.'

'Tell me, you provoking creature, or I shall box your ears!' she promised.

'It is Dr Obadiah Mansel.'

'Ah, yes,' she said, thoughtfully. 'I heard rumour that he had returned hereabouts.'

'He left the area, then?'

She nodded. 'It is perhaps twenty years and more since we last met. He worked with my father. It was thought, once, that we might have . . . But no!' she said firmly, 'it was a long time ago, and before the scandal . . .'

'What happened?'

'I do not know the facts, simply what was said at the time. The gossip, you understand? I know that it involved the death of a young girl.'

'Go on, tell me the rest of it!' commanded Joshua, as she paused.

'I know no details, save that there was investigation into his involvement, and that he was finally cleared. But it ruined his career. He was forced to leave the hospital. It is the first I have learnt of him, or his true whereabouts since . . . My father refused to speak of it, or discuss him.'

'You knew him well. What do you believe?'

'That he would never willingly hurt anyone. He was a good doctor. A kind man. He was incapable of physical cruelty . . . of that I am sure.'

'Will you see him? Pay him a visit?'

She shook her head. 'Water under the bridge, Joshua.' She settled heavily upon a chair. 'We are no longer the same people. It would not be kind. But tell me, how, and where, did you meet?'

'I am investigating a murder . . . a dead girl was found upon the shore.'

'You think . .?'

'Dr Mansel is doing the post mortem.'

'I should not have spoken. It was long ago, and should be forgotten!' She was clasping her hands tightly, as if she were cold, and there were high spots of colour in her cheeks. 'You tried to deceive me, Joshua. It was cruel of you, and unfair. You will forget everything I have told you!'

'I cannot do that.' He put an arm gently around her shoulders, and taking the fingers of one hand, found that they were indeed cold, as though the blood had drained away. 'I must speak to him.'

'He was incapable of a violent action. He was compassionate towards women ... respected them ... perhaps too greatly. I believe it was that which drew us apart in the end. If you are flesh and blood, and have a mind and feelings ...' She shrugged.

'What then?'

'A pedestal is a place for statues! But, come, Joshua,' she said, briskly, 'you are forgetting your manners. Have I not raised you to be a gentleman? Will you not offer your mother a dish of tea?'

Afterwards, by tacit agreement, they spoke of everything and everyone, except Dr Obadiah Mansel. Joshua asked news of his father and brother, Dr Handel Peate, former school friends, and minor relations. He enquired about the farm hands and the animals, the prospects for harvest, the affairs of the Vale, and affairs of the heart ... all the trivia and minutiae he knew that his mother would enjoy sharing. He showed her over the house, and even the small dirt yard with its well and privvy midden. She was already planning in her mind how she could improve 'this unspeakable hovel': choosing the bedding, the curtains, the linen, and those furnishings she would bring from the farm to make it habitable.

As she left, she ran her gloved hand over his bureau, and tutted disapprovingly at the dust, giving instructions that his cleaning woman from the village must be better directed. Then she unrolled Rebecca's drawing which he had placed upon it.

'A friend?' she enquired.

'No. The dead girl.'

She replaced it quickly. 'Who drew it? It is very real.'

'A girl who lives in the village.'

'A young lady whom you have met?'

'A cockle-gatherer.' He felt ashamed at his betrayal.

'Take care, Joshua. You were never much good at dissembling. Your father has indulged you in this ... escapade, because he believes it to be a whim; a young man's kicking over the traces. But take care, he would not tolerate a bad alliance. I know what his advice would be, "Sow your wild oats if you must, but they will bring you a poor harvest" ...'

He helped her into the curricle. 'No message for Dr Obadiah Mansel, Mother?'

'Say I have not forgotten him,' she waved and the light open carriage drew away, swaying on its slender wheels, the horses rested and refreshed, prancing delicately. He did not know why he thought of Rebecca and the rough cockle-filled cart.

Dr Obadiah Mansel greeted him with pleasure but no apparent curiosity. He was in the garden dead-heading some Zepherine Drouhin roses, which had been trained against the house's south-facing wall. He was wearing a battered wide-brimmed straw hat, endearingly at variance with his over-formal clothes. He carefully gathered the fallen heads from the earth, rolled them in a sheet of newspaper, then scattered them on a compost heap in a far corner of the garden. Then he neatly folded the newspaper, and invited Joshua to come indoors.

There was no sign of the raw-boned serving girl, nor of his wife, as Dr Mansel led him into the library. He gave Joshua a chair, then sat at his desk, fingertips touching, mouth pursed, as if summing up a patient at a consultation.

'You have something to ask, about the dead girl?'

'Another girl ...'

'I see ... so you have found out about that. I wondered when you would come.'

'You realize that I have no option but to question you?'

'We had best get on with it.' The pale opaque eyes looked tired under the thickly-haired brows, and he seemed to be altogether older, less in command.

Joshua took out his notebook and pencil. 'Will you tell me about her?'

'There is so little to tell ... I spoke to her only the once. Although I had seen her before. There was a young surgeon who worked with me at the hospital. Burrel, his name was. He was married to the daughter of a colleague, the professor of surgery. Burrel was not a man I liked. He was arrogant. Indifferent in his work, and to his patients, but skilled at flattering his superiors.'

'And the girl who died?'

'She was some shop-girl from the town. I don't know how they met, but it was the usual, trite story, except that this ended in tragedy.'

Joshua had stopped writing.

'Well ... it was a long drawn out affair. The girl became pregnant, expected him to marry her ... grew more and more demanding. He persuaded her that he would leave his wife, but that they would have a better life without the child. He performed an operation to abort the foetus.'

'But how were you involved?'

'The operation was botched ... an incomplete abortion. She returned to the room she shared with a friend, and began to haemmorhage, and her friend brought her to me, in a horse and trap belonging to their employer.'

'Why did she come to you?'

'I told you that I had met her once before. It was as I was leaving the house. Burrel was putting her into a carriage. I passed the time of day with him. She must have remembered where I lived, and asked to be brought to me.'

'Why did you not order her to hospital immediately?'

'She was already dying. Shock, and the loss of blood. She died in my rooms. I simply tried to bring her comfort ...'

'And Burrel?'

'He denied all knowledge of the girl,' he said bitterly. 'There was no evidence that he knew her, except the word of her friend, and she had never seen him.'

'So there was a police investigation, and one by the medical authorities. But you were exonerated?'

'Burrel's nurse, who had previously been a nurse at the hospital, stood up in the witness box and testified against him. He could hardly believe it. Swore that she had been in love with him, and did it out of malice and jealousy ... "Extracting her pound of flesh".'

'With what result?'

'He was found guilty and imprisoned. But of manslaughter ... he could afford a good advocate. And I, though adjudged innocent, was for ever damned.' Mansel gazed around the panelled, book-lined walls, but Joshua knew he was not seeing them, only the bleak room with the girl lying bloodied and dead.

There was a peremptory knocking on the door, and his wife came in, saying irritably, 'Obadiah, why is it that you never finish anything you start? You said that ...' She broke off, staring at Joshua in surprise, then regained her composure. She nodded, perfunctorily, and turned to her husband, 'Well, I will not disturb you any further, my dear, I did not know that you had ... company.'

'No, stay!' The doctor had regained his authority, and she stopped at once, alerted by his tone.

'Constable Stradling knows ...'

'Why did you have to tell him? You fool!' Anger forced blood under the sallow skin, giving her a vitality that emphasized the lifelessness of hair, skin and eyes. She turned furiously upon Joshua. 'Why do you keep persecuting us? Haven't we been through enough? Why don't you leave us in peace? Do we have to spend the rest of our lives running away, hiding from people? Fearful that they will find out and believe the worst.'

'It will not be through me,' Joshua said, but she had already rushed away and slammed the door behind her.

The doctor seemed to have shrunk inside his elegant clothes. He ran a hand through the tufts of fly-away hair, and wetted his lips with his tongue. 'It hit her hard.'

Joshua nodded.

'She had so much to lose. Come, I will see you to the door.'

They shook hands, and Dr Mansel said, 'We will meet at the inquest, then.'

'What happened to the nurse? The one who gave evidence against him?' Joshua asked.

'I married her.'

Joshua walked out through the great iron gateway, feeling unaccountably tired and confused. He wondered if he were any nearer the truth of the matter. There were so many things left unanswered. Had she, in fact, been Burrel's lover and perjured herself out of pique and jealousy? Or, perhaps, she had been Dr Mansel's nurse, or paramour, and defended him out of loyalty. Who was to say that it was not Mansel who had performed the operation and panicked when she had died as a result. Had he married the nurse merely to buy her silence? They seemed to live uneasily together, but that might be because of the strain of the past, and the fear of detection ...

He believed that Dr Mansel was telling the truth, but if it were not so, then he must certainly be a practised liar. Why did he feel that there were yet things that had not been spoken? Joshua resolved to try and obtain a written account of the testimony of the trial, and to study it minutely.

Of one thing, however, he was in no doubt. It had not been the time, nor the place, to deliver his mother's message, 'I have not forgotten you, Obadiah Mansel.'

Long after Joshua had left, Dr Mansel sat at his desk in the library, staring unseeing before him. He was not sure that Joshua believed him. He sighed, and tried to shake off the languor which possessed him. It was a long time ago. He had told the truth, as he saw it, but he was no longer that arrogant, crusading youth, so assured of his own infallibility ... He wondered if now, given the same circumstances, he would marry Madeleine. A futile, heroic gesture. His mouth twisted, wrily. As futile as speculation about Charlotte Stradling, and what might have been.

And the dead girl? When he had first dissected a cadaver, as a medical student, he had vowed to inure himself against any involvement with the lifeless carcass before him. He would not think of it as human flesh that had once lived, breathed, and had had a vital intimate life of its own. It would be to him an empty shell, a husk, no more. Neither male nor female; not young or old; ugly or beautiful; pitiful or obscene. He believed that he had succeeded. Yet, now, for this dead girl he felt a grief as lacerating and swift as the scalpel he wielded; as if in exposing what lay within her, he laid bare his own soul. He buried his head in his hands, as if for protection. Was it age that sharpened his perception? Or some memory, half hidden in the past, which would not let him go?

'Obadiah.'

He looked up, startled, unfocussing. 'Madeleine?'

'He has gone, then?' She asked and he saw that the swift rage which possessed her had vanished, leaving her calm. 'You think he will return?' Her voice was polite, disinterested.

'He has no choice. We will be expected to work together.'

'You think he has news of Burrel?'

'My dear, how could he? He has been in gaol for over twenty years ... before young Stradling was even born!'

'Yes, you are right, of course.' She hesitated. 'He asked nothing else? You are sure?'

He looked up, sharply. 'What should he ask? His interest is in the dead girl, solely. It cannot concern you.'

She nodded, satisfied. 'I shall require some money, Obadiah.'

'There is something particular you need, my dear?'

'Nothing but removal from this God-forsaken hole!' Her voice was hard, petulant, 'I sometimes believe that you bury me here deliberately.'

'You know why it is necessary.'

'Necessary? Is it necessary to burden me with illiterate clods of peasants, who have neither wit nor breeding? I have been accustomed to better.'

'But you have the Crandles, my dear, and other friends.'

'I have no friends. Acquaintances, only ... and those boring and déclassé. Why will you not cultivate the people at Nottage Court. You attend them, do you not? Or Robert Knight?'

'The justice? I think you know the answer, Madeleine.'

'Damn you, Obadiah! You make a hermit of me. A recluse. I believed, when I married you that ...'

'Yes. What did you believe, Madeleine?' His voice was dangerously quiet, 'That I would be rich, successful? That our life together would be warm and loving?'

She grimaced, wrily. 'Never that! I knew that you were dull, pompous, provincial ... I married you merely to escape.'

'From the past, or yourself, Madeleine?' he asked, gently.

'Is there a difference?'

'You know that better than I.'

She shrugged, dismissively. 'Does it matter?'

'It does to me.'

'Then you are either more stupid or more naive than I thought. If I lived in France ...'

'You are not in France, and you may thank God for it! If people look upon you with reserve, it is because the war is still fresh in their minds. Many of these peasants, as you call them, still suffer the wounds and losses. You will do well to remember it!'

'Shall I ever be allowed to forget?'

He took a small bag of sovereigns from a drawer in his desk, and handed it to her. She took it without a word of thanks, and put it in her reticule.

He looked at her keenly, objectively, studying her in the detached way he strove to regard his patients. He saw her pale angularity, the thin petulant line of her mouth. A woman as devoid of feminine softness as of flesh.

'Is there something wrong with my appearance?' she asked, sharply.

'No, my dear. You do not change. You are still the woman I married.'

She shrugged. 'I go to the Crandles for some congenial company, to escape boredom.'

'Then have a care for what you say.'

'I am not a fool!'

'No, you are certainly not that . . . but remember, "Old sins cast long shadows".' He watched her go with mingled exasperation and pity. Then his thoughts returned to the unknown girl, and a life ended by violence almost before it had begun. He could not say why the old proverb came into his mind, or judge its relevance, but he found himself muttering it aloud, 'Take what you want,' said God, 'and pay later.'

Chapter Six

Joshua lingered over his breakfast of bakestone bread, thickly spread with salted farm butter and spiced with the strong, rough flavour of ducks' eggs. To add to the luxury of his mother's bounty, there was a letter from his friend and mentor, Dr Handel Peate, delivered by the Pyle mail coach.

As he opened it, he marvelled anew at the copperplate neatness of the writing. Joshua thought it characterized him perfectly, physically and mentally. Compared with Joshua's broad-shouldered, six-feet-three-inch frame, Dr Peate's was neat and compact as a child's. His features were fine-drawn, under skin with the waxen, almost translucent, paleness of some invalids, or scholars who spend too much of their time indoors. He walked with the familiar stoop of the pedant, long hunched over books. His eyes were gentle, and often abstracted, as if, with his thoughts, they were concentrated on some inaccessible, secret place. If his outward appearance marked him as a dreamer, he made no effort to change it; it suited him to appear unworldly. His mind and tongue, as Joshua knew well, were sharp and incisive as well honed blades. Of all the people he knew, Joshua loved and respected Dr Peate most dearly, for, unlike his own family, this was a friendship of his own choosing. It made no demands of blood, sentiment or duty. Age was irrelevant. It needed no explanations; no declaration of its worth. It was enough that it existed.

Dr Peate congratulated him upon 'taking the first step in your great adventure. It pleases me,' he wrote, 'that the good vestrymen acknowledged you as being "literate and of good character". I confess that as your tutor and cleric, I am hard-pressed to choose which accolade affords me the greater pleasure.'

Joshua was still aglow with its warmth as he rode out of the 'Crown' courtyard, and took the route from Newton village over Dan-y-Graig Hill, with its swathe of woods skirting the edge of Stormy Down, where sheep and cattle plumply grazed, as they had from early centuries.

'History, Stradling, is not a dead thing, desiccated and lifeless, like a mummified corpse, to be preserved in funeral wrappings. History is alive!' Dr Peate had exclaimed. 'It is here! This minute! All about you . . . You are living it!'

Dr Peate was right, Joshua thought, urging on the grey. Was he not now witnessing the birth of a new port and the death of an old one at Newton Creek? Iron ore for the foundries, coal and limestone replacing the old cargoes of wheat, beans, pigs, sheep, cattle, butter and the knitted woollen stockings fashioned in old cottages by candlelight as early as the sixteenth century.

Even now rang past echoes of smugglers, wreckers and seafaring men, and before them, from the ninth and tenth centuries, the Black Pagans and Danes, whose raids brought a terror and havoc Joshua could well imagine. To those who dwelt here, as Dr Peate had said, these were not the cold facts of history, but the living reality of 'Now'.

He reined in his mare as he approached Tythegston and, as before, entered the manor house drive where his mount was swiftly stabled.

His request was received by the Reverend Robert Knight coldly, and for some time in silence. 'I cannot see,' declared the justice, tartly, 'how it could benefit you to journey to Cardiff to see the court records.'

'It is to satisfy a curiosity about a case.'

'And what case in particular?'

'An early case, sir. One which concerns Dr Obadiah Mansel.'

'Mansel, you say. Surely, Constable, you cannot suspect him?' The deceptively tired eyes were hostile behind the gold-rimmed glasses.

'No more than I suspect you, sir, but you instructed me to spare no one, exempt no one.'

A flicker of humour touched the justice's mouth. 'I did not expect such swift or literal interpretation. However, if you are set upon it.'

'I should be greatly obliged, sir.'

'Then I shall write you an authorization, without delay.' He opened the drawer of his desk and brought out a sheet of paper, and took up his quill. He looked up. 'You feel that this will help in your investigation?'

'I cannot be sure that it will, but my hope is to eliminate Dr Mansel, rather than convict him.'

He nodded, and began to write, then dried the note, and sealed it with wax, making an impression of his seal. 'It must be difficult being the first constable ... no rigid procedure to follow, no precedents?'

'Yet it has advantages, sir. I need not become too hide-bound. I may use my initiative with the ready cooperation of those in authority.'

The Reverend Robert Knight looked at him, sharply. 'Yes. I see that you are able to do that, Constable. But one word of advice. You said you did not hope to convict Dr Mansel. You do not convict. You merely help to bring to justice. The judge and jury convict, or declare innocent, and sentence accordingly.'

'Yes, sir. A slip of the tongue, I should have said "involve". I apologize.'

The justice looked mollified. Joshua had no doubt that he was aware of Dr Mansel's past.

'Do you think it might help you to read the newspaper reports of the trial, Stradling?' he asked, abruptly.

'If it were possible.'

'It might save the good vestrymen and the parish the burden of your coach trip to Cardiff! You may inspect the copies, and my personal notes upon the matter. They are neatly ordered and preserved by my clerk at Pyle courthouse.' Seeing Joshua's incredulity, 'Come, Constable, do you think we are so insular and parochial that we admit of no wider world beyond the three hamlets? The law, and justice, as religion, should have no boundaries. Do you agree?'

Joshua nodded.

'However, I have little doubt that our frugal vestrymen would prefer to limit your excursions and expenses to Pyle, unless it proves essential.' And he smiled. 'I fear my sermons sometimes fall upon thorns. I think I did not see you at church on Sunday, Stradling?'

'No, sir. I was at my duties.'

'Not a dissenter, are you?'

'No, sir.'

'Do not let your temporal duties divert you from your spiritual obligations.'

'No, sir, I shall try to pursue both with the dedication and effort each deserves.'

The Reverend Robert Knight's eyes twinkled, his mouth twitched, and his jowls and plump belly trembled with laughter. The image of a benevolent frog was fully restored.

'I believe that we understand each other well enough, Stradling. I believe that I am going to like you.'

'And I you, sir.'

'Keep me informed of your enquiries locally, and at the courthouse. You will find that the authorization I have given you grants you general access, with my bond upon your integrity and discretion. Use it wisely.'

He pulled the bell-rope and the morose footman, Leyshon, appeared, to show Joshua out.

Joshua enquired, civilly, about the condition of his spine and the state of his teeth, and was promptly offered refreshment, which he declined, truthfully pleading pressure of duties.

'A martyr to pain and suffering, I am . . . a veritable martyr,' the footman was confiding, as the groom brought Joshua's grey to the door. Joshua hoped that the good rector was sensitive to his good fortune in harbouring a saint under his roof.

When he arrived at Pyle, Joshua went, first, to the 'Pyle Inn', where he made enquiries of the landlord and the ostler and the serving maids, about the dead girl. No one recognized her from Rebecca's drawing, and it was certain that had she alighted there, or taken refreshment between coach stops, then she would have been remarked. Remembering his conversation with the justice's housekeeper, he enquired about guests being transported to the bathhouse at Newton Weare.

The coachman to the inn was firm, 'No, sir, I have never driven that young gentlewoman. I would certainly not have forgotten her. Besides which, I greet by name the coachmen upon both mail coaches, and the stages, and see their passengers alight. We are a small inn, but well kept, and personal. You understand? No, sir, she has not been here.'

Defeated, Joshua made his way to the courthouse.

His authorization from the justice carefully scrutinized and approved, he was guided, with due reverence, into the dusty catacombs which housed the skeletons of long-dead cases. He perused the brittle, yellowing newspaper accounts of the trial and Robert Knight's notes upon the case, for he had witnessed the trial.

Twenty-five minutes later, dishevelled and dirt-streaked, Joshua returned everything to order, then rode reflectively away. The vestrymen, at least, would be satisfied.

Instead of returning immediately, he decided to take the road to Bridgend and seek information at the coaching inns. Surely, if the girl had travelled by public, rather than private, carriage, she must have alighted there. His initial enquiries having proved fruitless, he rode to the stopping place for the weekly mail coach. It was 'due within the hour'.

Joshua decided to wait and he delivered his mare to the ostler, a wall-eyed, pocked old fellow, with a clenched-up fist of a face. He took the grey, admiring her lavishly, and with such delight upon his worn features that Joshua was constrained to give him a sixpence, whereupon the ostler promised, 'No beast shall be better groomed, fed and watered, not in all of Glamorgan.' Joshua, feeling the heat of the day, and the warmth of his helmet, removed it and took himself to the corner of the yard, to the windlass and rope well. The innkeeper, a cheerful, red-faced fellow, hurried out to make himself known, and invited Joshua into the kitchen. There, at the stone sink, Joshua enjoyed the luxury of water flowing from an iron pump, which the landlord demonstrated with such fierce abandon that Joshua was all but drowned. The portly innkeeper was so overcome by these exertions that he had to be helped to a chair by a scullery maid and the sweat wiped from his face with the hem of her apron.

Joshua, having apprised the innkeeper of his quest, was granted the use of a small, private parlour, where he might conduct the interviews in confidence and quiet.

'I wish you joy of the interviews, sir,' his host said, 'for some of the coachmen riding the "Royal Mail" believe themselves vastly superior to those upon the cheaper stages. They think no small liquor of themselves.'

The Swansea to London 'Royal Mail' coach, suitably emblazoned, arrived on time, the guard armed, Joshua was sure, with blunderbuss, pistols, bullets and powder horn, and sounding his post horn to herald his approach, and to warn the inn to prepare the horses for the next stage of the journey.

'Five minutes will be all you may count on,' the innkeeper had warned, 'for that is all that is allowed for the changing of the team. The world is mad for speed, since speed is money . . . although, alas, not for me! 'Tis no wonder coachmen grow fat on porter and make wind enough to sail a schooner, then complain of our victuals.'

The coach entered with a clatter of wheels and hooves upon the cobblestones of the courtyard. There was a confusion of noise and bustle. An opening and slamming of doors, a flurry of passengers disembarking, luggage being handed down, and the uncoupling of the leaders and wheelers by the ostlers.

Through the window, Joshua saw the guard step down, resplendent in his scarlet coat and gilded hatband. He kept his armaments close, sedulously protecting Her Majesty's mail, locked within a strong box. A serving maid brought him out a tray of porter.

The coachman was standing beside the handsome, leather-covered coach, raising his flat hat as the passengers alighted and receiving many a sixpence and shilling for his civility, and the blessing of a safe journey. He wore an onion-layering of garments, topped by an ankle-length overcoat with shoulder capes, its neckline cheerfully enlivened by a rolled kerchief, the colour of holly berries. He was, as coachmen always will be, surrounded by an admiring coterie of would be imitators: grooms, ostlers, pot boys and, most besotted of all, the runny-nosed sweepers and urchins of the place. He brushed them aside good naturedly, to enter.

The landlord ushered him in, enquired about refreshments needed, and returned almost immediately with a tray bearing two tankards, brimming with ale, and some veal pies which the coachman, a lean fellow with a bony, high-ridged nose and long, cadaverous face, devoured as if to fill all his vacant places. As he ate and drank, Joshua showed him Rebecca's drawing.

The man studied it, minutely. 'Yes. I am sure that I transported her on the coach. I recall it because she travelled alone. A small, delicate thing, she was, and soft spoken.'

'When was this?'

'Let me think ... Wednesday, it must have been, for we make this journey but once a week. I stay, then, overnight at Cowbridge, although the guard travels on. Yes, it was certainly Wednesday.'

'Alone, you say? You are sure she was meeting no one on the coach?'

'I am sure of it, for she scarce spoke a word, except to enquire the time of our arrival.'

'Where did she board the coach? At which stopping place? Do you remember?'

'Yes, certainly. At the very first stage of the journey, Swansea. She was ready and waiting at the post inn.'

'And nobody came to bid her goodbye?'

'No, for I aided her with her luggage.'

'Can you recall of what it was comprised? How many pieces?'

'I can, sir, for I found it remarkable. It was but one small portmanteau, small enough to hold in the hand with no difficulty. Most ladies have travelling trunks and those rosewood boxes, fitted with bottles and jars, for unguents and lotions and such ... vanity boxes, I believe them to be called, and meant to beautify, although, for some, it would need more than a miracle!'

Joshua smiled as the coachman continued.

'You would not credit the parcels and packets. I have seen a dead goose, salmon, song birds in a cage ... indeed, I mind once, a passenger died of an apoplexy, and the guard forbade me to stop until we reached the post inn, for fear of attack. But your question was of the young lady.'

'You are sure she carried nothing else?'

'Nothing, save for a small reticule, in which she kept her money, for she paid me her fare from that. I remember thinking that someone had already taken her luggage, or that it awaited her elsewhere . . . for no woman would travel so lightly equipped, not even for one day.'

'Do you recollect what she wore?'

'I am not one for remembering details of dress, as my good wife so frequently chides me, but I thought she was a pretty maid, refined and appealing, with her dark cloak and bonnet against her pale hair. A light, thin material, I recall, for I said that I hoped that she would not take cold, and lent her my warm travelling rug.'

'Did she say what her final destination was, or the purpose of her journey?'

'No, and I did not ask, for there were other passengers and by the time they were assembled and ready, it was the hour to depart.'

'Where did you leave her?'

'Why, here. At this very inn. She thanked me prettily, and gave me a shilling for refreshment.'

Joshua, mindful of his manners, recalled the innkeeper, and ordered, 'More ale, if you please, and whatever the coachman desires for his sustenance,' but the driver protested that two veal pies were more than sufficient, for he would fall asleep upon the box, or feel them lie like lead upon his belly, at which the landlord left, much affronted.

'I believed,' the coachman continued, supping his ale, unabashed, 'that she might rest here, and take the other mail coach journeying from Carmarthen to London . . . but she did not.'

'You are sure of this?'

'Indeed I am. As I came into the yard to speak to the ostler, did I not see with my own eyes that she stepped into a cabriolet?'

'And the driver?'

'A young gentleman, dressed in grey!'

'A gentleman, you say?'

'Certainly. No farm labourer or quarryman.'

'Was there anything distinctive you remember of him, of the carriage?'

'Only that his hair was the brightest copper-red and his skin so bathed in brown spots, freckles, you might call them, that they seemed to blot out his face. But enquire of the ostler, Constable, for he harnessed the horse. Now, I fear, I must be away, sir, for the horses stand ready, and the "Royal Mail" cannot wait.' He swilled down his ale at a gulp, and fulfilled the landlord's prediction by belching, flatulently, without shame.

Joshua took note of his name, lest he should need to question him further, and thanked him, courteously, for his time. As they spoke, the guard, splendid in his scarlet and gold, came in to remind them that the horses had been changed, and they must, at once, be on their way. Then Joshua, saying goodbye to the landlord and settling his bill, made for the stables.

The ostler brought him the grey, proudly. His pitted, brown face broke into a smile as he surveyed his handiwork. 'Did I not say he would be better groomed than any beast in Glamorgan?'

'You did indeed,' said Joshua, putting his foot into the stirrup and swinging himself astride. 'And you told the truth. I have never seen her look finer, and I thank you for your trouble.'

'Not trouble. Pleasure, sir.'

'Tell me,' Joshua enquired, unrolling the drawing, 'do you remember seeing this young woman?'

The ostler studied it with concentration, eyes awkwardly focussing before saying, 'I do, sir, she came by Wednesday's mail coach and left in a gig; one of those pretty two-wheelers with a hood and matched black horses.'

'Did you know the young man who drove her?'

'No, he was a stranger to me. I know most of the young gentlemen hereabouts; but, no, I have seen him neither before, nor since.'

Joshua thanked him and, reflecting that he had, at last, made some progress, adjusted his helmet, and resolutely set his mare upon the road home.

Rebecca de Breos, in her secluded cottage behind the church and edging the Burrows, was washing herself in the open air.

It was a fine day, and the sky a clear, periwinkle blue, the clouds high, and soft as curled goose feathers. Even the breeze which washed in from the sea was warm upon the skin.

In winter, bathing was a long, tedious business, for it meant winching countless buckets from the well at the rear of the yard, beyond the stables. They were heavy, and awkward to carry, and often the surface of the water became filmed with ice, and fingers grew chapped and swollen. After a time she had purchased for herself one of the rough, wooden yokes, used by the dairy maids to carry their pails of milk from the dairy. With this upon her shoulders the burden was more balanced and her journeys halved. But there was still the wretched business of lighting the wood which fuelled the brick oven. Friction matches were a luxury to those who were sore pressed to buy food, clothing and shelter. Usually, Rebecca used a flint from the shore, which she struck repeatedly against a steel, until a spark fired the linen rags which she housed in her tinder box. Once aglow, she used them to ignite a brimstone match. The rags were swiftly snuffed out, for she was a frugal girl and such tinder could be used again. Her knuckles, though, were often grazed raw, for the tinder was slow to fire, and her cold-numbed hands made her clumsy. Sometimes, itinerant wood-sellers came, offering their gleanings. They were invariably old and unfitted to do any hard, manual work, so they gathered bundles of faggots from the woods and hedgerows. They came with them strapped to their bodies, backs arched like hunch-backs. It was hard to turn them away, but the shore was strewn with driftwood after the storms, and there for the taking. Occasionally, there came dark-skinned Romanies, who tried to barter for food and warm clothing with their juniper twigs and dried spills, dipped in sulphur, or sweet-burning cones of pine or larch.

But today, winter was a memory, and there was no need to bathe in an outhouse. With her clean petticoats, dress and drawers spread upon a bank, she was able to stand in the wooden tub, naked as a fledgling, the sweet washball of tallow and lye secured in her mother's soap box of pierced silver. What did she care for the soap tax? Let it swell the coffers of the Treasury! Today promised to be special. She splashed in the tub, the water tingling upon her skin, cold and invigorating.

Then she dried herself upon a piece of rough linen, put on her clothes which had been carefully laundered in wood-ash, and hurried indoors, watched intently by the curious Welsh cob. She combed her hair, pinched some extra colour into her cheeks and, from the little earthenware jug in the larder where she kept her savings, took out a golden sovereign. A fortune. A bonebreak of cockling and boiling, but she did not hesitate. She placed the coin in a drawstring purse in her reticule and, locking the door, set off for the village.

The people of the area were hard-working, frugal, devout and independent. If they worked for others, as farm workers, servants, quarrymen, or in the brickyards, they were not owned by them. With the coming of the charity and church schools, and those of the dissenters, like Wesley, their cottages remained tied, but their minds were unleashed. Some might argue that it was a limited freedom, that they were guided and schooled by their new masters into the paths of religion. Yet the choice was their own. Like unbroken animals, they might be outwardly subdued by a stronger hand or mind, but the spirit remained independent and inviolate. It was this same independence which they recognized in Rebecca. A separateness. Like them she was hard-working, self-reliant, and in love with her books. For this she was respected.

She walked into Newton village, her head held high, her back erect. There was about her a certain arrogance, as Joshua had seen when he had first looked upon her. It was not born of any brash sense of superiority, nor was it conscious. It was the natural dignity of one who is aware of her own worth, secure within herself.

At a house with wooden beams criss-crossed in its white pargetting and with its entry made awkwardly over a small stone step and stile, she paused. Then, drawing up her skirt, she stepped across and walked to the door.

The seamstress was a small, rounded old lady with a shape like a well-baked cottage loaf. She wore a frilled cap over her grey curls, and metal rims to her glasses. Behind them, her eyes were embedded in flesh, like deep-set currants. The bodice of her black dress was thickly patterned with pins.

'Ah, good day to you, Mistress de Breos.' She pronounced it

'Dabrosse', in the usual way of the villagers.

'And how may I be of service to you?'

'I should like to have made a full set of clothing, if you please.'

The four little apprentices, sewing painstakingly around a table in the dim light from a single window, paused in their labours. One of them, bolder than the rest, giggled. The seamstress stared her into silence.

'What exactly were you proposing, Mistress de Breos. A gown, perhaps, and some lace-edged petticoats?'

'A dress, petticoats, a cloak, some bodices.'

'Oh, I see. Then perhaps you would care to look through some drawings. I have a book of the latest fashion. You would not find neater stitching, or more modish style, even in London. Indeed, we have made for the gentry. We pride ourselves upon the delicacy of our handiwork.'

The apprentices sewed more assiduously.

Rebecca and the seamstress scoured the pictures, discussed, suggested and came to a compromise on style and cloth.

'A wise choice,' approved the seamstress, 'showing taste and discrimination. They will be completed within the week, but first, I must take your measure.' The task completed to the curiosity of the apprentices, who chattered like starlings about her choice and her fine, upright figure, Rebecca opened her reticule.

'I shall pay you now,' she pronounced, producing her sovereign, 'for I shall find it more convenient.'

The apprentices fell silent. The seamstress demurred. No, it was unnecessary. There was no obligation to do so. None at all ... she would not hear of it! Then, resistance dissolved, she accepted with alacrity.

As she replaced her purse, Rebecca let fall a folded paper. 'Oh, how clumsy!' she scolded herself, as the seamstress reached for it and handed it to her, letting it lie open. 'It is nothing of consequence, simply a drawing I made of a dress I once saw ...'

The seamstress studied it, currant eyes alert behind her lenses. 'It is pleasant enough,' she agreed, 'indeed, quite ladylike, although a little dull, perhaps. You have made a wiser choice, I feel.'

Rebecca nodded.

'You drew it, you say, Mistress de Breos?'

'Yes, from life.'

'It is excellently executed, most accomplished. I wonder,' she paused, 'if you are amenable, and have the time to spare, I should be obliged for your services. It is better drawn than any I can show you. You will be going, perhaps, to the corset-maker?' she asked, dropping her voice, lest her indelicacy be overheard by the young seamstresses.

'Indeed, no!' confessed Rebecca, smiling, 'for I fear a corset would hardly be fitted to my cockle-gathering!'

The dressmaker smiled too. 'You are sure you would not like a small bustle added, for they are becoming quite the mode?'

'I think nature has provided me with padding enough.'

'In truth, Mistress de Breos, you have excellent deportment. It is a pity that the tight-bodiced dresses of the Regency have fallen into disfavour . . . they would suit you quite admirably. I even hear tell that some young gentlewomen wore them when taking a bath, for the water caused them to cling most becomingly . . .'

'Less becoming when you are dead of the ague!' said Rebecca laughing, and all the little seamstresses laughed, too, and even the dressmaker unbent enough to join in, wiping her spectacles on her bodice, for they became misted. And so Rebecca left them in great good humour after begging a small pattern of the fabric for cloak and gown, and stepped to the straw bonnet maker.

The shop of the milliner was in a cottage in the centre of the village, and occupied the front room, with a workroom and living quarters behind. It opened directly on to the pathway, and in the window were displayed a collection of prettily trimmed bonnets. For those too pious for such frivolous excesses, or too poor, there were austere plain ones set in baskets within, and for any cottager of an original mind, or who was forced to refurbish an ancient bonnet, there was a cornucopia of frills, laces and trimmings. Prettiest of all, Rebecca thought, were the delicate filigree collars and cuffs of lace to brighten a dull gown, hand-pieced by tired-eyed, industrious cottagers, by the guttering light of rush and tallow candles, or their fish-oil cruses.

Once within, Rebecca glimpsed, through the open doorway, three women busily occupied in their respective tasks. One, elderly, and hunched with some disease of the bones that made claws of her hands, presided over an open fire bearing trivets with flat irons. Above them, a steaming kettle hung from a chain. She uncoupled it clumsily, and hot water slopped into the fire, where it hissed and spat globs of water onto the hearth. She held it above a wooden block, upon which she was helping to shape a bonnet crown in its vapour. A girl who looked scarcely more than a child was weaving straw into plaited lengths, while in a corner, a third woman, her hands raw-boned and flecked with blood, was stitching assiduously at a brim. Rebecca wondered briefly if it was the steam that had shaped the old woman's hands as rigidly as her own now shaped the stiffening crown.

A woman came from the living quarters behind the work-room in answer to the jangling shop bell. She was thin, spare-fleshed, and wore a dress of grey, finished with a frill, from which her neck emerged like the neck of a tortoise. Hooded eyes and sparse lashes compounded the likeness.

'Good day to you, Mistress, and how may I help you?'

Rebecca produced her snippets of cloth, and their business was rapidly transacted.

'I had considered a dress of this design.' She produced the drawing of the girl.

'Strange ...' the woman said, 'for that young lady in the drawing was here but a day or so since, wearing that very dress. I am sure of it.'

'She came to buy a bonnet?'

'No, a collar and cuffs in lace. You are a friend of hers?'

Rebecca nodded, 'From school.'

'I hesitated simply because she bought them as a gift . . . "for a friend of long standing", that is what she said. If it is you, then I feel guilty at spoiling the surprise.'

'No,' said Rebecca, 'it was not I. She gave no name?'

'None. And I asked for none!' She looked indignant. 'It was

not my affair. I have only recently taken the business. It would not do if my patrons thought me rude and prying!'

Rebecca calmed her by buying a collar and cuffs in lace, which were wrapped for her and tied with ribbon.

'I have not seen her for such an age,' Rebecca said, sadly, 'I wonder if she is staying hereabouts? Visiting friends?'

'Indeed, I cannot say. I only know she came and left on foot.'

'In which direction?'

'Towards the church.' The milliner was tiring of the conversation and began to fidget, tidying the bonnets.

'Her voice? Did she speak as the village folk do?'

'Indeed. I thought you were friends from school? She spoke like you. How else?'

'She has been many years abroad. In Italy,' Rebecca improvised. 'A great tragedy ... too sordid to speak of!'

The milliner began to show an interest, and stopped fidgetting with her bonnets. She leaned over and asked, confidentially, 'A gentleman?'

'Is it not always the case?'

The tortoise eyelids blinked rapidly and Rebecca hastily gathered up her parcel, leaving her agog with agony and suspense.

Joshua, returning from the courthouse, saw her leaving the milliner's doorway. He reined in his horse, and saluted her formally, for the sake of the milliner, ostentatiously arranging a bonnet in the window.

'Good day to you, Miss de Breos.'

'Good day to you, Constable.' She inclined her head, stiffly.

'I see you have been shopping.'

'For information,' she said, very low.

'And did you obtain what you wanted?'

'Yes, I believe I did. And you, sir, were you well suited?'

'With more success than I expected.'

The milliner had been joined in the window by one of her sewing women.

'It would do me great honour if you would dine with me, tonight, at my house with our friend Mr Jeremiah Fleet.'

'I accept, sir, with pleasure, and anticipation.'

'Will seven o' the clock suit you?'

'Perfectly well.'

They parted, with formal bows of the head, and the leave-taking of modest acquaintances, to the chagrin of the milliner, who drove her accomplice back to the workroom, shrewishly berating her for wasting time.

When Joshua arrived at Jeremiah's simple stone cot, which was little more than a shelter, he entered the yard to a stench so overpowering that even the grey wrinkled its nostrils in distaste and stopped abruptly, refusing to advance.

Jeremiah was sweating over a huge iron pot, above a fire contained within bricks. On the ground at his feet was a vast wooden platter of fish, their bellies slit and degutted. From the bloody mess of entrails and offal, he was hacking the livers with a sharp knife and putting them into a lidded clay jar. Joshua was hard put not to clap his handkerchief to his mouth, and was half afraid to speak, lest he vomit.

'Fish liver oil for the lamps,' said Jeremiah, 'I boil them only when they are rancid. The fresh ones I keep until they rot.'

Joshua nodded, unwilling to trust his mouth.

'I make my own, and sell the spare in the villages: Newton, Nottage, The Port.'

Joshua was only grateful that his mother provided him with expensive wax candles and friction matches from the chandlers ... for he feared that fish oil would turn his stomach!

The dog, Charity, showing no signs of distress, was esconced at Jeremiah's feet, worshipping. It lifted its head towards Joshua, and wagged its whip of a tail, but made no effort to rise.

'You will be here for the dog?' ventured Jeremiah, 'I planned to bring him, directly.'

'No, I came with an invitation for you. Will you sup with me, tonight, with Rebecca de Breos? We have much to discuss.'

Jeremiah's fine eyes shone with pleasure, and he fingered his greying beard. 'At what time would you require me?'

'Seven o' the clock.'

'I shall be there, never fear. But there is much to do to make myself respectable. I shall not disgrace you, or the little maid.'

Joshua nodded, and made to leave.

'The dog?' Jeremiah asked.

'Bring him with you, when you come.'

Jeremiah stopped stirring with the wooden paddle for long enough to salute him, then returned to his foul-smelling brew.

Joshua, in the fresh, clean air, gave the grey her head. He was with these people, but, as yet, not of them. He could pity them, try to understand them, but not share their real lives; he was set apart. And he did not know if it was a curse, or an advantage.

Chapter Seven

If anyone had described Joshua's temperament as 'nervous' or 'mercurial', Dr Handel Peate would have been astounded. While admitting that as a scholar he had a quick, enquiring mind, he would have argued that his disposition was 'placid to the point of bovine phlegmatism.' Or, as his brother rudely paraphrased it, 'Our Joshua is docile as an old milch-cow.'

Tonight, neither would have recognized him, for he was in a state of extreme nervous agitation. The decisiveness which usually marked his thoughts and actions had deserted him. His close-fitting 'unmentionables' were elegant and creaseless, flaring over boots shiny as polished jet. His pristine shirt was immaculately frilled and starched. And his frock coat, of a darker, slate grey, was set aside upon a 'butler', its quilted collar impeccably rolled. Yet, he was not satisfied. He found himself in a quandary over the waistcoat ... to match, or contrast?

'Fool!' he exclaimed aloud, 'what does it matter? It is not some elegant soiree, or grand ball. It is simply an informal meeting of three good friends.' Yet he was plagued with doubts. If he dressed too grandly, would it embarrass Rebecca and humiliate Jeremiah? If he wore his ordinary workaday uniform would they think their coming of so little import, it deserved no effort on his part?

Eventually, he chose a toning weskit of patterned grey and white brocade and, taking a candle, went downstairs. He had prevailed upon his cleaning woman to come and prepare a meal, on the promise of two shillings and sixpence, should it be well done. An absurd extravagance! She was in the kitchen now, and there was a flurry of noise with pots and dishes, and a tantalising aroma of bacon sizzling upon a weight-jack spit. There would be vegetables, and a pudding, all boiled together in an iron pot behind the jack, and separated one from the other by nets of string.

Joshua regarded the table with satisfaction. Upon it he had placed the pewter plates which he had brought with him from the farm, and which his mother had pronounced 'more serviceable than that cheap earthenware produced by the potteries.' Beside them, he had placed tankards for ale and cups and saucers for tea, should Rebecca prefer it. Cutlery, which he had inherited from his grandfather, and some condiment dishes of silver gleamed beneath the candlelight. Even the candles were special, of beeswax and spermaceti, they glowed more brightly, needed no frequent snuffing of the wick, unlike tallow candles, and gave out no foul, fatty smell.

Jeremiah had called upon Rebecca to escort her. They arrived at the door promptly at seven o'clock. Rebecca wore her black, sprigged gown, but decorated with new lace collar and cuffs, and a fine soft shawl. But it was in Jeremiah that Joshua saw the bravest and most dramatic change. He wore a coat and trousers of darkest grey wool and a soft fronted shirt, ruffed and fitted with a cravat of paler grey. Above it his face gleamed pink and scrubbed as a babe's. His fine grey eyes shone brightly. Even his beard and grizzled head looked newly laundered and bleached with lye.

They stood there, awkwardly, for a moment, then Joshua ushered them in, beaming with delight.

'You look charming,' he told Rebecca, truthfully, 'and you, Jeremiah, a gentleman to your fingertips.'

'Skin-deep?' asked Jeremiah, smiling. 'Well, that is good enough for me. But you, Joshua, you look a gentleman born, down to your very bones.'

Joshua eased the stiffness of his well starched collar. 'Sharp enough to slice a hen . . . or through my ears,' he said, and they all laughed and relaxed properly.

The meal, served by his delighted cleaning woman, was declared by Jeremiah, 'to be fit for the Queen herself, dear lady,' and they toasted her health and prosperity, liberally, in cwrw da.

Later, his helper, paid handsomely and laden with leftover food, departed. Then they gathered around the fire and exchanged their gleanings of the day.

'So tomorrow,' said Joshua, 'I shall hunt for the man with copper hair and the cabriolet.'

'And I,' promised Rebecca, 'shall not rest until I have discovered more of him, and of the girl.'

'And you, Jeremiah?'

'The quarries, to question the men, and find if anyone knew the dead girl, and after, to the inns.'

Joshua nodded his approval.

They stood to take their leave with many avowals of pleasure and gratitude.

'I will see you safely upon your way,' said Joshua, taking the horn lantern, and lighting it with a friction match, to Jeremiah's outspoken admiration. 'But before you leave, Jeremiah, a small favour?'

'Gladly, if I can.'

Joshua opened the door into the yard, and walked to where Jeremiah had left the dog chained. The dog pulled at its shackles in an effort to get to the old man, its lean tail wagging, slanted eyes bright.

'If you would take him, it would be a kindness to both him and me,' said Joshua, 'for, with all my coming and going and travelling on horseback, I scarcely see him, and give him no exercise.'

Jeremiah looked at him steadily. 'If you are sure it would be better for him.'

'Of that, I am very sure.'

Jeremiah unchained the dog, which trembled with delight and licked his hands and face desperately. In the light of the horn lantern, Jeremiah's eyes were strange and unnaturally bright.

They went out through the yard door, and Joshua felt an ache of regret at losing the dog, and for its not caring.

Rebecca slipped a small, roughened hand into his and held his fingers tight. 'You are a kind man,' she said, 'and I thank you for it. It is a loving gift you have made to Jeremiah.'

He felt her lips brush his fingers, and was content.

When Joshua awoke, it was already day. Sunlight filtered

through the high window, the dust in its beam darting ceaselessly, like a swarm of trapped midges.

He had left the candle to burn in the candlestick, and it had guttered to the base, its wax a frozen waterfall from lip to saucer. He must remember to replace it before nightfall. If he should be called out at night, it would not do to blunder down the staircase in darkness.

His clothing of the night before lay folded upon a chair. It had been a good night . . . and the memory of it warmed him with pleasure. He had two good friends and, if pressed, might have added the goodwill of the justice. Of Dr Mansel's feelings, he was less sure, but of his wife's, he was in no doubt: she both feared and disliked him. Well, he must get used to it. There would certainly be many others before the murderer was trapped. He washed his face and hands in the cold water from the bedside bowl and jug, carefully drying the ball of soap and putting it on the saucer. Later he would scrub himself down at the well in the yard, in comfort. A hip-bath, with his six-foot-three-inch frame was a useless toy. It rendered him all angles and joints, elbows and knees, like a hearthside cricket!

He put on his uniform and boots, and walked downstairs, his boots scraping noisily on the bare stone. He ate an oaten cake and some cold bacon, clearing a space in the bleak debris of last night's table. He did not attempt to build a fire to heat the kettle, but drank some buttermilk from the larder stone and, taking his helmet from a hook behind the door, went out into the street. He missed the ritual of taking food to the dog and sharing its warm pleasure. He would return, always now, to a house empty of any living thing. But Jeremiah was glad . . . and Rebecca, too.

As he walked to the 'Crown Inn' to fetch his grey he was clarifying in his mind the things he needed to do. He did not know whether the fact that the man he sought drove a cabriolet would prove an advantage or a hindrance to him. It was the type of lightweight French carriage, as Joshua knew well, used by unmarried men to go out at night visiting, or to the theatre, or to dinner. An elegant contraption, shell-shaped and hooded, and so finely balanced upon its slender wheels, that it needed the stability of two horses . . . hence, he supposed, the matched black pair. Perhaps the young man was more used to a town life. Or did he use it, with raised hood, to guard the privacy of his female acquaintances?

Now where should he begin his search? The manors and large houses, of course, for they would own gigs, as well as the broughams and larger carriages. Then, there were the more affluent merchants, the administrators of the docks and the ship-owners, the iron masters, not to mention the owners of quarries and brickyards. And who was to say the red-haired man's journey with the unknown girl mattered? It could have been a simple kindness; a mild unplanned excursion for someone living in another place, well away from the three hamlets.

At the 'Crown', Ossie saw that Joshua was troubled. He took his mare with scarce a word of thanks, or a greeting and titbit for the animal. It nuzzled his pocket, now, with no response from its master.

'Your work lies heavily upon you, Constable.'

'There is much to do, I fear it would be less daunting to seek a needle in a haystack.'

'Who do you seek, sir? I ask because I know most families hereabouts.'

'That is the difficulty. I have no names. I know only that the man I seek is young, red-haired, and has a skin clustered with sun spots. I know little else, save that he drives a gig, or cabriolet.'

'Why, sir, that is no difficulty. I know well who you mean, for I made enquiries, myself! It is the young gentleman from Dan-y-Graig House. I have seen him but the once, but I know from your description that I cannot be mistaken. He is as covered with freckles as a trout with spots!' The ostler's face creased with a gap-toothed smile. Joshua had to hold himself in check, lest he hug him close.

'Where is the house?'

'If you ride over the Clevis Hill, and take the main way out to Tythegston, you cannot miss it. It lies but a few hundred yards to the right as you ride, under the lea of the woods. A big, grey, stone, rambling place, built by the Reverend Robert Knight, the justice.'

'Is this some relation of his, then?'

'No, sir. I believe that the house has been rented by some rich gentleman. He has come from elsewhere but a few weeks ago. I know nothing of him otherwise, save that the young man is his son.'

'What manner of man is the son?'

'As I say, I have seen him but the once, when he drank here at the inn. I unsaddled his horse. A rude, ill-mannered fellow, who treats both horses and servants with roughness, if you will forgive me for venturing an opinion.'

'Come, I asked you. Anything more?'

'I have heard that he treats those of his own station, gentlemen, with courtesy; which seems to me a greater fault.'

'How so?'

'If he had no manners at all, sir, he could be forgiven on the grounds of ignorance.'

Joshua smiled. 'You learn more of life and people than many who travel the world, Ostler, and I thank you for your help, and your lesson in philosophy. Tell me, what do they call you?'

'My name is Oswald, but Ossie the Ostler I am called hereabouts. Although like a good beast, I will answer to any kind word or command, sir.' Brown eyes twinkled in the creased face, and he walked away, back bent, and smiling cheerfully at his own joke.

Joshua mounted swiftly, determining to apprise Dr Peate of their exchange. Then, saluting the ostler from the archway, he rode out.

As Joshua turned into the carriageway of Dan-y-Graig House, past the small stone lodge, with its pretty, arched windows, and a tangle of glossy creeper softening its walls, he was grateful to the ostler. The prospect of knocking upon countless unknown doors, demanding, 'Does a red-haired man, stippled with freckles, live here?' did not appeal to him as either a dignified or fruitful occupation. It would certainly have earned him a reputation for eccentricity; a trait which was only tolerated, indeed, expected, in the upper classes.

The house was larger, grander, than he had expected it to be, from the pathway. It was as settled in the shelter of the woodland which grew up the hillside as if it had been flung up there naturally, like some outcrop of grey stone. It was gracefully proportioned and low lying, with many elegant windows, (despite the imposition of an iniquitous window tax) and its façade was softened with lavender-blue clusters of wisteria and fragile ivy trails.

It was a house Joshua would have liked to own, with its extensive shrubberies, walks and lawns, and the curved pathways which swept on either side to the stables and rambling stone outhouses. Privately, he thought it altogether more elegant and welcoming than the justice's house, although lacking its history and atmosphere. Perhaps the wintry circumstances surrounding his visits there had frozen his critical sensibilities!

He was surprised to see no servant about, and none at the lodge. He tethered the grey to the branch of a stout, chestnut tree, and paused outside the fanlighted door, then tugged on the bell-pull. It was some time before the door was opened by a liveried manservant, who looked at Joshua in some bewilderment, as if debating whether to dispatch him to the servants' entrance.

'Your business, sir?'

'I wish to see the master of the house.'

Joshua's voice and manner unexpectedly confirming him as a 'gentleman', the servant grew more amenable.

'I shall inform Mr Crandle that you are here, sir. Please come into the hall, and wait. If you would care to tell me your business?'

'My business is with Mr Crandle.'

The man walked away, back rigid, and returned within minutes. 'Mr Crandle will see you in the library, sir.'

Joshua thought, wrily, that he would soon be able to write a monograph on the libraries of the district. He wondered if men, perhaps, felt more in command in such places. As if being surrounded by books, maps and scholarships of others lent them a cerebral distinction, more fitting than the mindless frivolity of the drawing room.

The man who greeted him and bade him sit was a thick-set, grizzled individual with the high colour of an habitual drinker. He might have looked impressive, except for the monstrous excrescence of his nose. It dominated his face. In fact, it seemed to dominate the whole room, drawing the eye, unwillingly, from the elegance of his frock coat and trousers and the silk cravat with its grey pearl stock pin.

'Perhaps you will state your business, Constable, I am a very busy man.'

'And I, sir. So I will waste no time. I should like to interview your son.'

'The devil you would!' Then, realizing that he had been uncivil, Crandle attempted a heavy playfulness. 'Well, what has the young limb been up to this time? Some tomfoolery with the village maidens?'

'You would know that better than I, sir. My business concerns a journey your son took with a woman, now dead.'

Crandle's face drained of colour, save for the blotches stranded on his cheeks, and the awful nose, then became suffused again.

'You will excuse me, a shock ... you cannot think ..?'

'I think nothing, sir. As I said, I merely wish to interview your son.'

'You will have no objection to my staying during your questioning, I hope?'

'None, sir, if you will allow him to speak without interruption.'

'Of course. Of course.' He pulled at a bell-rope. 'You will excuse the house being somewhat disorganized, my wife and daughter are away, so I have dismissed some of the servants until their return.'

'A visit, sir?'

'A brief holiday, unfortunately marred by illness. My daughter has contracted some minor fever and so their return has been delayed. A great inconvenience.'

'I hope that there will be a speedy return to health,' said Joshua, smoothly. 'I have no doubt there is an excellent doctor in ..?'

'Porlock.'

'An excellent resort, with good clean air, most suitable for a convalescence.'

The manservant entered, and Crandle instructed, 'Please tell

Mr Creighton that I wish to see him here, without delay.'

When Creighton Crandle entered, he first stood in the doorway, languidly, then adjusted his cuffs and strode arrogantly in. He ignored Joshua, and looked at his father as if seeking some clue to the way he should respond.

'You wanted to speak to me, father?'

'The constable has some questions to ask of you.'

'Well?' His voice was abrupt, disinterested, as if addressing an inferior.

'I believe that on Wednesday of last week, you visited Bridgend,' Joshua said.

'So?' Creighton looked amused, 'have you come to tell me that it has become a punishable offence?' He took a chair, and sat astride it.

'I believe that on that day you picked up a young lady passenger from the "Royal Mail" coach.'

'Picked up? A quaint expression ... I am not a coachman. I do not hire my services.'

'You drove with her to Newton?'

'And if I did?'

'Her name, sir, if you please?'

He looked unutterably bored. 'I did not enquire. It was of no interest to me!'

His father gave him a warning look, which Joshua intercepted.

'You did not meet her by arrangement, then?' Joshua asked.

'I did not. I merely did her the honour of conveying her in the cabriolet.'

'She was coming for what purpose?'

'I did not enquire. It was of no interest to me,' Creighton repeated, arrogantly.

'Was she staying with friends, perhaps?'

'I have already told you, I know nothing of the girl.'

'You made no conversation during the journey?'

'None that is worth repeating. Why do you persist? Are you hard of hearing ... or merely stupid?'

'The young woman is dead. Murdered. I am seeking to establish her identity.'

'So? She is dead. Since I know nothing of her, I can hardly be expected to mourn. Now. If you will excuse me, Constable.'

'Sit down, Creighton!' his father instructed, harshly, 'you will help the constable.'

The young man flushed angrily, but sat. 'How can I help if I know nothing?' he muttered, peevishly.

'Keep a civil tongue,' his father retorted.

'Well! What else do you wish to know?' he asked Joshua, rudely.

'So far, you have told me nothing.'

'Very well. I offered to convey her to Newton, for that is where she wished to go. I did not ask her her name. I did not ask her where she came from, or where she was bound, or with whom she was staying. I did not see her again, nor did I wish to. And I certainly did not kill her. Does that satisfy you?'

Joshua refrained from answering.

'Now, if you have no further use for me, perhaps you will allow me to leave.'

'You have always been free to do so . . . but I would ask one more question.'

'Well?' Creighton did not attempt to hide his irritation.

'What exactly were you doing at the coaching inn?'

'I was doing what people usually do at such places, seeking refreshment.'

'You had been where?'

'To the market. The cattle market.'

'We have thoughts of building up a herd,' interposed his father, quickly.

Joshua nodded.

The older man had pushed his chair back behind his desk, looking awkwardly for a way to bring the interview to a close. For a moment Joshua could almost feel sorry for him, with his bulbous, strawberry-pitted nose and graceless oaf of a son.

'Good day to you, sir,' Joshua said civilly. 'I thank you for receiving me.' He returned to the son. 'It would be insulting, sir, to thank you either for your help or your courtesy. I bid you good day with the firm assurance that we shall meet again.'

Creighton flushed angrily, skin ugly under the freckles and shock of copper hair, but stood aside for Joshua to pass.

Mr Crandle pulled the bell-rope for the servant, but Joshua had already gone.

'You fool.' The father rounded, furiously, upon his son. 'Are you completely devoid of all sense? Did that expensive education teach you nothing but boorishness and loutishness? Does your conceit and vanity drive you to risk everything?'

His blazing fury made his son shuffle and look sheepish. 'He knows nothing ... suspects nothing. What is he but a village constable? Stupid! Muddle-headed! There is nothing to fear from him.'

'It is you who are stupid. If you cannot see that he is a man of guile and intelligence, then I can hope to teach you nothing!'

'I told him the truth,' Creighton objected, petulantly.

'You told him nothing. But he learnt more than if you had written in every last detail. Get out of my sight. I have work to do and your perversity puts me off it!'

His son shrugged petulantly. 'I am off to the "Ancient Briton" then, as in Mama's absence, luncheon is likely to be cattle fodder. If you need me you will know where to find me.'

'If not there, then in any alehouse or whorehouse where your credit is still good! I warn you, sir, keep a guard on your tongue!'

'Always,' the tone was mocking, 'and you, sir, on yours.'

As Joshua took the wide driveway to the lodge, he was surprised to see Dr Mansel's carriage negotiating a curve, and reined in the grey to let it pass.

He was more surprised to see not the doctor, but Mrs Mansel peering out, her sallow face pinched and querulous. He had no doubt that she recognized him, but she gave no sign.

A pretty adventure, he thought, amused, timing her visits to when the women of the household are absent! Well, it is hardly young Crandle she has come to moon over, since he is but half her age. Although, he recalled the wild conservatory, some women nurtured strange fancies! None stranger, though, than a passion for the older Crandle, and his monstrous encumbrance of a nose! To be so burdened, and then saddled with an arrogant lout of a son ... and the unspeakable Mrs Mansel.

'Dear life,' marvelled Joshua out loud, 'it must be very hell on earth!'

When Joshua returned to the 'Crown Inn' to stable his horse, he was still smarting at young Crandle's studied insolence. Although he had galloped the horse over the warren to rid himself of his spleen, after reaching the village, he still felt murderous. Only one thing lifted his spirits, seeing Jeremiah and the dog, Charity, walking together on his way.

Jeremiah carried a large parcel, clumsily tied and tucked insecurely under one arm, the other hand holding the dog's leash. When Joshua reined in, and stopped, the dog wriggled its backside and whip of a tail in welcome, pink-rimmed slits of eyes bright.

'Well, I'll be damned!' exclaimed Joshua. 'I believe he likes me better now that we are apart.'

''Tis said that absence has that effect,' returned Jeremiah.

'What are you carrying? From what has escaped from the wrapping, I fear it is your shroud!'

'I would not have one so laced with frills,' Jeremiah objected, 'indeed, I would put the rest of the angels and the resurrected to shame. It is my shirt of last evening.'

'What? You are wearing it to delight the quarrymen? Or the widow ladies of the parish?'

'Neither. I returned it to Rebecca with the shoes and stockings which she lent me, for they were her father's, but he was a smaller man, fortunately with enormously disproportionate feet.'

'And?'

'It necessitated slitting the shirt from collar to hem in order that I might wear it, agape at the back.'

Joshua began to laugh immediately, his ill temper swiftly waning.

'But,' continued Jeremiah, 'Rebecca gave me this bundle of them, frilled and furbelowed as a bride's drawers, and I am to choose those which suit me best, and she will put great patches upon the backsides of them.'

'Take care!' said Joshua, 'for she will turn you into a dandy, and the fish will take fright and swim to deeper waters.'

'Speaking of deep waters, is there news or progress?'

'I have found the red-haired gentleman ... No, I lie, for "gentleman" he is not.'

'But is he involved in her death, do you think?'

'I think not, although he is as unpleasant and ill-natured a fellow as I have ever met. He is called Creighton Crandle.'

'Perhaps it is his name with vexes him, causes a flux,' said Jeremiah, smiling. 'It is a hard cross to bear. Did I not tell you of a maid I knew called Mistress Gentle, as sour as a crab apple, and a voice like a rook!'

Joshua laughed, humour restored, and rode on with a salute to Jeremiah and the dog, and a pat for the grey.

He left his mount with Ossie and returned home to find the justice's groom waiting at the door.

'I bring you a message, Constable, from Mr Robert Knight.'

Joshua tore it open, breaking the seal.

> 'I have arranged a coach for your witnesses, to convey them to the inquest on Tuesday. It will be at your door at nine o' the clock. Will you please inform them of the time and place. I have news of the person of whom you enquired. The answer is "Yes", the date one week since. There will be no need to prepare a parish funeral for the dead woman. When the inquest decides that her body may be released for burial, I shall arrange it and meet all expenses. I have agreed to read the funeral service at the parish church of St John the Baptist.
>
> Robert Knight.
> Priest and Justice'

'There is no answer,' said Joshua to the groom, 'save to say the note was safely delivered. I shall thank your master myself.' A good man, thought Joshua, a fine justice, and a better priest. He was glad about the girl, yet troubled about the answer to the question he had posed the justice.

I foresee conflict ahead, he thought, and perhaps the threat of bloodshed. For the moment, it was a matter he must keep to himself. He hoped that his fears would prove unfounded.

Chapter Eight

Within the hour, upon an impulse, Joshua stripped himself naked in his yard and, taking water from the well, rained it by the bucketful over his head and flesh until he had leached away all traces of the day. Then he turned indoors, laid his uniform aside, and carefully dressed himself in his party clothes of the night before.

He knew that by stepping out dressed up like a boar's head upon a platter, he would not go unnoticed. Every inch of his pilgrimage would be covertly watched and remarked upon; every detail of his attire assessed as to the pence it had cost. Nonetheless, he hoped that his errand might excite approval upon the way, and not rancour or ridicule. He would go openly, and suitably presented, to pay his compliments to Miss Rebecca de Breos.

Those acquaintances he met upon the way exchanged greetings with him pleasantly, remarking to themselves that their tall young constable was every inch a gentleman, and not a whit the worse for it.

The russet-cheeked old lady, who had shovelled the horse droppings for her garden, peered at him from her gateway, unsure of the elegant stranger.

'Why Constable, sir. 'Tis you. My old eyes do mist, sometimes, and play me tricks.'

Joshua bade her a civil good day.

'If it is not a rudeness, sir, the day is brighter for seeing you so finely clad. I mean no offence.'

'And it would be churlish, ma'am, to take it, for the compliments of friends are one of life's pleasures, and I thank you most humbly.'

The old lady smiled broadly, and despite the ache in her bones, fairly flew along the path to her door, fleet as a swallow, to tell any who would listen that young Constable Stradling was as elegant in speech as in dress.

From the doorway of the 'Ancient Briton', the landlord regarded him with interest, 'A fine day for a walk, is it not, Constable Stradling?'

'It is, sir.'

'I see you travel in the direction of the Burrows.' His florid face creased in humour, 'It is said the area is remarkable for its flora and fauna. Is it of interest to you, sir?'

'Passing,' replied Joshua, straight-faced.

'Is there perhaps a particular flower that you seek . . . to add to your collection? Perhaps I can advise you where to search, knowing the area.'

'Thank you, but I am already aware of its location.'

'Then I hope you may find it at home.' He broke into laughter, right eye disappearing into the creases of a knowing wink. Then, still laughing, he entered the inn, striking his large hand upon his thigh, convulsed with his own wit. Gentleman though he be, he thought, he gave as good as he got, putting on no airs and graces. Whether in humour, or combat, he would be a worthy adversary.

Rebecca, tending her small front garden, and seeing him coming, stroked the creases from her faded cotton skirt and blouse, put a hand to her hair and resolutely went out through the wicket gate to greet him.

Joshua doffed his high silk hat courteously. 'Good morning, Rebecca, I hope that I have not called at an inconvenient time?'

'There is no inconvenient time for welcoming friends,' she said, warmly. 'Will you not come into the house?'

He followed her into the coolness of the drawing room. 'I have come to tell you that your likeness of the murdered girl has brought results.'

'You have found the man?' she asked, anxiously. 'The one who brought her here?'

'Indeed, and a more arrogant, insolent dog . . .' Anger inflamed his skin at the memory of the encounter.

She motioned him to a chair. 'You believe he killed her, Joshua?'

'He is vicious and offensive enough in all conscience! I have never met a more rude or disagreeable fellow, but my contempt for him does not prove him a murderer.'

'No.'

'He is a stranger to the place. His father has taken the big house at Dan-y-Graig ... Crandle. You have met him?'

She hesitated. 'I do not know the name.'

'It is no loss, for I swear to you, Rebecca, the man is no respecter of women. Of that I am certain.'

'And I,' she agreed emphatically. Colouring, she added, 'If that is your belief, Joshua.'

There was a silence between them that lengthened into awkwardness.

'To tell the whole truth, Rebecca, the drawing was but part of my errand.'

She waited, puzzled.

'You have no parents, no one to ask ...' He broke off, fingers tracing the brim of his silk hat, looking embarrassed. 'God's truth, Rebecca, I do it clumsily.' He took a deep breath, 'I have come to pay you my respects.'

She gave him no help.

'Damn it, Rebecca,' he exploded. 'I have come to ask permission to court you.'

'Then I give it freely.' She began to laugh. 'Oh, Joshua, if you could but see your face ... so grave and embarrassed ... as if it were a funeral you attended, and not a wooing!'

He said, stiffly. 'I am not familiar with the practice.'

'And I even less so ... for I swear that you are the first who has so addressed me. Since we are both novices at the game, perhaps you had best kiss me and, if it proves agreeable to us both, then we may continue from there.'

Obediently, he took her in his arms, and kissed her gently and respectfully upon her soft mouth.

'Yes,' she said, drawing away, 'it was quite satisfactory, but I think, Joshua, that you have not put your whole heart and effort into it. Will you not try to improve upon your performance?'

'Minx!' he exclaimed, drawing her to him. 'I will show you how competent I am!'

When she was able to catch her breath, she said, demurely, 'Already, I begin to enjoy it.'

*

Jeremiah and his dog, Charity, were content. As they followed the dunes across Newton Burrows, they could smell the strange, powerful aroma of the sea. It was like no other smell on earth. If anyone had asked Jeremiah to describe it, he would have said, 'How do you describe God? Or happiness? Trying to explain it is like trying to hold grains of sand in your open hand, a profitless endeavour. Best accept it, and be glad.'

From their vantage point, at the summit of the highest dune, the Burrows unrolled before them, acre upon acre of fine white-bleached sand, curves and hollows shaped by the wind and tide as the coast subsided. Man and dog surveyed their kingdom, sniffed the air, and looked at each other with pleasure and anticipation. Far off in the bay, Jeremiah glimpsed Rebecca's cob and cart, silhouetted like a child's wooden toy. He was part of the world, and yet apart. The day stretched before them unspoiled and inviting, like the land. Then, without warning, the dog stiffened. A growl erupted low in its throat, and Jeremiah felt the quick jerk of his arm muscle as the leash grew taut.

Below them, in the curved bowl of the plain, something was moving. Jeremiah, following the dog's gaze, saw it too; a figure weaving its way through a tangle of willow shoots and scrub. It bent to the sand, something gleamed, and with a cry torn from his throat, Jeremiah, and the dog charged down the hillside like two avenging angels of wrath.

The figure, hearing their strange and savage cry, froze, then saw the two descending in a storm of sand and fury, too terrible to withstand. He tried to get away, stumbling over roots and brambles, whip-lashed by willow. Then his foot twisted in a rabbit hole, and Jeremiah and the dog were upon him. Jeremiah swung him up by the collar of his coat and the powerful arms held him aloft, struggling in the air, legs and arms jerking feebly, like a trapped black beetle, while the dog, released, darted and barked, making lunges at the dangling feet.

'Now I've got you,' Jeremiah exulted. 'Let's see how you like being trapped. Worm! Maggot on the flesh of the earth! Carrion!'

He looked into the terrified eyes of Ezra the Box.

'You!' Jeremiah's grip tightened so that Ezra's eyes bulged in their sockets, and his mouth gaped; then he let him drop to the sand. The dog stood menacingly above him, teeth bared in a snarl, daring him to move.

'Get that beast off me,' Ezra entreated, body rigid, lips barely moving. 'He'll murder me!'

'Murder would be too good for you, you scum!' Jeremiah wiped his hands as if touching Ezra had defiled them. 'What is the matter with you, man? What is this blood lust that you have? Aren't the bodies that you deal with enough for you?'

Ezra's small, beady eyes moistened with tears. 'It wasn't me ... I didn't do anything, I was just walking here and found the trap. I thought I would throw it away.'

'A likely tale!' Jeremiah grabbed him by the collar and jerked him to his feet.

'Since when have you taken up walking? And dressed up like a cock pheasant.'

'I was on my way to a funeral.'

'Pity it wasn't your own.'

Ezra dusted himself down, sniffing and wiping his nose on his cuff. 'You've broken my sleeve.'

'It should have been your neck!' said Jeremiah, unfeeling.

'I could tell the constable ... complain to the vestry. Say how you assaulted me.'

'You just try it and you'll feel the full weight of my fist!'

The dog growled agreement.

'Now, get going, you little weasel, before I change my mind and beat you unconscious.'

Ezra scrambled away, glancing back apprehensively as the dog was leashed in. 'You haven't heard the last of this,' he called, from a safe distance.

'Here!' Jeremiah threw the gin trap after him. 'Take your bloody trap and start running before I set the dog on you, or you'll need to start to praying.'

Ezra started running.

'Come back! Pick up that trap!' Jeremiah ordered.

Ezra edged back and grabbed it, then he was off, up the sand dune, slithering and falling as he went.

Jeremiah began to laugh. He laughed until the tears ran

down his chin, his ribs ached, and he had to hold on to a willow sapling for support. The dog leapt high on the leash, barking with excitement, trying to lick Jeremiah's face, to share in his pleasure. 'I've never seen a man move so fast,' he said, brushing the tears from his eyes, 'if all the fiends of hell were after him with pitchforks, he couldn't have gone quicker. I'll remember that sight to my dying day.

'Come, Charity,' he instructed, 'we've a good day ahead of us.'

The slanted, intelligent eyes looked enquiringly into Jeremiah's.

'You did well,' Jeremiah told the dog. 'Menacing, but restrained. I think Ezra was impressed.'

They walked together, across the plain, in perfect understanding.

Rebecca, intent on her shellfish-gathering upon the shore, thought what a strange, unexplored world there was in the rock pools and in the wake of the tide. The beach was strewn with the flotsam of the deep. White cuttle fish bones, that the cottagers put with their caged birds to sharpen their beaks, the brittle egg-cases of ink fish, seaweed, shells, and sometimes, green glass floats and cork from the fishermen's nets. Then, there were the living creatures: crabs, lobsters and the stranger hermit crabs that stole the discarded sea shells and used them as wandering homes. Prettiest of all, Rebecca thought, were the rock pools which, when they dried in the sun, left the rocks glittering with crystals of salt, like hoar frost. The deeper rock pools were the haunts of sea-anemones, jellyfish, prawns and small darting fishes, perfect in every detail, but no bigger than a finger nail. Sometimes she found a stranded starfish, shaped like a small child's outstretched hand, a hollow sea-urchin, or a pinkly transparent jelly fish, large as a platter, waiting patiently for the tide to return it to pulsing life. Sometimes, the cottagers gathered the mussels clustered under the crevices of the rocks and pools, wrenching away the ferny growths which fused them there and which all the power of the sea had been unable to loosen. They gathered, too, the strange, edible seaweed peculiar to the place, which they boiled and ate as laver bread. To Rebecca, in its finished state, it looked like wet cowpats, dingy and unappetizing. Yet, when rolled in oatmeal and baked in melted bacon fat, it was a dish to humble the gods.

She looked up, aware of being under scrutiny, but seeing no one. She felt unaccountably afraid and, getting up on the cart, pulled at the reins and clicked her tongue, to make the pony trot. They had reached the Burrows when a stranger pulled out from behind a clump of marram grass. He did not speak nor attempt to detain her; in fact, she could not be certain that he even saw her, so deep was his concentration. He was well enough dressed, but neglected and ill-shaven. A man of fifty, perhaps, it was difficult to tell. All that she remembered was the burning fierceness of his eyes, and the defeated lines of face and body. Rebecca was deeply troubled. She felt that she should have stopped and spoken some words of friendship or comfort. Perhaps he was unwell, or recently bereaved. But she knew, somehow, that what pained him was too deep to be eased by a passing stranger. Just as she knew that he had been watching her.

When she had crossed the flatter, more open ground of Picket's Lease, and reached the village, the feeling of apprehension lifted, and she was angry with herself for her foolishness.

Once home, she busied herself with unloading the cart, washing the cockles in their shells, preparing the fire, and unharnessing and stabling the cob.

Her tasks completed, and the cockles steaming in their iron pot on the brick stove, she drew some water from the well to wash herself. When she straightened up, the stranger was there, at the wall, watching her. She never understood why, but as she looked at him, all fear left her, and she said, gently, 'Will you not come in and rest for a while, for I can see that you are either sick or tired, sir?'

'A little of both,' he replied. 'I have indeed suffered an illness for many years, and I have walked too far, and too long. I shall be grateful for the chance to rest.'

She nodded, and opened the gate which led to the Burrows. 'Please come into the house. I have little enough to offer you of refreshment, but what I have you are welcome to share.'

He thanked her, and she gave him her arm as support, for he seemed to be walking with effort, his strength used up. She helped to seat him upon a chair and fetched him some buttermilk from the larder, and some oaten cakes, and sat beside him and watched him drink, for he refused all offers of food.

'Are you restored, now?'

He nodded, and when he looked up, to her surprise, his eyes were filled with tears, and he began to cry, rocking to and fro like a child, his head buried in his hands. She waited until the spasm had passed, neither touching him nor saying any word of comfort. She had never seen a man cry before, and she felt his pain and hopelessness as if it were her own.

'I am sorry,' he said, at length. 'It is a physical weakness, the illness has left me tired and depressed. I beg your pardon, Mistress, and ask you to forgive me.'

She nodded,.not trusting herself to speak.

'You are so like someone I knew a long time ago, and the memory brought me pleasure and pain I had thought buried with her.' He thanked her most courteously for her kindness, and said, 'I will go, now. I have abused your hospitality, I fear. Again, I beg your pardon most humbly, for I know that I have distressed you.'

'If you are sick, sir, I believe that there is a doctor who lives nearby. I have not had cause to seek his help, for he did not dwell here until after my father's illness and death, but the reports I hear of him are good, and he appears to be kind. He is called Dr Mansel.'

He rose to his feet. 'Thank you, Miss ..?'

'De Breos, but my chosen name is Rebecca.'

'Thank you, Rebecca. You have given me drink and shelter, and told me all I need to know.'

She walked with him to the garden gate, for he steadfastly refused her pleas to drive him to the village in the cart, or to the doctor's house. He left, as he came, over the Burrows.

Rebecca returned to the house. He had been gently bred, of that she was sure, well spoken, and his gratitude had been real. She was afraid that the illness which he suffered was grave, for his fatigue was extreme, and his colour pallid and unhealthy.

She wondered what condition caused a man to weep with such terrible wretchedness and depth of feeling. She was no longer afraid of him.

As he walked up Clevis Hill to Dr Mansel's house, Joshua was so deeply engrossed in thought that he passed by the iron gateway, unwittingly, and had to return, somewhat sheepishly, hoping that he had not been observed. He was not, however, dwelling upon the meeting with Dr Mansel, or even the dead girl and the morrow's inquest. His thoughts were of the world outside his small, triangular kingdom.

He had received, that morning, a letter from his friend, Dr Handel Peate, giving him news of the secret researches Joshua had persuaded him to undertake. The progress report pleased and excited him. He hoped that the object of the investigation might be equally pleased. The other information, however, was less sanguine.

There was a persistent rumour of a cholera outbreak in the cities, which threatened to spread as swiftly and devastatingly as the great epidemic of 1832. Those in authority strove to suppress the news lest it caused panic and disorder.

'It is a disgrace,' wrote Dr Peate, 'indeed, a public scandal, that Chadwick's report upon the appallingly insanitary conditions endured by the poor, with the damning evidence of squalor, sickness and decay in the cities, have wrought no changes. The recommendations are dead and forgotten, as are the tragic victims of our neglect. For now,' Dr Peate continued, 'a London doctor, by the name of John Snow, has proved that some epidemics are spread by the excrement of victims polluting sewers, public wells, conduits and other shared water supplies. In the name of pity, how many more must die, before we act?'

Joshua thought of the privvy middens seeping their contents through the surrounding soil, contaminating wells and springs, and the drinking water of the three hamlets. He thanked God that, at least, they were not wholly dependent upon a shared river or brook, although many poor cottagers drank, laundered and, no doubt, bathed in Newton Pool, or the freshwater streams that emerged in the bays. It needed but one affected visitor to the Port, by cargo ship, or even by coach to the inns or lodging houses, to bring disaster.

He would seek the advice of Dr Mansel, but keep the news well hid from Rebecca and Jeremiah, for no purpose would be served by alarming them. For the moment, it was a more immediate and personal concern which drew him to Dr Mansel's door.

The underfed house maid, whom he thought of as 'the nervous shrew', opened the door, but it was Dr Obadiah Mansel who came into the hall and ushered him into the light, elegantly proportioned drawing room. Dr Mansel offered him a handsome black and gold chair of the Regency period then seated himself, face pinkly flushed under the fly-away hair, which reminded Joshua, irresistibly, of dandelion clocks.

'I watched you coming, from my window,' Dr Mansel observed, 'you seemed lost in thought.' The pale-gooseberry eyes were alert, questioning. 'Something about the inquiry, perhaps?'

'No, there is nothing new of that business, save that we have found the young man who drove her here.'

'Involved in the murder, you think?'

'No. I think not. An accidental involvement only. But the justice has told you of his plans for the girl's burial?'

'Yes. It is arranged. Yet, I puzzle over his motives.'

'How so?'

'Does he take responsibility as a priest . . . or as a justice?'

'As a man,' said Joshua, instantly. ' I believe that he cares for people. It is as simple as that . . . his roles as priest and justice depend upon it, surely?'

'You suspect no deeper reason?'

'I have not yet been corrupted by corruption,' Joshua replied, easily. 'If I suspected everyone who behaved well in life, then I could wish, most devoutly, that such work might occupy me night and day.'

'Well said,' approved Dr Mansel, 'but in my worldly experience, you would be sadly under-occupied.'

They both laughed.

'Then why have you come?' Mansel enquired. 'You seek my help in some other case of yours?'

'No.' Joshua's face grew serious, 'It is about another case, certainly, but that involving you and your wife.'

'I see,' Dr Mansel sighed, 'so that is once again to be resurrected. I had thought it all decently buried, at last.'

'I have been at the courthouse reading the files.'

'I am sorry that you found it necessary.' His voice was stiff.

'It was as well, sir, that I did.'

'How, then?'

'I learnt that at his trial, Dr Burrel threatened you and your wife. He promised vengeance.'

'It is not uncommon for a man under stress ... but that was more than twenty years ago.'

'Twenty years for a sick man to brood and plan revenge.'

'Come, you cannot be serious?'

'Dr Burrel was released from prison a week since. Upon leaving, he again swore to seek you both out.'

Dr Mansel seemed to have shrunk, grown older. 'So. It begins again.'

Joshua nodded.

'It is my wife I fear for. Already, as you have seen, she is nervous, agitated ... her behaviour unpredictable.'

'You do not mean to tell her?'

He shook his head, the pale, opaque eyes looked tired, defeated. He blinked rapidly. 'I do not wish her to be pushed beyond her limits.'

'I understand. It is your decision. I must respect it. You have greater experience and knowledge of these things.'

'Have I?' the tired eyes came to life suddenly. 'Half my time as a doctor is spent convincing people of it. The other half is spent in convincing myself. I leave you to judge which is the harder.'

Joshua nodded.

'Do you not find, Constable, that people expect too much of you?'

'I do indeed, sir.'

'The trouble with playing God is that, unlike Him, one is unable to perform miracles.'

Joshua smiled, glancing around, and thinking that for someone playing God, Dr Mansel had chosen an appropriate setting. The whole impression was one of great lightness and delicacy. The silk curtains were held clear of the large windows, streaming in light. The furniture too was restrained, delicate in the Regency fashion, and occupied, mostly, the centre of the room, giving an impression of infinite space. Above them hung a fine chandelier, already set with wax candles. Joshua imagined it glowing with flame, its crystals aglitter with rainbow-coloured light.

Joshua looked down to see Dr Mansel watching him good-humouredly, fingertips held together, pressed to his lips.

'Well, and do you approve, Stradling?'

'I am sorry. It was unpardonable of me . . . but, yes, it is a beautiful room.'

'My wife is a woman of the utmost sensibility. Her refinement is absolute. Her taste impeccable. The only discordant thing in the room is me.' He rose to his feet, waistcoat buttons straining over his rounded belly. 'Things are not always what they seem, Stradling.' He held out his hand.

Joshua did not know if he meant himself, his wife, or the case he had won. Joshua took his hand, and Dr Mansel shook it firmly.

'I thank you for coming to warn me of Burrel. You will tell me if there is news of him in the vicinity?'

'Of course.'

'We meet at the inquest, then, tomorrow.' Dr Mansel walked with Joshua to the door. 'They told me I had won my case,' he said, unexpectedly, 'They were wrong. There were no winners or losers, only survivors and, sometimes, survival is the hardest thing to bear.

Jeremiah and Rebecca, did Joshua but know it, were gathered upon the village green, in the lea of the clock-tower, in company with those of the cottagers who were not at their labour, or household tasks.

As was his custom, the Reverend Robert Knight had instructed a vestryman to read to the parishioners suitably expurgated accounts from the previous day's newspaper. It was a practice born during the wars with the French, when word of battles and triumphs had seeped through but slowly, for there were no mail coaches and no company stages to bring news, merely the few private carriages, and those of the inns. There was an air of suppressed excitement in the crowd, a cheerful holy day atmosphere. The readings were popular, and a welcome diversion from the cares of the day. Even the reports of public whippings, and the gallows, were distant enough to be salutary. A good excuse for gossip. 'Indeed,' the Reverend Robert Knight had been heard to remark, 'were my sermons so well attended, and faithfully followed, then my parishioners of the three hamlets would, undoubtedly, all be saints!'

Now, the vestryman, being one of the few who was literate, and determined to demonstrate the fact, grew over-enthusiastic, departing from the prepared text, and wilfully including the reported rumour of cholera.

At first, the crowd remained silent, motionless, then a whispering and rustling swept through them like the wind through a cornfield.

'Dear God!' said Jeremiah, speaking for them all, 'Is it possible?'

'You think it will spread here?' Rebecca's voice was child-like, frightened.

'No, we must pray not,' he said, to soothe her.

''Tis a vile, stinking affliction,' declared a neighbour, ignoring Jeremiah's efforts to quieten him. 'I mind hearing how the victims choke upon their own vomit. They are afire with fever ... and lie in their own filth, unable to eat or drink, and so dry up and die, living skeletons. A stench of decay, and their faces swell and grow black.'

Jeremiah took Rebecca's hand firmly, feeling it cold in his own, despite the warmth of the day. 'Come, little maid,' he said, 'the tide calls us, and we have work to do.'

She nodded, asking hesitantly, 'Is it true, Jeremiah? What he said?'

'True? Why he has the brains of a gnat, and the mouth of a dog-fish. The braying of an ass would make more sense!'

She was not reassured.

They walked in silence to her cob and cart.

Jeremiah climbed up beside her, settling his sack amidst the woven frails.

‘Yet it is a cruel disease, Jeremiah?’ she persisted.

‘Yes, Rebecca,’ he said, gravely, ‘it is certainly that. Pray God you never meet it.’

Chapter Nine

The justice's small coach rumbled along the highway above Newton Downs, watched by a flock of curious sheep. The trundling of wheels upon uneven ground, the creaking of springs and the swaying of the monster, made them pause in their chewing, protuberant, brown eyes amazed. In a moment the coach had passed, a receding jangle of harness and hooves, and they returned to their grazing.

Inside, bumping about in considerable discomfort, Rebecca and Jeremiah, dressed in their best, considered the inquest.

'Damn me!' complained Jeremiah, as the wheels struck a deep rut. 'I am nothing but bruises. I wonder the justice has the strength to stand up! I would sooner walk.'

'His bones are better cushioned,' observed Rebecca, 'but I warrant he has to be lifted out at the end of the ride; we are like two small peas on a very large platter!'

They both laughed, then Jeremiah grew serious. 'The findings were not surprising. Murder by a person or persons unknown.'

'I hope that they will not remain unknown.'

'No, poor little maid.' He shook his head. 'But even if they bring them to justice, it will do her no good.'

'I think she will know,' said Rebecca, 'and it will bring her peace ... for they say those who die violently roam the earth, constantly seeking rest. You think she will find it, Jeremiah?' Her voice was anxious.

Jeremiah stared out of the window. The windmill on the Downs was catching the wind, its sails cutting the air, like a bird's wings.

'There, my girl. You see your answer.'

Rebecca looked at him, not understanding.

Jeremiah explained, solemnly. 'It is written, "The mills of God grind slowly, but they grind exceeding small"!'

She had a vision of someone trapped between the great stone

millwheels, bones crushed and ground fine as flour. Like Jeremiah she was a true believer and yet it was a thought which brought her no comfort.

The liveried coachman reined in the horses as they approached the constable's house, and they drew up in a flurry of noise and flung sand. The coachman alighted and, to the delight of the passing cottagers and the drinkers at the 'Crown' and 'Ancient Briton', opened the door of the coach, and helped them both climb down, bowing obsequiously.

Jeremiah bowed to the onlookers, and Rebecca made a deep curtsey, which pleased them greatly, and when Jeremiah made to tip the coachman a sixpence, it threw the crowd into fits of good-humoured laughter.

'Where do you go now?' Rebecca asked Jeremiah.

'To the quarries again, for yesterday I found no answers, and yet I am sure there is something hid . . . and you?'

'I shall finish stitching your shirts, and then to the pool, or the well, claiming mine is dry.'

'Indeed,' said Jeremiah, 'a veritable gossip shop! A quarry and mine of useful information. Take care that they do not get you married to our bow-legged ostler.'

'And you take care I do not stitch your tongue along with your shirts,' warned Rebecca, and they parted smiling and reluctant, as friends do.

Jeremiah returned to his cot, changed his clothing to his workaday garments, and unchained the dog, Charity, from the yard. He was greeted by such a paroxysm of noise and enthusiasm that he was forced to caution the animal, although not severely, for his heart was warmed by it. Then, together, they returned to Newton Downs.

The limestone quarries, on the Downs, had been there so long that no one was sure who had started them, or why. It was certain that much limestone had been used for the building of the old manor houses and farms, and there was rumour of it being shipped with coal and iron ore from the creek of Newton in the seventeenth century. All these cargoes must have been mined or quarried from the immediate hinterland, but even so, their transportation must have proved perilous and expensive. Now, however, its main use was as manure on the land. It was taken away by sea, either as quarried or reduced by burning and sent ready for use. This trade was mainly carried out with Minehead or Porlock. Some, however, was taken to build the new Port, or used as a flux in the iron works at nearby Tondu.

Jeremiah knew some of the men labouring in the quarries, but many were itinerant workmen, who had drifted in with the building of the docks. They came from Ireland, Bristol, from the sea ports of Somerset and Devon and remoter parts of Wales; their customs and character as diverse as their accents. One thing they shared was a willingness for hard work and a fondness for the local brew; theirs was fierce, demanding work and the stone dust which filled the eyes, mouth and lungs had to be constantly 'wetted down'. The labourers were paid from twelve to fifteen pence a day, depending upon results. The rivalry between them was intense, as was their unity in the world outside. Jeremiah had often been called upon by the landlord of the 'Crown' or 'Ancient Briton', to 'rip them apart!' when brawling upon the premises, or to 'knock their silly heads together!' It was an aspect of law keeping which he gratefully surrendered to Joshua, for they were likely to turn upon the peacemaker and leather him soundly. At least Joshua had the authority of his uniform.

As Jeremiah approached the quarry, walking with the cur down the ramp of compacted stone, he saw below him in the flat crater of the quarry floor that the men, stripped to the waist, were gathered around a small wood fire, eating and drinking. Above and below him the green flags were hoisted, showing that work had ceased and there was no threat from explosives to the innocent passer-by.

The men were brown-skinned from the sun and air, their arms and chests muscled, hair whitened with stone dust. Their bodies were damp; sweat streaked in runnels to their trousers, held firm with leather belts, over thick boots. They greeted Jeremiah, some by name, as he approached, and one threw the dog a piece of bread, which he devoured gratefully. One man left his pony and cart and came over to him.

'Well, Jeremiah?'

'Well, Emrys?'

'Come to see some real men working, have you?'

'Indeed, Emrys, they are all working as hard as I have ever seen them! It makes me quite faint just to watch such activity.'

There was a shout of laughter from the fireside, and Emrys punched him companionably on the chest.

'Come,' he said, taking Jeremiah's arm, 'we will walk a little, I am eager to stretch my legs.' He called out orders to a young boy, who went to take charge of the pony and cart.

'Well?' asked Jeremiah, when they were clear of the others, unable to be overheard. 'What news, then?'

'I have done as you said, and listened to the talk. I do it because I have pity for the little maid who died.'

Jeremiah nodded his understanding.

'It is said that one of the men, an Irishman by the name of Doonan, has been spending freely.'

'You think he has been paid for some other work? Outside the quarrying?'

'If so, then no one knows the source.'

'What manner of man is he?'

'Violent. Foul-mouthed ... ever eager for a brawl. He has few friends, and those only because they fear to cross him.'

'Point him out to me,' said Jeremiah, 'but do it circumspectly, for I do not wish to leave with my head cracked open.'

Emrys smiled, and did as he was bid.

The Irishman was huge, red-haired, and barrel-chested. The enormous fists that held his tankard were raw-boned as hams.

'By heaven and all the angels!' said Jeremiah, 'I would be loath to tangle with him! Put him in a yard with South Farm's bull and it would be hard to tell them apart!'

He and Emrys talked for a while, turning about and walking, the dog walking happily with them. Then, suddenly, there came a screeching and shouting from beside a wooden hut across the quarry, and a general confusion of yelling and shouting that took them running towards it. The dog ran with them, barking and yelping, adding to the uproar. In a small circle of quarry stones, the big Irishman was urging on a cock-fight; the birds, spurred with metal, were tearing at each other, shrieking and clawing, pecking wildly, in a flurry of blood and feathers.

Jeremiah pressed the dog's leash on Emrys and, without a

thought, grabbed at Doonan. Fury lent him strength. He could not fasten upon clothing, for the Irishman's body was bare and slippery with sweat. He grabbed the shock of red hair and swung him around. The Irishman wrenched away, eyes smarting with tears, leaving Jeremiah standing with tufts of torn hair in his hands. Then Jeremiah felt a blow upon his face which seemed to dislocate his spine, rocking him back on his heels, and Doonan started raining blows upon him, fists flailing, kicking, crushing, as if he were a beetle.

Furiously, Charity wrenched himself out of Emrys's hands and, with the snarl of a tiger, leapt high and clamped his teeth on the Irishman's backside. Round and round Doonan went, screeching with pain, the bull terrier hanging on grimly.

Jeremiah, seeing his advantage, summoned the strength of the righteous, and with one massive swing, sent Doonan to his knees, and with another, the Irishman fell forward onto his face, dazed. It was only then that the cur released him.

Emrys and Jeremiah then leapt into the ring and, grabbing the cocks who were still in battle, swifly de-spurred them. Before Doonan could recover, Jeremiah, his hands bleeding from the battle with man and cockerel, tucked a writhing cock under each arm, shouted to the dog to follow him and was off across the quarry, in a gale of laughter and encouragement. As Doonan rose, dazedly, to his feet, to give chase, the whistle blew a warning that work was to start. To ignore it brought a threat of dismissal, which even the Irishman dare not ignore. With ill-grace he opened his belt and inspected his bleeding backside, to the delighted cheers of the quarrymen, who roared even louder and more raucously as he doused it with water from the horses' bucket.

In the distance, near the top of the ramp, Jeremiah was still running, cockerels under his arms, the dog beside him. To their credit, not one of the quarrymen protested that Emrys had blown the whistle five minutes early.

'Well,' said Jeremiah to the dog, when they had reached the top of Dan-y-Graig Hill, the cockerels' legs and beaks secured with strips of rag from his shirt ends, 'what am I do do with them? Make a present of them to some villager with a hen or two? You tell me ... for as sure as there is a hell, after all that we have been through, I would never have the heart to eat them.'

'Saints preserve us!' exclaimed Joshua, opening his cottage door, and seeing Jeremiah's battered face, 'Who have you been doing battle with? A carriage and pair?'

'Worse,' said Jeremiah, through swollen lips, 'a mad Irishman, and a couple of spurred cockerels.'

Joshua ushered him inside, and bade him make himself comfortable. 'If there is as much as an inch of you that is not bruised or bloody!'

The adventure of the day recounted, they laughed together over a jug of ale.

'I have since discovered that Doonan has lodgings in Port. It is said that he has some sort of understanding with his landlady's daughter. He frequents the inn known as "The Ship Aground", near the docks.'

'I hope it will not prove prophetic!' said Joshua fervently.

Jeremiah's right eye was rapidly closing, his whole face swollen and bruised as a fallen apple. 'I will come with you,' he volunteered.

'Hold hard!' Joshua cautioned, 'Have you not taken enough of a beating? Would you seek more?'

'Pulped as I am,' said Jeremiah, philosophically, 'another bruise or two would hardly matter. I will come!'

They set off together, as unlikely a pair as ever breathed: Joshua, immaculate in his uniform and helmet and carrying a staunch, wooden truncheon, and Jeremiah in his old working clothes, face mis-shapen and sinister.

'Beauty and the Beast,' called out a wag, as they passed the 'Crown'. Jeremiah made a mock threatening gesture, at which the culprit crowed like a cock. Joshua's exploit was already folklore.

As they crossed the horse-drawn tramway, to walk to the 'Ship Aground', Jeremiah asked, 'What is to be our plan of action?'

'If you can somehow manage to contain him in the bar,' Joshua suggested, 'I will search his rooms . . . try to find some evidence.'

Jeremiah nodded, thinking hard.

But then Joshua observed, 'I fear though that you would have difficulty in warning me if he should return. What would I do then?'

'Start praying!' advised Jeremiah, fingering his face, 'and if that fails, run like the devil.'

Jeremiah peered through the window of the tavern and saw his friend, Emrys, sitting with a pint pot, at a small bench nearby. Leaning upon the bar was the bellicose Irishman, his broad shoulders and fierce red hair, now slightly less profligate, making him unmistakable.

Jeremiah tapped gently upon the window, praying that Doonan would not turn and see him. Emrys looked up and nodded, then slipped out unnoticed.

'By all that's wonderful,' he said, admiringly, 'what an eye he has given you! Like a piebald's backside! I don't think I've ever seen a finer ...'

They held a whispered conversation, and Jeremiah handed him a half-sovereign, gleaned from his brewings of fish-oil, 'Are you sure that you can do it?'

'No doubt about it. I've never known him turn down a wager. He'll gamble his wages on the throw of a dice ... or two flies upon the wall, for that matter!'

Jeremiah thanked him, but Emrys waved it aside, swearing, 'S'truth, Jeremiah, I should be thanking you. If I live to be a hundred, I'll never forget it! That game little cur of yours, hanging on to his backside, and you, off like the wind, a cock under each elbow ...' He was still laughing as he went back into the tavern, while Jeremiah went swiftly away.

Joshua had very little difficulty in tracing Doonan's lodgings. His questions to port workers and random passers-by quickly established Doonan's notoriety as a 'brawling, hell-raising, ale-swilling, heathen of a man'. Joshua had only to mention a 'big, red-headed Irishman', to release a torrent of abuse and invective, which left little doubt about Doonan's standing in the place. It was hardly surprising to Joshua that in the eyes of such industrious, law-abiding, God-fearing folk, Doonan's licentious ways smacked of the Devil incarnate.

His lodgings, in Lias cottages, a small deep-windowed row,

seemed remarkably innocuous and respectable. The woman who opened the door was clean, large-bosomed, and clad in speckled brown. With her quick, brown eyes and incredibly thin limbs, she reminded Joshua of a thrush; an impression intensified when she cocked her head nervously, demanding to know his business with her.

This established, she took him swiftly to Doonan's room, an unexpectedly neat little cell, with the ammonia smell of urine, and sheep-fat from the tallow. Joshua searched minutely, even under the mattress, but found nothing. Feeling defeated and sick at heart, he was on the point of apologizing, and taking his leave, when there was a commotion at the door. He reached for his truncheon, bracing himself.

The girl who came in was slight, fair-haired, with skin so palely delicate that it showed the blue of the veins beneath. She was weeping noisily, and without restraint, her reddened eyelids and nostrils the only colour about her. Beside the flamboyant vitality of Doonan, she might almost have disappeared.

'You mustn't take him,' she was sobbing. 'You mustn't! It was I who took it. I persuaded him . . .' A fresh paroxysm of sobbing made her unintelligible.

When her mother's bullying, and Joshua's reassurances, had calmed her sufficiently to make her coherent, she went out on to the landing, and returned with a reticule of silk.

'We were walking in the Burrows, Cavan and I.' She glanced, apprehensively, at her mother, 'I am not allowed there, you see, my mother forbids it . . . We found this purse.'

Her mother had sat down heavily on the bed, face colourless as her daughter's.

'You stole it?' Joshua demanded.

'No, we kept it. We were getting married, you see.'

'And the money?'

'It's there. All of it. I didn't touch a penny. Cavan wanted me to wear the locket. I couldn't, it wasn't right to. Then I heard about the girl, and got frightened. What will they do to me? Oh, Mama, I'm so frightened.' Her whole body shuddered with sobbing, and her mother drew her to her ample breast, stroking her hair, trying to bring comfort.

'Hush now! Hush!' she said. 'Let the constable see it.'

Joshua emptied the reticule on to the bed. The contents looked pitiful in their sparseness. In the drawstring purse there were ten new-minted gold sovereigns; a little velvet envelope contained a silver comb and a small silver hand mirror. There was a pretty lace handkerchief with the initial 'M' embroidered by hand in the corner. In addition, a small key which might have belonged to a valise or hatbox and, finally, a square box in shagreen lined with velvet, which held a gold ring with a garnet, and a cluster of seed pearls, a matching brooch, a stock pin in the shape of a running fox and a heart-shaped locket in gold. When he opened it, Joshua drew in his breath, for there, painted on ivory, was the dead girl's face, now radiant with life. Opposite, lay a matching miniature of a man in his mid-twenties or so, with the same soft hair and delicate colouring, and bright, questioning eyes. A brother, Joshua wondered, or her father, perhaps, captured some decades before? The likeness between them was remarkable. He had almost forgotten the two women, so great was his feeling of recognition and kinship with the unknown man and girl.

'Were there any letters, documents?' he asked, finally.

'Cavan burnt them.'

'When?'

'When we found it ... there on the dunes. He had some friction matches, you see.'

'Do you remember anything about them? Names? Places? Anything?' Joshua asked desperately.

'No.' The girl started to sob again, noisily.

'You will have to show me exactly where you found the reticule. You understand?'

The girl nodded. 'I will, oh, I will. I promise. Will they take me before the magistrates? To jail?'

Joshua shook his head, wearily. 'No, I think not. We have recovered the girl's belongings ... but it was a cruel, heedless thing to do, burning her things, for we might never learn her name.'

There was a rattling and banging outside which had the three of them running anxiously to the window. There, by the light of a guttering candle lantern, they saw Emrys pushing a wooden handcart with Jeremiah's help, while another, smaller fellow with a hunched back and large head set upon a wry neck held the lantern upon a long pole. On the cart, sprawled upon his back, snoring like a comatose pig, was the vast bulk of Cavan Doonan.

'He's dead! They've killed him! Murdered him!' The girl ran from the room, skirts flying.

'Dead drunk, more's the pity!' her mother observed. 'The worst day's work I ever did was to let that ... that ... limb of Satan set foot upon my doorstep! The girl is besotted with him, lost all sense of decency. If I were a man, I'd take a horsewhip to him!'

There was a noise of grunting, tramping and general bedlam on the stairs, and the three man struggled in, bearing the unconscious Doonan. Jeremiah and Emrys held a vast leg apiece and the unknown hunchback his head, while the girl carried the lantern. Even so, the dead weight of the Irishman defeated them all, and his huge backside thumped, then dragged menacingly across the floor. A carefully timed swing to the left and right, and the inert body rose upwards, and on to the bed.

Joshua thought that there could never have been a more droll or macabre sight than that reflected by the lantern. Jeremiah's battered face with its closed eye, the grotesque misshapen shadow of the large-headed man, the girl weeping, Emrys laughing, while the red-haired Irishman snored on, oblivious.

By some curious juxtaposition, the good men had become evil and menacing, and the villain slept innocent and peaceful as a babe.

While the four of them walked back to the 'Ship Aground', to return the handcart and lantern, Joshua told them what had befallen, and Emrys explained Doonan's helplessness.

'When Jeremiah handed me the money, I determined to use it to the best advantage. I chose the crudest, brashest drunkard in the bar and got Illtyd, here, to say that Doonan had said he was a weak-kneed, lily-livered apology for a man, and that he could drink him under the table, any time. Then Illtyd took

Doonan the same message, and said it had come from the drunk.'

Joshua smiled. 'Why choose Illtyd?'

Emrys tapped the little fellow affectionately on the shoulder. 'Well, they were both bullies. Ugly, aggressive louts. How could they believe that a small, inoffensive little soul like Illtyd would lie to them? Men ten times his size run away from them when they see them coming, but there was one thing they didn't know.'

'What was that?' asked Jeremiah.

'That Illtyd's got a heart bigger than both of theirs put together!'

In the light of the lantern, the little man's smile was broad and satisfied, a blush of pure pleasure spread under his skin.

'And you,' said Emrys, turning to Joshua, 'I admire you. You went, alone, to his lodgings, not knowing what you would find, or when he would return. It took real courage. But most of all, I admire you for not taking her to court. A silly, thoughtless slip of a girl, with no real malice. It was a kind act. A good, Christian thing.'

'Indeed,' admitted Joshua, 'You do me too much honour. As for the little fellow, his heart is braver than not merely two, but three. I knew that there was no way on earth to take Doonan, keep him in my custody or get him to the courthouse. When the vestry appointed me, they gave me no cell, no instruction, and no transport, and I readily admit, I had not the wit to ask!'

Illtyd, the little man, began to laugh, then Jeremiah, Emrys and, finally, Joshua, until the handcart rattled and the cobbles rang with the sound of their mirth.

Chapter Ten

It would have surprised Joshua to learn that the local villagers held him in respect and high esteem. Of necessity, they were frugal, hardworking and, with the exception of a little mild poaching, excused on the grounds that it helped to maintain the delicate balance of nature, they were law-abiding. True, with the opening of the new Port, there had been an infusion of new life, fresh blood. But the villagers of Newton and Nottage remained aloof. Separated geographically and by occupation and custom, their lives were unchanging as the land and sea. Strangers who visited the place for the bathing, or to benefit from the sea air, found the people scrupulously polite, but reserved in their manner. Insular, devout, not given to wild excesses, save an occasional flirtation with cwrw da, they were articulate with each other and awkward with outsiders. When Joshua found an occasional hare or pigeon upon his doorstep in the early morning, its body still warm, he knew what honour they did him. It said, more openly than any speech, 'We are grateful for what you are doing. We accept you as one of us.'

Strangest of all was Doonan's attitude towards him. He became Joshua's fiercest champion, ready to defend him verbally and physically against the onslaughts of others. It would have been pleasing to attribute some remarkable conversion to Joshua's sympathetic handling of his case. In truth, he remained belligerent, surly and argumentative as ever, although his offer that the constable might depend upon him by night or day, to accompany or defend him, was well received.

Doonan and the pale-faced girl, inaptly named Rosa, accompanied Joshua to the Burrows to show him where they had found the reticule. It had been flung into a tangle of scrub and brambles, and had remained well-hidden until Doonan had uncovered it. With delicacy, Joshua refrained from enquiring their purpose there ... and neither had volunteered any explanation. The place where it had been found was but yards from where the dog had unearthed the girl's clothing in the rabbit hole. It seemed likely that, either in a panic, or to help those who would come seeking her, she had flung it with all her strength, before her attacker had finally overpowered her.

Doonan had seemed remarkably chastened and grieved by it all. 'Anyone who beats a man in a fair fight is following nature ... doing what animals do by instinct. But a man who could beat or throttle a helpless girl to death ...' He put his arm protectively about Rosa, 'Well, he is no man, just a rotten, filthy, snivelling apology for one!'

He looked down at Rosa, and she up at his broad, unlovely face, with such devotion that Joshua was forced to conclude that, unlikely as it appeared, theirs might well prove to be a lasting marriage. Doonan found in her a gentleness and dependence which aroused his protection, like a rough boy tending a wounded bird. She saw him as he was, wilful, feckless, filled with aggression and wild schemes. She would expect nothing from him that he could not give.

As they walked back across the sand dunes and the sandy wastes of Pickets Lease to Port, Rosa darted ahead, and Joshua, taking his chance, asked Doonan, 'Where did all the money you were spending so freely come from?'

Doonan fidgeted, and looked sheepish. 'Cock-fighting and gambling. I swore to her that I had given it up ... for she thought the fighting cruel, and said I must choose between it and her. Oh but what a cockerel I'd bought, man! Nothing on two legs to beat it. Why, I'd wager you ...' he stopped and Joshua, and then Doonan, burst into laughter.

Rosa, hearing their mirth, turned back to them. 'And what amuses you so much?' she asked Joshua.

'We were talking about the evils of gambling.'

'Ah, but that was all in the past,' she said firmly. 'For Cavan has done with it. To prove it to me he has given his cockerels away ... to some poor fisherman who has need of them. Do you not think, Constable Stradling, that it takes a generous and loving spirit to make such a sacrifice?'

'I do indeed, Mistress,' said Joshua, gravely, 'I do indeed.'

That same day, Joshua requested, some might say insisted, that a special meeting of the vestry be called, to discuss the protection of the district. Since many of the vestrymen were farmers, and agriculture mainly contained in the fertile land at Nottage, it was decided, for convenience, to hold the meeting there. The venue was the "Lamb" tavern, which met with general approval. The Nottage vestrymen were as much at home there as upon their own hearths, and the Newton vestrymen were not averse to a change of scene, the ale being the same.

The half mile or so to Nottage on horseback was a very pleasant ride, for the way was wide and leafy, and the land productive and well-tended. Joshua skirted the solid, square-faced house, Old Shortlands, and stopped to admire the great pool, its edges clotted with yellow and white petalled marsh buttercups, and surface reflecting the blue of the sky. There were newts and frogs moving in its depths which amused and pleased Joshua with their graceful antics. In the meadows around, there were the sounds of bees and small hidden animals, and larks hovered and sang overhead. He saw a moorhen spurt across the water into a clump of reed mace, and the darting circles as a mayfly rippled the surface. Then, feeling that he had tarried long enough, he went upon his way.

Outside the walls of the manor house, women were busy at the Great Well, filling pitchers and buckets of water. Some used yokes and hoops to carry their burdens, and a few carried pitchers upon their heads, walking gracefully so as not to spill a precious drop. Without exception, they greeted Joshua courteously, and stopped to allow him to pass by. The prettiest was Rebecca, who, straightening up from her labours, becomingly flushed, pleaded with him, mutely, by means of her fine eyes, not to acknowledge her. He glimpsed her cob and cart set in a leafy grove nearby and knew that she travelled this far to aid him.

The memory of their time together warmed him, curving his mouth into a smile. Rebecca remarked it and hugged it to herself as secretly and fiercely as their lovemaking. Of all the women there, she alone spoke no word of admiration for the young constable, but how eagerly she savoured and digested every crumb of their praise.

Joshua, looking back from the brow of the hill, saw the high stone wall of the Court, curved like a sinuous grey snake exploring a green landscape. At its outer curve, Rebecca and her companions stilled and diminished by distance. Within, the restored Elizabethan manor house upon a hillock, its gardens and lawns flowing downwards like cool water.

Joshua felt for the moment part of its timelessness: the fusing of past, present and what was yet to be. The flesh and warm blood of Rebecca busied at the well, as women had been since time before Christ. Her backcloth the sold grey stone of Noce Court, Grange of Margam Abbey since the fifteenth century, inner walls hung with rare tapestries brought, or plundered, from Tewkesbury Abbey.

On another hill, at Clevis, Madeleine Mansel sat writing at her small elegant bonheur-du-jour. Two splashes of colour burned high in her cheeks, rounded and symmetrical, as if hot pennies had been pressed to the skin. Her hand shook, so that her quill grated, spattering the page. She sat for a moment, biting her lip, then crumpled the paper in her fist, threw it into the basket at her feet, and began again.

She could not shake off the feeling of coldness and foreboding. She hated this place; the savagery of its coast and climate were alien to her. As alien as the stiff, joyless people with their strange language and voices. She had furnished her drawing room as a replica of her grandmother's house at Rouen. Now, instead of bringing her comfort, it heightened her feeling of isolation and exile.

She was not sure how much of her fear sprang from what she had overheard the young constable say of Burrel's release. There was no doubt that the threat to her life was real. She had done what was necessary but, even now, she did not know how much of her past was open to him, and what danger he could pose.

She opened the curved satinwood door atop her desk, and took from a small silver casket an empty bottle from which she drained the last drop of liquid, then slipped it into her reticule. As she waited for the laudanum to take effect, she finished the letter and, sealing it carefully, tugged the bell-pull. To her disgust, it was the pinched, stupid, little housemaid who answered her summons. She stood there, uncertainly, eyes raw-rimmed, nose moist, and sniffing nervously.

'Ma'am?'

'Take this to the coachman. It must be delivered to Dan-y-Graig house. Tell him to go immediately. It is urgent.'

The maid hesitated, awkwardly.

'Don't dither, girl, go!'

'I think the coachman is not here; he has taken Dr Mansel ...'

'You think? You are not paid to think. Just take it!' She gestured, impatiently, towards her desk.

The girl, frightened into clumsiness, leaned over, the sleeve of her dress sweeping a small, crystal scent flacon to the floor. She stooped to pick up the fragments.

'Imbecile!' A stinging blow sent the girl stumbling against a chair, and she fell, awkwardly, to her knees. A small glob of blood sprang from her cheek, where Mrs Mansel's ring had pierced it, running to the corner of her mouth as she stood upright.

'Now, go ... before I dismiss you for insolence and stupidity! And if you dare to discuss it with the other servants, I'll make you sorry. Now, send Mrs Pritchard to me!'

The girl made her way downstairs determinedly opening her eyes wide, not blinking, lest the tears spill. There was the warm salt taste of blood in her mouth, and the sour taste of humiliation. Her mother, she knew, would bid her, 'Come you home, my girl! You are not some animal to be kept in harness and whipped. We will manage somehow.' But how? Where? The poorhouse? Scant pickings, there, for a widow woman with four young children to feed and clothe. No, she was no longer a child, she was nearly fourteen. Old enough to take responsibility for herself and others, to learn that life owes you nothing.

How she despised Mrs Mansel! Not for the blow to her face. She could survive that. But when she had first come to Dr

Mansel's house, and the housekeeper had taken her before her mistress, Mrs Mansel had demanded, 'What is your name, girl? Speak up!'

'Lily . . . ma'am.'

'Lily?' She turned to Mrs Pritchard, lips twitching with malicious pleasure, 'Have you ever heard anything so absurdly inappropriate? One might almost suspect a sense of humour in these people. She shall answer to "Daisy", Mrs Pritchard! All my housemaids have been Daisy; I find it less effort than remembering their names!'

'Well,' decided the little housemaid, as she made her way back to the kitchen, 'she can call me Daisy until she is blue in the face, and I'll even condescend to answer to it. But where it matters, inside my head, I'll still be Lily. Even she can't change that!'

Mrs Pritchard, summoned peremptorily into her mistress's presence, went at once. She had learnt the wisdom of swift obedience to Mrs Mansel's demands, and the folly of delay.

To all appearances the housekeeper was austere, stern and entirely forbidding; a very model of rectitude in her plain black dress. She glanced at Daisy, saw the blood congealed upon her cheek, and the pale eyes, sore-rimmed with weeping, and felt pity and irritation with the child. A child was all she was, thrust from the warm, enclosed safety of a family into this arid place, with neither love nor warm flesh for comfort. For a moment Mrs Pritchard was that child again, vulnerable, afraid.

'Daisy!' she called out sharply.

'Yes, ma'am?'

'Tell cook to make you up a parcel of left-overs . . . You may slip home for an hour. An hour, I said, no more! See that you are clean and presentable . . .'

'Oh, Mrs Pritchard . . .' Daisy's sallow face grew pink, and almost pretty. 'You are the kindest woman in all the world! Truly . . .'

'Nonsense, girl!' declared Mrs Pritchard.

'I don't know what to say . . .'

'Try "Thank You"' said Mrs Pritchard as she continued upon her way.

As she lingered outside the door to Mrs Mansel's room, the housekeeper was reflecting upon her mistress, and her treatment of Daisy. She was a foreigner, true ... and therefore different. There was something in the blood ... yet it could not account for the wild swings of mood, from blackness to fierce elation; from febrile, glittering excitement to an apathy so deep that she would lie upon her bed, powerless to eat, sleep, or even to wash and tend to her person ...

No. There was something other than blood. It gnawed at her constantly, eroding, laying bare ... but there were rare times of lavishness, when she thrust money and gifts upon Mrs Pritchard: jewellery, a pretty scarf, clothes she no longer wore ... yet even her giving lacked spontaneity. It was neither generous nor impulsive, merely an act calculated to pacify, to secure not friendship but obedience. The housekeeper took no pleasure in these acquisitions. They lay neglected and unworn, in a drawer. They seemed to bear the imprint of Madeleine Mansel, as if her flesh and emotions permeated them still ... But it was the master Mrs Pritchard grieved for ... a kind, loyal man, who deserved better. She sometimes felt that he was the real reason why she remained here in this house, where contempt and mistrust poisoned the air ...

Her thoughts were brusquely interrupted, when she heard a sharp voice from inside the room.

'Come,' Madeleine Mansel commanded, impatiently.

Mrs Pritchard, with the habit of long training, assumed the mask of the archetypal servant: unobtrusive, dependable, with neither opinions nor emotions of her own.

Joshua left the "Lamb Inn" well pleased. The vestrymen had approved a plan to convert a stable block behind the "Crown Inn" into a place of temporary detention. They would employ a stonemason, blacksmith and locksmith to make it safe and, in addition, an able-bodied pauper from the workhouse would be engaged, as necessary, to act as gaoler. Meals would be provided, at usual cost, from the kitchens of the "Crown". The landlord, a vestryman himself, was about to replace one of his carriages, and would be pleased to offer the services of his old coach, to transport prisoners to the courthouse or cells. This being agreed upon, an order was given to employ Ezra the Box and any other craftsmen found necessary to make it safe for the purpose intended. As for the horses, they would be provided, as needed, from the stables of the inn, at minimal cost, with no charge for feeding, a plan which met with the unanimous approval of the frugal vestrymen. The permanent services of a coachman being considered an unnecessary extravagance, the entire vestry volunteered to undertake the task in turn, with a proviso from the farmers that should this be at harvest time a reliable substitute would be provided.

Joshua, astride the grey, as it cantered along the wide highway of Newton-Nottage, with its fine grass verges, wondered if it was true that in early times the great Sutton stones for the Abbey at Margam had been drawn along this very route by oxen, from the quarries at Ogmore-by-Sea. Of one thing he was certain: any vestryman required to transport Doonan to the cells at Pyle would need more stamina than the oxen! As for the able-bodied pauper, pressed into the service as his gaoler, he would not for long be a burden on the parish. He would take to the road, vowing never to return, with Doonan's great boot to speed him on his way!

Rebecca had collected her gown and petticoats and cloak from the dressmaker's house in the village. The little round seamstress had come forward eagerly when she had seen her, her face ringed in smiles, cheeks like polished red apples. Rebecca thought she would have been an ideal model for the plump Mrs Noah on a child's wooden ark.

'Your garments are quite ready, Miss de Breos. Will you try on the gown and petticoats, to see that they fit well?'

She led Rebecca into a tiny room, which might have once served as a pantry, or game larder, then left her to divest herself of her own clothing, and to try on the new. She emerged feeling like a butterfly which has just shed its chrysalis, but is not sure of its wings.

The dressmaker's eyes were bright with real pleasure. She stepped back, admiring both Rebecca and her handiwork, tweaking a fold here, a seam there.

'Perfect,' she announced, straightening up with some effort, 'quite excellent. I declare, Miss de Breos, if it were not immodest of me, I would claim that there is no better made gown in all the county. You have a fine, upright carriage, and the blue of the gown shows your eyes and complexion to great advantage. Yes, indeed, a gown to be proud of.' She fastened the cape over Rebecca's shoulders. 'There, a perfect finishing touch. Come, ladies, you may leave your stitching for the moment.'

The little apprentices crowded around, but at a discreet distance. At first, they hung back, shyly, until the boldest of them declared, 'It is a pleasure to sew for you, Mistress, for you are young and pretty, and the gown becomes you . . . So many of our ladies are fat and hard to please!' The dressmaker rounded on her directly and boxed her ears hard, and she returned to her place red-faced and tearful, feeling ill-used for being truthful. The others, however, drew nearer, expressing pleasure and pride that 'their gown' was so successful.

When the dressmaker ventured into the little dressing room upon some errand, Rebecca gave the apprentice, who was still snivelling quietly, a sixpence, which served to dry her tears quite remarkably.

The dressmaker returned, eyes still cross behind her metal framed spectacles. 'A stupid, impetuous girl, who could lose me good custom,' she grumbled. 'However, she will make a good enough seamstress.' The deep set eyes sparkled in their pouches, as she whispered, confidentially, 'To tell the truth, I am much in sympathy with her, Miss de Breos, for some of our ladies are shaped like bolsters, and others like herons, and they all require that they should look like you!' She smiled, and handed Rebecca a small, neatly-wrapped package, saying discreetly, 'Those other necessities, which you bade us provide,' meaning the lace-edged drawers. Then she gave her a bulkier parcel, containing her old clothing. They parted amicably, with exclamations of satisfaction on both sides, and many good wishes.

The dressmaker, guilty at her impetuosity in boxing the bold apprentice's ears, remarked upon the neatness and superiority of her stitching, and bade her, 'Go, this instant, and prepare us all some tea.'

Rebecca went to collect her blue straw bonnet, and on to the cordwainer's to order for herself a pair of delicately unserviceable shoes.

She wondered now, as she stood dressed in her purchases in the long room at the cottage, and trying to glimpse them from every angle in her mother's silver hand-glass, if there would ever be an opportunity to wear them and, if she did, whether Joshua would think her beautiful. Then, berating herself for being as vain as a peahen and an extravagant fool, she undressed, and put the new clothing carefully away.

When Joshua rode back into Newton village from the meeting with the vestrymen, he saw her crossing the village green to St John's Well, two wooden buckets dangling from a yoke on her shoulders. She wore her black-sprigged party dress, but without the lace collar and cuffs, and with her fall of dark hair and her erect carriage, he thought she looked striking and graceful in her movements ... although he suspected that she could provision the whole village with well-water! He greeted her formally, aware that they were being observed.

'Good day to you, Mistress de Breos.' He reined the grey in beside her.

'Good day to you, Constable.' Her fine, extraordinary eyes looked into his, mischievously. 'A fine day, is it not?'

'Will you permit me to help you with your yoke?'

'No, sir.'

'May I enquire why not?'

'If you did, sir, those ladies watching us so avidly from the well would have us yoked in matrimony before you had set foot from your stirrup.'

'Then I will detain you no longer ... I would not add fuel to the fires of their gossip!' He raised his helmet, extravagantly.

'Stay, sir.'

He paused enquiringly.

'I wished to ask you about a stranger I have met,' she said hesitantly.

'A stranger? A man?' he asked, sharply.

'Yes. It is of little consequence ... but he seemed sick, ill at ease; as if he had suffered a bereavement, perhaps.'

'It is of every consequence! What manner of man, would you say? Old? Young? Well-spoken?'

The anger in his voice alarmed her.

'As to his age, I do not know, for I did not think it civil to ask him,' she said haughtily. 'As for his voice, yes, he was well spoken ... and courteous.'

'Where did you come upon him? At the beach, the well?'

'I saw him once upon the Burrows. He did not speak. He looked as if he were sick, troubled. Then I saw him at my gate. I invited him in.'

'You did what?' He leapt down from the saddle, and took her arm, gripping it tightly.

'If you will release me, sir.' She wrenched herself free. 'You are making a laughing-stock of us both, and I do not relish it!'

'It was a stupid, irresponsible thing to do.' Fear made his voice hard. 'A stranger! I had thought better of you, Rebecca.'

'Your good opinion is of no relevance to me!'

'You are a foolish, headstrong girl.'

'And you, sir, are a self-opinionated boor.'

'You will not see him, or speak to him, again. You understand?'

'By what right do you command me, sir?'

'By my right as a constable, and ... friend.'

'You are no friend of mine, sir, and I am guilty only of charity to a poor, troubled creature who had not the strength to ... to climb into a chair.'

'If you see him, in future, you will tell me, at once.'

'That I will not! I will speak to whomsoever I please whenever I please.'

'Rebecca! I think only of your safety ...'

'My safety is none of your affair. What do you suspect him of? Murder, fire-raising?' she asked scornfully. 'It was as much as he could do to raise his head.'

'I am not at liberty to tell you.'

'Then it is better that we keep our own company, and our own counsel. I bid you good day, sir, with the fervent hope that your manners will improve.'

'And I, Mistress, return that hope for your sense and your temper!'

She turned abruptly, and made her way, not to the well, but

back to her cottage, calling, 'If you seek him, I sent him to Dr Mansel ...'

He urged on his horse, muttering, 'Damn the woman! Damn her to little, wild pieces!'

The women at the stone well went stolidly, silently about their business until the young constable was out of sight.

Instead of riding out to Weare House, the bathing annexe to 'Pyle Inn', as he had planned to do, Joshua turned the grey towards Clevis Hill and Dr Mansel's house. He could not be sure if the man Rebecca had seen was Dr Burrel, yet he dare not ignore the threat his presence might bring. He argued that it was better to alarm Dr Mansel unnecessarily than to leave him unprepared for an encounter.

When he reached the house, the door was opened, not by the nervous little housemaid, but a housekeeper, a tall, angular woman with sharp features, and a mouth pursed like a button. Only a white apron over her black dress gave indication of her position as a servant in the house.

He enquired as to Dr Mansel's whereabouts.

'The doctor is not here, sir. He has been called to Nottage Court for a consultation.'

'Will he be away long?'

'That I cannot say, sir.'

'It is imperative that I speak to him. A matter of great urgency. Will you give him my message?'

'Certainly, sir.'

'I would prefer to write it, for it is a matter of strict confidence ... personal. Will you furnish me with paper and pen, if you please?'

She led him into the library, and indicated ink and paper in a cabinet, upon the desk.

'I will leave you to your business, sir. If you will ring for me when you are finished, I will take your letter, and escort you out.'

Joshua nodded. A short time later, his task completed, he pulled the bell-rope as he was bid, reiterated the urgency of the message, and left the house.

As he mounted the grey, which the groom held for him, he fancied he saw a movement beside the curtain of the drawing room, as if something slight and dark blurred into the shadows. It was only after he had ridden out, through the ornate, iron gateway, that he wondered if it were Mrs Mansel, how much she had heard, and if he had been wise to write that he believed Dr Burrel to be already here.

Jeremiah, meanwhile, was finding that his triumphant flight with the cockerels, while establishing his heroism in the alehouses, presented certain practical difficulties at home. The pair shattered the early morning peace with their never-ending crowing; demanded food incessantly, and terrorized poor Charity, until the wretched animal was afraid to venture into the yard. They tormented the dog ceaselessly, pecking until they drew blood, and even leaping upon its back, and spurring it on with their claws, 'For all the world,' as Jeremiah said, 'like the devil riding a mare!' When they were not attacking each other, they were menacing Jeremiah, their deliverer, which he considered to be the basest ingratitude. Even separating them in crudely made wooden pens only served to increase their viciousness, and the noise they created grew into such a cacophony that both Jeremiah and the dog were glad to escape to the shore.

Now, he was having no more of it. After one bellicose attack, which left him bleeding, Jeremiah bundled the particular offender under his arm, and set off to present it to the Widow Cleat, who lived near the old windmill at Nottage. Her husband had been a blacksmith, a huge sinewy man, with muscles made hard by his craft. His relict, being a frugal woman, had made a parcel of his clothes, and delivered them to Jeremiah, vowing that he was the only man in the three hamlets who 'could fill his shoes.' Fortunately, the honest creature meant it literally, and had no matrimonial designs upon him. Had she done, Jeremiah would undoubtedly have developed a turn of speed which would have made the Doonan escape resemble a slow march. In return for the clothing, and the occasional shared meal, Jeremiah repaid her with fresh fish, crabs, lobsters and fish-oil for her lamps. And now, with a very large cockerel. So it was that, attired in the late blacksmith's second-best coat and trousers, and clutching the ungrateful bird,

Jeremiah was flung to the ground by Joshua's horse emerging at a canter from Dr Mansel's driveway.

With profuse and extravagant apologies, Joshua dismounted, dusted Jeremiah, who was still a trifle dazed by the suddenness of it all, and helped to retrieve the furious bird, which pecked him severely for his trouble. They chatted companionably for a while, and Joshua, in laughing reference to their encounter with Doonan, told him of the vestry's plans for a jail house and transport.

'About as much hope of getting Doonan into that as an elephant into a nightshirt!' said Jeremiah, cheerfully.

They fell to a general discussion on the appointments of a parish overseer, highway surveyors and an overseer of the poor, when Joshua happened to let fall that the vestry were about to appoint a hayward, to prevent the straying of sheep from other parishes on to the local commons.

'The Widow Cleat's son!' exclaimed Jeremiah. 'Illtyd. It would be God-sent for him.'

'Little Illtyd? The small man?' Joshua was incredulous, 'It would be impossible!'

'How so?' demanded Jeremiah, settling the squawking cockerel more firmly under his arm, 'he is as strong as an ox!'

'I don't know,' admitted Joshua, doubtfully, 'for he would be required to ride a horse.'

Jeremiah considered in silence for a moment. 'You are right. With legs like his he would be hard-pressed to mount even this rooster! Well, it was but a thought. He is a brave fellow, as you saw, ever ready to do a service for others. I mind well, last year, seeing him on the village green for the feast of Mabsant. They had dressed him in a cap and bells, to sell some tomfoolery to the children. With his bent back and that awkward head, they laughed and made him the butt of their humour. It so sickened me, that I returned home, and the Widow Cleat was in tears for shame and pity.' He smote his large fist into his palm, and the cock squawked, and ruffled its feathers. 'It demeaned the little man!' He made to move off.

'Wait!' cried Joshua, 'Not so fast!' He caught Jeremiah by the arm.

'I have a good friend, a farmer, who for his own pleasure,

and profit, breeds a miniature strain of horses, perfect in every particular. They sell well to the aristocracy, for their young children, and have even been bought by royalty.'

Jeremiah looked interested.

'I'm damned if I will not persuade him to sell one to me! If the vestry agree to it, and I will certainly press them hard, then our little knight shall have his charger!'

They shook hands upon it, laughing delightedly at the prospect of Illtyd the hayward, rounding up sheep on a ram-sized mount.

'Your bruises are faring well,' remarked Joshua, 'I am glad that my hasty exit did you no more damage.'

'In truth,' said Jeremiah, fervently, 'if you had trampled me flat, for ever, it would have been a small price to pay for witnessing the Widow Cleat's pleasure.'

He settled the unruly bird firmly under his arm, and went on his way, whistling.

Chapter Eleven

Joshua awoke after a disturbed night of dreams in which Illtyd, seated upon a ram, fought a pitched battle with Doonan. Rebecca was there, holding Joshua by the throat and pushing him deeper and deeper under the water of the well, while Jeremiah stood upon the dog to unsettle a rooster from the branch of a tree.

He awoke, sweating, and not surprisingly confused, to an urgent knocking upon his front door. He dressed hurriedly and went down to find Ossie standing upon the doorstep, fidgetting in his boots, and looking awkward.

'I would not have disturbed you this early in the morning, Constable, for I know that you prepare for the funeral today, but I must hurry and be about my business.'

'How can I be of help?' asked Joshua, bidding him enter.

'No, for my boots are full of stable filth, and I have little time. I have seen something odd, which I cannot explain. I do not know if it is of consequence.'

Joshua waited.

'This morning, early, at perhaps four of the clock, I was easing a sick horse. It seemed to me that I saw lights, not one, but many, moving in the churchyard across the green.' His brown face creased in perplexity, and he scratched his head. 'I am not a fanciful man, you understand, and I am not superstitious of spirits and devils.'

Joshua nodded in sympathy as the ostler continued.

'Although, I admit there are those things which allow of no rational explanation. The lights were not supernatural, but lanterns held in human hands, of that, I am quite certain.'

'Did you see anyone? Recognize a face perhaps?'

'No, for it was dark and the glow of the lights was all I could make out. I could not summon you, or call to anyone at the "Crown", for I was unable to leave the poor animal.'

'What did you suppose the lights to be?'

'Ah! That I can only guess, but I thought grave robbers, or body snatchers, for there are those who are evil enough to desecrate the dead.'

'I thank you for telling me,' Joshua said. 'It shows a rare public spirit. I shall certainly search there, after the burial today, and keep watch at night.'

The ostler nodded, his weathered face creased in his gap-toothed smile. 'As I am to attend to the horses of the new gaol-coach, and your own, sir, I count myself as much an aide to the constable as I am an aide at the inn. I shall be proud to consider it my duty.'

'And I to have your help.'

Joshua took the ostler's hand and shook it, solemnly. He did not think it fitting to tip him a sixpence, for he was loath to wound the good man's feelings.

After the ostler had returned to his duties at the 'Crown' and Joshua had washed himself at the well in the yard, and eaten, he began to prepare himself for the funeral of the dead girl. His laundry woman had pressed the better of his two uniforms, which had been copied for him, at his own expense, by the local tailor. The woman had first held it in the steam from a boiling kettle, then ironed it with a heavy flat iron taken from the fire. To ensure that it was the correct heat, she had spat upon its under surface and watched the spittle form into a water bubble, which hissed and flew off. Experience had made her expert, for Joshua had never found cause to complain of a singed shirt, or suit ill-ironed.

He was grateful to the justice for accepting responsibility for the girl's burial. It was a generous act. A parish funeral, such as those given to paupers and inmates of the workhouse, seemed bleak and impersonal, although willing paupers were sometimes paid a few coppers to act as 'mourners'. When Joshua had enquired of the relief officer what could be done for the dead girl, he was told that twenty-one shillings were allowed for the burial of an adult, of which fifteen shillings must be used for a coffin. Of all the things that had occurred, strangely, it was this which had moved and angered him most.

He did not know if anyone else would attend the funeral, but at least the Reverend Robert Knight would see to it that her burial would receive the dignity and Christian charity which her death had not. Would her murderer be there? Unlikely, Joshua thought; but who could fathom a disordered mind? He took his helmet, and walked out across the village green, and into the churchyard.

It seemed to him that most of the non-working population of the three hamlets was gathered there, in their good, black clothes. Old men and women, younger women with children at their skirts, and some carrying babies cocooned in woven shawls. What touched him was the quiet dignity of the waiting. They stood singly, or in groups, neither speaking nor moving about, patient, respectful, as if mourning one of their own. Some of the children and women held small posies of garden flowers, culled fresh and not yet drooping. One man, white-haired and with the ringed opaque eyes of the aged, held a single, perfect flower of the rose, and Joshua, standing beside him, could smell its delicate, elusive fragrance.

Through the gateway to the churchyard, he saw Rosa and her mother arriving, the Widow Cleat and Illtyd and, later, Jeremiah and Rebecca: he like an Old Testament prophet with his grey beard and fine eyes; she, neat and unusually subdued in her gown of sprigged black. They nodded to him, and went to stand in a far corner, where an oblong of sandy loam had been excised, edges piled with earth. It seemed that Joshua recognized someone from every inn, every farm, and every trade and craft in the hamlets, all come together to show their regret and sadness at the manner of her passing.

Joshua heard the clopping of horses' hooves, and the rattle of wheels approaching, and moved to the gateway. The horses drawing the cortege were paired blacks, coats and harness gleaming, mourning plumes at their heads. The driver, elegant in top hat with banding and fall of crêpe, black frock coat and gloves. Behind the carriage and coffin walked the vestrymen, overseers of the poor, surveyors of the highway, with administrators of the dock and tramway. Joshua was surprised to recognize Dr Mansel and, at the rear of the mourners, Ezra the Box, and Leyshon and other staff from Tythegston Court.

The six silk-hatted pall bearers lifted the coffin from the hearse and bore it to the graveside. The Reverend Robert

Knight read the burial service, his beautiful, warm voice giving richness and compassion to the age-old words.

'"I am the resurrection and the life, saith the Lord ... The Lord gave, and the Lord hath taken away ... cometh up, and is cut down like a flower ... Earth to earth, ashes to ashes, dust to dust."'

There was a spatter of earth upon the coffin lid, then the void filled. The grave edge was scattered with flowers, and the mourners left, the carriage departed.

Joshua waited for a time, then sought out the rector, waiting for him in the porch of the church. Joshua thought that he looked care-worn and tired, as if part of his strength had flowed out to strengthen those around him.

'Well, Constable, have you news for me in this unhappy business?'

Joshua told him of Dr Burrel, his dealings with the Crandles and the finding of the reticule. The rector smiled when Joshua spoke of the vestrymen's plans for a cell and gaol-coach, but grew serious when told of the lights in the churchyard.

'You think that the ostler told the truth?'

'I am sure of it, but I am at a loss for a reason.'

'Grave robbers perhaps. Or seeking some of the church plate. We have few treasures, but those we have are sacred, bequeathed to us in love, and so their value is limitless. I should be saddened to think any man would stoop to such sacrilege. Come,' he said to Joshua, 'we will look inside the church to see that all is as it should be.'

He called the verger to stand at the porch door to see that no one disturbed them.

Together, they inspected every inch of the small church, including the new vestry behind the pulpit. They ascended the rood-loft staircase, even examined the embattled tower with its saddleback roof. They trod carefully and with some trepidation, for it was in a sad state of repair, its four bells cracked and silent. They found nothing.

It seemed to Joshua that the church had an air of serenity, peacefulness, as if the devotions of those who had worshipped there since Norman times had infiltrated the very stones and flags of the building. Yet it must have known conflict, or threat, for high in the eastern wall of the tower, below the battlements, remained a small door; its purpose to give vantage and egress to those who, aloft upon a wooden platform, sought to defend the church, while the tower bells pealed the alarm.

'Whoever they are,' the rector was saying, as if in response to Joshua's thought, 'I will not close the door of the church. There are many who come here in sorrow or despair, seeking God. I cannot cut them off from His comfort. I would be failing in my duty as a priest.'

'I understand.'

'Look around you, Stradling. What do you see? Great wealth, opulent furnishings?' He shook his head, 'Simplicity of stone: the walls; the stone altar with its five crosses cut into its very heart; the pulpit with its crudely carved relief of the flagellation of Christ; the simple, octagonal font. Ordinary things, made by ordinary craftsmen. What makes them so beautiful, so remarkable, is that they were made with love. Sometimes, when I am here alone, I look around me and think, "these things were made by humble men, some of them in the thirteenth century, six hundred years ago; just as nearly two thousand years ago the father of Christ fashioned things by hand in his carpenter's shop."'

'Yes,' agreed Joshua, 'It gives a feeling of continuity, changelessness.'

'Come,' said the rector, 'I am in danger of preaching you a sermon.'

'Sermons in stones,' quoted Joshua, 'and good in everything.'

'No, my boy, a great deal of evil, I fear.'

'I will keep careful watch, here,' promised Joshua, 'and, if needs be, get some strong men to help me in my search.'

'Thank you, Stradling. The worshippers here are like the church, itself . . . good, simple, honest and unadorned. Fishermen, craftsmen, farmers. I would not like their peace, nor that of the sanctuary, to be violated or defiled.' He put his hand on Joshua's shoulder. 'God go with you.'

Before leaving the churchyard, Joshua looked about him, carefully, to see if there were any signs of intrusion; damage to gravestones, crosses broken or misaligned. There appeared to be nothing. He could not be sure, because the influx of mourners had trampled and disordered the earth, obliterating all else. Similarly, he knew that at the gate, the carriage and horses would have churned the soil to dust. He took one last look at the newly-dug grave, standing stiffly, his helmet in his hands. He said a silent prayer for the repose of her soul, promising that he would not stop searching until someone had been brought to justice.

As he returned to his cottage to change into his working uniform, a horse came out of the archway to the stables of the 'Crown', its rider striking its flanks hard with a whip. Joshua stepped back to avoid the hooves, and looked into the grinning face of Creighton Crandle. 'You will have to move faster than that, Contable, if you mean to catch anyone.'

'I am content to wait.'

'Take care you do not wait as long as that girl, then. Eternity is a long time!' He spurred his horse and was away, back arrogant, red hair flying.

Ossie, standing in the yard, shook his head. 'There are times,' he said, 'when I thank God that my work is with horses, and not their masters.'

'Amen to that!' agreed Joshua, fervently, 'although I fear that it would make my task much harder, for horses are altogether more intelligent, resourceful and brave.'

The ostler cackled, appreciatively, and asked, 'Shall I saddle your horse, sir?'

'If you please. I shall return directly. Should I need your help in that matter we talked of earlier, will you be free?'

'Free and willing, sir, by night or day.'

Joshua nodded and, bidding good day, he rode out to Weare House, the seventeenth century house, built high upon the sand of the shore. It stood alone, on a beach of shells and minute pebbles, ground by the tide into a multi-coloured shingle. No one remembered for whom the house had originally been built, or for what purpose, but now, almost lapped by the encroachment of sand and tide, it was the 'Bathing House': an annexe for visitors to the 'Pyle Inn'. The season was short, for the Atlantic brought gales and huge breakers for all but a few months in midsummer and, even then, the sea remained cold and uninviting. The rocks and tides of the Bristol Channel produced fierce, unpredictable currents, and even the most experienced mariners treated its coastline with respect. Should they forget, the many wrecks scattered around the creeks, cliffs and the infamous Tusker Rock were a grim reminder. But on this day, the sea was calm, its surface barely rippled by a southerly breeze, and reflecting the clear blue of the sky, its edges lapped with milky foam.

As Joshua approached, he saw two figures, deep in conversation at the rear of the house. As he came nearer, one helped the other, bulkier man to mount his horse and, with scarcely a glance in Joshua's direction, the man spurred the animal and rode away over the dunes, to skirt the limestone workings beyond. From what he had glimpsed of the rider, Joshua was sure that it was the elder Crandle.

As he brought his horse to a halt, the man remaining came forward to take the bridle. He was unknown to Joshua, a compact, dark-haired fellow with the pink and white complexion of a girl, hair growing in a widow's peak over restless pale eyes.

'Well, Constable, and to what do we owe the honour of your visit?'

Even as he spoke, he eyes focussed everywhere save on Joshua's face, a mannerism Joshua found irritating.

'Who was the man who rode away?' Joshua demanded, without preamble.

The other looked disconcerted, but quickly gathered his wits. 'A visitor, come to make arrangements for a stay.'

'Mr Crandle? But why? He lives not a mile distant.'

'He makes arrangements for his guests, not himself,' the man answered, sullenly.

He called upon a groom to take Joshua's horse. 'People come here from many places ... persons of rank and substance, often. We put notices in those newspapers read by the nobility and gentry.' His tone implied that a constable would hardly be cognizant of the practice.

'Your name?'

'I, sir, am Mr Thomas Gwilliam, manager of this bathhouse.'

'Very well, Mr Thomas Gwilliam. Show me your register of visitors,' instructed Joshua, hiding a smile.

Gwilliam led him inside to a small sitting room, his back stiff with resentment. 'I would not have our guests think we have dealings with the law.'

'Or outside it,' agreed Joshua, leafing through the pages of the book, 'I see you have visitors from Porlock.'

'Yes, the owner of a cargo ship, Mr Stanton Gould and his wife. They are our only visitors for the moment . . . We expect many more.'

'And Mr Crandle's guests?'

Gwilliam looked discomfitted. 'It is a reservation for some weeks' time.'

'The name?'

'That I cannot say, it was a tentative enquiry, only. In general terms, you understand?'

The pale gaze wandered restlessly about him. 'Merely to see if accommodation is freely available.'

Joshua did not believe him, but wondered if, perhaps, the evasiveness of the man's eyes was making him prejudiced.

'What accommodation does the bathhouse offer?'

'It is small, six bedrooms only, with cabins which may be wheeled to the shore for protection and disrobing . . . We are purely a bathing annexe to the "Pyle Inn". We pride ourselves that ours is a personal, family service for those who desire privacy and appreciate such refinements.'

Joshua evidently did not qualify for such esoteric delights.

'You have a boathouse, I observed, and stables,' Joshua said.

'Only what is necessary to take the gentlemen on fishing expeditions in the bays, or to the estuary of the Ogwr. We stable the coach and horses from the "Pyle Inn", and one or two mounts of our own.'

'And you have cellars, beneath?'

'Enough to house the barrels of ale and wines our patrons expect . . . If you will excuse me,' the man had been glancing through the open door to the entrance hall, and moved out to where a middle-aged man and woman were standing. They were well, but not fashionably, dressed, in the manner of yeomen.

'Ah, Gwilliam,' the man's voice was pleasant, cultivated, with the underlying soft burr of Somerset speech. 'Has Crandle been enquiring after us? We were delayed ...' but Joshua heard no more, for Gwilliam had dexterously removed them out of his hearing. He saw the woman glance at him, enquiringly then, purposely, as if rebuked, look away. Joshua could not know if the man grew nervous, or merely wished to mind his wife's manners.

'You will excuse me,' Joshua stepped forward to confront them. 'I fear, Gwilliam, that I must leave, now, for other duties. I shall return very soon.'

He turned to the woman, 'Mrs Crandle and her daughter have returned, I trust?'

'Why, no.' She looked confused, 'I am not apprised of their intentions.'

She glanced at her husband for guidance, but he gave her none.

'I will bid you good day, and trust that your stay here will be rewarding in every particular.' Joshua bowed lightly and left, not knowing why he had spoken as he did.

The groom brought his horse from the stable.

'A fine beast,' he said admiringly, as Joshua mounted.

'High spirited,' he agreed, 'like Mr Crandle's.'

'Sir?' the groom asked, puzzled.

'The gentleman who rode off as I arrived.'

'I do not recollect having seen him, sir, or having care of his horse; not at any time.'

'Then he is not a visitor here? Does not ride in frequently?'

'If he does, then it is at night, for my hours of work are from six of the clock each morning until dusk.'

'There is a night ostler, then?'

'No, for it is not necessary, sir, not even in June, July and August. There are never more than half a dozen guests at any time. In the winter, it is as quiet as the grave, and as bleak and cheerless. I wonder that Mr Gwilliam and his wife are able to bear the solitude, and the violence of the gales ... I swear that I could not.' He stopped speaking and stared back towards the house. Joshua followed his gaze.

'Ah, Gwilliam,' he said, easily. 'I was about to return to see you.' He unbuttoned the tunic of his uniform, and unfolded the drawing of the dead girl. 'Perhaps you will tell me if this face is known to you?'

Gwilliam took it and, briefly glancing at it, returned it to him. 'No, I have never seen her.'

Joshua handed it down to the groom, who studied it intently, forehead puckering in concentration.

'I thought at first,' he began, ' but no, I was mistaken, I have never seen her. I am sure of it. She just had the look of someone I fancied I knew. I am sorry.'

Joshua thanked him and rode away, not over the dunes, but along the rough pathway that bore the ruts of the coach from the 'Pyle Inn'. It seemed to him that the proprietor of the inn must be absurdly generous, or merely counted the bathhouse as an extra amenity for his guests, disregarding the cost. Gwilliam might be shifty-eyed and reticent, but that was hardly a crime! As for Crandle, there was no reason why he should not be making an enquiry on behalf of his friends, particularly as his wife was not at home to entertain them and why should he not be acquainted with the Goulds? He decided that seeing both Crandles, father and son, within the hour had put him out of humour, making him jaundiced and suspicious. For the moment, his activities must be centred on the churchyard. He could only hope for some greater satisfaction there.

Doonan, Jeremiah and the dog, and Joshua were crouched in the living room of Joshua's cottage in the darkness, taking turns at the window. The clock on the church tower had struck three and was now reaching the quarter hour. They were bored, restless and stiff of limb, all save the dog, which was snoring and snuffling contentedly before the fire. Cavan Doonan had an unlighted candle-lantern beside him, and some friction matches provided by Joshua. He and Jeremiah also had a pint jar part filled with ale, Doonan's having been emptied within minutes. The Irishman's mutterings about the awful dryness of the air were met by the rebuke that they would need 'all their wits about them!' He stretched his massive frame, rubbing his cramped legs, and sighing extravagantly.

'Hush!' called Jeremiah, from the window, 'I see something . . . a light.'

The other two were alert instantly, and crept to join him.

'By God, you are right!' cried Doonan, tiredness forgotten. 'I'll light the lantern. Quick, let us be off.'

Jeremiah swiftly gathered up the dog's leash and, armed with thick staves, the trio left the house. With Doonan shielding the light behind his coat, they moved stealthily and purposefully across the green, Jeremiah motioning to the dog to be silent.

As they passed through the gateway to the churchyard, a figure on watch with a lantern let out a cry of alarm, and lunged at Jeremiah with a stout stick, beating him across the shoulders, and knocking him off balance. The dog's chain tightened as he fell and, taken by surprise, Doonan flew over it, lantern, man and stave crashing noisily into a gravestone. Joshua alone remained standing and attempted to beat off Jeremiah's assailant with his truncheon. Within minutes the whole churchyard erupted with noise and fury. There was a tangle of limbs and bodies, a confusion of shouts and groans and a fierce cracking of sticks and heads. By the light of a pole lantern thrust into the earth of a grave, Joshua saw Doonan pick up a man bodily, and hold him high above his head, turning slowly to drop him upon the path with a mighty crack of bone. A kick hurled at the dog made it yelp aloud, and Jeremiah, incensed beyond reason, rushed at the aggressor and, grabbing him by the neck of his jacket, thrust him towards another man running to join the fray with such force that their heads banged together with a furious crack and they sank, dazed, to the ground. The dog joined in the brawl enthusiastically, barking and snapping encouragement with every blow struck.

Finally, when the four villains lay vanquished and bloody upon the ground, pleading, 'No more!' Doonan, Jeremiah, Joshua and the dog took inventory of their wounds. No bones broken but, in the flickering light of the lanterns, their many bruises, lacerations and lumps were nakedly revealed. Doonan had lost a front tooth, and his upper lip was split and bleeding; one eye was already closing and a trickle of blood was seeping from his nostril. Jeremiah had a lump on the back of his head like a plover's egg, a gashed cheekbone and one eye little more than a slit. Joshua, still wearing his helmet, had come off better, although he had a very bloody nose, and an eyebrow split apart.

Doonan spat blood, and said, with satisfaction, 'Damn me! That is what I call a scrap!' He settled a massive boot upon the chest of a man who was trying to struggle upright.

'Well,' ventured Jeremiah, 'We would none of us win any prizes for our beauty, but I think they got the worst of it.' He started to laugh, and soon the three of them were laughing weakly, then louder, slapping each other upon the back, alternately clinging together and wiping away tears and blood. The dog barked and jumped, joining in the fun, and making darting runs at the men upon the ground. One of them yelled, 'Keep that flaming animal away from me!' Doonan jerked him to his feet, and the man, groaning, covered his face to ward off an expected blow from the great fists.

'Tell the constable what you were doing,' Doonan bellowed.

The man stayed silent.

'Damn your eyes! Tell him before I knock your head clean off your shoulders!'

'All right. All right. We were smuggling,' the man mumbled sullenly.

'Smuggling what?'

'Brandy. Kegs of French brandy.'

'Right,' commanded Joshua, 'Get to your feet, all of you and show me where it is hidden. Come on! Come on! We can't stay here all night! Shape yourselves.'

They struggled to their feet, groaning with pain and effort, helped on their way by prods and kicks from the indefatigable Doonan. One, who was obviously the ring leader, led the way to a large stone coffin, ornately engraved and topped with a cross. With the combined strength of Doonan and Jeremiah, it was moved aside to reveal a flight of stone-hewn steps, leading into a small vault. Joshua, bearing the lantern, descended warily, to discover a cache of wooden barrels, from which rose the unmistakable aroma of fine French cognac.

'How did you get it here?' Joshua demanded, when he had mounted the steps.

They remained silent, eyes fixed upon the leader, awaiting some sign. He gave none. Lips remained clamped tight on the swollen, discoloured face, one hand lying awkwardly from the wrist, at an angle which showed it to be broken. Doonan moved towards him with fist upraised, threateningly.

'We rolled them over the dunes, from Newton creek,' the man admitted reluctantly.

'Where did they come from?'

'We rowed out ... to a ship anchored off ...'

'Which ship?' Joshua demanded.

'Come on, man. Talk before I thump it out of you,' Doonan growled. But not even Doonan's threat to break his other arm, or Joshua's patient questioning, could make him say another word. Eventually, defeated, Joshua walked across to the churchyard, and signalled with his lantern, waving it steadily to and fro, before receiving an answering sign.

Within minutes Ossie was beside them in the churchyard, awaiting instructions. As he approached, he saw the battered face of the ringleader in the glow from Joshua's lantern.

'Packwood!' he exclaimed, perplexed. 'What are you doing here?'

'You know him?' Joshua asked sharply.

'Yes, of course, he is the stonemason who sees to the church, repairs the graves, makes the headstones.'

'Shut up!' cried Packwood, harshly, 'or I'll shut you up!'

'No, I don't think you will,' said Doonan, evenly, 'now, or in the future ... for if you as much as lay a finger upon him, you will have me to reckon with. Understood?' He flexed the muscles of his thick arms, warningly, and Packwood's blustering ceased abruptly.

'Will you go to the Port, Ossie, and bring the exciseman?' asked Joshua, 'You can take my grey ... Go, saddle her!'

The little bow-legged ostler seemed to grow visibly in height and authority. His weathered face glowed. 'I will go at once.' He turned to Doonan, 'I thank you, sir, for your offer of protection, for I know it was offered in the spirit of friendship.'

He went to stand within range of Packwood and seemed to draw himself almost erect in the lantern light, 'If you so much as look at me sideways in the future, Gomer Packwood, I shall kick your backside every inch of the way from here to Nottage. Now, as aide to the constable, I will be off on his horse, to deliver his message.'

'A proper little fighting cock!' said Doonan, admiringly, as he watched Ossie's retreating back.

'Aye, much like the one I have at home,' Jeremiah interjected, slyly, and Doonan, his red hair ablaze in the haloed light, let out a bellow of laughter fit to fracture the slumbers of the dead.

When Ossie returned with the exciseman, bursting with pride on Joshua's grey, the prisoners and their assembled booty were ceremoniously handed over.

An hour later, the mutilated victors and their messenger were ensconced in Joshua's living room, drinking liberal quantities of cwrw da, and congratulating themselves with becoming modesty upon the evening's work. After a while, Jeremiah roused the dog which had been dozing before the fire, and with much laughter and goodwill from all sides, left the cottage for home.

Doonan and the ostler, now firm friends, took their leave soon after and Joshua finally went to his bed. Within minutes of undressing, he heard a bumping and rattling that had him rushing to his window. Beneath the lantern light at the archway to the 'Crown', he saw Doonan trying to bowl a brandy keg through the ostler's bow legs. He rapped hard upon the glass of the window, and they paused to wave briefly, raising gap-toothed smiles, then they and the barrel rolled, companionably, along the highway and out of sight.

Chapter Twelve

Although Joshua's intake of ale the night before had been moderate to the point of abstemiousness, he awoke feeling unusually liverish. His head ached abominably, his mouth might have been dredged with sand and gravel and he found difficulty in opening his left eye.

The euphoria of the capture had evaporated and, in the crisp, clear light of morning, he saw that, although he had aided the exciseman and enhanced his personal prestige, he was no nearer a solution to the murder. His jaundiced view was aggravated by the reflection in his looking glass. The gash on his eyebrow had congealed and crusted, the swelling almost closing his eye. His nose was bruised and appeared to have spread almost to the size of Crandle's monstrous carbuncle. In addition, every rib, vertebra and inch of flesh felt as if it had not only been belaboured with sticks, but scraped raw upon a flintstone. He wondered how on earth Doonan would survive a day in the quarries, with every hammer blow and pick-strike exploding, not on the rockface, but inside his head! As for Ossie, his acrobatics with the brandy keg, and presumably its contents, would make his mucking out of the 'Crown' stables decidedly less savoury than anything Hercules attempted.

Nevertheless, mindful of his duties as constable, though deprived of sleep and unable to stomach food and drink, Joshua put on his uniform and helmet, and rode away to Port and the 'Knights Arms' alehouse. Rawlings, the exciseman of the night's adventure, was waiting for him at the bar, with a pint pot ready to be filled by the landlord upon his entry.

'Ah . . .' said Joshua, after greeting him, and taking a deep, refreshing draught, 'I have never needed a drink more . . . for I feel as if I have been thwacked by Bando sticks, every inch of the way!'

The exciseman, with great restraint, forebore from comment. 'You did well for us last night,' he said, warmly. 'We are deeply grateful. How did you stumble upon them?'

'Literally.' Joshua fingered his eye, and they both smiled. 'In truth, by accident. It was the ostler from the "Crown" who saw the lights and suspected grave robbers.'

'That bent creature who rode out on the fine grey to fetch me?'

Joshua nodded.

'Well, I daresay he received some reward,' commented the exciseman, drily, 'for I discovered him in a ditch but two hours ago, a little more bent, asleep and reeking of French brandy!'

'A case for the constable, or the exciseman, would you say?'

'More for sleeping it off in the hayloft. In any event, I do not think we will come to blows over his capture . . . we have larger fish to catch.'

'And last night's haul?'

'Minnows and fry; a small ineffectual little shoal. Running a few barrels for their own use . . . although, I fancy the man they call Ezra the Box might be implicated.'

'An odious little fellow.'

'Agreed. It will be hard to prove, however, for none of them will talk. I suspect he managed some unholy substitution with his coffins, and the hearse-carriage was never remarked at the churchyard gate, for the stonemason was repairing the vault and he the family coffins.'

'I am sorry,' confessed Joshua, smiling, 'but I cannot but be amused at their devilish audacity. A deathly alliance in every sense!'

'Indeed! Our hope is that they might have knowledge of the real villains we seek; men who hide behind cloaks of respectability, power, influence, those we would least suspect . . . They are as cunning as foxes. Even those who work for them are unaware of their names.'

'How, then, could the stonemason help?'

'The small people would not dare poach upon their preserves. They must therefore learn when it is not prudent to strike, and where . . . you understand?'

Joshua nodded, 'You will allow me to replenish your drink?'

'No, I thank you. I must keep a clear head, or there will be rumours about a keg of missing brandy! I fancy we will be working much together in the future. You may return your refreshment then. I have only one fear.'

'What is that?' enquired Joshua.

'That without that nose and your splendid eye, I might fail to recognize you!'

When he returned to Newton and had stabled his horse with an unknown but obliging ostler at the 'Crown', Joshua crossed the village green to the parish church. The rector had been celebrating the Eucharist and, the small congregation having dispersed, he was standing in the church porch, staring out at the churchyard. His fine brown eyes were clouded, unfocussing without the gold-rimmed glasses, and Joshua knew that he was seeing nothing around him, only some scene created, or recreated, within his mind. He started, visibly, as Joshua approached, and took some time to recollect himself, before saying, warmly, 'Constable Stradling, I believe that I am to congratulate you.'

'Thank you, sir.'

'You certainly bear the honourable scars of battle!'

'I fancy the enemy sustained worse injuries and greater casualties.'

'So I understand,' the rector's eyes twinkled. 'As a man of the cloth, you realize that such violent conflict is wholly abhorrent to me. Yet, I fancy a few rousing martial hymns on Sunday night might not go amiss with the congregation. Come now, what do you say, Stradling? What shall it be? "He who would true valour see"? or, "Fight the good fight"?'

Joshua answered, smiling, 'Are we not exhorted to show magnanimity to our enemies: charity even?'

'Certainly. And since it begins at home, we must therefore give the parishioners what they expect, and not disappoint them!'

'I fear that one of the wounded men suffered a badly broken wrist ...'

'Quite so. It has been attended to with all the other disabilities. It will be paid for from The Fund Apportioned to the Medical and Surgical Relief of the Poor. From what I hear, there will be very little left in the coffers afterwards! In any event, I feel that is quite magnanimous enough for us both, in view of their blatant villainy. Now, Stradling, let us revisit the scene of the crime ...'

They walked together to the vaulted tomb. The coffin-shaped stone and cross had been lifted aside and the steps and coffin shelves were visible.

'I am to hold a re-interment service, later, for the sake of the family. At their request ... It is no small matter, the desecration of a tomb, and it causes much distress. Although, to be fair, I think they are stupid creatures, thoughtless and greedy, rather than wicked. I do not believe they contemplated sacrilege ...'

'No, sir, I am sure you are right.'

'Come, I will show you a grave which always fills me with more sadness than any other, for it is the grave of three small boys ... brothers. The sons of J H Jackert, drowned on board a Dutch vessel which sank off Newton in 1770. They were bound from the Indies to school in Amsterdam when the *Planters Welward* was driven ashore in a fierce gale.'

'A great tragedy to lose three sons ... and buried in a strange land.'

'Yes and, what grieves me more, a strange land where the people fought to steal and destroy all that came ashore. The wreck and cargo of food were protected by night and day, and yet they threatened death to those who, in doing their duty, would stand in their way. Human nature does not change ... nor greed.'

'But they were poor, and the food was there ...' reasoned Joshua, 'and those unhappy boys, and the crew, were already dead.'

'Not only the poor ... have you never heard the story of the Vaughans of Dunraven Castle? How the master of the castle, in the sixteenth century, took to the wrecking of ships? He ordered his men to fasten lights to the heads of animals, grazing upon the cliffs, so that the moving glow would lure ships on to the treacherous rocks below. One night, in a fierce gale, he hurried down to a broken ship to pillage and to rob the drowned. The ring he tried to wrench from a dead man's hand was that of his own son, long absent.'

'If it were true,' said Joshua, 'then it is a greed more vicious and cruel than any other.'

'As vicious and cruel as the greed or lust which killed the girl I buried yesterday. One or one hundred, known or unknown, it is all the same. A life is all we have.'

'You believe the story of the wreckers to be true?'

'Well, it survives, and there were wreckers upon this coast, and they were savage times, as now.'

'You have heard nothing of your enquiries in Swansea and thereabouts, sir?'

'No, I fear not, Stradling. I have sought information from constables, justices, and friends to no purpose. There is something in this matter which troubles me deeply, for it is as if the girl had no family, no friends to mourn, or even care.'

'From a workhouse, you think, or farmed out as a child? And yet, from her clothes and hands, I would not have believed so ... I cannot reconcile it with the gold locket and the miniature found in her reticule. No, I think she must have been deeply loved and one of a close-knit family, for she carried the likeness of herself and someone she held dear ...'

'Some tragedy, then, rent them apart? It grieves me, Stradling, to think of someone perhaps seeking her, not knowing she is dead.'

'I will visit every remaining farm, and the workhouse, and make enquiries further afield, sir. I fear the chances of finding someone who knew her are remote.'

'And I, Stradling, will continue to pray to Almighty God for the repose of her spirit, and the comfort of those who seek her.'

'You do not believe, as the cottagers, that a soul taken in violence cannot rest?'

'I believe she is at peace with God. It is the soul of the one who committed the violence which will remain restless, in terror of life and eternal death. That is his hell.' He put a hand on Joshua's arm, and they turned and walked back along the pathway to the church door. The intelligent eyes were filled with hurt as he admitted, 'I fail in my duties as a priest, Stradling.'

Joshua made to protest.

'No, hear me out. My gospel is of forgiveness. Yet I cannot

find it in me to pity him. How then can I preach it to others . . .?' He shook his head, sadly. 'I love God, but then that is easy. I suspect that even He must find it hard to love some of my fellow men.'

He turned, abruptly, and walked into the church.

No one, seeing the constable sitting firm and upright on his fine grey horse, his splendid uniform and helmet catching the sun, would have dreamed that he was depressed. Yet he was possessed by a lethargy which owed nothing to lack of sleep, or the physical battering he had taken. Like the good rector, he suspected a spiritual malaise, born of a feeling of helplessness and inadequacy for the work he had chosen.

What on earth had possessed him to think that he would make a constable? What arrogance, an absurd self-delusion. His life, education, experience made him totally unfitted for the responsibilities thrust upon him. True, he had achieved a modest success with the smugglers, but how would he have fared without the alertness of Ossie, the ostler, and the strength of Jeremiah and Doonan? He would very likely have been beaten unconscious and entombed in the vault, with all the other relics of decay and uselessness. He was still musing upon this, and the mutability of all earthly things, when he realized that he was riding in the direction of Rebecca's cottage. As he reined in his horse, to turn back, she came out of the doorway, with a bucket in her hand.

'Good morning, Constable Stradling,' she said, coolly. 'I was about to soft-stone the doorway. Was there something you wanted?'

'No, I thank you, Mistress de Breos.' He was of a mind to ride off, then he pulled the horse round, abruptly, 'Yes, dammit. There was!'

'Then you had better come inside to cool both your horse and your temper, sir.'

He tied the grey to the gate post, and followed her indoors.

'Rebecca, you are a damnably obstinate, pig-headed, wayward and altogether irresponsible girl.'

'Perhaps you had better tell me why you think so highly of me?'

'Because, miss, your spirit and your reckless trust in strangers could bring you great danger, that is why!'

'Will you explain, sir?'

He told her of his fears about Burrel, and the part that Dr Mansel and his wife played in the affair, adding, 'Do you not see the difficulty it put me in? I had sworn secrecy to Mansel, but I feared for you . . . felt responsible.'

'There is no need. I am responsible for myself.'

'There is every need.' He put his two hands firmly upon her shoulders, and swung her round to face him. 'Will you not listen, and try to understand, you infuriating creature?'

'I understand that you hound a man, and condemn him on the word of others.'

'He was tried and convicted. He killed a girl. You must understand?'

'I do not believe it!'

'You will promise me that you will never speak to him again. Have no contact. If you should meet him, then you will tell me at once!'

'I cannot give you that promise. Will not. By what right do you ask it?'

'The right of someone who loves you. There. I have said it. I have thought it for a very long time. Laugh if you will. Call me a fool!'

'Why should I laugh? As for calling you a fool, then if you do not know that I love you, you are either that, or blind, for it is as plain as the nose upon your face.' She looked at him, and broke into laughing. 'Well, perhaps not quite so plain as the nose upon your face, for that is monstrously evident!' She removed his helmet, gently, and kissed him upon his bruised lip.

'Oh, Rebecca,' he said, helplessly. 'I love you so dearly. The thought of any man hurting you, doing you harm . . . like that poor dead girl!' He shook his head as if to shake away pain. 'I would kill him. I swear I would kill him.'

She saw his eyes were bright with tears. 'Hush,' she soothed, 'Hush, Joshua, my dear, my love. It is I who should be hurt and weeping, that I caused you grief. I was arrogant and headstrong . . . but I have been alone so long, with no one who loved me, or cared.'

'I swear that I shall love you and care for you, Rebecca, for all of my life.'

'And I for you.'

'Until death ... and even beyond,' he vowed, 'for I shall be joined to you in spirit when flesh has lost all power. I swear, Rebecca, that you will never be free of me!'

'Nor would I hope to be,' she said, softly, drawing his head to her breast.

He pulled away after a while and kissed her upon her eyelids, cheeks and her warm mouth, forgetting the bruising of his own in the pleasure and pain of love.

'Now, sir,' she chided, when he had released her, 'you have compromised me enough for one day, and I suspect your horse grows restive ... we must continue this ... exploration some other day.'

'You are right, Rebecca,' he said, reluctantly, 'I have much work to do before nightfall ... although my burdens are quite remarkably lightened.'

She smiled, and taking his hand in her small, roughened one, led him to the door.

He turned her hand over and kissed the palm. 'You promise me, at least, that you will take care?'

'Yes, Joshua, that I will promise.'

She watched him mount the grey, salute, and ride away. Yes, it was safe to promise him that.

Joshua, savouring the pleasure of their reconciliation, allowed the grey her head. He reflected upon how brave Rebecca was, and independent; how strong-willed. Like many a lover before him, he saw no irony in the fact that those qualities which he had berated in her as sins, he now held as her dearest virtues. His mood of depression and self-doubt had left him as quickly as it had come and, like the grey, he felt the power of strength and freedom, and a joy in living.

After Joshua had ridden away, Rebecca sat in the shield-back chair in the window for a long while, considering what to do. When she had made up her mind, she dressed for outdoors, harnessed the cob to the cart, and took the way through Picket's Lease, and on to the cart track through the dunes. She had seen Burrel twice since his visit to her house, and always in remote, uninhabited places. Each time he had encountered her, he had greeted her with civility and warmth, but little conversation, save to pass the time of day, or to make some mild observation about the weather. She had thought that, like her, he preferred solitude, the freshness of undiscovered places. Now she knew that there was an added reason for his withdrawal into himself. She did not know where he stayed, or with whom, but she realized that it could not be long before Joshua, or one of his aides, discovered it. If she had any misgivings about what she meant to do, or Joshua's reactions, she stilled them with the thought that she had been truthful. She had promised merely to take care ... She could not explain, even to herself, why she did not, at least, confide in Jeremiah.

It was some time before she glimpsed the thin, nervous-eyed figure she sought, walking some distance from the track, through the dunes. Without thought, she called out, 'Dr Burrel. Stop!'

He looked around, anxious, poised for flight, like some animal scenting danger ... then, reassured, walked slowly towards her.

'Rebecca. You have found out, then, who I am?'

'Yes.'

'Why have you come?'

'To help you.'

He glanced about them, uncertainly.

'Do not worry. I have come alone. I would not betray you.'

He nodded, satisfied. 'Who has told you of the affair? Mansel?'

'No, but that does not matter. What matters is that Dr Mansel knows that you are here. We must get you away ... to a safe place.'

'For me. Or Mansel?' he asked, bitterly.

'I cannot believe that you would harm him.'

'No?' His voice was harsh. 'The harm he has done me has been festering in my soul for twenty-three years.'

'It is over, now.'

'You are wrong. It is just beginning ... I would not want you to know what filth and squalor I lived in, the degradation of body and spirit. Men become as animals, brutes, feeling nothing but the need to survive.'

'But you did survive, Dr Burrel. Is it not enough?' she pleaded.

'Enough?' He looked at her as if seeing her for the first time. 'When he took away everything that gave any meaning to my life, and left me to rot, without any pity or compunction? My work, my freedom, even my hopes for the years ahead. Can you understand that?'

'Yes, I believe that I can,' she said, gently.

'Then you will understand why I fought to stay alive. I wanted to live to see them suffer ... Mansel and his whore!'

'I had best be going,' Rebecca said, 'for though I pity you with all my heart, I cannot help you, Dr Burrel.' She shortened the reins in her hands, and stood, looking down at him. 'I know of a safe house ... an old shepherd's hut on the Downs. It is an isolated place, where no one goes ... You would be secure there, and able to think things out.'

'Regain my sanity, you mean?' he asked, abruptly.

'It would not be strange if your ordeal and your suffering had made you bitter and vengeful, but as for your sanity, I do not doubt it, or that you are incapable of the cruelty inflicted on you.'

'Then you have more faith than I.' He turned his head away, awkwardly.

'Dr Burrel ... please listen. I do not wish to know where you are living. I simply ask you to go there and to do nothing to harm yourself or others. If, after thought, you feel that you would welcome a place where you can allow your wounds to heal, then I will gladly take you there. I shall go now, to prepare it. Be here, at the same time tomorrow, with whatever you need to make life comfortable.'

She flicked at the reins, and the cob obediently moved away.

'Goodbye,' she called out to him, but he was already trudging across the drift of sand, deep in thought, as she had first seen him, thin shoulders hunched in defeat.

In the carpenter's and coffinmaker's shop in the village,

Joshua was seated on a wheel-backed chair, watching Ezra the Box as he lavished care upon an ornately carved coffin lid. The floor was littered with curled wood shavings, sawdust and strangely shaped offcuts of wood which, Joshua thought, would give the poorer of the cottage children a great deal of pleasure. He knew better though than to suggest it to the oily, little man. Outside, in the yard, he could see the stacked timbers, left to 'season' and 'breathe'; the blended colours and grain an endless fascination. Indoors, around him, the benches were spread with woodworking tools and the air with the scent of pine, and the oils and unguents of the woodworker's craft. These, and the dryness of dust and sawdust, caught in his nose and throat, making his eyes burn.

'You were saying, Constable?' Ezra, busy gouging a rivulet along the lid, paused, and brushed out a shaving with his fingers.

'I was asking if you knew the stonemason, Packwood?'

'Only in passing, so to speak, being craftsmen. It is only a love of beauty, and our artistry, we have in common,' Ezra's thin, ferrety smile showed pointed teeth.

'Why do you ask, sir? Do you wish to commission a coffin, or memorial?'

'I fear he will not be carving memorials for some time ... although he might be set to less artistic breaking of stone, since he will, doubtless, end in prison.'

'Indeed?' The small eyes blinked rapidly. 'You surprise me, for I thought him to be a man of the highest integrity. What was his ... failing?'

'Crime, you mean?'

'If it pleases you.'

'It can hardly please me, since it is the reason why I arrested him! His crime was smuggling, or his "failing", that he didn't do it well enough!'

'Dear! Dear!' Ezra clicked his tongue regretfully, 'I am sorry to hear that.'

'You have no knowledge of it yourself?'

'Indeed, no ... my time is given to providing for the last needs of those about me ... I do my humble best to see that they have a suitable last resting place.'

'It seems we are in the same business, then!' said Joshua without humour.

'I see that you were brutally attacked, sir. Some men are wickedly unholy villains!'

'Yes,' agreed Joshua, wrily.

'Indeed, were you not so busy, I would have approached you on that very subject, myself. Only a day or so since, I was attacked most violently by the fisherman, Jeremiah Fleet, the man they call Lamentations Fish, and his vicious dog. It is getting so bad that no man can safely be about his lawful business.'

'What lawful business were you about?'

Ezra looked disconcerted.

'Would you, perhaps, care to lodge a formal complaint?' Joshua asked coldly.

'I would hesitate to add to your burdens,' Ezra replied virtuously, 'for I know the cares of a heavy workload.'

'I imagine that the smugglers, too, found theirs a heavy load to carry ... How would you think they managed to conceal it, and what type of carriage would be least noticed at the church?'

'That I cannot say.'

'No matter. I am sure that I will learn the answer very soon. You are shaping that coffin for a villager?'

'Oh, no! Most of those are cheap, plain wood, like the pauper's, with no embellishments.'

'I dare say that any lack of decoration would be of supreme indifference to them, given the circumstances.'

'This is my own coffin,' said Ezra, coldly. 'Fashioned from a single piece of oak. I have worked upon it for many years getting it perfect ...'

'In life as in death,' said Joshua, ironically. 'Ah, well, I will not keep you from your labour of love. I go to interview the smugglers. I believe they have information for me.'

Ezra's spokeshave slipped on the coffin lid, and his thumb oozed blood. He held it to his mouth and sucked noisily.

'Wounded?' cried Joshua, solicitously, 'Take care ... it would grieve me if you were unable to continue working on your coffin. Who knows how soon any one of us might be struck down by the actions and cruel words of other men?' he added piously.

As Ezra made to rise and see him to the door.

'No! I beg you. Do not disturb yourself, for the work you have recently been engaged in requires a period of calm and sober reflection. Almost, one might say, the solitude of a cell!'

Chapter Thirteen

The following morning, having interviewed the smugglers in their cells in the presence of Rawlings the exciseman, Joshua determined to ride out to the workhouse in Bridgend, as he had promised the justice, the Reverend Robert Knight. In his questioning of Packwood and the others, he had sought, in vain, for some small sign of recognition, or guilt, which would link them to the dead girl. Their puzzlement seemed genuine. Unlike the wily Ezra, who was as slithery and difficult to trap as a conger eel, they were simple creatures. Both Joshua and the exciseman were convinced that any lack of cooperation was caused by ignorance, rather than obtuseness, and now that the four shared the deprivation of a cell, the stonemason had lost his authority as leader. The others no longer feared him; rather, they held him responsible for their plight, and treated him, if not with contempt, then certainly with condescension. What good was a leader who could only lead you into disaster? However, on one thing they were united, not one of them would implicate Ezra the Box.

'There must be honour, even among thieves,' said the exciseman, smiling.

'More likely, bribery,' replied Joshua, 'for I have, honestly, never met a more sinister, slimier, less attractive little reptile in my life!'

'He hasn't the most salubrious occupation in the world ...'

'Neither have we, but we manage to remain human and civilized ... would you believe that when I left him, he was actually carving his own coffin!'

'If he intended filling it with French brandy, I can't say that I blame him,' said the exciseman, good-humouredly.

'At least it would give literal meaning to being "dead-drunk!"'

They saluted each other, laughing, and rode their separate ways.

Joshua had never in his life had cause to visit a workhouse, and he did so with no great enthusiasm, for it seemed to him an austere and restrictive way to live. To men like Jeremiah, he knew, it was a constant and real threat. Jeremiah was an independent man, strong in body and character. He lived in dread of becoming sick, feeble, or having an accident which would render him incapable of work or caring for himself. 'To live on charity,' he declared, 'would be the final humiliation, stripping a man of dignity and manhood.' Nothing Joshua could say would persuade him otherwise.

Joshua had spoken to the relieving officer for the poor of the three hamlets, and found him to be efficient and compassionate. In the few years since the Elizabethan Poor Law had been amended, he told Joshua, earnestly, much had been done to help the destitute financially. The greatest change, however, had been in helping them to retain their dignity and self-respect. It was a message, Joshua thought wrily, which had failed to convince Jeremiah, and, very likely, those in the workhouses, too. Under the new act, 'out-relief' was to be paid only to 'the impotent and aged', and all able-bodied paupers and children were to be transferred to a central workhouse to earn their keep. At least, Joshua conceded, inwardly, it was better than moving the sick and helpless to their 'places of settlement', if they were not born within a parish and became a charge on the poor rate. He wondered, as he rode along, how such inhumanity could be. How many homeless and disadvantaged had walked these ways in despair for the morrow, knowing the humiliation of a public rejection?

He was aware that he was entering Quarella Road, winding alongside the river Ogmore; its waters, which rose clear and sparkling in the Welsh hills, were here brackish and clouded with the slops and detritus of living. He thought again of the cholera outbreaks in the towns, and wondered how these people could hope to survive, should it become polluted with a victim's excrement.

He reined in his horse at the entrance to the workhouse, and dismounted. It was a squat, sprawling building of rough-hewn stone, grey and uninviting. There was a solidity about it, an air of permanence which belied its newness. It was as if the guardians of the poor had instructed the architect, 'Build something that will last. No frills, mind. These people are paupers. They are here to work, to eke out a frugal existence. Make it austere to remind them of their circumstances; bleak as an augury of the future; strong to show them what they must learn to be.' Joshua only knew that, as an outsider, he found it soullessly depressing.

He delivered his grey to one of the inmates, a tall whey-faced fellow, who kept looking down at his own shoes, as if they alone could give him the answer to some question which occupied his mind constantly. When he spoke to Joshua, his voice was mumbling, almost inaudible; yet when he had taken the horse, and led it away, Joshua turned and saw him stop, and stroke the beast, looking steadily into her eyes, and talking to her warmly, reassuringly.

Joshua pulled the brass bell-pull and heard it ring and echo within. The woman who answered the door was old; the hair which escaped her mob-cap white and so sparse that it showed the pink scalp beneath. She wore a heavy-spun apron of grey, which almost hid a dress in the same rough fabric. Another younger woman in similar clothing was scrubbing the flag-stones with a mixture of lye and coarse soap, in a rhythmic steady motion. She did not look up as Joshua passed, so intent was she upon her task, but he bade her, 'Good day,' thinking even as he did so, that it was a singularly inapt greeting.

The manager of the workhouse, or the 'workmaster', as the old woman had called him, was expecting Joshua, 'Sit down, Constable,' he said, 'Walter Bevan, the relieving officer, has told me of the murder, although I am at a loss to know how I can help you.'

Joshua produced the drawing of the dead girl. 'I wondered if, perhaps, she had been a resident here, a visitor, even?'

The man studied it for a moment, as Joshua, surreptitiously, studied him. As a workmaster, he seemed ill-cast, with his plump face, pink and white skin and over-full lips and cheeks. With them both seated, and in full face, he had the look of an elderly cherub. Now, as he bent over the drawing, Joshua could see that vanity caused him to heap up the few remaining curls upon his forehead, while across the top of his bald head, thin strands of hair were stretched taut as piano wires. His eyes, when he looked up, were cold.

'No, not one of mine,' he stated, positively. 'Not the type. You are wasting your time.'

'Is there a type?'

'Certainly, the losers in life ... those who are too feckless, ignorant or simple-minded to make their own way, or provide for their families ... so we have to persuade them.'

'Surely, a harsh generalization? What of those who fall sick, or, through no fault of their own, lose a tied cottage, or their livelihood?'

'I see you are unconvinced. Let me tell you that in a room full of unknown people, I could immediately pick out the weak and the misfits in society.'

'Then you are privileged to help them,' said Joshua, stiffly.

'We are not here to help them. Our aim is to make them help themselves. We do not seek to give them a comfortable existence, rather to act as a deterrent to laziness and apathy. This is the expressed policy of the commissioners. Otherwise we would be filled to overflowing with the shiftless and degenerate.'

'And the families, the women and children?'

'We are not harsh, Constable. When reasonable, then they must work, too, as you would expect: the children in the woollen mills, the women on farms, in sculleries, or where they can. We try to keep them together, but it is not always convenient to do so, you understand?'

'I understand,' said Joshua, rising.

'Come, sir, you are not a stupid man. You realize that our purse is not bottomless. We do the best we can. If it is inadequate, then it is better than nothing.'

As Joshua made to pick up the drawing from the desk, the workmaster cautioned, 'Wait. Do you not wish me to show it to the paupers when their work is done and they assemble for the evening meal?' He stretched out his hand, and Joshua, though strangely reluctant to let the drawing out of his possession, gave it to him.

'If you reflect upon it, objectively and dispassionately,

Constable, you will see that our attitudes and aims are right. As for this, I will do what I can, and return it by way of the relieving officer.'

Joshua thanked him, nodded curtly and went into the hall. The woman was now at the other side of the flagged hall, and he hesitated to walk over the stones she had scrubbed so clean. She looked up and smiled. He saw that she had the wide, flat cheekbones of those they called 'Mongols'. Her voice, when she spoke, was deep, hoarse even.

'Clean. Very clean,' she said, with pride.

'I declare,' said Joshua, smiling in return, 'it is the cleanest floor I have ever seen in all my life.'

He could not, at first, think why a picture of Jeremiah's dog came, unbidden, to his mind, or why he said the words aloud, 'Charity suffereth long.'

Rebecca too had been engaged in scrubbing, scouring, sanding and trying to make the abandoned shepherd's hut habitable; it was a daunting task. When she had first forced open the door, and heard it scrape upon its sunken hinges, the stench had been overpowering. Released, it swept out in a nauseous wave, compounded, as it was, of damp, animal excreta, stale urine and the accumulated filth of stray wild animals and passing vagrants. From the droppings and leavings of fleece and briar, Rebecca supposed that the shepherd had shared his hovel with his flock, either for warmth or to keep them safe from predatory foxes.

She had returned home, harnessed the cob to the cart, and put into it the besom she had fashioned from birch twigs, her dusters and mop of shredded rags, and the brush of hog's hair, a gift from Jeremiah's friend, the Widow Cleat. She had filled her wooden buckets with water from the well, and lye, included a pile of kindling and her tinder box, and a sackful of dry sand.

When, eventually, it looked habitable, she tore down the strip of decayed sacking from the hole in the stone wall, which served as a window, and replaced it with the clean, well-brushed sack. She had already swept out the sand, spread upon the floor to soak up the grease and dirt, and replaced it with a new layer, covered with fronds of dried bracken.

Her final drive home had been to collect a sacking mattress, stuffed with straw, together with a few small pieces of furniture, a wooden bucket, dishes and pots well scoured with stone from the quarries. Her visit to the chandler's and grocer's added a frugal offering of food and drink, plus candles and friction matches. At the last moment, she put in a tankard of her father's and a bottle of home-made elderberry wine.

When she closed the door of the hut, it was with relief, satisfied that she had done all that was possible. Upon the small stool, which served as a table, she placed a posy of herbs; rue, parsley, applemint and thyme to absorb odours and scent the air. As she climbed up into the cart, her only fear was that Dr Burrel would not come ... but as she drove, her spirits lightened when she visualized the face of the long gone shepherd, should he suddenly return.

On reaching their promised meeting place and finding it deserted, she jumped from the cart, and climbed to the top of a sand dune. Below in a rift, she saw him walking, a slight hunched figure, in clothes altogether too large for him, struggling to carry a small trunk, and stopping every few yards to put it to the ground. She returned to the cart and waited.

'Good day, Rebecca,' Burrel greeted her, 'as you see, I have come.'

She nodded.

He lifted his trunk on to the cart, the strain creating a beading of sweat above his lip and he looked ill and drained of energy. He climbed up, to sit beside her, with audible relief.

'I think you and your luggage would be better covered.' Rebecca said. 'Alone, I will arouse no curiosity or comment. Will you lie upon the floor of the cart? It will not be comfortable, but the journey is short.'

'I daresay many in the tumbrils leaving the Bastille wished theirs longer,' he responded, with a smile.

She spoke to him from time to time as they rode, telling him where they were, cautioning him to be silent as they approached the village, or passed a waggon or horseman. He clambered out stiffly at the end of the journey, stretching his cramped limbs. They walked together into the hut, and he stood quite still, looking about him.

'It was the best I could do,' she said, simply.

'After my former home, it is a palace.' He took her hand and turned it over, seeing its roughness. 'You have worked hard for me, a stranger ... and I thank you for it.'

'You will be lonely, I fear.'

'It is something I have grown used to.'

She nodded. 'I have tried to think of all that you might need. The food is meagre, but I will return as often as I can with whatever can be spared. There is a bucket filled to the brim with water, but I think there must be a stream close by, for the watering of flocks. The kindling is set for a fire and you will find plenty more in the woods. As for clothing, I shall bring some of my father's if you are not averse to wearing it ... as and when it is needed.'

'You are a good, brave girl, Rebecca.'

'Brave, sir? How, when I have nothing to fear? I would trust you with my life.'

'As you have already done.' He looked hard at her for a moment, as though about to speak again, but said nothing.

'I will go now. Will you take your trunk from the cart?' She handed it down to him, with a small parcel, saying awkwardly, 'It is nothing, simply some books I have chosen to make the time less tedious ... a catholic selection, for I do not know your tastes.'

'Full of good works, uplifting, and meant, like music, to soothe the savage breast?' he asked, wrily.

'No, but if you wish it, sir, I could swiftly return with *A Pilgrim's Progress*.'

'Are you not bent upon observing that yourself?'

'That is my hope.'

She flicked at the reins and the cob moved off. Burrel watched her until she was out of sight, then re-entered the hut. He unpacked his few possessions from the small trunk, opened up the parcel of books, and made a simple meal. As he ate, he was surprised to see the tears dropping from his chin and on to his hands. He felt neither sadness nor pain. All he thought was how strange it was that through all the years of loss and hopelessness, his eyes had been dry, yet kindness from an unknown child had twice brought him to the edge of weakness, blunting the sharp thrust of revenge. He lay his head upon his arms, and slept.

Creighton Crandle grew bored and restless as he awaited Madeleine Mansel in the room he had furnished as living and sleeping quarters above the coach-house at Dan-y-Graig. He knew that when he was bored he drank too much, as he did now, reaching again for the decanter of brandy, then swilling it down like rough ale, not tasting it.

God! How he missed London and its diversions: the excursions, gaming tables, the women, even the grime and crowded streets, arattle with horses and carriages. He was not a man for solitude. He needed the stimulation of people, and excitement. Well, it would not be long coming and, when his part was played, he would return to his friends, and the whore-houses and drinking dens would know of his coming! He would make sure of that ...

He heard the Mansel coach halt in the stable yard and, putting down his glass, descended the stone steps to greet her. She bored him now, too. Being part French, he had expected ... well, what had he expected? Vitality? Coquetry? Beauty, even ... with the sensuous warmth of that race which seemed to emanate from the flesh, as if it stored the sun ...

He watched her dismiss the coachman and walk across the yard, austere, angular and graceless. He composed his features carefully into a welcome.

'Good day, Madeleine. I received your note. I have been expecting you.'

She nodded, marking the unsteadiness of his gait as he approached her, and when he took her hand, the stale, overpowering smell of drink upon his breath. She turned her head away, involuntarily, then forced herself to smile at him. She feared he had sensed her recoil, and it would not do to offend or irritate him. He was necessary now, but if it were not for his father, she would castigate him for what he was, a drunken clod, shiftless and devoid of both intelligence and manners. He motioned towards the stone stairway, and she preceded him to the upper room. It was little more than a bedroom. From its furnishings she judged it to have been planned by him. It was as showy and vulgar as he, quite unlike the restrained elegance of the main house.

'Well?' he asked, when she was seated, 'what do you think of my little love-nest?'

'That it reflects your character perfectly!'

He looked gratified.

'I did not come here to discuss your personal affairs, but my own ...'

'Ah.' He offered her a drink which she declined, and poured one for himself, 'and how am I involved?'

'There is someone I wish to dispose of.'

'Dispose of?' He was startled. 'You mean kill?' His glass struck the table top sharply, liquid spilling. 'Is this some sort of jest?'

'No jest. There is a man who seeks to do me harm. I want him stopped ... threatened.'

'You want me to frighten him away?' Creighton's mind was fuddled, slow-acting.

'Not personally, you fool!' she stopped, irritably, 'I want you to hire some strong men who will put the fear of God into him!'

'The Devil,' he corrected. 'The fear of the Devil.'

'You can do this?'

'It will need money.'

'That is no problem.' She removed the purse of coins which her husband had given her from her reticule and handed it to him. He pocketed it, face expressionless. 'And the man?'

'Someone from my past ...'

'Ah ...' he said, leaning over and gripping her wrist with mock playfulness, 'so the lady has a past? A lover, perhaps?'

'Don't you ever try to touch me again!' Her voice was dangerously quiet as she wrenched herself free, 'I am not one of your harlots or back-street doxies!'

'A joke ...' he said, flushing and mumbling as if in apology. 'A joke!'

'Then you had best not repeat it, for it does not amuse me!'

His face grew flushed, resentful under its covering of freckles. 'Who is this man? How shall I recognize him?' he asked, sullenly.

'I have written down all the facts about him which you need to know, his height, features, colouring ... although he might well have changed, since it is more than twenty years, but I think you will recognize him.'

'And if I do?'

'Then you will do what is necessary ... and inform me, at once!'

He poured himself another brandy, slopping it awkwardly over his fingers, sucking them clean. Already she saw signs of his degeneration, a puffiness and thickening of face and chin, a slowness in movement and thought, a barely perceptible tremor of the hands.

'You had best forego the drinking.'

'I am man enough to take my liquor ... and anything, or anyone else I choose!' he said childishly.

'A real man does not need to try so hard to prove it!'

'And a real woman ...' he began, savagely.

'Yes?' she asked coldly.

'Nothing,' he mumbled, sullenly. 'Nothing.'

'You will order your carriage to return me to my house,' she instructed, 'but first, the laudanum.'

He walked unsteadily to a small wall-cupboard, extracted a phial, and gave it to her.

'The money?'

'You will make enough from your commission, I have no doubt. Remember that I have paid you well. I shall expect value.'

Without a word, he went out and summoned the coachman, and proceeded to take out his surliness upon the groom, bidding him saddle his horse. When Madeleine Mansel had gone, he took the purse which she had given him and emptied it upon the table, replacing half of the gold coins and locking it in the wall-cupboard. The key he put into his pocket with the remainder of the money.

'Damn the woman! She is a stupid, shrivelled-up old bitch! Not even an apology for a woman,' he sneered. Well, he would show her that he was not as stupid as she thought! There were plenty of other women, younger and prettier, and altogether more willing! He went out to fetch the mare.

*

From the day when Cavan Doonan had willingly, and formally, asked Rosa Howarth to be his wife, everyone was declaring that he was a changed man. Rosa was under no such illusion. In fact, had he been, she would very likely have spurned his proposal, for the splendid truth was that she loved him as he was: fiery, hell-raising, profligate and as unreliable as the church tower clock. She, alone, knew of the tender Doonan. That bewildered small boy who found himself in a body too huge and powerful for him, and responded with rage and aggression, or penitent tears. It was true that his brawls and alehouse evictions had grown less. This heralded no conversion to peace. He had simply changed sides in the battle, belabouring Joshua's foes with the same force and enthusiasm he had shown to his own. As for his working, it was said by the quarrymen that he was the equal of any three men, and could split a rock face with one blow of a sledge ... Rosa was only grateful that he was not splitting skulls. He had always been fiercely competitive, but now his winning had purpose. The money he earned he gave to Rosa, who kept it securely under lock and key. Not that he would have broken into it, any more than he would have violated an alms dish. But Rosa was a prudent creature, and believed in removing temptation. She was also wise. She never enquired about what he gambled away, but greeted his offerings with such joy and praise for his labours, that his gambling declined as his sense of virtue increased. Soon, she knew, there would be enough to marry and rent a small cottage of their own and, one day, perhaps even to buy one.

She was deep in thought about him, and the appealing prospect of their future together, as she waited by the pool at the bottom of Dan-y-Graig hill, to meet him from his work. She knew how surprised he would be and hoped that he would also be pleased. She had been granted a ride by carrier's cart as far as Newton village and her uncle, the carrier, had said that she looked 'as pretty a piece of muslin' as he had ever seen! As she stood dreaming and watching the antics of a moorhen and chicks as they spurted into a clump of reed-mace, she heard a clatter of hooves and, instinctively, jumped aside.

The man who looked down at her from the saddle was

dressed in the clothes of a gentleman, but there was sweat on his face, and his red hair clung damp on his brow. As he leaned towards her, she smelled drink upon his breath, and saw that his eyes were reddened and unfocussing.

Rosa stepped back hard, looking for some way of escape, or someone to help her, but there was no one, and her way was barred.

'What is your hurry?' he asked, tapping his riding crop against his boot. 'A pretty little creature like you should be riding with a gentleman, not walking the roads alone.'

He leaned sideways in the saddle, and put his arms about her waist; she wrenched herself free. Anger and fright had forced colour into her pale, almost transparent skin and Creighton Crandle, even in his befuddled state, found her mightily appealing. He made the mistake of stepping down beside her.

'Come, I shall lift you up.'

'You will not, sir, for I swear that if you do,' she stamped her small foot, 'I will kick you hard, and painfully!'

'Methinks the lady doth protest too much!' He laughed and caught her by the arm, fingers bruising her flesh beneath the thin cotton sleeve. 'Now, let us see how you like being kissed by a gentleman.'

His grip tightened, and she caught the odour of ale and stale sweat as he drew closer. She struggled to free herself, but could not, as his freckle-blotched face drew nearer, and his lips pressed painfully against her own. For a moment she was terrified, unable to breathe, then she bit with all her force upon his lip. He swore and wrenched away, raising his crop to strike her. She tore it from his grasp and, fury giving her strength, lashed him about the neck and shoulders. Then, before he could recover his drunken balance, she shoved him so hard across the chest that he went reeling backwards, to collapse in the pond.

Rosa threw the crop after him in disgust and, without stopping to look back, lifted up her skirts and ran. Safely in the village, she fell, sobbing and incoherent, into the arms of her uncle, the carter. His fury knew no bounds and he was all for fetching the constable and lodging a complaint, or taking a few of his friends to 'give the young varmint the lesson of his life!'

But Rosa wisely dissuaded him, saying that if it came to the ears of Doonan, he would very likely murder the fellow, and then where would she be? She would rather have a husband than her maidenly virtue to keep her warm on a cold night. This way she managed to protect both.

The carrier, seeing that her distress about Doonan equalled her distress about her adventure, calmed her down with gentleness, vowing to himself that he would, nevertheless, relate what had happened to the young constable. He would tell him, too, that Crandle was despised by the maidservants at his house, who were careful to avoid being caught by him near that room he kept in the old stable block. He was an arrogant, ill-mannered little coxcomb of a fellow, fit only to frighten the wits out of helpless young women. It was a pity that Doonan could not get his hands upon him; he would teach him a lesson that he would never forget! For the moment, however, the carrier was only concerned for his niece. He lifted Rosa up beside him and, watched by a quietly sympathetic audience, drove her away. It was when they were nearing Port, and Lias cottages, that the humour in the situation suddenly caught him. He visualized the scene as the palely delicate Rosa bit young Crandle upon the lip, set upon him fiercely with the riding crop, and pushed him into the pond-weed.

'By heaven, Rosa girl,' he said, laughing admiringly, 'there is nothing wrong with your spirit, I'll give you that. Doonan does not know what he is letting himself in for!'

Rosa, who had by now recovered herself, began to laugh with him, and they laughed so helplessly that the carrier was unable to manage the reins, and was forced to stop the cart.

'I tell you, uncle,' she said, giving him a kiss upon his cheek, 'that poor horse was as pleased as I to see him unseated and the whip thrown after him. As for Cavan, he is more of a gentleman than Crandle will ever be!'

'I would not wager upon it, should he find out what happened today,' said the carrier. 'Stay clear of Crandle, Rosa love, for he will bring you nothing but grief, believe me.'

Doonan, riding home with Emrys, on his horse and cart, saw Crandle riding past, 'for all the world,' he told Rosa later, 'like a bat out of hell. He was in the foulest of tempers, and as wet as a gossip upon a ducking stool. I said to him "Good day to you, Squire," and made as if to touch my forelock, but he kicked his mount, having no whip, it seemed, and drove through his gates as if possessed. It looked to me as if the mare was a spirited creature and had thrown him.'

'Very likely, Cavan my dear,' agreed Rosa, demurely.

Chapter Fourteen

Life for Ossie at the 'Crown Inn', had never been more exciting or filled with promise. Once, his world had been encompassed by the four bleak walls of his stable loft, and the stalls beneath. He had no family, for he had been farmed out from the earliest time he could remember, working at anything and everything, often for no more than a place to lay his head and his meagre keep. When those he had worked for were, by his own standards, rich, some strange alchemy had rendered him quite invisible to them; if they were poor, their energies and emotions were used up in providing for their own large brood. When he had entered service as a stable lad at the 'Crown', and walked beneath its archway into the yard, it was a spiritual revelation; almost like entering the Kingdom of Heaven. He still remained invisible to those who arrived in their coaches, but now he had a room of his own, food enough, and something living to care for, and to care for him.

The horses at the 'Crown' were known to be the best groomed and the best tempered for miles around. It grieved him to see the winded, broken-down animals which came to him with some of the public, and even the private coaches. Many were blind, or already too old, or wearied by ill-use, but it was commonplace to run them until they died; their average life span less than three years. When the poor creatures came into his hands, he would lavish upon them all the care and love they had been denied, as if, alone, he could make up for the deficiency in their lives, and his own.

He would still sit up at night with a horse that was sick, or to ease a mare in foal, but now it was not only animals who saw in him his true worth, but people: Jeremiah, Doonan and Rosa, Rebecca, Emrys, and Illtyd, the little man. It was to Illtyd that he felt closest of all. Perhaps it was an affinity of outcasts. He did not question, simply accepted it gratefully. But it was to Joshua he felt he owed most: the friendship, his new-born fame in the village and, above all, the distinction of being the constable's honorary aide. Consequently, he supervised the conversion of the room over the coach house into an escape-proof cell and the fortifying of the old carriage, with a zeal that left the workmen exhausted. He chivvied, harried, probed and inspected until they were glad to finish the job in half the time allotted, the foreman swearing 'It would have been less work to build the pyramids single-handed!' Now, as Joshua came to claim his grey, Ossie brought her forward, proudly, saying, 'The horses for the prisoners' carriage will always be prepared, and I with them. You have only to call me, by day or night ...'

'I shall remember,' Joshua said, 'but may I depend on you for a more immediate favour?'

'You have only to ask.'

'It will mean a day's journey.'

'That is of no account. The ostler from Weare House will take my place, for he told me yesterday that there are no visitors for the bathing.'

Joshua nodded, and explained the mission.

The ostler's smile grew wider and more expansive, his weathered face creasing into delight.

'You shall be well rewarded.' Joshua added.

'The act will be reward enough! I will take no payment. Indeed, to do so would be an affront.'

'Then I will make sure that your ostler friend does not lose by it.'

'That would indeed be a kindness.'

Joshua thanked him and, with a brief salute, rode off under the arch. Ossie watched his benefactor until he was out of sight, then, warm with pride and anticipation, sent a stable boy to summon the Weare ostler.

Joshua had, that morning, received a visit from Walter Bevan, the relieving officer for the poor. Littlepage, the work-master, bade the constable return, for he had news of some importance to convey.

Joshua thanked the officer and said, carefully, 'I suppose the workmaster needs to be a special kind of man ... resolute, inflexible, would you not say?'

'I say nothing, save that hardness and strength are not the

same thing ... You may make of that what you will.'

Joshua nodded. 'And your own work? What made you choose it?'

'I know the people here ... their needs.' Bevan's earnest, sallow face grew animated. 'They will talk to me because I am one of them. I understand their pride, their desire to be independent, not to be beholden to anyone.'

'Yes. I see that.'

'I am restricted in what I can do. It is pitifully inadequate ... and what I can offer could be withdrawn at any time, at the discretion of the guardians. Today, a paralysed man, bedridden, and with four young children, was granted but five shillings, and eleven yards of calico; an eighty-two-year-old widow was given ten shillings to be spent only on clothing, or else withdrawn ... and the guardians allowed a lunatic parishioner four shillings. Many more were refused help, and told that their children must provide.'

'It must be difficult to refuse help?'

'The most difficult of all is to persuade them to apply for charity, to convince them that it is their due; owed to them for a lifetime of working, or caring for others. I try to let them keep some small shred of dignity, some belief in their own worth. If they are refused, it is more than money they lose.'

'Their self respect?' Joshua asked.

Bevan nodded. 'When I came into this work, I thought that I would be able to create miracles; to move heaven and earth. Now I would be content merely to move the Board of Guardians!' He grimaced expressively and bade Joshua, 'Good day.'

As Joshua rode out over Dan-y-Graig Hill, and past the low, rambling house of grey stone where the Crandles lived, he was thinking of what Evans the carrier had told him about his niece, Rosa. The thought of the fragile, pale-skinned girl setting about young Crandle with his own crop, and throwing him into the pond, brought a smile to his lips, and he found himself laughing, delightedly, aloud.

'Most unbecoming conduct for a constable,' he said to himself, unable to stop smiling. 'Any guardian, sitting in judgement, would certainly deem me a "lunatic parishioner"!' He was well aware, however, that there was another, more serious, side to the encounter. If, as it was rumoured, Crandle was meeting other young girls from the village, it was a dangerous practice. A little high-spirited fun between a country girl and boy was an essential part of everyday courting, to be looked upon indulgently by their elders. It either ended in swiftly dried tears, or wedding. But Crandle was a putative gentleman ... seeking cheap amusement outside his class. It could end in nothing but trouble, especially if his victims were servants, employed in his house, and vulnerable. If resentful fathers or brothers should plan to 'teach him a lesson' one dark night, Joshua did not give much for his chances of surviving unscathed. As for any confrontation with Doonan!

It seemed strange that Rosa and the dead girl should be so similar in colouring and physique ... Was this what had excited Crandle to accost them both, if, in fact, he had done so? Was it their fragility and, in Rosa's case, deceptive look of vulnerability and helplessness which attracted him, or had it simply marked them out as easy targets? Joshua determined to find out whether it had been mere coincidence, or had any others Crandle approached fitted the pattern.

He was still musing about this, and regretting how his intense dislike of Crandle fuelled his prejudice, when he entered the gateway of the workhouse.

He delivered his horse to the same whey-faced fellow who had tended the grey before. This time the man raised his eyes briefly from an absorption with his shoes to say, shyly but audibly, 'Good day to you, sir. A fine horse. I will take good care of her.' Joshua was disproportionately cheered by this sign of progress. The same sparse-haired old lady greeted him at the door and led him to the workmaster's office, where he knocked authoritatively and was bidden, 'Enter'. Littlepage rose from behind his desk to greet him, pushing at a drawer as he did so. His elderly cherub face was unbecomingly flushed. As he leaned forward to take Joshua's hand, the thin strands of hair across his scalp were awry, and he smelled of alcohol. He appeared flustered, but quickly regained his composure.

'I did not expect you quite so soon, Constable ... Stradling, is it not? You have me at a disadvantage.'

'I believed the matter to be urgent.'

'Quite so.' He tugged at a bell-pull behind his desk and, when it was answered, gave orders to, 'Fetch Mistress Randall from the laundry. Tell her she is needed at once. See that she is neat and tidy!'

Joshua sat in silence.

'It is a continual battle to keep them clean and well turned out. They seem to take so little pride in themselves; it reflects upon us as an institution. The guardians see that they are adequately clothed, but get very little thanks for it.'

Joshua did not trust himself to reply.

'It is a symptom of their general inadequacy, I suppose. A sloppiness ... apathy. You see it in the way they dress, eat, work; the way they walk and stand, even.' He smiled. 'These things are sent to try us, I daresay.'

'As long as we are not found wanting.' Joshua's voice was dangerously calm.

Before Littlepage could reply, there was a firm knock upon the door, and he called, 'Come!' imperiously.

The woman who entered was perhaps fifty years old, small, slim and fine featured. There was nothing wrong with her posture. She held herself erect with a natural, easy grace, and she moved in the same way. Joshua could only have described it as 'a fluid elegance'. She wore the ugly coarse-textured dress of the other women, but without an apron covering, and she had added a small lace collar with a mourning brooch of jet.

'Emily Randall?' Joshua rose to his feet, but Littlepage remained seated.

'That is my name.' She looked down at the workmaster with an almost imperceptible twitch of the lips, which Joshua read as amusement. He held her chair for her, and she thanked him and accepted it. He could see that beneath her controlled manner, she was tired. It showed in her eyes, and the slight tremor of her hands, which were reddened by heat and moisture. Her face, too, was flushed with heat, and her dark brown hair, knotted at the nape of her neck, escaped in damp tendrils about her face and brow. She made no effort to touch it, but sat calm and composed.

'Go on, woman, tell him!' said Littlepage impatiently. 'It is what you are here for!' He took the drawing of the dead girl from beneath an inkstand on his desk, smoothed it briefly, and handed it to her.

'You know her?' asked Joshua.

'Yes, I really believe that I do ... although I cannot be absolutely sure, for she was but a child ...'

Joshua brought the locket from his uniform pocket, clipped it open, and put it gently into her hand. Her face, as she studied it, softened with delight and recognition.

'Yes, now I am quite sure. She is so like her mother. It was one of my charges, Mary Devereaux. I was her nurse and governess when she was very young.'

'And the other? The man?'

'Her brother, I believe. He was some twelve years or so older than she. I saw so little of him. He was for the most part away at school ... Roland he was called. Yes, Roland Devereaux. It must be! They were so alike, even as children, and now I see it even more ...' She looked up at Joshua, pleased, enquiring. 'You have news of her? She has asked to see me?'

'I did not tell her why ...' mumbled Littlepage, in answer to Joshua's look, 'It did not seem to be necessary.'

'I am afraid that I am the bearer of bad news for you, Mistress Randall.'

'She is dead, of course ... that is why you have come,' the woman's voice was dull, lifeless. 'I thought at first ...' Joshua moved as if to help her, but she shook her head. 'What is it that you wish to know?'

'Her parents. Are they alive?'

'No. Her father, a sea captain, was killed at sea. Her mother died a year later of a sickness. That was when I was forced to leave.'

'How old was the girl, Mary?'

'Six years old, no more. She left Carmarthen then, to live with a great aunt at a village near Swansea. An aunt of her father's, I believe.'

'And the boy, Roland?'

'That I cannot say, for I became governess to another family and I all but lost touch. She was a dear gentle-natured child. It broke my heart to leave her so bewildered and unhappy. She clung to me, I remember, weeping bitterly and begging me to stay, saying that now she had no one. I tried to comfort her as best I could, saying that her brother would look after her, care for her, always ... but she was not to be pacified. She barely knew him, you see. They were so much apart and, to her, he was already a grown man. I remember that I unfastened the brooch from my collar and pinned it upon her dress, to distract her. She had always liked it. It was a pretty thing in chased silver, with the words *Ever Thine* engraved upon it. It was willed to me by her mother ... a gift from her husband when they were very young. I felt that it belonged to Mary, rather than to me.'

Joshua saw that her eyes were bright with unshed tears. 'That was kind of you. It must have been a comfort to her.'

'Do you think so? I would like to believe that.'

'You may be sure of it. It was pinned to her dress when she died. She must have treasured it over the years.'

She hesitated. 'Her death?'

'Murder. By person or persons unknown.'

She rose to her feet, pushing herself upright on the edge of the desk. She had not lost her poise. She seemed perfectly in control of herself, save that her face was now unnaturally pale except for two circles of colour which burned high on her cheeks. She held out her hand to Joshua.

'Thank you for telling me. I hope that I might have been of some help to you.'

Joshua took her hand firmly, marvelling at her self-control. She was the kind of woman, he thought, who would only cry when alone. He did not let go of her hand, but drew her around to face him.

'I will bring your brooch to you ... It is what she would have wished.'

She nodded, but did not speak.

'You will return to the laundry.' Littlepage instructed, 'and resume your duties, Randall. While you are here, others are forced to do your work for you. You must make up the lost time as best you can.'

She looked at him, and then at Joshua.

'It is a sad thing for anyone, a child, or a woman, to be alone and friendless. I grieve for her with all my heart ... but sometimes it is almost as sad never to be alone.'

She went out, closing the door quietly behind her.

'What was she blathering about?' demanded Littlepage, irritably. 'I could make neither head nor tail ...' But Joshua had already moved into the hall, and was hurrying after her, down the corridor. When she turned, he saw that the tears were running down her cheeks, although she was making no sound.

'Mistress Randall,' Joshua said brusquely, 'if work were to be offered to you, and a place to live, however poor and unpromising ..?'

'Then I would accept it humbly, and with gratitude, sir. I would work at anything, go anywhere.'

'But if it were merely an old coachhouse ... a converted cell ..?'

She looked about her meaningfully, brushing her cheeks dry with the heel of her palm.

'Even if it were unconverted, it would be a good exchange for what I have now.' She smiled. 'Prisons do not always have bars ...'

'Then I will arrange it.'

As he rode home to Newton, over Three-Step-Hill and past Tythegston Court, Joshua wondered what the justice would have to say if he knew that his newest and lowliest of constables had so exceeded his duty as to offer the cells as a lodging house to a female pauper. 'Damn it!' he thought, 'I am my own man. If I cannot make it right with the vestry, then my powers of persuasion have atrophied and I am unfitted for the job! In addition to the cell above the coachhouse, there is a huge barn-loft of empty space ... just wasting, and gathering dust ... If I get Ossie and Jeremiah to help me clean it, then furnish it with any sticks of furniture I can borrow or coax ... perhaps the vestrymen will pay her a small sum for cleaning the cell and acting as caretaker of the place. If not, I shall pay rent to the innkeeper secretly. It cannot be much, for he is a kind-hearted fellow and has no use of the loft, of that I am sure. As for work, perhaps, since she was a governess, they will let her teach in one of the schoolrooms ... or a family in one of the yeomen's houses might have need of her services. If not, then I shall claim that I need a daily housekeeper who will prepare my meals. He suddenly remembered that he had not asked her about the small scar which Dr Mansel had mentioned in his post mortem report and the oak leaf birthmark. It was the sort of thing a nurse would see and recall, but not a brother. Well, birth, death, it was all the same now to Mary Devereaux.

He was abruptly shaken from his introspection by the unusual sight of Rebecca's cart at the base of the hill, taking the way that led over the downs. He saw its back wheels, in silhouette, as they took the corner that disappeared from view behind the high hedges. He was at first puzzled, then intrigued. He wondered if he should follow and surprise her. What was she doing so far from the cottage, and in such an isolated place? He actually reined the horse in at the entrance to the lane and stopped while he deliberated his course of action. Then, regretfully, he set the grey upon a course for the 'Crown'.

He must speak to the innkeeper of his plans ... invite his cooperation. As for Rebecca, she was very likely gathering berries, or wild herbs, for some concoction, or as a flavouring. In any case, her independent spirit would not take kindly to over-solicitous care, or to being spied upon. Still, it was high time he invited her upon an outing or celebration. She was young and pretty, but had known little enough of frivolity and childish pleasure. The Mabsant Feast? Yes, that would please her. Rosa and Doonan must come, too. But, of course, all the villagers would be there. It was the brightest day in the calendar. He was resolved upon it. He must make it a day that Rebecca would always remember.

Smiling, he rode under the archway to the 'Crown', and dismounted. Ossie had not returned yet from his errand, and it was the ostler from Weare House who came out eagerly to take his horse. Joshua, after much persuasion, managed to make him accept a sum of money for his services, as substitute for Ossie and, the transaction concluded to their mutual satisfaction, thanked him for his readiness.

'A pleasure, Constable. To tell the truth, it is more congenial to be here with company.'

'It is quiet at the bath house, then?'

'As the grave, sir. Next week I shall not be required at all.'

'I am sorry, for when that happens, unexpectedly, you must be sadly out of pocket, Ostler.'

'It is not easy, with a family to support, there is so little work, and none at short notice, but, as you know, my duties at the Weare are seasonal.'

'What will you do?'

'Well, that is the strange thing; when I protested to Mr Gwilliam and said that it was unfair as I had been hired for the season, I expected him to upbraid me for my insolence, or even dismiss me.'

'He did not?'

'No, indeed,' the ostler chuckled, 'I could scarcely credit it. He gave me my full wages for a week. I tell you, sir, I took that money and ran off fast as a pig sighting acorns! I expected to awaken and find myself in bed, dreaming, or to learn that Mr Gwilliam had suffered some seizure to the brain!'

'Well, I am pleased at your good fortune.'

The ostler looked at him consideringly, then nodded. 'Yes, but, perhaps like me, a little puzzled. .?' He took the grey, and led her to the stables.

Jeremiah had finally found a home for the remaining bellicose cockerel. Deprived of its adversary, it had at first reacted with louder and even more raucous crowing, to proclaim how cleverly it had vanquished its rival. Its skirmishes with the dog became wilder, more bloody, until the wretched cur had to be coaxed to set its nose over the doorstep and into the yard. Jeremiah and Charity bore it with resignation and fortitude, feeling that it was a Nemesis of their own creation. But when the cock's eyes grew less bright, its feathers dulled, and it refused to eat, its jauntiness deserting it, they grew concerned. It was, after all, a guest in the house. The dog ventured, once more, into the yard, even trying a few mock forays to encourage it, but it lay there, dully, its proud coxcomb wilting and sere.

'It needs company,' Jeremiah commented to the dog. 'The poor creature is pining to death. It needs a mate; to show off to a brood of admiring hens.'

No sooner had he made up his mind than he bundled it,

sagging and unprotesting, under his arm and set off to the cartwright's in Nottage, to remedy affairs.

Like most of the cottagers in the three hamlets, the cartwright's wife had a small garden at the back of the house in which she grew potatoes and a few modest vegetables, to see them through a lean year. She kept a few hens which scratched, half-heartedly, in the bare earth, and laid occasional, fragile-shelled eggs, which she sold, or bartered, at the market for butter or cheese. The pride of her life was a large pink and black sow, which wallowed in the mud of its thatched sty, its small teats for all the world like neatly spaced buttons upon a waistcoat. Today, being sunny, Jeremiah saw that it wore a cotton sunbonnet, to guard its sensitive head from sunstroke. It came to the cottage wall to watch him pass by, peering through narrow, slit eyes, flat snout twitching inquisitively under its bonnet brim.

'Just like one of those gossipy old biddies at the well,' Jeremiah said to Hannah, the cartwright's wife, as she came to the door to greet him. 'I am sorry about the rooster ... he seems a poor cowed creature.'

'No doubt he will revive and show off alarmingly with a little encouragement from the hens ... like most of his sex!' said Hannah, tartly, 'But come in, Jeremiah, your nose must have led you, for I have just made some oat-cakes. I will butter them warm and pour you some ale. You look tired!'

'I am,' he admitted. 'I do not know whether it is old age or the time of the year, but I seem drained of my energy ... like the old rooster.'

'I will take him into the yard to introduce him to the ladies. I would do as much for you, if it would restore your vigour!'

'My days for courting are long over, Hannah. The excitement would very likely bring on apoplexy!' They laughed companionably and after the rooster was ensconsed in his new home, they sat down to exchange their news of the villages.

'I hear you played the hero the night of the smuggling, Jeremiah, laying about you with a stick, like a fool on a donkey. It is no wonder you lack energy, you are no longer a stripling.'

'Not dead yet, either.'

'Talking of the dead, there are rumours of Ezra the Box. Someone who came to have his cart mended told Daniel that Ezra has one special, finely-carved coffin which he works upon constantly. He says it is to be his own! It is no wonder, for it is believed to be filled to the brim with brandy, tobacco, and other contraband. You might mention it to the constable, should he have a mind to visit him. I would not inform upon a neighbour, as well you know, but Ezra is such a mean, slimy-tongued, little toad of a creature.' She leapt up, and looked through the window into the yard.

'Well, would you believe it! Come here, Jeremiah. Just look at that cockerel up to his old antics.' The sow's snout was resting on the wooden fence of her pen as she watched the rooster, jaunty as ever, chasing a squawking hen in a blur of feathers.

'Not much wrong with the old devil. Just like you . . . only waiting to get his second wind!'

Jeremiah left for home, much cheered that the game old rooster had revived, for, perversely, he had grown quite fond of the troublesome bird.

'You will be very sorry to see your old sow go at Christmas, Hannah,' he said at the gate, for he knew that the cottagers could rarely afford to eat meat, except at Christmas, when they killed a 'bacon' of their own rearing.

'*If* I let her go . . . for Jemima is like one of the family. I have reared her from a piglet. I could no more eat her than I could eat you, Jeremiah. And I have no yearning to turn cannibal.'

Jeremiah walked as far as the well outside the wall of Nottage Court, and then felt so strange and light-headed that he had to cup his hands to drink some water, and dip his kerchief in and put it to his head, which ached as though he had been set upon by footpads with sticks. He sat for some time upon a stone, then resolutely stood up, and went on his way. By the time he reached the village he was shivering violently, and his eyes were blurred. His forehead felt hot, but when he wiped it with his palm, it was damp with sweat and cold to touch. His throat ached too, and there was a raw pain in his chest which made breathing difficult. He hoped that he would not meet anyone that he knew.

When he entered the yard, Charity rushed at him with its usual boisterous, ecstatic welcome. Jeremiah unleashed it, and the dog stood trembling, sensing its master's distress and not knowing what to do to bring him comfort.

Jeremiah walked indoors to his bedroom and, without taking off his boots and jacket, lay with his head upon the straw-filled pillow, tears of weakness filling his eyes. The dog leapt up beside him, licking his face gently, and whimpering softly. They lay there together until the sun went down and the night grew dark. When the dawn broke, filling the room with red light, the dog awoke and leapt to the floor, then it began licking Jeremiah's hand. Charity started to bark, small yelps of anguish and agitation ... and leapt back upon the bed, and began licking its master's face frantically, in an effort to make him open his eyes and speak. Jeremiah tried to tell the dog he was all right, but the words made no sound.

Chapter Fifteen

Jeremiah alone of the folk of the three hamlets was unaware of the great gale which whipped the coast of the Bristol Channel, lacerating all which dared to stand in its way. What it could not sever, it bowed and bent, like the trees and hedges, twisting them into strange shapes that leaned into the land, as if fleeing the wrath of the storm.

It was the sea which took the full brunt of the wind's fury. The water seethed and rose up, battering itself against the rocky shore. Its force was terrible. Fierce waves clawed the edges of the land, hollowing out cliffs, gouging bays and inlets from the rocky outcrop, eroding fertile soil. Man and beast were driven inland to escape the excoriating rawness of sand, wind and spray. For those upon the sea, there was no escape. Craft, great and small, were sucked down, then spewed upon the shore as effortlessly as the jetsam of shell, bladderwrack and stone ...

Joshua, washing himself at the well in the yard, looked up to see the seabirds crowding upon the village green, their agitated cries a brief warning. He felt the first coolness in the summer breeze, and shivered. Huge spots of rain rippled the surface of the water and left dark stains upon the stone. He felt them sting his flesh, and the strengthening and cooling of the wind, as he dressed and hurried indoors.

Within minutes, it seemed, the sky grew bruised and angry. Rain spattered like ice upon the window-panes, as the wind rose, howling, to circle the house. The cottagers made sure that their animals were secure, then hastened to their own shelter, fastening windows and doors, building up their fires, cocooning themselves against the force of the storm. All night it raged without ceasing or losing strength, tearing at roofs, uprooting trees, whipping a crust of salt over earth and stone. The cottagers lay awake in their beds, hearing the rattle of glass, the wind's moan in chimney and tree ... fearful for those who walked abroad, their livestock, but, most of all, their menfolk at sea. When the dawn came the wind suddenly stilled, and the silence was as ominous as the storm.

Joshua, dozing after a sleepless night, thought, at first, that the gale had risen again. As his senses returned, he realized that what he had heard was a rattling and shouting at his door.

He dressed quickly and, lighting his lantern, hurried below. Upon the doorstep was Dr Mansel, shouting incoherently, face flushed, his breathing raw with the effort of hurrying against the storm. Joshua pulled him inside and shut the door.

'She's gone, Stradling. Madeleine, she's gone!'

Joshua led him inside, trying to calm him, and settling him upon a chair.

Mansel thrust him away, striking out in his agitation. 'Can't you hear me, man? I said she has gone. Left ...'

'When?'

'Now! Tonight! It must have been in the storm.' He buried his face in his hands, and began to weep. 'I fell asleep, do you see? She hated storms. They frightened her. Where would she go?' He struggled to his feet. 'What are we doing just talking here? I should be out looking for her, man! We are wasting time.'

'The storm has eased,' Joshua said. 'There will be shelter from the wind, but we will go and search for her. Wait, I will get my clothing, and take some spirits to warm her, and a blanket; the lantern is already lit.'

For an hour and more they searched, across the green, and the path to the Burrows, even the churchyard and the church itself, lest she had sought sanctuary there, but they found no sign. Together they retraced the way Mansel himself had come, making his search through the storm. Finally, they hunted through every inch of his shrubbery and garden, the coach house and outhouses, even the great conservatory, but again they found nothing. Then they went indoors, the servants were up: the housekeeper grimly silent; the manservant loquacious with shock; the little housemaid weeping nervously, her pinched nose raw. They assured Dr Mansel that no room in the house had been left unentered. Even the attics had been searched.

Mrs Mansel was nowhere to be found.

When the servants had been dismissed, and gone to their beds, Dr Mansel said, wearily, 'I am at a loss to know what to do, Stradling. I am very afraid ... You know what a nervous state of mind she was in?'

Joshua nodded.

'The note you left me ... about Burrel ...'

'I delivered it to the housekeeper.'

'The seal was broken.'

'You believe that your wife read it?'

'I am sure of it. After that, she became even more withdrawn, more agitated, unable to sleep at night, or to relax by day. She seemed to be always watching, waiting for something. If Burrel has taken her, harmed her ...'

'Hush!' Joshua said, 'You are talking wildly. How could he have known that she would be distressed by the storm, run away?'

'He could have planned to meet her ... lured her away with him.'

'Why?' asked Joshua. 'If she was terrified? Take a grip upon yourself, sir! You are not thinking clearly, and it is no wonder, for you are exhausted and afraid.'

'Yes,' agreed Mansel, dully, 'You are right and I apologize.'

'I do not blame you, Dr Mansel, that you are confused and shocked, but we must be practical, do what is most likely to find her. She has friends hereabouts?'

'I know so little,' Mansel admitted, helplessly. 'You will understand that our lives were separate. I have heard her speak of the Crandles and some other acquaintances ... but they would have sent word to me.'

'Perhaps the storm prevented them.'

'No, they would have found a way. I know it!'

'Is there then some place which she particularly loved? Somewhere with memories of happiness, perhaps?'

'I know of nowhere.'

'Then we must raise a search party as soon as it is properly light. If you will bring a manservant, I will get together some people from the "Crown Inn". We will cover the area systematically, from the seashore to the pools and Downs.'

'Yes, that would be best.' Mansel's face, florid after the rigours of the storm, and the search, was now unnaturally pale, the opaque eyes tired. Bereft of his air of command and purpose, he looked old and rather pathetic.

'If your coachman could, perhaps, cover the road over the Downs?' Joshua requested.

'Yes, of course. He is asleep over the stables. I will awaken him if the storm and the search have not already done so.'

'You will want to be there yourself?'

'Of course, she is my wife. I am responsible for her.' He broke off, running a hand through the white fly-away hair.

'If you will be at my cottage at seven o'clock, with a lantern, and whatever will be needed?'

He nodded. 'There is something I would like you to know, Stradling, of my wife and me.' As Joshua made a movement of dissent, 'No, hear me out. It is necessary that it be said. I would like you to know how things are. It might seem to you a strange relationship. Habit, and the past, have held us together for many years. We have shared sorrow and pity, it can bind you more closely than a brief passion or love. What I am trying to say to you, and to myself, is that I do care.'

'I had never thought otherwise,' said Joshua, gently.

'I thank you for that, my boy. But since I am being honest, and have no other soul to say it to, I must also admit that I do not truthfully know what will bring me the greater sorrow: to find that she is dead, or disordered in mind, or to have the rest of our lives before us.'

Joshua left him there, seated upon one of the elegant Regency chairs, looking out of place, and rather ridiculous. He had made no attempt to accompany him to the door, or even to bid him goodbye, so lost was he in thought. Joshua believed that it was tiredness and shock which had made Mansel reveal so much of himself, and hoped that he would forget what had been spoken between them.

Just after the church clock struck the hour of seven, the search parties set off, instructed by Joshua as to their destinations and needs. All the servants who were not required to wait upon the guests at the 'Crown Inn' had assembled at Joshua's cottage, together with the innkeeper and Ossie, and a few of the stable lads. Some were to travel on foot, to inspect the grounds of cottages and inns, taking care to search the stables and messuages. Others left on horseback to scour the Burrows and country lanes, or the seashore edge. Dr Mansel's manservant took the carriage upon the highway over Dan-y-Graig, and to Newton Downs, while Joshua and Dr Mansel left to search the pools, and Ossie and his men the buildings upon Clevis Hill.

Joshua and Mansel rode off together, their tools and equipment strapped to their horses' saddles, Joshua with a grappling-iron wrapped clumsily within a blanket. Mansel had brought with him his bag of medicines, some brandy in a flask, and fresh, warm clothing, provided for Mrs Mansel by her maid. They spoke little as they rode, their minds fixed upon the task ahead and the tragedy of what they might find. They made first for Newton Pool, separating to skirt the edges, then dismounting to search the clumps of reedmace and its weeds, and peer into its deeper, clearer waters . . . Joshua prayed to God that Mrs Mansel had not perished there, and that they would find nothing.

For three hours the parties searched minutely, painstakingly, with the ready help of every cottager, workman, and traveller upon their way. After two hours, Joshua and Dr Mansel, having visited every pool, and even the public wells and conduit, returned to the cottage to confer with the others, as planned. If no trace of Mrs Mansel had been found, it would mean extending the search to the boundaries of Nottage and Port. Joshua was determined that even if it took until nightfall, the three hamlets must be covered, cottage by cottage, until the missing woman was found, alive or dead.

As Joshua and Mansel dispiritedly neared the church, the innkeeper from the 'Crown' and one of his men were galloping full stretch along the path from the Burrows, their faces taut, bodies charged with nervous excitement. As they glimpsed Dr Mansel, they instinctively slackened their pace, then halted altogether, each urging the other to go forward and speak.

'You have found her?' asked Joshua, reining his horse towards them.

'A body.'

'Is it Mrs Mansel?'

The innkeeper glanced apprehensively towards Dr Mansel who, drained of all colour, was leaning forward in his saddle.

'I do not know. The body is wedged in a crevice in the Black Rocks ... the tide has not receded enough to ...'

Joshua heard the sigh of Mansel's exhaled breath as he slumped across the horse's neck. He dismounted, and ran forward to help him, but by the time he caught at the animal's reins, Dr Mansel had recovered himself a little. He was still pale, and appeared to be shivering with cold, although his upper lip and brow were damp with sweat.

'Will you not rest in my cottage?' asked Joshua, in concern.

'No, I thank you, Stradling, but I will ride to the bay with you.'

'At least, sir, take some spirit from your flask.'

Mansel took the flask from his hip pocket, and Joshua heard the sound of metal as it struck his clenched teeth. As he drank, the liquid dribbled from the corners of his mouth, and his hand shook.

'Well, I am ready,' Mansel said, replacing his flask, 'Shall we go?'

Joshua nodded to the innkeeper, who sent his pot-man to tell the rest of the search parties to disperse to their homes. Then the three of them took the way over the Burrows, and down to the sea.

The worst part of it, Joshua thought, afterwards, was waiting for the sea to ebb enough for them to wade to the rocks. The turn of the tide was a treacherous one; currents swirled and sucked around the rocks, and there were deep hollows in the sand, and fissures to trap the unwary. All the time they waited, Joshua was fearful that some violent swirl of water, or giant wave, would take the body out of reach, or mutilate it cruelly upon the jagged rock.

Eventually, he started into the surf, bidding Dr Mansel to stay upon the shore and the innkeeper with him. Within minutes, they were there beside him, splashing through the sea, scrabbling with him onto the wet rocks. Joshua, more sure-footed, but slithering over seaweed and through spray, got there first. The body, impelled by the force of the sea, was wedged sideways into a crevice, only an arm and a swathe of dark hair showing.

'Thank God!' Joshua shouted aloud. 'Oh! Thank God! It isn't Mrs Mansel!'

The innkeeper and the doctor were there beside him, and he felt a surge of shame at the obscenity of welcoming the death of an unknown man. He muttered quickly, 'A sailor, by the look of him, and his clothes.'

'Washed overboard in the storm, perhaps,' ventured the innkeeper. 'It will be the Devil's own work to get him out of there!'

It took sustained and harrowing effort to carry him to the beach. It left the three men, their wet clothing clinging to them, sickened and exhausted. Joshua knew that he must search through the man's pockets to establish his identity, but he had little stomach for it. Unexpectedly, it was Dr Mansel who seemed to pull himself together and take charge. He appeared to have forgotten the original purpose of their search, necessity and training re-establishing his authority. Joshua and the innkeeper having nerved themselves to hunt through the dead man's pockets, and heap the contents on a blanket higher up the beach, Dr Mansel made a preliminary examination of the body.

There was little of note in the man's pockets, and nothing that would serve to identify him. Altogether, it amounted to a few coins of small denomination and one half-sovereign, a comb, a kerchief, and a small silver medallion bearing a likeness of St Christopher. Joshua turned it over, hoping to find some inscription. There was none.

'Stradling!' called Dr Mansel. 'Here! I think I have something.' He held out a small pigskin bag, fastened with a leather neck-thong. It felt slimy with sea-water. Joshua opened it, and poured on to the blanket fifteen gold sovereigns.

'A good reward for a mariner,' said the innkeeper in astonishment.

'Too good,' agreed Joshua.

'Smuggling, perhaps?'

Joshua turned to Mansel, 'You have discovered ..?'

'His injuries from the rocks are severe, and it is difficult to say from a cursory examination. I would need to do a post mortem to be sure he died from drowning . . . that there is water in the lungs.'

'But an educated guess?'

Mansel smiled. 'Guessing has never been my function, Stradling. But in my opinion, and it is only that, he died no earlier than yesterday. Now I suggest that we leave him here and instruct that unpleasant little undertaker from the village to transport him to my house, so that I can begin a post mortem examination.'

'But under the circumstances . . .' Joshua broke off, 'I mean, do you feel, sir, that . .?'

'Come, Stradling, out with it! You are questioning whether I am capable of operating under stress?'

'Not capable, sir, merely wise.'

'I have full confidence in your capabilities, Constable, I am sure that you will do all that is required of you . . . as will I. As to the wisdom of it, that is outweighed by the necessity, for me as much as for him. If I am occupied, then I will have less time to think of other things.'

'Of course.'

The three of them walked to where the horses were waiting at the edge of the Burrows and mounted them. Joshua's shoes and stockings squelched miserably as he thrust his feet into the stirrups, and his wet trouser legs chafed against his calves and the horse's ribs. From the pathway, he looked back at the dead man, and the scar of black rock that erupted into the bay and beyond it, just visible, the red brick and stone bulk of Weare House.

'Dr Mansel,' he began, 'I will continue to search for your wife . . . the search parties will be recalled, and I will ask others to help. We will search until it grows dark.'

'You may count upon me and my workmen,' offered the innkeeper, 'I will gladly help for as long as we are needed, and provide food and drink for the searchers.'

Dr Mansel nodded. He looked as if he were about to speak, but said nothing. His face had grown pink, and his eyes bright under the heavy brows. Without warning, he spurred his horse and rode on, a portly, rather absurd figure, with his shiny scalp and crown of baby-fine hair.

'I hope,' said the innkeeper, 'that our searching may prove less bloody than his.'

Rebecca, like many villagers in the three hamlets, had spent a restless night, emotions rubbed raw by the fury of the storm. She had made certain that the cob was secure in his shelter of thick-walled stone, but his usual phlegmatism had deserted him. He was nervous, high-spirited, sensing the coming of a natural violence which he could neither understand nor escape.

While the storm raged, she had resolutely taken her candle and made her way to bed, determined not to be intimidated, a prey to superstitious fear. At length, she was obliged to dress and return to the fire, glad of the driftwood from the shore to keep it bright. Even now, when coal was being brought into the Port, and more easily secured, she could not make use of it. The chimney of the cottage would need to be rebuilt, a costly business which more often than not left clouds of billowing smoke, and layers of filthy soot. At least driftwood was clean and cost nothing. Many of the older villagers still burned dried cow-pats, horse manure, or even pig-droppings. They gave out a steady heat and bright flame, but Rebecca preferred to harvest the cob's droppings to serve her garden. She wondered if the smell of the burning was nauseous, like the candles of cheap hog-fat, which filled the whole house with their acrid stench. Thinking upon this, with the fire warming and soporific, she finally fell into an uneasy sleep in the chair, the sound of the gale moaning in the chimney, and screeching around the house, a fading background ... Her last conscious thought made her lips twitch with the humour of it all. Instead of the vast ungovernable power of the elements making her dwell upon life and eternity, she had been taken up with manure!

When she awoke, awkward and stiff, the storm was over. She put on a shawl and went first to see the cob, and then to inspect the house for damage. The garden was thick with drifted sand from the dunes beyond, and a few bushes and small trees uprooted, or with branches torn ... The roof of the house seemed intact, but she would need to inspect the front to be sure. When she opened the stable door, the cob came to her eagerly; now his nervousness had gone he was his usual self, placid and serene. All was once again right with his world, and with hers.

Directly after breakfast, she determined to visit Jeremiah, for there was little either of them could do on the beach after the storm, save, perhaps, gather kindling. There was some washing of his to return, and he would very likely have saved her a fine crab or pouting. She harnessed the cob and set off for his cottage.

Bearing his parcel of washing, she knocked sharply upon the door, without response. Was it possible that he had gone fishing, after all, she wondered. But, surely, in such a storm, he would not have set his night lines? They would have been torn adrift and lost. She was about to walk away when she heard a faint tap upon glass and a frantic barking from above. Of Jeremiah there was no sign, but the shrill barking of the dog continued, urgent and alarming. Rebecca tried the latch and, finding it unsecured, opened the door and went inside. She heard the bull terrier running downstairs, scrabbling and slipping in his eagerness, then he was beside her, licking her hands, jumping, and yelping excitedly.

'Jeremiah,' she called up the stairway, 'are you there? Are you all right? It is Rebecca.' The dog had fallen silent now, and appeared to be listening as intently as she, but there was only silence. With a sense of unease, she began to mount the stairs, the bull terrier pushing past roughly, and running ahead. She followed him through the open door.

Jeremiah was lying upon the bed, fully dressed, his face pale and soaked with sweat, breath making a harsh, rasping noise in his throat. Rebecca ran to his side and took his hand, which was damp and icily cold, rubbing it between her hands to give it warmth and calling his name over and over again. Once, he opened his eyes, briefly, and looked at her without recognition, then his eyelids closed again.

'Oh, Jeremiah, my dear friend, my dear friend,' she kept repeating. 'Don't die . . . Oh, please don't die!' Then realizing the futility of staying there doing nothing, she ran downstairs to try and summon help. The bull terrier ran behind her, rushing into the yard, to urinate upon a patch of grass. She tried to persuade him to leap on to the cart, but he would not and instead ran back to the door, howling dismally, until she unlatched it and let him enter.

Once in the cart, she flicked the pony into action and drove to Joshua's house. Not finding him, she went to the 'Crown', in search of Ossie, but one of the stable boys told her that they might be anywhere, searching for Mrs Mansel, who had disappeared into the storm.

She remounted the cart, and set the cob in the direction of the quarries where, upon finding Doonan and Emrys, she began to weep with relief and blurt out her fears for Jeremiah. Within minutes, it seemed, Emrys and his cart were following her through the Downs and over Dan-y-Graig Hill, then Clevis Hill, to Jeremiah's cot.

Within half an hour, swaddled in blankets, and carried by Doonan as tenderly as a babe, Jeremiah was settled in the cart, the dog beside him, and on his way to Rebecca's house. The two men helped her to set up the bed for Jeremiah, beside the fire, and to see him settled, then returned to their work at the quarries, vowing to come back as soon as they could. They knew, from Rebecca, of the search for Mansel's wife, and that there would be no doctor available to minister to Jeremiah, even if the money needed could be raised. As for appealing for help to the poor-law charity, each knew it was unthinkable, and so the question was not even broached.

Rebecca, seeing their cart leaving, returned to bank up the fire with driftwood and bathe Jeremiah's head with a wrung-out cloth, which had been immersed in cold water. Then, with much difficulty, she removed his clothes, washed and dressed him in a cool, voluminous nightgown of her father's, kept neatly packed away since his long illness. Like most of the cottagers, Jeremiah had no nightwear of his own, sleeping instead in what he wore by day. Indeed, many had but the one set of clothing which, by custom, was washed, dried and smoothed with a flat iron upon a Saturday, that they might attend church on the morrow, clean and fragrant in the eyes of God. Rebecca prayed now that God would look mercifully upon his servant, the freshly-laundered Jeremiah, and spare his soul a little longer. The Lord must surely know that the messiness and squalor of their occupations were unavoidable, and in no way sullied their purity of heart. If He did not, then she was not over-eager to enter into the Kingdom of Heaven! She smiled wrily and settled herself beside the bull terrier and its master. Her long, lonely vigil was beginning. She would not consider how it might end.

Doonan and Emrys returned to Rebecca's house when they had finished their day's work in the limestone quarries. They were tired, and their faces streaked with stone dust, for they had not wasted precious time in awaiting their turn at the water-filled buckets the quarry lads sluiced at the stream, and brought back to the quarry floor. Doonan presented her with a brace of pigeons, and Emrys with a skinned and gutted hare, the innards of which he had thoughtfully replaced, that Rebecca might feed them to Charity the dog. She did not feel it civil to enquire of them how these delicacies had come into their possession, but accepted them gratefully. They would, as Emrys vowed, 'make a rich, nourishing soup to keep up Jeremiah's strength.'

She watched them through the window, skylarking in the yard, as they hauled up buckets of water from the well. Soon they were intent upon washing away the dust and fatigue of the day before leaving to join the search for Mrs Mansel. They refused all offers of food, Emrys jesting, with a sly look at Doonan, 'My poor horse would surely drop between the shafts if he had any more weight to carry!'

'Besides,' added Doonan, wickedly, 'doesn't everyone in the three hamlets say that Rebecca's bread could be used for cannon balls?'

'Or ballast upon a ship!'

Rebecca pretended outrage at such insults, grateful to the two men for trying to lighten her spirits with their banter.

'Indeed,' said Doonan, as they left, 'I declare that if Jeremiah should awaken, and find himself in that nightshirt, he would think himself an angel, and start to sing like a bird.'

'A crow,' she heard Emrys declare, as they went upon their way, laughing.

'A large raw-voiced crow.'
'As long as he doesn't try to fly!' said Doonan.

By early morning, Rebecca began to feel afraid. Jeremiah's breathing was worse and he seemed to be in great anguish, tossing and turning in his bed, his skin burning, yet clammy to the touch. She could not make out what he was saying, for his voice was harsh and unnatural. Rebecca did not know what nightmares possessed his mind, or what demons he fought within himself, but he kept striking out with his arms, and screaming as if to exorcize or frighten them away. She kept bathing his face and head to cool him, but the cloth dried in her hand with the fevered heat of his skin. Finally, frightened and feeling that she was unable to help ease his torment, she made him as comfortable as she could and, harnessing up the cob and cart, took the road to the Downs and Dr Burrel.

As she breasted the top of Dan-y-Graig Hill, she heard the muffled sound of hooves in the distance, and was able to glimpse the two riders leaving the great house. She had no doubt at all that it was Crandle father and son, making off in the opposite direction. She wondered, briefly, what business could occupy them so urgently at such an ungodly hour, then, dismissing them from her mind, concentrated on taking the cart safely around the treacherous corner to the Downs.

When she knocked upon the door of the shepherd's cottage, she did not know if Dr Burrel would be there. She believed in him, and trusted him, but Mrs Mansel's disappearance had left her anxious and confused. Would one of the search parties have found his hiding place and informed Joshua, or taken him into custody themselves? If the searchers had come upon him accidentally, not knowing of his connection with Mansel, would their questions have caused him to panic and flee? Where would he then go? What had he decided to do about taking revenge? If he had gone away what would happen to Jeremiah? Without help, he would surely die. Dear God! How could she bear it all?

When the door opened, and Burrel stood there in the candle light, her relief was so intense that she was unable to speak. Physical sickness rose in her throat, and she tasted it in her mouth, sour as gall. Burrel, seeing the whiteness of her face, and the shock, took her arm and hurried her inside, shutting the door.

'What is it, child? Are you ill?'

She shook her head, numbly. 'No, it is my dear friend, Jeremiah . . . I think he is dying . . . and I don't know what to do to help him. I thought of you. Please will you come to him?'

'Of course. I will do whatever I can,' he said, immediately. 'But why did you not call upon Dr Mansel; surely he would not refuse to come?'

'Mrs Mansel is missing.'

'Missing?' There was no mistaking the surprise in his voice. 'How, missing?'

'She left the house in the storm and cannot be found. There have been search parties out all day. I was afraid.'

'That I had done it?' he asked, sharply.

'No, that they might find you here, and I had no chance to warn you. If you come to Jeremiah, you will be putting yourself at grave risk, for now they have reason to search for you, knowing the past.'

He put his hand under her chin, and lifted her face towards his.

'Rebecca,' he said, 'you have a great devotion to your friends, both old and new. I do not know your friend, Jeremiah, but I know that, like me, he is a very fortunate man. You risked much in helping me; it would be a poor return of friendship if I could not now help you. Come, let us not waste time, for I fancy that if we were intercepted my presence would be required elsewhere.'

'I have the pony and cart outside.'

'As I, indeed, have the bruises from my last encounter with it.'

When they were settled in the cart, he said, 'You realize that, apart from the little help I was allowed to give my fellow prisoners in gaol, it has been many years? I bring no instruments, no medicine.'

'It is you I came for,' she said, simply, 'and it will be enough. I am sure of it.'

He shook his head. 'If he needs special treatment, surgery

even, then I shall go to Mansel, and ask for his help.'

'You would do that?' Rebecca asked, startled.

'If it is necessary.'

They drove in silence for a while.

'This Jeremiah, where is he?'

'I have taken him to my cottage.'

'He is a young man?'

'Oh, no. Old. Very old ... older even than you.'

Dr Burrel laughed aloud, clapping his hands together in amusement.

'Well, Rebecca,' he said, 'I will do my best for this venerable gentleman. Having survived to such an extraordinarily great age, we have much in common, it seems; but you will not feel yourself compromised in caring for him?'

'How compromised, sir? He is old enough to be my grandfather; but if he were not and but one and twenty, then it would make no matter. Evil tongues cannot create evil where there is none. I would hope always to have the courage and good sense to do what I felt to be just and proper, whatever the consequences,' she responded, tartly.

'I am chastened, and much obliged to you for the lesson, Mistress,' he said, smiling broadly.

She smiled at him in return, 'Then I hope, sir, that you will benefit from it!'

Chapter Sixteen

Joshua, immersed in the search for Mrs Mansel, wondered if life would ever return to normal. His sleeplessness through the night of the storm, and the search all day, and into the night by lantern light, made him tired and irritable. In addition, there were the formalities concerned with the body of the dead man: interviews, reports to the justice and the vestrymen, questions to be asked at the docks. The hunt for the killer of Mary Devereaux went on, as well as the trivia of the daily routine. Alehouse fights, domestic squabbles, things stolen or lost, complaints from neighbours, fraud, debt, all had to be sifted and resolved by him, or referred to others.

On a personal level he was missing Rebecca, and now Jeremiah was sick and taken to her cottage. Joshua had vowed to himself that he would visit them sometime during the day, but his duties were too harsh. He had sent a small parcel of food from the farm for the invalid, with some flowers he had bought from a cottager's garden for Rebecca. A stable boy from the 'Crown' had delivered them, together with a note of apology and affection, but it was a poor substitute for his presence, and the comfort he might bring them.

Even now, with the light fading, his work was not done. He must hurry to Dr Mansel's house to report on the fruitlessness of the day's search, and to seek news of the post mortem upon the man from the sea. Joshua's eyes felt raw and gritty through lack of sleep, and exhaustion seeped from the marrow of his bones. He had been forced to change his uniform after wading into the surf to dislodge the body from the rocks, but his flesh remained chilled, and his leg muscles ached from riding and walking. Tomorrow, the weary round of searching would begin again.

Dr Mansel was at the door to greet him, his usually immaculate clothes crumpled, eyes sore-rimmed.

'You have news, Stradling?'

'I am sorry, sir.'

Mansel nodded, defeat deepening the lines of face and body. 'It is as I feared. If there is no sign, then she will not be alive. It is the sea we must look to.'

'Is there not some friend, or relative, perhaps, who might have taken her away to safety?'

'With no word of explanation? Who would be so cruel?'

'It was only a hope I was clinging to, rightly or wrongly. Something to explore in my own mind. I did not mean to distress you any further.'

'You will not do that, Stradling,' Mansel's voice was rough with hurt. 'I have been in a hell of my own these past days, not knowing how much of this is owed to me. Whatever the reality ... the outcome ... it cannot be worse than not knowing.'

'We will begin the search again at daylight,' promised Joshua, 'and keep it up until it grows dark.'

'Please forgive me,' Mansel said, as if he had not heard, 'I am forgetting my manners. I see that you are exhausted beyond endurance. Come into the library and let us sit down.' He opened a cupboard behind his desk, and poured two measures of brandy, handing a glass to Joshua, and taking one himself.

'Drink it,' he advised. 'It is too late to claim that you are on duty. I order it as a doctor and a friend.'

Joshua thanked him, and drank, feeling its warmth spread through him, comfortingly.

'You have performed the post mortem on the man, sir?'

'Yes. There is no doubt that he died from drowning. His other injuries, broken bones, lacerations, contusions, all occurred after death, probably by being battered against the rocks by the force of the sea.'

'Nothing else?'

'Nothing of relevance, except a drawing upon his arm. The usual thing ... a tattoo. Flowers, a snake, a scroll with the words *Foget Me Not.*' He smiled wrily. 'Either he was unable to spell, or the tattooist unable to copy. You are interested? You would care to see it, Stradling?'

Joshua rose to his feet, quickly. 'No, I thank you. I am content to take your word for it. It would confirm then, that he was a seafaring man, as we supposed. I will arrange to see the harbour master, and check upon the ships he might have been lost from.'

Mansel walked with him to the door. As he stood beneath the oil lamp, bracketed upon the wall, Joshua could see clearly that his trouser legs were still damp from the sea and his shoes streaked white with dried crystals of salt. Mansel laid a hand upon Joshua's arm, detaining him, and said, face bleak, 'Stay ... there is something I have kept from you, Stradling.'

'Sir?'

'I do not know if it has any bearing ... is relevant, you understand?'

Joshua waited, but Mansel stood, wiping a tired hand across his eyes.

'Is it, perhaps, about the dead sailor, sir?' Joshua prompted.

'No. My wife, Madeleine ... I believe that she was being supplied with laudanum ...'

To Joshua's unspoken enquiry, 'No. Not I ... although I prescribed small doses, to quieten her nerves, for she seemed obsessed with Burrel. It was long ago. When he first went to prison ...'

'And now?'

Mansel shook his head despairingly. 'I do not know how, or from whom, she gets it. I had long suspected, from her manner and actions ... so strange and unnatural, and the physical signs. Like a fool I thrust the thought from me. I did not want to believe.'

'You have proof?'

'I have found bottles ... empty, unmarked ...'

'You think it is bound up in some way with her going? That someone has harmed her?'

'I fear it might be so ... for some time she has been demanding sums of money.'

'You did not ask her why?'

He shook his head. 'I thought perhaps small gaming debts, between friends ... some jewellery or small luxury to raise her spirits. Even difficulties with the household accounts ... some stupid extravagance. I do not question her about her friends or movements, Stradling,' he said with dignity, 'it would avail me nothing.'

Joshua nodded, understanding.

'I only know that she left taking only the meagre jewellery and clothes she wore.' He recalled himself with an effort. 'You have news of Burrel?'

'None. I have people watching, but he has not been seen.'

'His reason for coming has gone.' Mansel said bleakly. 'Madeleine. She has cheated him of his revenge.'

As surely as she cheated you, thought Joshua. 'You had best have a care for yourself, sir,' he said aloud. 'Burrel, I mean. He might still return to you.'

'Then I will be ready for him,' said Mansel, unemotionally.

After Joshua had gone, he returned to the library, and poured himself another brandy, which he drank at a draught. Then he opened the drawer of his desk and looked down at the pistol which lay there, ready primed.

Let him come, he thought, for now we both have a score to settle.

Creighton Crandle, too, was thinking of Madeleine Mansel, and the furore and speculation about her disappearance. 'Well, let them speculate until kingdom come, they would be no wiser!' At least he would be richer by the sovereigns set aside to hire men with strong fists and weak scruples! Where she was, there would no longer be need for protection.

The thought amused him and he grinned stupidly, as he poured a measure of brandy from the decanter at his elbow. He had outwitted that arrogant young constable too, denying all knowledge of her, or what had happened to make her desperate enough to flee into the storm.

He wondered about the man who had threatened her. Some lover perhaps? God knows, she was skinny and unappetizing enough, with her sallow skin, and fierce angularity, all bone and gristle, like an old boiling fowl, he thought contemptuously. Still, it was over twenty years ago ... time enough, surely, for old passions to die!

Madeleine Mansel had been thinking much the same thing as she stared into her looking glass, after breaking open the seal of Joshua's letter to her husband. The ravages of twenty years had altered her face and body, but not her hatred of Burrel. She despised and scorned him now, as he had once scorned her, and the tentative love she offered. Memory of his disgust, and the humiliation of rejection, could still make her raw with shame. Well, much good it had done him! He had paid a harsh price, rotting for twenty years ... and she could have wished him twenty more! She had lied about him, and she would do it again. Let him share the pain and despair of being rejected, the slow disintegration of hope.

She loathed and despised him, as fiercely as she had once loved him! That he had taken that girl from the streets, loved her, given her a child. A common slut! A trollop with no intelligence or breeding!

She hated all men, whether strong as Burrel had once been, or weak and pliant as her husband. It had suited her purpose to marry him. He had given her the cloak of respectability she needed for her work.

My God! Once she had even suffered that drunken oaf, Creighton, to invade her body! She shuddered, recalling his foetid breath and sweating red hands, clumsy and demanding ... the smile of lasciviousness upon his lips.

It was her need for laudanum that made her endure. She lusted for it, as he lusted after women's flesh. It was her only escape and salvation.

She was bitterly aware that Creighton had taken her money to squander upon drink, the whorehouses and gaming dens ... He was a weak, spineless creature! Yet, if Burrel had learnt the full depth of her betrayal ... She began to shake uncontrollably, gripping the edge of her dressing table so fiercely that her knuckles gleamed white as bone ...

There had only been one true man. Memory of him haunted and drove her on. Vengeance was her spur ... revenge for his death at the hands of the English; for the loss of a father who had loved her for what she was, demanding nothing, seeking neither to mould nor change her. 'I am not a cold Englishwoman!' she cried to her reflection in the glass. 'I am French, as he was ... passionate, warm, loving! This face and body belong to someone old, ugly. They are nothing to do with me!' She cradled her head in her hands, and wept loudly and bitterly. What did it matter if Burrel came? He would not even know her now. She fetched her cloak, and with it the small, mother-of-pearl-handled pistol, which she kept so carefully hidden, and slipped it into her reticule.

Then, without even a final glance, the tears untouched upon her face, she walked out into the beginnings of the storm.

When Rebecca and Burrel returned to her cottage, the church clock was chiming the hour of three. Although it was summer, the early morning air was chill, and a breeze from the sea shivered the leaves and grass. Rebecca went to Jeremiah at once, and saw that he was feverish still, his face flushed unhealthily, and his nightgown drenched with sweat. She wiped his face, gently, with the dampened cloth, and stood back for Burrel to examine him, her face taut with anxiety.

'You have the cob to attend and stable,' he reminded her, quietly. 'Had you forgotten?'

'Will you not need help?'

'No, it will be better if I am left alone.'

She nodded, and went reluctantly, calling the dog to follow her, but Charity remained. Rebecca thought that the animal could scarcely have moved since she left, still lying in the same position, inert save for the intelligent, slanting eyes, which never for a moment left Jeremiah's bed. The dog watched Burrel as he worked, wary, but showing no animosity to this stranger, pushing, prodding, and wreaking indignities upon its master's flesh.

When Rebecca returned, Burrel was heaping driftwood upon the fire. He turned when he heard her, his expression giving away nothing.

'You have warm blankets and other clothing you could use to cover him?'

'Yes, but he is so hot, and the room so airless. His clothing is soaked to his flesh.'

'We must bundle him up, keep the fire stoked high. He must sweat out the fever, get rid of the poisons within. Do not be alarmed, child! I will stay with you until the fever breaks. You shall not stay alone. I shall do all that I can to help you.'

'What is it that he suffers from? What manner of sickness?'

'What did you suppose?'

'I had thought cholera ... for he was so strange, screaming aloud, striking out, not even knowing me when I spoke to him. There is so much cholera in the towns, and so many deaths.' She studied him anxiously, face white. 'It is not that?'

'No, I am sure of it, for there is no sickness, no extreme loss of body fluids, save through sweat. It is some congestion of the lungs which hinders his breathing. Have you herbs, Rebecca?'

She nodded.

'Boil up some water upon the fire ... we will make an infusion of them in a bowl, then a tent of cloth to cover it and keep the steam contained. He will inhale it and that will help clear his lungs. You must hold it safe, so as not to scald him, while I will hold his arms and try to keep him restrained.' He smiled at her. 'Do not look so frightened, child. I admit that I am a poor, puny creature, and he has the strength of an ox, but I daresay we will find a solution.'

So it was that with the fire roaring up the chimney, swaddled like a newborn baby, in his makeshift tent scented with herbs, at seven o'clock, Jeremiah awoke to see three pairs of eyes staring at him with concern. He tried to move his arms and legs, but found it impossible, for they were firmly tied with shredded rags to the four corners of the bed. He saw their faces change from concern to delight as he looked about him with mild astonishment and recognition. His voice, when he tried to speak, was cracked, and the words slurred over his swollen tongue.

'Take this bloody nightgown off, and untie me! What are you grinning at? Have you all gone mad?' Then he fell into a tranquil sleep. Rebecca thought they were the most beautiful words she had ever heard. The dog leapt upon the coverlet beside him and would not be moved.

Dr Burrel, exhaustion pinching his features and setting dark shadows around his eyes, said, 'Well, nurse, I think he will do.'

Rebecca ran across the room, embracing him, then kissing him upon the cheek, and dancing him across the floor in her delight.

'A little decorum, Mistress, please!' he admonished, laughing. 'I only countenance such familiarity when my bill is paid, in full, and promptly.'

'What, then, is your fee, sir?' she asked gravely.

'I will settle for a bowl of that stew, which you have warming upon the hearth, for the smell has been tantalizing me from the moment I entered the house. Besides, it will line and strengthen my stomach for the ride back in your pony and cart, although, I swear, I would be better served in a suit of armour.'

Their journey back to the shepherd's cottage completed in safety, Rebecca was able to relax her vigilance as the cob settled into a rhythmic trot along the homeward road. She felt a warm gratitude to Dr Burrel, for his selflessness. His help had been immediate, and unreserved, although it could have brought him into great personal danger. She was saddened that his long-time feud with Mansel was unresolved. He no longer spoke of revenge ... but whether this was because the need for it had diminished, or because he was planning it in secret, she did not know. Perhaps Mrs Mansel's disappearance had made him realize that life or, more tragically, death, had resolved the conflict for him.

For the time being, she must devote her energies to making Jeremiah well. She would be unable to leave him for a while, so the beach and the shellfish would have to wait. It was fortunate that the seamstress in the village had asked her to sketch and make copies of gown styles culled from journals, and to blend them with ideas of her own. It would distract her from over-solicitude towards Jeremiah, who hated 'to be cosseted'. She could work at them at the cottage, and the little money she earned would pay for their food. It was a pity she could not tell Joshua of Burrel's kindness, and worse that she was forced to deceive him. There was no possibility of telling him of her early morning glimpse of the Crandles, either, without explaining why she was abroad at such an ungodly hour. It had been kind of Joshua to send the parcel of food, and the flowers. The note, too, had been warmly affectionate, and apologetic about his duties, although he begged her to accompany him to the Mabsant celebrations, should Jeremiah be well enough.

He was an honest, loving, compassionate friend, as she had

seen in all his dealings with Jeremiah, Illtyd, and the others. Rebecca knew that what she felt for him was deeper, and more intense than friendship. She loved him deeply, as he loved her. As a realist, she knew that nothing could come of it. Such a liaison would alienate him from his family, whom he loved, and a society which he affected to despise. He was strong enough to over-ride the pressures, of that she was sure . . . but was she? Would there be a time in the years ahead when, despite his loyalty, like Dr Mansel, he saw her as the architect of all his discontent, and grew to despise her, or himself? It was not a hypothesis she was eager to put to the test.

Joshua, after another day of abortive searching for Madeleine Mansel, was obliged to conclude that everything which could have been done to find her had been put into practice. He steeled himself to tell Mansel of his decision, thanked all who had helped him in the search, and absolved them from any further involvement. He would still keep a watch upon the shore, and ask the manager of Weare House, and the excisemen, to do the same. The keepers in the newly-built lighthouse, upon the cliffs at Nash Point, might also help, and the local fishermen, having knowledge of the currents and tides along the coast, and where a body might be cast up by the sea. The words came into his mind, unbidden, 'A good friend, but an implacable enemy.' He could not, now, remember when he had used them, or about whom. That they applied to the sea, there was no doubt. It had played a grim part in the lives of two of the dead. Did it now hold the secret of a third?

He wondered about Mary Devereaux and her brother. Had they kept in touch, since, apart from the aged great-aunt, they were the lone survivors of their family? Perhaps he was living abroad. Or had his business taken him to another part of the country, where, in marrying and raising a family of his own, he had lost touch with the girl? Well, he supposed that he would soon know, and, like a broken pitcher, the pieces would again fit into shape, the final pattern revealed. Emily Randall's testimony had brought its completion nearer, and now those who were searching in the villages around Swansea would have a name, and a few fragments of information, to help them.

The loft at the 'Crown Inn' had been thoroughly cleaned, repaired, and whitewashed, thanks to Ossie, Doonan and their friends. Now all that remained was to make it habitable with a few sticks of furniture, and everyday utensils. Rebecca was too involved with her nursing of Jeremiah to take an active part in the transformation, but Rosa, Hannah and the Widow Cleat were tireless helpers, providing countless small feminine comforts, begging and borrowing what Joshua could not afford to buy, while his mother, marvelling at her son's guardianship of an elderly pauper, had indulged him with promises of small furnishings, bedding, linen, and good cast-off clothing of her own. He was not altogether sure that his mother's elegant frivolities would be of much practical use to a governess and laundress, confined to a coach house loft and forced to earn a living. However, her altruism did her credit, and he had no doubt that she would play the part of Lady Bountiful as to the manor born, dispensing food and largesse with her usual elan. It would be a churlish son, indeed, who could rebuff such eagerness to please.

As he turned now into the courtyard of the 'Crown', his thoughts were not on the dead, but the living. His spirits were light, for he had a meeting planned with the Widow Cleat, and had prevailed upon her to bring Illtyd along, for he was a great favourite with Joshua, who admired his ready physical courage, and his generosity of spirit.

The Widow Cleat was stitching curtains when he mounted the stone staircase that led from the yard, with Ossie close upon his heels. Illtyd was engrossed in repairing the wooden stretcher of a chair, carefully binding the jagged edges of wood, after fusing them together. His large head was bowed low over his task, and so intent was he that he did not hear the men enter. When Joshua touched his arm, he looked up, quickly, alarm turning to pleasure on his frank, childlike face.

'You are busy, my friend,' said Joshua, warmly. 'It is kind of you to give your time, and toil, to someone you do not even know.'

'I know that she is in need of friends,' said the little man, smiling. 'It is enough. I am sure that her home will fill her with surprise and pleasure.'

'I have a small surprise for you, also,' Joshua promised, 'and one which you richly deserve, for all the help you have given to me, and others.'

The Widow Cleat looked up from her sewing, and Illtyd rose to his feet, taking Ossie's outstretched hand gratefully for support. Joshua was always surprised by the sheer beauty of Illtyd's deep-set, intelligent eyes. It was, he sometimes thought, as if everything lacking in the deformed body and the awkward head had been somehow distilled into this one, perfect, arresting feature. Illtyd's clear eyes were now intent, puzzled.

'It is not a gift, exactly ... more a piece of news.'

'Oh, tell him!' cried Ossie, impulsively, 'for I am sure that we will all burst apart with curiosity if you do not explain, soon.'

'The vestrymen have appointed you hayward of the common land, Illtyd.'

The Widow Cleat had dropped her sewing, and grown pale, fearing it was a cruel joke, and Illtyd himself looked bewildered.

'You cannot mean it,' he said, 'for how would I do such work? They are no better than the rest. They see me as a figure of fun. Someone to be mocked and laughed at ... a fool to amuse them. I had not thought it of you, Joshua.'

'Do you think I would ever mock or humiliate you?' Joshua asked, gently.

Illtyd shook his head. 'But it is a job for a man.'

'Are you not a man? Worth any six men upon the vestry, and more? Illtyd, I swear I speak but the truth. The hayward's job is yours.'

'Ossie?' Illtyd turned to appeal to him, but Ossie had left the loft without being seen.

'I do not understand,' said Illtyd. 'How can this be? I did not apply to the vestry; for I would not have made myself look any more ridiculous ... How could I ride? How work? Tell me ..?'

Joshua took him gently by the arm and, putting his other arm around the Widow Cleat's shoulders, led them to the window. In the yard, below, Ossie stood proudly, holding a miniature piebald pony, its saddle of tooled leather with brass mountings gleaming with his loving waxing and polishing.

'It is yours,' Joshua said. 'Ossie will teach you to ride, but you will have no trouble, for you are intelligent, and will be quick to learn.'

The Widow Cleat's fingers were pressing into his clenched hand so fiercely that they were numbed from pain.

'Well, Illtyd, have you nothing to say?'

The wry neck lifted, and Illtyd looked at him, and shook his head. The raw emotion and gratitude in his eyes caught Joshua's throat with an actual physical pain, and he felt his eyes burn.

'Come,' he said roughly, 'you will want to meet your new friend, I fancy he has been awaiting a master such as you.'

Joshua and the Widow Cleat stood silently together as Ossie excitedly helped the little man to mount the piebald. Illtyd sat rigidly in the saddle, holding the reins, as Ossie carefully adjusted the stirrups.

'There,' he said, his weatherbeaten face glowing with pleasure, 'the perfect little horseman.'

Joshua saw genuine happiness and affection in the ostler's eyes, and the answering pride in Illtyd's. He thought that if ever, in future, he felt low or dissatisfied with life, he would recall the brave sight of his friend astride the piebald, the overlarge head held proud above the small twisted body. There was no sadness in the scene, and Joshua felt no pity, only pride, in sharing the radiant joy of communion between the two men. The Widow Cleat touched his arm.

'Illtyd has not thanked you,' she said.

'Yes, he has. In the best way he knew.'

She nodded. 'I thank you, too, with all of my heart, sir.'

'It is only a very small horse,' said Joshua, embarrassed and clumsy under her gratitude, 'and a smaller saddle. Although, I admit, Illtyd is as big a man as any I have met.' He turned and grasped her hand.

'It is more than a horse you have given him, Mr Stradling, it is friendship, and a recognition of his own worth. I shall not forget it.'

'Illtyd is a fine man,' he mumbled. 'I have much to thank him for.'

'Then you have amply repaid it. Many only see what is outside, and do not look beyond that part of him which is awkward and has not grown. I have always known his true worth.'

'Come,' said Joshua, 'for he is watching us. Will you not lead him home?'

Chapter Seventeen

It sometimes seemed to Joshua that he had known the dead girl, Mary Devereaux, as well as he knew Rebecca or any of his friends. At other times, he felt that he knew her not at all. He could recall the shock and pity he felt at seeing her amidst the frails on Rebecca's cart. It seemed so terrible a thing that anyone as fragile and beautiful should be touched by violence. There was a delicacy about her, an innocence almost, even in death. Joshua wondered if it was this very quality of being uncorrupted which had precipitated her murder. He remembered, from schooldays, those gentle creatures whose very passivity had awakened cruelty in the bullies and braggarts. There was a viciousness in animal and human nature which sought to destroy anything which was original or different; people like Illtyd who were physically imperfect; like Mary Devereaux who had purity of flesh or spirit. Was it because of some primitive fear of what we could not understand? Or because they reminded us of what we might yet become, or might have aspired to?

There had been so little known of the living Mary Devereaux, only such physical details as could be gleaned at her death. It was Emily Randall who recreated the small child of her memory, gentle, vulnerable, alone. Was this the woman she had become? Or had solitude embittered her? Had later life made her brashly promiscuous, or had she stretched out her hand, trustingly, to the first man who had shown her kindness? She was still an enigma. The picture of her life was gradually being painted, outlines being drawn, colour filled in, but it still lacked depth and definition. From all those involved in helping Joshua, constables, justices, friends, there was no clue to her character at all. The hamlet where she was delivered to her great-aunt was known. The old lady was insular, cantankerous with servants and callers alike, almost a recluse; the house was large, with gloomy extensive grounds, and set apart from its nearest neighbour by three miles or more. No one in the nearest village recalled seeing the child, except on the rare occasions when she was driven to church in her great-aunt's carriage, to sit quietly and gravely composed, her small figure lost in the depths of the high wooden pew. There were no servants to befriend the child, for they would not long tolerate the old lady's parsimony and irritable ways. One, who had been traced, fancied that she had heard somewhere that the little girl had been sent away to school, or perhaps it was to stay with some family and share a governess, she could not be sure. All that was known was that, eventually, the old lady became sick, the servants were dismissed, and the house closed. Of Mary Devereaux nothing was known after this time, and of her brother, nothing at all.

Joshua, in making a report on the matter to the Reverend Robert Knight, had been obliged to tell him of the disappearance of Mrs Mansel, and her dependence upon laudanum, the sighting of Dr Burrel, and the drowning of the unknown sailor. The justice had carefully adjusted his gold-rimmed glasses, blinked his intelligent, alert eyes and said, drily, 'Indeed, Stradling, another death, you say? I am at pains to decide whether such profligacy is coincidental, or whether you actually attract disaster to you.'

'I do not think that the last death has any bearing on the other two incidents, sir.'

'I am relieved to hear it! It would distress me if the entire congregation for my sermons were decimated overnight.'

'Then I shall do my part, sir, to see that they stay alert.'

The justice looked at him, intently, then began to laugh, appreciatively. 'I declare you had the better of me over that exchange, Stradling. But to more serious matters. You think Mrs Mansel has been abducted by the man, Burrel?'

'No, sir. I think it extremely unlikely. I think she has either fled to friends, or has become deranged and taken her own life.'

'I pray that you are wrong, Stradling, for it would be a grave sin against God, as well as herself. And what of Mansel?'

'He is distraught, as one would expect . . . but I fear for his physical safety, should Burrel seek him out.'

'You have warned him of this?'

'I have, sir. I shall keep watch upon him, of course, and continue the search for Burrel, but I fear I have neither the time nor the resources.'

'Well, do what you can, Stradling, and tell him to warn his servants, or put one on guard.'

'I have already suggested it, sir.'

'Good. And this sailor? Washed overboard in the storm, perhaps?'

'I ride now to the docks to enquire, sir.'

'Speak to the exciseman, Stradling. Tell him I have sent you, and that I instruct him to give you every aid and, if necessary, to take you into his confidence. He will take my meaning.'

He rose to his feet, smiling, wide-mouthed, corpulent. 'I trust, Stradling, that next time we meet, you will bring me news of crimes solved, rather than additional corpses. When arrangements have been made for the inquest, I shall inform you, and Dr Mansel.'

Joshua nodded.

'And, Stradling.'

'Sir?'

'If you do discover the secret of keeping a congregation alert, or even awake . . .' He smiled, eyes disappearing into his cheek pouches and under the heavy eyelids; a plump, benevolent frog.

'I will report to you at once, sir, and set it in writing.'

Joshua rode out from Tythegston Court, still smiling at his encounter with the justice. He had been accompanied to the door by Leyshon, the usual, taciturn manservant who, experiencing less trouble with his rotting teeth and aching spine, had grown expansive. He pressed Joshua to return with him to the kitchens for refreshment, an invitation which he again declined with some reluctance, truthfully pleading pressure of duties.

Once amid the bustle and clamour of the docks, he picked his way around hillocks of coal, minerals and limestone, heaped ready for loading. He stood a while, admiring the colour and vitality of the scene, and inhaling the mingled smells of coffee, pine-resin, tobacco and tea, with the clean iodine tang of ozone, then crossed the horse-drawn tramroad to the office of the harbour master, Captain Ayde Buchan, RN. It seemed to Joshua that the spare, weathered mariner, with his air of command and authority, had never really come ashore, merely surrendering his sea-going vessel for a spell in dry dock. He greeted Joshua warmly, and for a while they talked about the fascination of a port with its sailing ships, and the lure of unknown places, and the evocative smells of the coffee beans and spices upon the wharf.

'I shall be sorry to see it change,' declared the captain, 'but change it must, if we are to compete. There is already talk of the new Llynfi Valley Railway Company planning a broad-gauge locomotive railway. The horse trams will have to go. It will not be the same. But it will be the passing of the sailing barques I shall grieve most. There is nothing quite as beautiful as a fully rigged ship, but then, I suppose efficiency overrides elegance.'

'Change is not necessarily progress.'

'Exactly. But in what way can I help you, Constable?'

'You have no doubt heard of the sailor who was washed ashore at the Black Rocks?'

'Yes, a sad business. I feel for his family.' He shook his head, regretfully.

'I hope to find the vessel from which he might have been swept overboard. You have a list of the sailings to and from the Port at that time?' Joshua asked.

'Over how long a period?'

'Within twenty-four hours of the storm.'

'Then that is easily established.' He produced his books and records and, together, they sifted through the possibilities, checking times and tide tables. 'You will see that one coal cargo left in a barque to round Cape Horn for Valparaiso. If he sailed in her, *The Stormy Venturer*, it might be some months before his death is known.'

'And the others?'

'Mostly engaged in coastal trade, usually between here and Bristol or Minehead, occasionally Porlock. Small vessels, all under one hundred tons.'

'And the cargoes?'

'The customs and excisemen will have greater detail but, in general, coal and some minerals, but mainly iron, of course, from the Cambrian, Tondu and Cefn ironworks, on the outward journeys.'

'And the incoming cargoes?'

'High-grade iron ore for the foundries from Bilbao, and pit props for the coal mines from France.'

'I see,' said Joshua reflectively.

'Over half the incoming boats come in "light", or in ballast, to pick up cargoes.'

Joshua nodded. 'The possibilities, then?'

The captain handed Joshua a list which he had been writing sedulously during their conversation. 'Most of these I can check for you with the coal and iron companies, for they have their own vessels, or deal with larger charter companies. They will have lists of crews for each sailing. If a man had been swept overboard however, they would certainly have informed the authorities. It is a statutory duty.'

'The smaller, individual owners?'

'I have added the names to the foot of the list, there are only three for the day you specify. One, catching the edge of the storm, returned to Bristol, and its arrival was delayed for twenty-four hours, so it need not concern us. The other two are owned by the same joint owners. One of their vessels docked here from Minehead, the other one brought wooden pit props from France upon the same tide.'

'"The *Minehead Lady* and *Victoria*,"' read Joshua, '"jointly owned by Mr Stanton Gould of Porlock and Mr Hugo Crandle of Dan-y-Graig, Porthcawl". There was no report of a missing seaman when these vessels docked?'

'No, I would most certainly have been notified. No, Constable, it is not conceivable. I regret that you must look elsewhere. Some foreign vessel washed inshore, perhaps, but recovering to continue her voyage . . . or bound from Swansea to Cardiff? You must try further afield.'

'Perhaps.' Joshua held out his hand and clasped Captain Buchan's. 'I thank you, sir, for your ready help.'

'I regret that it was not more productive . . . the loss of a seaman is a tragedy that can demoralize a crew. You live in such close proximity; it is of necessity a closed and close-knit community and you become protective and united as any family. I speak as one who was a sailor for many years.' He shook his head. 'If a man had been washed overboard, it could not have been hidden. Someone would talk . . . I would know. Believe me, I would know.'

Joshua, making his way along the quayside, paused at the customs building to enquire after Rawlings, the chief exciseman, but was told that he had already left to meet him at the 'Knight's Arms', as arranged.

Joshua had stabled his grey there, upon arrival at the Port, so he went directly into the alehouse. Rawlings was seated upon an inglenook bench, at the right of the fire and, upon seeing him, signalled to the landlord to bring some tankards of ale.

'These are mine, I fancy,' said Joshua, placing some coins upon the tray, 'for upon our last meeting, you played host.'

Rawlings nodded. 'Well, your appearance has improved greatly since that encounter, Stradling. I hope I may say as much for the ale . . .'

'I recall,' said Joshua, ruefully, 'that the smugglers had so disarranged my features that you suspected a quarrel with a horse-drawn tram.'

'Well, you might have your revenge upon them next week, for they will be brought to trial at the assizes.'

'Did they give you the information you hoped for? News of the man behind the trade?'

'No. It would be more than their miserable hides were worth! We have plenty of suspicions, but very little real evidence. What brings you to the Port?'

'I am investigating a drowning; that of a sailor who was washed up at the Black Rocks . . .' Joshua paused.

'And?'

'I have just returned from a meeting with Mr Knight, the justice. He requests you to offer me every aid in the matter.'

'Does he, indeed?'

'His actual words were, "Say I instruct him to take you into his confidence, if necessary. He will take my meaning".'

Rawlings studied Joshua intently for a moment, as if making

up his mind, then said, resolutely, 'Drink up your ale, Stradling, and let us take a walk outside where the air is fresher.'

Joshua emptied his tankard, rose swiftly to his feet, and followed the exciseman outside.

'Now,' said Rawlings, 'let us take the pathway along the sea-edge, and towards Locks Common and Sker, for it will be deserted there. We must not be overheard, you understand? Then you shall tell me all you know.'

'I know nothing,' Joshua admitted, as they walked across the sea-washed turf, bright with the ling and the sulphurous yellow of gorse blossoms.

'What do you suspect, then?'

'I believe that, in some way, Crandle and his son are involved in the death of the sailor, and in the smuggling.'

'Your reasons?'

'I admit that they are slight, and would have no substance in law. First, two of the barques which sailed to the Port on the day of the storm are jointly owned by Crandle and a Mr Stanton Gould of Porlock. I saw Crandle leaving Weare House when I was investigating the murder of Mary Devereaux, and shortly afterwards heard Stanton Gould enquiring after him. In addition, Crandle's wife and daughter are said to be staying at Porlock for several weeks.' He paused, waiting for some reaction from the exciseman, but he asked only, 'There is more?'

Joshua nodded. 'The ostler at Weare House has been paid for two weeks' work, but has been instructed to stay away, as his services will not be required. Finally, the drowned man was washed ashore within sight of Weare House. Is it not feasible that since there is no record of any seaman being lost from any known trading ship, then he might have died when leaving the shore by boat, or when landing upon the beach?'

'More than feasible,' commented Rawlings, 'probable. I congratulate you, Stradling. You have done your work well, and much of mine for me. To tell the truth, we have been watching Crandle and his son for some time, as the excisemen in Somerset have been tracking Stanton Gould. We believe that the high tides next week will bring an increase in their smuggling activities.'

'You aim to catch them then?'

'I would be happier to know the time and date, with any accuracy ... but, yes, we will be keeping vigil, well armed. There is a great deal at stake, so it might prove to be a bloody confrontation.'

'You will allow me to take part?'

'I would welcome it ... and any reliable men you can provide. It is a small port, and we are few in number. Some must always remain on duty at the custom-house, for the life of the Port goes on. I need not impress on you the need for discretion.'

'No, it is understood.'

'It is probable that the dead sailor was in the pay of the Crandles ... but you think, perhaps, that they are implicated in the girl's murder, too?'

Joshua shook his head. 'I have no proof of it, or any hint of their involvement, save that the son met her once by accident. I admit that my dislike of the man makes me less objective than I should be, and I regret it. Animosity towards him clouds my judgement. But he is a proven womanizer, a molester of pretty young women.'

'As who would not be, given the chance?' asked Rawlings, ingenuously. 'If all the men whose thoughts were lewd or lecherous were laid end to end, I vow you could cross the Bristol Channel upon them without getting your feet wet!'

'Come,' said Joshua, laughing, 'we must at least wet our throats. Let us return to the alehouse and drink to a successful issue out of all our afflictions!'

When he had retrieved his grey from the stables of the 'Knight's Arms', and made arrangements to meet the exciseman, to plan and coordinate their watch upon Weare House, Joshua rode off to Rebecca's cottage. It was a warm sun-filled day, with the sky the clear, violet-blue of wild speedwell. There were few clouds, and those soft and high as downy underfeathers. As he passed, the cottage gardens blazed with marigolds and gilly flowers, and the air was clotted with the scent of stocks, mignonette, roses, and the twining stems of summer jasmine. Joshua, replete with ale and the satisfaction of work well done, thought that he had never been so contented.

As he approached the 'Ancient Briton' alehouse, the landlord, standing in its doorway, saluted him cordially, calling out, 'Good day to you, Constable Stradling, a fine bright day it is. I hear that your friend, Jeremiah Fleet is much improved. Would you take him a firkin of ale from me? To help his recovery? I would consider it a kindness.'

Joshua dismounted and took charge of the miniature barrel. 'That is kind of you, landlord.'

'No, sir, a neighbourly gesture, for the village people think highly of him. He is a good man, a generous one. I speak no disrespect if I say that it was not always so. After his wife and child died, he grew sullen and morose, keeping to himself, spurning all offers of friendship. It is a joy to see him so restored in spirit and in body.'

Joshua remounted the horse and, balancing his burden first upon the pommel of his saddle, then uneasily under his arm, rode away to Rebecca's cottage, and his friends.

He tied the grey to the gate post, allowing him freedom to roam and crop the grass and, with the firkin of ale resting on the doorstep, raised the knocker.

Rebecca came to answer his summons, face flushed, sleeves rolled up above her elbows, hair disordered, as if she had been running her fingers through it distractedly.

'Joshua,' she cried, delightedly, 'Oh, how pleased I am to see you!' She kissed him warmly upon his lips. 'Now our party is complete. Oh, Jeremiah, see who is here!' She ran ahead of him into the room, almost beside herself with excitement. Joshua followed more sedately, bearing the cask of ale.

The sight that met his eyes was bizarre in the extreme, and totally unexpected. Jeremiah, splendid in a freshly laundered nightshirt, was sitting up in bed, regally holding court. Across his legs the bull terrier lay asleep, snoring contentedly, its loose jowls trembling moistly with each exhalation of air. Doonan, perched precariously at the end of the bed near the fire, was playing some unrecognizable tune upon a whistle he had carved. The heat of the fire had reddened his face, and his shock of chestnut hair glowed brighter than the fire itself, as his huge fingers searched for the notes, forehead puckered in concentration. Emrys was seated in one of Rebecca's delicate chairs, clapping in time with the music and beating out the tempo with his booted foot. Circling the bed confidently, with Ossie at the leading rein, was Illtyd upon his pony, bowing serenely to right and left, and even attempting some mild acrobatics, spurred on by Jeremiah's extravagant cries of admiration.

'A born rider!' he was declaring, proudly. 'Just look at him; as natural to him as breathing. Oh, what a hayward you will make, my boy! Come quick, Joshua! Come and see Illtyd.'

'A brave little pony, and a braver little rider!' applauded Joshua from the doorway. There was a general clamour of conversation as the firkin was delivered with its message from the landlord.

'Well, I declare,' said Jeremiah, happily, 'I have never in all my life received so many gifts, and so much goodwill; it is almost a blessing to be sick!' He looked round at them appreciatively. 'Of all the surprises I have been given, I swear that none has pleased me more than the sight of Illtyd upon his little horse and his news from the vestry. It has lifted my spirits to the roof.'

'And will, very likely, drop them to the floor again if this bedlam and excitement continue,' scolded Rebecca. 'You shall all have some ale and some spice cakes, and then depart and leave the invalid to his sleep.'

Jeremiah protested mildly, but without much conviction, as she summoned Doonan and he lumbered after her into the larder to open the cask and bring in the ale for the party.

Glancing through the window into the yard, Joshua saw a bucket part-filled with miniature horse-droppings, a shovel beside it, and knew the cause of Rebecca's dishevelment at the door.

'I offered to leave him in the yard,' explained Illtyd, defensively.

'Leave him?' thundered Jeremiah. 'Nonsense! He is the reason for this celebration; that, and our affection for his master!'

Illtyd smiled happily, and twisted his wry neck awkwardly to look at Ossie. 'It was Ossie who taught me to ride ... and Joshua who gave me the pony and saddle, and pleaded with the vestrymen.' As Joshua made to deny it, 'Yes, I know it to be true, for how, otherwise, would they even consider me? If I have not thanked you both as I should, it is not because I am ungrateful.' He rested his ungainly head against the pony's neck and looked up, face flushed. 'There are no words generous enough, or loving enough, to speak of what I feel for you ... my true friends.' There was a moment of silence as he looked from one to the other, his beautiful, unexpected eyes bright. Then Jeremiah reached for the small, unformed hand and clasped it between his own.

'A toast, then,' cried Doonan, blundering in noisily with a wicker tray, his massive frame filling the doorway.

'To true friends.'

'Great and small,' added Jeremiah, contentedly, raising the tankard which Doonan had given him. His gaze rested upon Illtyd and Emrys, Ossie, Joshua and Doonan, and finally settled upon Rebecca, who was handing out a plate of spice cakes.

'To the best little nurse a man ever had,' he said, saluting her.

'I had best send for the physician, for I fear you have a touch of the brain fever!' she said, tartly. 'You would swear, Jeremiah, that it was you who kissed the Blarney Stone, and not Cavan there!'

'I don't know about the Blarney Stone,' said Doonan, draining his glass, 'but if Emrys and I do not return to that other stone, it will not be kissing we can expect, and that is a fact!'

They all began to laugh and prepare to go, taking leave of Jeremiah at his bed. The bull terrier awoke, bewildered by the uproar, and Rebecca fed him some spice cake, which made him slobber and sneeze. Doonan, taking advantage of the distraction, called Joshua aside.

'I have been hoping to see you ... for a labourer in the quarries approached me in the "Ship Aground", and asked if I would care to earn some gold. There would be little to do, he assured me, simply to move some cargo one night.'

'And what did you reply?'

'That I would think about it carefully. I delayed an answer, for I wanted your instruction upon it.'

Joshua nodded, 'Mention it to no one, but come to my cottage tonight, if you are able, and we will discuss it.'

Emrys signalled to Doonan that the horse and cart stood ready at the end of the yard, and they took their leave; Ossie and Illtyd followed close behind them, with the ostler leading the little hunchback proudly upon his mount. Joshua and Rebecca watched them go, and as they turned to go inside, Joshua saw that Rebecca's eyes were unaccountably filled with tears, which she brushed away roughly with the knuckles of her hand.

'What has upset you? Is it Illtyd? You should not grieve for him. He is happy. Can you not see the change in him?'

'I am not sad for him . . . at least, I do not think it is that. It is just seeing his poor misshapen body, and knowing that inside he is compassionate and warm and good. Life is unfair. For his feelings are the same as ours . . . Who will look past what he seems, and love him?'

'Ossie loves him, as you and I do, and Jeremiah and the rest, and the Widow Cleat.'

'I meant who will love him as a man? As I love you.'

'I know, and there is no answer that I can give you. You cannot weep for the whole world, Rebecca, not even for your own small corner of it, for you would never stop. Come, now,' he took out his handkerchief, 'dry your eyes, or Jeremiah will think I have been beating you cruelly.'

When they returned to Jeremiah and the dog, Joshua said, looking at Rebecca, 'I came to bring you not one but two invitations, Miss de Breos.'

'Oh, and where would they take me?'

'To the Mabsant celebrations, and then to my father's farm, my home, if you will come with me.'

She flushed, and grew pale, saying awkwardly, 'No, of course I cannot come. I must attend to Jeremiah. He is not fit to be left alone.'

'I would not be alone,' cried Jeremiah, cheerfully, 'for my good friend Daniel detests the Mabsant revels and would sooner be hanged on a gibbet on Stalling Downs than attend!

As for your visit to the farm, Hannah and the Widow Cleat would consider it a rare privilege to sit with me!'

'You see,' smiled Joshua. 'There are no obstacles to your coming, save in your own mind.'

She looked at him, sharply. 'Your parents have invited me? They know I am coming?'

'Of course,' he returned her gaze steadily.

'Then I shall be pleased to accept.'

'On Wednesday, then, I shall escort you to the frolics on the village green. On Friday morning, if you are agreeable, I shall call for you with the curricle at ten of the clock.'

So it was arranged.

As Joshua was taking his leave, Jeremiah said, 'Did I tell you that Illtyd has named his horse "Faith".'

'No, you did not. Why Faith, then?'

Jeremiah smiled, and patted the bull terrier which lay upon the bed-cover, awake and watchful.

'He said that you had given me Charity, him Faith in himself ... and we all must be left with Hope.'

As Rebecca returned the tray to the larder, he whispered, slyly, 'What he really said was, "He has given Rebecca Hope!"'

'You are a wicked old man,' Joshua chided, 'and your matchmaking ill becomes you. Besides, it is the other way around. It is Rebecca who brings hope to me, a hopeless reprobate. For I confess to you, Jeremiah, I love her dearly.'

Jeremiah heard it and was glad, but he was tired of the game, and pretended to be asleep.

Chapter Eighteen

Joshua's eager plans to please Rebecca with the Mabsant frolics were set awry by an urgent summons from the justice.

As Joshua rode out to Tythegston Court, the prolonged heat of summer filled him with a strange lethargy. Sunlight shimmered before him in a veil, bleaching cornfields, leeching colour from the meadows and hedgerows. It seemed to him that as it dried sap from all things green, so must it suck out his blood with his sweat, leaving him a poor, desiccated skeleton, incapable of thought or action. The way, although short, set him and the grey in a lather, and he was glad to dismount and see the poor beast watered.

The justice regarded Joshua quizzically from behind his lenses. 'You know why I have sent for you.'

Joshua scoured his mind for sins or omissions.

'No, sir.'

'The feast of Mabsant, Stradling! Midsummer Eve: the decollation of St John the Baptist.'

'Ah yes, sir. The celebrations.'

'Indeed. I confess, Stradling, that if it were not an irreverence, I could wish our good saint had been beheaded in the wintertime. Midsummer makes for hot weather and hotter blood. The rigours of icy blasts might serve to cool men's ardour.' He sighed. 'I have no doubt that there will be a spate of marriages at Michaelmas, with Lammas christenings to follow . . .'

'Surely, all grist to your mill, sir?'

'God's mill, my boy! I am but the miller's apprentice . . . or, at best, he who shapes the bread . . .'

'Then, sir, at least yours will be leavened!'

The justice peered at him sharply. 'What exactly is your meaning, Stradling?'

'Why, that your sermons and example are the yeast, sir.

They must cause the poorest and most flaccid dough to rise. I speak metaphorically, of course ...'

'Of course,' responded the justice drily. Then, 'Tell me, Stradling, yours is an honourable name. Is there, by chance, some consanguinity with the Stradlings of St Donat's Castle?'

'I fear not even "by chance" sir! I claim neither blood kinship, nor even the bend sinister ... and if I did profess to such distinction, and claim to be a gentleman, then my status would be even lower than it is now, in the eyes of the villagers! Begging your pardon, sir ...'

The justice's eyes twinkled. 'I grant it unconditionally and declare, Stradling, that many a self-styled "gentleman" might envy you your wit and understanding. Now to business! You will keep a special watch upon the churchyard. You are free to hire any help which you might consider necessary. The cost will be borne by the vestry. Take heed, by night, of the fires at the wells. The villagers declare they drive away dragons which pollute and poison the waters. Pagan rubbish! Indeed, some of their practices come close enough to witchcraft!' As Joshua made to protest, 'No, I know none is intended. The origins of some traditions are too deep-buried to trace. The cottagers think of it merely as a feast day, a midsummer revel ...'

Joshua nodded.

'I freely admit the church is much the cause. We took the old pagan beliefs and superimposed our God upon them. We buried their idols, Stradling, but not deeply enough. The skeletons remain ...'

'And the erosion of time and habit bare their bones?'

'Exactly ... Watch them, Stradling. Protect them. They are children, trusting, impetuous, innocent of guile ... but there are darker forces. Evils of which they know nothing, but which, once unleashed ...' He left the sentence unfinished.

'I will do as you ask, sir.'

'Good. And the innkeepers?'

'They promise free ale, and diversions.'

'I wish I could believe in their altruism, Stradling! There will be many a drunken brawl and broken head before the night is out! Do not let it be yours!'

'I shall endeavour to keep mine intact, sir.'

'And your heart, Stradling.'

'I think there is no risk attached to that!'

'Good.' The Reverend Robert Knight nodded dismissal, and watched him leave. He had not missed the slow stain beneath the constable's skin. He took off his eyeglasses and polished the lenses, thoughtfully, with his handkerchief. Time was when he, too ... He recalled himself abruptly. Regret for the past was profitless, an old man's salve ... the young were too busy living.

Before midsummer eve, the green sward without the church walls had been a hive of urgent, and all too often irreverent, activity, and Joshua noted, with some misgivings, the growing pile of kindling and faggots beside St John's Well.

He had done as the justice instructed, and hired five stout men to aid him. Well, strictly speaking, four stout men and Illtyd, who, although puny in stature, qualified through sheer stoutness of heart.

Doonan had excelled himself by selecting and chopping the finest Mabsant birch that the village had ever seen. The women had prettified it with streamers of ribbon, and garlands of silk flowers, leaving, Joshua suspected, many a Sunday bonnet bare of ornament. The planked tables were set with cottage garden flowers pressed into damp moss, or potatoes, to ensure their freshness, and everywhere there were crude stalls and marked-out courses for the children's games and donkey races.

Doonan, Daniel, Emrys, and the new blacksmith had set up the birch in the centre of the green. Denuded of branches, well sunk and hammered into the ground, it stood like the mast of a tall ship, rigged overall. If its raising had been the cause of some levity, and not a little bawdiness, Joshua wisely chose to ignore it.

'Children' the rector had called them, and children they were; absorbed, happy, and as swift to laughter and tears. There is little enough laughter in their lives, Joshua thought, let them enjoy life while they may.

Ossie, nut-brown and proud as a squirrel, was to take charge of the nose-to-tail, although his was a coarser description, donkey-races. The thought of well-upholstered farmers' wives, facing backwards, and bouncing along clutching the asses' tails was enough to make him hug his stomach, and roll upon the grass in mirth.

'What a day I shall have of it!' he confided to Joshua, eyes aglow at the prospect, 'Bosoms wobbling like jelly-fish, backsides billowing like sails in the wind! Upon my oath, Joshua, I should be paying them for the sights ... not charging them!'

Doonan and the blacksmith, victualled by the 'Ancient Briton', and 'Crown Inn', slept beside the birch tree, lest it be snatched away by envious marauders from outside the three hamlets. At least, such was their intention, but so prodigal were their hosts that their snores were heard as far away as Nottage. Indeed, if they, too, had been spirited away, it was doubtful if they would even have noticed.

The dawn of Mabsant was crisp and clear. Doonan and the blacksmith, had they been so minded, could have washed their faces in the early dew. It misted the grass to silver, and lay upon the spiders' webs in fragile drops of crystal, yet not, perhaps, as fragile as their respective heads! Indeed, the pain of opening his eyelids made Doonan wonder if he had died in the night, and been somehow transported to hell. Small fiends seemed to be stabbing at his eyeballs with pitchforks.

'Dear life!' groaned the blacksmith, steadying his head with his palms, 'No need to look for the morris men, they are clog-dancing in my skull!'

'At least the birch pole is intact ...' grunted Doonan, squinting upwards, and using it to haul himself to his feet. The ribbons fluttered about his massive frame like many-coloured butterflies.

'*So chaste a maid, full fair of face, shall be the May Queen of this place*,' mimicked and postured the blacksmith, only to be grounded by a massive blow from Doonan's fist.

Mabsant had begun.

Despite the justice's forebodings, the day passed sunny and cloud-free as the weather. There were the usual good-natured fisticuffs: a few drunken brawls and a broken head when a quarryman impugned the maleness of a morris dancer, who demonstrated the lie by clouting him with his stick, without missing a beat, to the delight of the onlookers.

The more nubile of the village maidens danced around the birch-pole in a swirl of prettily starched petticoats, while their swains lumbered beside them, damp with sweat and concentration. Rebecca and Doonan's Rosa, Joshua thought, were the loveliest, their colouring making them a perfect foil, one for the other: Rosa so palely delicate, and Rebecca ablaze with dark vitality.

'Rose Red and Snow White,' murmured the Widow Cleat, coming to stand beside him. 'What a perfect day it has been, Joshua. The sort of day to remember when you are old, and the flesh and bones grow cold and in need of summer warmth.' Her eyes clouded with tears. Joshua put a comforting arm about her shoulders. 'Silly,' she said, 'to weep for beauty and pleasure, when I am unable to cry for what matters most.' She looked towards Illtyd, awkwardly running beside a small child upon his pony, Faith, the child's face and his aglow with pleasure.

There was a sudden commotion at the birch-pole as one of the farmboys, losing his rhythm, stumbled, cracking his boot upon his partner's instep. She unleashed her ribbon and crouched in pain. The dancers collided, and fell in a tangle of flesh and streamers. Joshua rushed forward to pull Rebecca to her feet, laughing and disarrayed, cheeks flushed with dancing. She put a hand to her hair.

'My ribbon ...'

Joshua beckoned to the pedlar who was standing, watching. The music stopped, and the scene seemed frozen, timeless. The cottagers saw their young constable take a gold sovereign from his pocket, and without even glancing at it, thrust it at the astonished pedlar, scoop up the entire contents of his tray, and rain them upon Rebecca, who gathered up her petticoats to catch them.

'I shall buy you a ribbon for every day of the year ...' Joshua cried rashly, and all the good souls of the three hamlets cheered, smiled and applauded. Then he took her in his arms and kissed her soundly, while the ribbons spilled unheeded to the grass.

Jeremiah, had he been upon the fringes of the crowd, watching his friends, would have reflected, like the justice, that midsummer blood indeed flowed hot ... Unlike the justice, after such a public declaration, Jeremiah would have prayed, most earnestly, that cold winds, and bleaker days, might never come.

With the onset of darkness, the mood of the revelry had changed. Children were abed, sated with excitement and sweetmeats; their dreams of fiddlers and penny whistles, fights and donkey gallops ... The more nervous of them stayed awake, and begged for taper or rushlight. Yet it brought no comfort, only sombre shadows in the looming shapes of dragons, breathing sulphurous fire; lizard tongues flicking and darting with the fitful light.

Outside, Joshua and his small band of peacekeepers were hard pressed to prevent a conflagration between the people of the three hamlets and the 'itinerants': sailors and workmen from the port. They brought with them their own customs, own values, not always shared by the insular cottagers. The harvesters from Somerset also brought their own cider and apple brandy. Over-indulgence, while dulling their homesickness, sometimes dulled their wits, or made them boastful and aggressive. Either way, they were fair game.

Joshua knew that the night's revelry, and in particular the bonfires, would prove irresistible to them. 'Like moths to a flame,' he thought, hoping that they would not show the same urge for self-destruction! He feared that the justice was right. The villagers pretended the fires were an extension of the Mabsant celebrations, nothing more. Yet such roots were deep and atavistic. Their Mabsant and paganism were inextricably mixed: harvest; fertility; the burning of animal bones to recall the holy relic – the saint's hand which, alone, had survived the flames of martyrdom in a far-off land; the ritual leaping over flame; the passing of infants over the glowing embers, as Illtyd remembered, 'to make him grow ...' The villagers pleaded ignorance of the origins of the rites, yet they still hung bunches of St John's Wort over their lintels to keep away evil spirits, and covered their wells to shield them from the poisonous breath of dragons. It would not do if the itinerants mocked their traditions. Like the bonfires so deprecated by the justice, a single spark would serve to ignite ...

Joshua and his men moved between the appointed inns and bonfires, keeping steady but unobtrusive watch, while, in the churchyard, the blacksmith, all too mindful of youthful ardour, kept vigil over mossy tombstones and the church porch. Seeing him erupt in wrath, from behind a monument, Joshua thought, would make the most ardent lover swear celibacy ...

Doonan, in both 'Crown' and 'Ancient Briton', shared jokes and ale with rare good humour, bringing reason to argument. If reason failed he banged heads together with strict impartiality. Some he knocked sober; some he knocked senseless. Joshua wasn't convinced that the justice would have approved such ethics, but wisely deferred any judgement of his own.

Just when it seemed that the night had passed without serious incident, Emrys came running to the 'Ancient Briton', breathless, hair awry, almost too agitated to find words.

'Quick!' he managed, grasping Joshua's arm. 'Plover's Plain ...' He subsided onto a stool, holding his ribcage.

Joshua all but shook him. 'Who, man?' he demanded impatiently.

Emrys, unable to speak, wiped a smear of blood across his cheek, fighting to get his breath. His bottom lip was split and one eye closing. Blood from his nose dripped remorselessly down his shirt front.

'Who?' repeated Joshua, irritably.

Emrys shook his head helplessly, but managed, 'Rosa ... Rebecca ... Quick man! Do something! Get after them ..!'

Doonan had already lumbered to his feet, and lunged towards the door. Joshua followed fast, accompanied by half a dozen cottagers, wielding rough staves from the innkeeper's armoury. Doonan was nearly out of sight. For a heavy man he moved incredibly fast, and lightly, although bogged down by the fine sand of the dunes. He pulled himself upwards, clutching the marram grass, unaware of it lacerating his clenched palms. On the topmost hill, above the green bowl of Plover's Plain, he saw the blaze of a bonfire rising high and the two women close by, hedged in by a crowd of men.

Rebecca had plucked a burning brand from the flames, and was lunging and swinging it at any man who came too close. Rosa was clasped in the vice-like grip of a big, brutish-looking stranger, his teeth bared in a grin as he swung her around, giddily, her face flushed, petticoats awry.

She was kicking, spitting, raging at him impotently, trapped in the air ...

With a bellow of rage, and a red mist before his eyes, Doonan rushed towards him, only vaguely aware of the circle of bleached animal skulls; he punched the man so hard that he heard the cracking of bone, like the splintering of a twig, and Rosa fell to the ground, petticoats flying. Doonan had no need of a stave for his fists and feet were battering rams, smashing and splintering all who dared to stand in his way. Once, he looked up briefly, to see Rebecca throwing a lighted brand at an oppressor, and heard the scream of pain and an oath, as the fire burnt into flesh ... A plucky little maid, Doonan thought, as a mighty blow felled him to his knees, but he shook himself like a dog from the sea, and waded in again.

There was a yell from above as the blacksmith and his boy arrived and ran down the sandy slope to the plain, wooden branches flailing about them like threshing sticks ... When Joshua and his men arrived the action grew fiercer, and Rebecca and Rosa, no longer menaced, withdrew to the shelter of a willow copse to watch and ease their bruises. The resulting carnage silenced and shamed them, and when their assailants were routed, and those still able to walk had made their escape, Joshua and Doonan approached. If the women had expected praise for their courage and spirit, there was none.

'Well?' demanded Joshua, 'what have you to say for yourselves? A fine night's work you have made of it!'

Rosa was weeping silently, but Doonan averted his eyes. Rebecca, whose palm throbbed and ached, where the brand from the fire had burnt the flesh, stamped her foot in exasperation.

'Damn you!' she cried, blinking to stop the tears. 'Who asked you to interfere?'

'Not interfere ...' corrected Joshua, 'just gather the pieces.

You were warned most explicitly that you were to stay indoors, not venture abroad. Are you stupid as well as wilful?'

Rosa was weeping loudly, now, in fear and exhaustion. 'I'm sorry ...' she muttered. 'I was foolish, foolish ... I will never disobey you again, as long as I live, Cavan. I promise.' She ran to him and buried her face in his chest, and his arms slipped inevitably around her, while he murmured endearments, as to a frightened child, and stroked her pale hair.

'And you, madam?' demanded Joshua of Rebecca. 'Have you no word of regret?'

Rebecca stamped her foot in pain and frustration. 'None, save for your smug, self-righteous interference ... It had nothing to do with you!'

'It had everything to do with me! I am angry not because you disobeyed me, you brave infuriating little fighting cock, but because I love you and fear for your safety! Do you not see that I would die rather than have you harmed ..?'

Now Rebecca began to cry too, and Joshua wasted no time on further recrimination but gathered her to him, wiping her eyes with his handkerchief, then, seeing the raw flesh of her palm, bandaging it tenderly.

When Ossie came upon them, there was such a sobbing and comforting, and flurry of explanations, that he swore it was more unnerving than the battle.

'Be off home, my maids,' he said. 'It is not fitting that you are abroad on such a night. Come, I will take you to your homes, for I am sure that Joshua will spare me.'

Joshua nodded.

As Rosa and Rebecca strove to restore some semblance of order to their appearance, Ossie called him aside.

'I do not like it,' he said. 'I do not like it at all. What did they hope to do, Joshua? It does not bear thinking about ...'

He kicked at a skull. 'These must be buried, decently, in some other place.'

'You are right. I will ask someone to see to it,' Joshua promised.

Ossie shivered. 'This is not some Mabsant prank of which we speak, Joshua. It is evil, depraved.' Ossie's voice was raw, troubled, as he confessed, 'I had heard wild talk of witchcraft, animal skulls . . . the violation of virgin maidens, sacrifice even, and had thought it rumour and lies . . . Yet there is unspeakable corruption here, I feel it, as surely as I feel the night air upon my face. It is a wickedness so vile that it is tangible . . .'

'I feel as you do, the need to be cleansed of whatever forces corrupt this night.'

'Say nothing to the maidens. I shall see that they leave in safety. Have no fear . . . but afterwards, I shall go to the church and pray. I do not know what words to use, or what I pray to be delivered from.'

'Deliver us from evil . . .' quoted Joshua softly.

'I believe He has, this night,' said Ossie gravely, 'and I thank Him for it.'

Joshua was troubled as he watched them go, and he fought to subdue the fury which arose in him when he thought of how nearly tragedy had corrupted the lives of those he had grown to love. He did not know how best to deal with the human carrion before him. Every raw instinct and nerve urged him to meet violence with greater violence. A word from him and the villagers would teach them a lesson so bloody and lacerating that the scars would never allow them to forget . . . He was unaware that he was grinding his fist into his palm. Emrys, still bloodied, but elated by victory, came and stood beside him.

'I was wondering what to do with these . . . animals.'

'Do not insult God's creatures by calling them that,' said Emrys, 'for animals savage and kill to survive, knowing no better.'

'I am tempted to flog them and take them before the justice . . .' Joshua said bitterly.

'And if you do, Rosa and Rebecca must go too. They will learn of what was intended for them, and their lives will never again be as they were.'

'I cannot let them go unpunished!'

'Unpunished? See what a cowed and gutless pack they are, Joshua. Like whipped curs. They have no spirit. Let them go, for I swear they will not return.'

'Perhaps you are right. Yet my every instinct is to kill them. . .'

'A fine revenge,' said Emrys drily, 'if we lose you, too.' He put an arm about the constable's shoulders. 'Come Joshua, they are not worth the effort, or the loss of your self-respect.'

Joshua nodded reluctantly. 'Let us remove this filth and ordure which remains, then return to those other bonfires, and other conflagrations. I fear it will be a long, hard night, my friend.' As he spoke he felt the first splash of rain upon his face, and then the spatter of drops as its intensity increased, making the bonfire smoke and hiss.

'I think you have your answer.' Emrys lifted his face and outstretched palms to the sky as the first crack of thunder shook the air. A vivid fork of lightning ripped the sky. 'Yes. There is your salvation ...'

'It is more than I deserve,' confessed Joshua, as soaked but laughing with elation they fled the plain, and the Mabsant fires guttered and died.

The rector and Joshua stood beneath the shadow of the church tower, seeking coolness from the glare of the sun.

'The Mabsant celebrations, Stradling? They passed without tragedy or fatality, I hear.'

'Yes sir. There was nothing I could not contain.'

'I am glad to hear it ...' He looked at Joshua keenly, persisting, 'No outbreaks of violence then?'

'Nothing severe enough to bring to you, sir.'

'And the skulls of those dead animals? They have been removed?'

'Yes,' agreed Joshua, startled.

'And the young women concerned ... they are unharmed physically and emotionally?'

'Yes, thank God!'

The rector looked at him shrewdly from behind the gold-rimmed lenses. 'I am relieved,' he said drily, 'that you do not claim the entire credit for the night's work.'

Chapter Nineteen

Joshua was determined that Rebecca's visit to his father's farm would make up for his neglect of her at the Mabsant feast. He could not recall that night without an overpowering feeling of menace, and fear. If he had lost her, or she had been violated, or otherwise harmed, then nothing else in his life would have had meaning. He knew, without any doubt at all, that he loved Rebecca and wanted to make her his wife. He wanted this meeting with his family to be perfect. Besides, there was a surprise he had planned . . .

Rebecca was unhappy about the visit. Although Joshua's intentions were good, she was aware that they might well pave the way to a hell he had not envisaged. She was not naive enough to believe that his family would accept her. She was part of Joshua's 'other life'. It was one thing to smile over it with their friends, and discuss how liberal they had been in indulging him in 'this whim' of his; quite another to accept the reality. She, Rebecca, was the reality. She knew that she would disappoint them. In a way, she supposed, it was like people's reactions to Illtyd. They saw only the surface inadequacies and imperfections. To Joshua's family, she would be a social cripple; a cockle gatherer with no family, no money, background or place in the social hierarchy. She had wept for Illtyd because he was different, and the difference isolated him. Well, so was she different, but she was damned if she would cry for herself! If they could not accept her, then it was sad, but she would survive. It was Joshua she feared for; unlike her, he was torn by the demands of two separate lives, their needs, their expectations. For the moment, he was able to keep them apart. One day he would have to choose, for there was no known way to bridge them.

She determined that, for her own sake, and Joshua's, she would be pleasant, appreciative if the occasion demanded it, and prepared to like his parents. She would not lie, but neither would she denigrate her way of life, nor her friends.

Jeremiah, seeing her conflict and nervousness, was troubled, and sought a way to comfort and reassure her. He had asked Illtyd to beg the Widow Cleat to bring him one perfect rose from her cottage garden and a spray of her parlour fern, that he might give it to Rebecca to pin upon her dress. As fresh and lovely as a rose she is herself, Jeremiah thought, truthfully. He hoped she would understand what he was unable to say, and not feel awkwardness, or pity, at the commonplace offering of a sentimental old man.

'It is strange,' he said to Rebecca, 'but for the first time I seem able to think of my wife and the boy without sadness, or feeling bitter. Perhaps it is because I was so close to death myself. I feel nearer to them, as real people, you understand, not just a picture in my head. I have been shutting them out, when I should have been grateful for having them in my life, even for a little time. I was wrong; as soon as I am well, I will go to the churchyard and tell them so. Yes, that is what I shall do.'

'I am glad,' she answered, 'but if you wish to restore your energy, you had best eat that gruel upon your tray, then make haste to change your nightshirt, lest the Widow Cleat and your friend, Hannah, brand me sluttish. We shall have you looking as pure and appealing as an angel when they come to take charge of you.'

'I am not a helpless babe, that I have need of two nursemaids,' he grumbled, 'and they will gossip, gossip, until my head aches.'

'Then let them gossip together,' she said, briskly, 'and then you may talk to yourself, knowing you are in pleasant company.' Jeremiah tried to hide a smile, but failed, and soon they were laughing together, and the dog barking to add to the uproar.

Now, watching her through the window as she heated water in the iron pot above the brick oven of the yard, Jeremiah's mood was more sober. He had thought that Joshua's affection for her could bring only good. Now he was not so sure. If his family slighted her, or rejected her altogether, it would not break her spirit, for she was a proud independent girl, but it might well bruise her self-esteem. He hoped she would not reject Joshua because of it, for he was sure that the young man loved her dearly. Suddenly, Jeremiah felt bewildered and old.

Rebecca took the linen out of the wooden tub, where it had been soaking with coarse soap, and transferred it to the boiling water upon the oven, adding a lye of clean wood ash, wrapped in muslin, to soften and whiten the fibres. When it was clean enough, she would stir and pound it with a wooden dolly stick, to help loosen the dirt, then it would be rinsed in a final solution of blue or, for petticoats and her best bodice, and Jeremiah's nightshirt, a mix of starch. Tomorrow, she would iron her petticoats until they rustled and stood on their own. Her new blue dress and cloak were already pressed, and set out in her bedroom, together with her matching bonnet and unworn shoes. It was a pity about the burn upon her palm. She hoped that they would not ask about it, for she felt shame and regret that she and Rosa had behaved so recklessly upon Mabsant. Yet, the memory of Joshua's gentleness in binding it, and his warm kisses and declarations of fear for her safety, made her feel loved and secure, and brought a smile to her lips. Tonight she would rub some moistened oatmeal into her hands, and cover them with strips of linen to keep them soft. She thought they looked less raw and chapped since she had given up her shellfish gathering to care for Jeremiah. As she stirred the washing in the boiler, there came to mind the soft pale fingers of the dead girl, Mary Devereaux, as she had seen her first, upon the sand, with her pretty petticoats white above her naked flesh. She shivered despite the heat of the fire and the warmth of the day. Someone had coldly and cruelly taken a life. She could not believe it to be anyone she knew.

For the moment, Joshua's mind was occupied, not with the visit to the farm but with the planned watch upon Weare House, and the exciseman's hopes of trapping the smugglers. If it led to the identification of the dead sailor, and brought to justice whoever was culpable, then it would be an added prize.

Doonan, Ossie, Emrys, and the little man, Illtyd, were seated with him in the living room of his cottage, being apprised of the parts they were expected to play in the venture.

Each had a jar of ale set upon the table before him, and the mood was convivial and informal, as befitted friends. They chatted of Jeremiah for a while, and the pleasure and relief at seeing him restored to health, day by day.

'It is strange,' said Emrys, 'how much fevers act upon the brain, to bring strange fancies and confusion. I would have sworn that Jeremiah was the most solid and unfanciful of men.'

'Why, so he is,' declared Doonan. 'I have never known him otherwise. If he saw the devil with a pitchfork sitting on a milestone, he would but raise his hat, and enquire if he could help him.'

'Well, he seemed worried enough about a man he claimed he saw. He came to him in his sickness, or so he said. A doctor of sorts. Twice, he has told me of it: the last time so persistently, and with such vehemence, that Rebecca grew quite disturbed, and bade him speak no more of it, for his mind had been playing him tricks.'

'What did this fellow look like?' demanded Joshua.

'Who knows?' replied Emrys. 'I did not ask, for Rebecca was obviously distressed at the recollection of his mind wandering. She convinced me, if she did not altogether convince poor Jeremiah!'

'I fear that he grows a little forgetful, too. I do not know whether through illness or age,' ventured Ossie, 'for he told me most definitely that the two Crandles had been seen riding out from their house at three of the clock in the morning. When I asked who had told him of this, he confessed that he could not remember, but swore that he knew it for a fact. I quietened him by saying that I did not doubt it.'

'That may be so,' said Illtyd, quietly, 'but now, at least, he is perfectly in possession of his faculties and his memory, too, for he instructed me only tonight to tell Joshua that his friend Hannah bade him visit Ezra the Box and to inspect some ornate coffin which he carves for himself. He says that Ezra keeps his earnings in it.'

'If that is proof of Jeremiah's return to normality,' exclaimed Doonan, 'then I am a Dutchman! A more unlikely story I never heard!'

Joshua busied himself in pouring some more ale and said nothing, letting the talk swirl about him, but missing nothing that was said.

Finally, when the men stood ready to leave, their plan of action having been decided, Joshua impressed upon them all the importance of discretion. There was to be no careless mention of it to others; no discussion in public places where they might be overheard. The success of the adventure depended upon their silence.

Doonan, Emrys and Illtyd could be relied upon to be ready at a moment's notice, at any time of the night. Ossie, however, was limited by the needs of his work: if the night was quiet and no travellers were expected, then he could summon a stableboy to take his place and slip away. With notice, he could hire the ostler from Weare House to take his turn at the 'Crown'. However, if a horse became ill, he explained, then he must stay with the beast for as long as he was needed. This being agreed, and the entire group promising to provide themselves with defensive weapons, they went their respective ways: Emrys to his lodgings; Doonan to his Rosa; Ossie and Illtyd to pick up his pony from the stables of the 'Crown'.

After they had gone, Joshua sat and considered what had been disclosed about Jeremiah. Two of his three claims were almost certainly true. As to the man who had visited him, did he exist, or was he a figment of his fevered imagination? If he were not, then Rebecca was guilty, not only of deceiving him, but setting the lives of others in danger . . .

Rebecca had been up since daylight, too nervous and excited to waste time in sleep. She had spent a long time washing herself in cold water from the jug and bowl on the table by her bed, and brushing her hair excessively, so that it might look well under her new bonnet. Anticipation had brought an added sparkle to her eyes and, regarding herself in the looking glass, she felt that she looked almost pretty. Her hands were a disappointment; so little improved under the linen bandages and the oatmeal poultice. She had walked to the haberdasher's yesterday, after delivering her sketches to the dressmaker, and bought a good pair of cotton gloves, in a blue to tone with her dress, a vanity and extravagance she was not proud of. She wished that there was some way of keeping them on when she ate, or drank tea, but could think of no excuse for doing so, save confessing that she had some eruption of the skin, or contagion; a remedy which might well embarrass her more than the cause itself.

Everything in the house freshly dusted, the day's meals for Hannah, the Widow Cleat and Jeremiah arranged and rearranged a dozen times, and Jeremiah himself, and even the dog, pristine and without a hair disarrayed, she finally took heed of his command to 'be seated and rest awhile, for you are as restless as a moth at a candle flame.'

Jeremiah, watching her now, as she sat upon his bed in her pert bonnet and pretty gown, with dainty slippers encasing her feet, thought he had never, in all his life, seen anyone more beautiful . . . or worthy to be loved. She was indeed his treasure, his 'little maid'. The sheer freshness and youth of her caught tears in his throat and, for a time, he was unable to speak, so moved was he by pride and affection. He pretended to be engrossed in refastening the bull terrier's collar, keeping his head low to blink away the unmanly threat of tears. Then, his composure regained, he thrust his hand under the pillow, and brought out a small leather-covered box.

'Here,' he said, abruptly. 'It is something to go at the neck of your gown. It seemed a bit plain . . . the collar. I sent Illtyd to the cottage to search for it, and bring it to me.'

Rebecca opened the lid upon a small silver brooch of hearts entwined; at the centre of each, a tiny seed pearl.

'Oh, but it is beautiful, Jeremiah! I could not take it. It is too much.'

'I fancy, my girl, that it would wait a long time to be worn by me. Take it . . . there is no one I would want to wear it, but you.'

'It is very special to you, Jeremiah?'

'I pinned it upon my wife's dress when our son was born. Now, I pin it upon my daughter's dress . . . for that is how I think of you.' He fastened it clumsily upon her collar, his large hands awkward with weakness, but she did not repin it. She simply took his hand and laid it against her cheek.

'There is no one I love in the whole world as much as you,

Jeremiah,' she said, earnestly, 'save, perhaps for Joshua, and that is a different kind of loving. I shall wear your brooch every day until I die. I shall never be without it.'

'Come, little maid,' he chided, gently, 'you grow too serious for such a happy, special day.'

There was a knocking upon the front door and she hurried to open it, to many exclamations of pleasure and admiration from Hannah and the Widow Cleat.

'I declare, Rebecca, you are as pretty as a picture.'

'Like a spring flower, as fresh and clean.'

'How well the colour becomes your eyes . . . I declare, I am sure that Joshua will hardly be able to take his eyes off you!'

'Stop!' cried Jeremiah, loudly, from his bed, 'for any more flattery will make her head swell so much that she will scarcely fit into her bonnet. It will sit like a pimple upon her head.'

Since time was getting short, they begged her to put on her bonnet, gloves and cloak, and Jeremiah gallantly fastened upon the ribbon trim of her bonnet the white rosebud and fern which the Widow Cleat had brought fresh-cut from her garden and parlour, whereupon the excitement and congratulations broke out anew.

When Joshua came, driving the curricle with its matched, chestnut horses his parents had sent to convey them, he simply studied her gravely and said, with his mouth curving into a smile, 'Miss de Breos, will you do me the honour of gracing my humble carriage?' He left her and the two good ladies admiring every aspect of it, while he went to exchange brief greetings with Jeremiah.

'Take care of her,' Jeremiah said. 'I would not see her hurt.'

Joshua did not pretend to misunderstand his message.

'She is as dear to me as she is to you, Jeremiah; no one shall wound her, or make her feel out of place, I promise.' They clasped hands upon it.

Joshua drove off, the horses trotting in unison, heads tossing, harness jangling. Rebecca, sitting upright in the elegant curricle, her remarkable eyes bright under her bonnet brim, smiled at Joshua, then waved happily to the two women standing entranced upon the doorstep of the cottage.

'This is the happiest day in all my life,' she exclaimed,

clutching Joshua's arm impetuously. 'I could wish it might never end.'

The Widow Cleat wiped her eyes upon her apron, sighing with satisfaction. 'What a lovely sight, Hannah. I am sure that I have never seen two people as well-matched, or two such horses. Rebecca was so excited, she could scarcely sit still.'

'Smiles before dawning, tears before morning.'

'Damn fool women! Forever weeping or wailing,' said Jeremiah. 'You've got more sense than the two of them put together!' As he patted Charity's head, the bull terrier wagged its tail and cocked its head, intelligently. Jeremiah would have sworn it winked an eye.

As the carriage and horses drove through the edge of the village, past the church of St John the Baptist, and skirting the village green, Rebecca saw Ossie standing under the archway to the 'Crown', obviously awaiting a glimpse of them. She waved to him gaily, and in reply he delivered a bow of such grandeur that it all but swept him off his crooked legs, and into the yard.

It seemed to Rebecca, as she watched Joshua's deft hands stroking the reins, and the gleaming rumps and the tossing manes of the horses as they moved in unison, that the whole of life beat with a warm, insistent rhythm, a pulsing of life and blood. The summer breeze was warm upon her skin, and the air clotted with the sound of insects and bees, and the music of harness and hoof.

As the lanes grew narrower, from her perch above the hedgerows she saw the fields flecked with thistle and mallow, and cows wearied by heat, dozing udder-deep in buttercups. Their tails were whips, flicking away the flies which clouded their eyes. Once she watched a vixen and four cubs playing near a stile, with the fox running anxiously atop a dry stone wall. When he heard the sound of their carriage, he leapt down and scolded the family through the stile, and when they were safe, streaked for a gap in the hedge; he turned his tapering head as he ran, brush streaming behind him, never pausing nor slowing his pace. A colourful cock pheasant jumped from a wall ahead of them, preening himself and trailing his iridescent tail, then, in a clash of sound and a blur of feathers, he flew off again. Rebecca clapped her hands in glee and Joshua, looking into the vivid eyes with their fringe of black lashes, saw how luminous and touched with blue were the whites of her eyes.

He steadied the curricle, gentling the horses as they approached the stone dipping bridge that spanned the river Ewenny. Through the sheep dipping holes, Rebecca could see the course of the river as it flowed between woods of sycamore and ash, and the sudden metallic gleam of a kingfisher. Along country lanes dappled with light, past the ancient priory of Ewenny, then up the steep hill which had the horses sliding and the curricle bobbing like a shell upon a wave. Below them, a view of the countryside which caused her to draw in her breath, lost in admiration of the richly-patterned fabric of green, ochre and deep, earthy brown. Like a tapestry of carefully woven threads, Rebecca thought. They turned off the highway into a wooded incline, which, in the spring, Joshua told her, was a sea of small, wild daffodils, and then a darker tide of bluebells. Through the stony ford at Castle-upon-Alun, with the splash and graze of the horses' slithering hooves and the flung spray of the carriage wheels, then the rumble of dry land again. Joshua reined the horses close, stopped, then climbed down. He put his hands to her waist, and swung her from the carriage.

'There is someone I want you to meet. A dear friend of mine, my tutor, Dr Peate.'

Dr Peate emerged from the shadowed porchway of the church, a small, delicate-boned figure, with the stoop of one who spends too much time at his books. He held out both his hands to Rebecca, and she took them, remarking their frailness. Surprisingly, his hair was long and fine as a child's, an impression heightened by the unwavering, childlike candour of his eyes.

'Miss de Breos,' he bowed, 'Joshua has told you of the task he has set me?'

'No, sir, he has told me nothing.'

'Then that is remiss of him. He has asked me to trace your family history.'

Rebecca was very still, then looked at Joshua enquiringly.

'Dr Peate has found a line of descent. An unbroken

genealogy from a Norman called de Breos, one of the twelve knights of Glamorgan.'

'More. I have actually traced a record of the wedding of your parents, they are named on the register, here at this very church. I can show you the graves of your forebears; your grandfather and others of your family live here still, within the vale, Miss de Breos.'

Seeing that her face was flushed and her hands trembling, he said, contritely, 'Come, sit for a while, here in the church porchway, for I can see that you are unsettled, shocked. We should not have blurted it out so nakedly. It was thoughtless and clumsy.' When she was seated, he asked, anxiously, 'Have you any papers of your father's? Letters? Documents, perhaps?'

'None. He burned them all in one great blaze before he died. He warned me to ask nothing of anyone, expect nothing.'

'Then he was a sad mistaken man.'

'No, a good man. His secrets were his own, as his life was his own.'

'But your life was not his to bargain with, or order; he should have given you the choice,' insisted Joshua.

'I have taken my choice. I want nothing of these people. I am nothing to them, or they to me. If they wronged him, then they wronged me. There is an end to the matter,' she said, with dignity.

She turned to Dr Peate. 'I believe, sir, that what you have done, you did in kindness, with the best of intentions, and I thank you for it. But as you know, they sometimes pave the pathway to a hell not of our own making . . .'

Dr Peate asked gently, 'Will you at least let me tell you who seeks you?'

'No, it is better not. Now I must be away to Joshua's farm, for his family await me. I fear I shall discomfort them enough, without adding unpunctuality to my sins.'

Dr Peate took her hand. 'You will not disappoint them, for you are a very remarkable woman, Miss de Breos. Had I the rare privilege of meeting someone like you in my younger days, then I might not have chosen to become fossilized within my books.'

Joshua looked startled, then bade Dr Peate a civil goodbye.

'If, at some time, you should again visit your friend at Tythegston,' Rebecca said with dignity, 'it would give me great pleasure to receive you at my house.'

'Then I will most certainly come. You have my word upon it.' Dr Peate bowed and walked away.

When she was again seated in the curricle, and Joshua had taken up the reins, she asked, white with fury and hurt, 'Is that why you asked him to research it, because you wanted to offer something better than Rebecca the cockle-maid?'

'No! It was never in my thoughts!'

'I wish I could believe it. You will not tell them what you have discovered.' It was a command, not a question. 'For I am the same girl you first saw with Jeremiah, the same as this morning and yesterday. If they accept me, it is for what I am and not whom I might be. I am a person in my own right, not my father, or my grandfather, or whoever has gone before me.'

'They have helped to make you what you are, Rebecca, your blood, your character.'

'What I am now they have forced upon me. Have they done my work for me? Fed and clothed me? My character, for good or ill, is my own. If you cannot accept me as I am, then I beg you to drive me home, for there is no point in our being together. If you wish to continue this visit, then drive on.'

In silence, Joshua tugged at the reins, and drove on.

When she thought about it, afterwards, Rebecca could never be quite sure when the visit had begun to go wrong. Perhaps, she admitted to herself, her encounter with Dr Peate, and Joshua's attempt to establish an acceptable background for her had made her prickly and more susceptible to hurt. Or it might have been, simply, that they were all trying too hard to find some common ground, for Joshua's sake. He, awkward and ill at ease, was anxious that the people he loved best in the world should make a good impression, consequently, he became over effusive and unnatural, and ended by irritating them all. When Rebecca had been asked, 'Did you find the journey tedious?' and 'Was the carriage comfortable?' she replied, honestly, 'No, it was not tedious, I found it most enthralling. I have never been beyond the village before. As for the carriage, when you travel to the beach each day to gather cockles by cob and cart, it was a luxury beyond belief!' There was a brief, but strained, silence, before they all rushed in to fill it with innocuous chatter.

'What a pretty dress, my dear,' Mrs Stradling said. 'You have made it quite beautifully. I see that you are used to working with your hands.'

Rebecca, acutely aware of her roughened skin and that her dress, although pretty, was unfashionable and appeared home-made, was put at a disadvantage. Joshua, trying to ease her distress, announced that her drawings were so fine that she actually sketched and designed patterns for the local dress-maker. His mother, realizing her mistake, but unable to rectify it, gave a nervous smile, which Rebecca construed as superciliousness.

'I wonder, with all your . . . activities, that you find the time.'

'Oh, I do it out of necessity,' Rebecca explained, 'for since I have nursed Jeremiah Fleet at my house, and in my bed, I am no longer able to go cockle-gathering.'

'Jeremiah is a very old friend ... of us both,' Joshua explained, uncomfortably, 'Rebecca has taken him into her house, for he is alone, and there is no one else to care for him.'

'I see. What exactly does he do?' Mrs Stradling asked helplessly.

'He catches fish, when he is well and able to do so and he also makes lamp-oil from boiled fish livers, when they are rancid enough.'

Joshua's brother, Alex, who was balancing a plate of cake in his hand while seated upon the sofa, let out a snort of laughter, catching a crumb in his throat which made him cough so much that Joshua had to thump him uncommonly hard upon the back to dislodge it.

Aled caught Rebecca's eye and his laughter was so spontaneous and good-natured that she could not help but laugh with him.

'Oh, Rebecca,' he said, eyes still streaming, 'how refreshing you are after all the prim, namby-pamby young ladies we know. They have not a thought in their heads, other than fashion and flirting. I can see that we will be firm friends. Joshua tells me that your library and reading habits put him to shame.'

There followed a more general discussion of books and poetry, which led to good-natured argument over philosophy, languages and other less contentious and workaday topics. It was during this exchange that Joshua's father made his entrance from the farm.

Physically, and in character, he was as unlike his two sons as it was possible to be. While they were tall, fair and fine-featured, he was stolid, dark and a little under average height; he was firm in his views, authoritarian, and demanded respect as head of the household. Rebecca, the individualist, was unable to give it to him, believing it to be a tribute to be earned. Although the meeting, until then, had been sometimes awkward and unsatisfactory, all was not irretrievably lost. It was when he remarked to Joshua, 'So this is the friend you were bringing to see us, Joshua. You did not mention who. I had thought one of the delightful young ladies we had entertained before.'

'No,' replied Rebecca, her lovely voice level and two spots of colour burning high in her cheeks, 'I have not been entertained here, sir.'

He looked at her, keenly, 'I take it that you are the young woman he has been visiting in the village.'

'I am a friend of Joshua's, yes.'

'You work upon the shore?' he asked, abruptly.

'As you, sir, work upon the land. It seems that we have something in common.' His lips tightened. 'Really? Apart from a fondness for Joshua, I confess I am at a loss to see it, Miss . . .'

'de Breos,' said Aled, quickly. 'Will you have some more tea, Rebecca? A piece of cake, perhaps? You, father?'

His father took the cup of tea he offered. Rebecca declined, smiling.

'I believe that you approve of this . . . escapade of Joshua's?'

'His work as constable, you mean, sir? Yes. He is able and conscientious, and much respected for it.'

'As you are respected for yours?'

'I would hope so, sir, for it is honest work, honestly done ... however, it helps me retain my self-respect, which is more important to me.'

'And what do your parents think of it?'

'They are both dead, sir, but were they alive, I believe that they would be grateful for my independence and resourcefulness. It is not work I would choose to do. I do it from necessity, merely to live. If, like Joshua, I had the good fortune to be offered work I loved, and was able to do it well, then I am sure that they would be glad for me.'

'I think, Father, that Rebecca has had quite enough of a catechism for one day,' said Joshua, barely controlling his anger. 'As a guest in this house, I am ashamed that she has been treated with such discourtesy. Will you not come, Rebecca, and see the animals and some of the farm? Aled, will you come with us?'

'Of course, it will give me pleasure. Shall we not start at the piggery, Rebecca, for the air there is purer, and the atmosphere altogether less stifling than in here.' And Aled winked at her, companionably.

With a brother upon either arm, Rebecca went out into the yard.

'Joshua was right,' said his mother, 'you were unpardonably rude. It was unforgiveable. You will not only antagonize, but alienate your son. Is that what you want? She is an intelligent, kind girl, honest and full of spirit. I am sure that given time, and instruction ... example ...' she broke off, helplessly.

'She will not do, Charlotte! I told you so when you first mentioned her to me, when you visited Joshua. Is she, truthfully, what you had in mind for him?'

She shook her head, wordlessly. And then admitted, 'No, my dear, she simply will not do.'

Chapter Twenty

The return journey to Newton had been, for both Joshua and Rebecca, a disappointing and chastening affair. Aled had been unfailingly kind, and supported her openly during her visit to the farm, at the risk of increasing his father's displeasure and bearing the brunt of it, later. Rebecca was grateful to him. She knew that, in part, his solicitousness was a reaction against his father's churlishness and a kind attempt to soften her feeling of rejection. But he made no secret of the fact that he liked her for herself. He found her funny, intelligent, and courageous, as well as remarkably pretty, and Joshua was sure that he would remain a staunch and articulate advocate.

Joshua was not surprised by his father's opposition, for he had faced it in many small battles, and the greater one of becoming a constable. His commitment to Rebecca was equally strong and he had already determined that, if necessary, he would break with his family rather than lose her. Joshua's greatest disappointment had been in his mother's attitude. He had always considered her to be intelligent, fair-minded, and honest with herself and others. Overtly, she had treated Rebecca politely: there was no single incident which he could cite to show her disapproval, which she could not have defended by pleading innocence of the circumstances, or an over-eagerness to be kind, yet her reservations were obvious. He supposed that her upbringing and the strictures of society meant more to her than she had previously allowed. She was unable to face the criticism, or amused scorn of her peers; judgements which she had formerly affected to despise. She had always impressed upon her sons the need to do what was honest, without being swayed by the opinions of others. 'Well,' thought Joshua, tugging the reins unnecessarily hard, 'perhaps she was being honest with herself and believing that an alliance with Rebecca could only bring grief, and ultimate disaster.' He only knew that, without Rebecca, his work, family, and the whole of his future would hold such little meaning that he could not bear to think of it.

He reached out a hand and touched hers, briefly, before returning to the reins. The glance she gave him, and the smile, were candid and warm, as she fingered the brooch which Jeremiah had given her, as if it were some sort of talisman. He wanted to tell her that he had been wrong about asking Dr Peate to search for her family. He had done so out of affection; that she might have the comfort of 'roots' and history. He realized now that she had need of none of these things. She was, as she claimed, a woman in her own right, secure in the knowledge of her own worth. He had been wrong, too, in putting forward her skills at drawing. It had been said out of simple pride at her achievements, yet had the effect of making her feel dull, and ill-dressed, and suspicious that he was ashamed of what she was. His mother, elegantly gowned, charming, had played the part of hostess impeccably. Had she, perhaps, been a little too fastidious in her preparations? If she had not, would he then have thought that she had not considered Rebecca worthy of special care? And his father ... If Joshua had actually told him that it was Rebecca he was bringing, would it have given him time to accept her more gracefully, or merely time to whip up stronger resentment? Damn it! he thought, angrily, for the mess it is!

Rebecca was scarcely aware of the countryside through which they passed: the hedges alive with sound and movement, and pink with ragged robin, early foxgloves, and a white frosting of Queen Anne's lace. She was thinking of her humiliation at the farm, and recognizing that she was unacceptable to Joshua's parents. She was deliberating, too, on what Dr Peate had told her of her family. From what she had seen of the discord and unkindness of the Stradling family, blood relationship was not always a blessing. Most of all, she was thinking of Jeremiah, and the two women waiting at the cottage, convinced that everyone at the farm would immediately love her as unreservedly as they. As they approached the cottage, a small tear ran down the side of her nose, and she scooped it into her mouth with her tongue, so that Joshua would not see it, and sat up straight.

At the door she bade him good-day, thanking him for his kindness, and the pleasure of the journey, and seeing the farm. He agreed, helplessly, when she begged him not to come in but to contact her on the morrow.

There was no need for Jeremiah and the good Hannah and Widow Cleat to ask anything of her. As soon as she entered she began to weep, then ran to Jeremiah, pulling off her bonnet with the browning rose, and drenching his nightshirt with her tears, while he soothed and hugged her, helplessly. Then she was packed off to her bed, sheets warmed with a hot brick wrapped in flannel, as the Widow Cleat dressed her in her nightgown, after undressing her like a small child. Hannah kissed her goodnight and insisted that she keep the candle burning at her bedside for as long as it was needed.

'They are stupid, ignorant people,' the Widow Cleat said, dismissing them briskly, 'stuffed full of their own importance and prejudice! Do not dignify them by even giving them a thought, much less a tear!'

Rebecca wondered how many times she had said the same words to Illtyd, then hugged him for comfort. She could still hear their voices, and Jeremiah's raised in sorrow and anger, when she finally fell asleep.

Dr Burrel put on his overcoat, and looked around him at the simple, cell-like hut which had been his resting place since Rebecca had brought him here, hidden under the blankets in her cart. The time for concealment was past. Perhaps ebecca
her cart. The time for concealment was past. Perhaps Rebecca was right and what he had needed was time to recover his strength, and strength of purpose, in this bleak, monastic calm; isolated, and free from distraction.

Now, resolute in his mind and intent, he selected an ash-branch from those which he had carved, to use as a walking aid, looked down approvingly at his comfortable walking shoes and, closing the door to the shepherd's hut, set out for Mansel's house.

Rebecca had told him that she would be away at the constable's farm in the Vale, and Joshua with her, on a journey that would take most of the day. Burrel felt a vague stirring of unease and guilt at deceiving her. She was a gentle girl, loyal and honest. She had risked enough by befriending him; it would have been cruel to put her in further jeopardy by betraying his intentions. If she did not know what he planned, then she could not be held culpable for any repercussions which might follow the act.

He decided that he would keep, as far as possible, to the lanes and footpaths through the fields, rather than the open road. It was likely that the constable had told others of his involvement with the disappearance of Madeleine Mansel. Having made up his mind, he did not want to be deflected from his purpose; it had taken him a long, bitter time, and much soul searching. He hoped that Rebecca would understand.

When he arrived at Mansel's gates, he felt tired, and the old weakness and sweating began, with the palpitations in his chest. He paused for a moment, sick and light-headed, leaning upon the ash-stick, then forced himself to walk through the gates and up to the front door.

He saw no gardener or groom as he had feared he might, and turning the knob of the front door found that it opened easily, but with a noise which seemed to screech in his ears and head interminably. He found that he was trembling uncontrollably from fear and anticipation, but he forced himself to cross the deserted hall and then open the door which faced him. Once inside, he leaned heavily against it, willing it to close silently, and when he had nerved himself to look up saw Mansel watching him, perplexedly, but without alarm.

Burrel realized then, that Mansel did not recognize him.

'Well,' Mansel demanded, brusquely, 'who are you? And what do you want of me? This is a private house. You have no business here.'

'I have every business,' said Burrel, walking forward slowly to approach the desk.

'How did you get in here? Did you ring the bell? The servants should have stopped you ... I see patients only by appointment!' Dr Mansel said, irritably, and stood up to reach for the bell-pull.

Burrel eased swiftly around the side of the desk and grabbed his wrist, preventing him. Mansel turned upon him furiously, trying to wrench himself free, but unable to throw off the fierce strength of Burrel's thin fingers.

'Damn it, man! Have you gone mad? Who the hell are you? What do you want?' A vein throbbed at his temple, and his face was flushed with anger, 'For God's sake, tell me what you want!'

'Sit down.' Burrel's voice was calm, reasonable, but it seemed to disturb Mansel more, and for the first time Burrel saw a glimpse of fear in the opaque eyes, and a sense of realization.

'Burrel? You!' For a moment Burrel was almost sorry for him, for his features seemed to dissolve into formlessness and his whole body sag, until he made a conscious effort to control himself.

'Mansel, I have come to do you no harm, I promise you. I am here to tell you that I know nothing of Madeleine, or her whereabouts. I want you to believe that . . . for it is important to me, you understand?'

Mansel nodded, bewildered and silent.

'It is of no account, now, and whether you believe it or not is immaterial, but I did not operate upon Ella Pearce. I did not kill her . . . I wanted that child. I would have died myself rather than have either of them hurt. Are you listening, Mansel?'

Mansel still did not speak, running a hand through the wispy, fly-away hair and simply nodding again.

'I swear before God that I knew nothing of the operation, or why it was done, or who persuaded her. I could only think, at first, that it was you, and when it had gone wrong . . .'

'I?' Mansel almost screamed it aloud. 'You think it was I? What reason would I have, man?'

'Or I?' Burrel demanded. 'For my wife knew of the child and that I intended to go away, make a home with Ella and the child, until I was free to marry her . . .'

'That was not said at the trial!'

'Should it have been? There was no longer a need . . . and my wife was the innocent one, caught up in a nightmare which destroyed three people. She had suffered enough.'

'Then in the name of God, man. Who . .?

'Someone she knew: a person she trusted through association; someone, perhaps, who despised or actively hated me and wanted to see me suffer ... It had to be someone vicious and cruel enough to persuade Ella to murder the child.'

He saw the terrible comprehension in Mansel's eyes before the man lay his head upon his arms and wept.

Burrel sat there silently, and after a few moments, he looked up.

'I had wondered ...' Mansel admitted, helplessly, 'but I thrust the thought from me. I could not bring myself to believe ...' he broke off, bleakly.

'Now,' said Burrel, rising, 'all is open between us. There is no more to be said.'

Mansel looked at the figure standing awkwardly before him, gaunt, sick, unrecognizable as the young man whom, he realized, he had distrusted jealously, but without cause.

'I am sorry ... I am truly sorry, Burrel, I swear I had no knowledge of this. I beg you to believe me.'

Burrel nodded slowly, and Mansel continued.

'To me you seemed to have everything: success, money, a wife who ...'

Burrel's mouth twisted wrily, 'You want to ask if she stood by me? The answer is yes ... but she died three years later, in the cholera outbreak, as hundreds of others. I do not know if things would have been different if she had lived; or if the child and Ella had lived. Perhaps I would have found Ella's dependency cloying, the simplicity which attracted me to her, tedious and empty ... Or perhaps we would be living together still, with a son or a daughter little younger than I was then. But for you, Mansel, there is always the thought that your wife will return.'

Mansel looked at him uncomprehendingly.

'You will not spend twenty-three years trapped in a prison from which there is no escape. Now I will leave you, and I will find my way, openly, for I have hidden long enough. I will remain here for one more day, for there is a friend I must speak to. After that, I promise you that you will see me no more. Goodbye, Mansel. Believe me when I say that I wish you well.'

After he had gone, Mansel sat for a long while at his desk, his face registering no emotion. Then he roused himself, and pulled open the drawer of the desk. He lifted out the gun, feeling it cold in his palm, then replaced it and locked the drawer.

Rebecca, to Jeremiah's great relief, seemed to have recovered from the disappointment of her visit to Joshua's family. He supposed that it was the natural resilience of the young, like shoots of grass which, crushed underfoot and seemingly broken, spring back into green life. He was glad that he was old. Time put things into perspective; softened and blurred the edges of hurt. Or was it simply that with the aging of the body, and the dulling of eyes and ears, came a dulling of feeling? The numbing of emotions? Nature's way, perhaps, of protecting the old when the spirit and fire of youth had gone. No, he did not regret the passing of the rage and passion, the swift change from ecstasy to the depths of hopelessness, he only regretted the passing of people ...

Jeremiah wanted, now, to be back in the normal tide of life. He was missing the ebb and flow of routine. He yearned, first of all, to walk with the dog upon the wet sand, feeling the sea-wind upon his skin, and to thrust his hands into the cold of the rock-pools and set his night-lines on the edge of the shore; idleness was no life for a man. When Rebecca was out for any short space of time, he had taken to getting up and walking around the bed and then, as he grew stronger, sitting upon the chair and looking through the window into the yard, and the sand dunes beyond. Yesterday, he told Rebecca, proudly, he had even persuaded his 'two gaolers' to bring him his clothes, then hide themselves in the larder while he dressed. He had stayed up for a whole hour and, as it was a mild day and warm, had taken a turn outdoors to see the cob, the bull terrier barking with excitement around his feet ... She scolded him for his recklessness, claiming that he was undoing all her good work, and was 'an obstinate, ungrateful old man', and she had no patience with him! Jeremiah knew that she was as delighted as he that his strength was returning and he felt a need to be free.

As she went about her usual tasks of sweeping and dusting, he bided his time, and when she was engrossed in making her bed upstairs he dressed and went to sit at the window again.

She heard the hoarse urgency in his cry, 'Rebecca! Quickly!' and ran down the staircase, fearful of how she might find him. He was staring incredulously into the yard as she ran to the window to join him.

'It is him! The man I told you about. Look, girl, he is coming here to the door. Quick! Hide yourself away. Let me answer it.' He jumped to his feet nervously.

'No!' She put her arms about his shoulders, and gently settled him back into his chair. 'I know him. It is Dr Burrel. He means us no harm, Jeremiah.'

'No harm? But Joshua is searching for him!'

'Hush, I will explain later ... for now, simply accept him as a friend, for it was he who came to you in your sickness. He helped you, Jeremiah. You were right ... you did not dream it! I could not give him away ...'

She ran to the door and opened it, exchanging greetings, and Dr Burrel came into the room with them. He smiled at Jeremiah and held out his hand. Jeremiah took it, but looked ill at ease and confused.

'You have improved greatly, Jeremiah, since last I saw you. I am very glad of that, for your young nurse had all but despaired of you ...'

'Dr Burrel sat with you through the night when your fever was at its peak ...' Rebecca's eyes pleaded with Jeremiah. 'He tended you, and would not leave until the fever had broken and he believed you would mend ...'

Jeremiah looked from one to the other helplessly, and she continued.

'He risked much in coming here ... for they were searching for him. Do you not recollect what he did to help you?'

Jeremiah shook his head. 'I remember so little ... save that I saw you then. But I must thank you, sir, for your kindness. If I have been remiss in expressing my gratitude, or lacked warmth, it is because all this is new to me and I am bewildered and slow to understand.'

'Then I will explain it to you. How Rebecca has trusted me, and cared for me ... and what has transpired since, for I would have you both believe that her trust was not misplaced.'

They listened, feeling pity, and with a sense of shame for the injustice he had endured for so long. When he had completed his story with the visit to Dr Mansel, Jeremiah asked, his voice rough.

'What will you do now, sir?'

'I shall leave today, as I promised Mansel.'

'Where will you go?' asked Rebecca, bleakly. 'For now you have no home, or family. You are welcome to make your home here with Jeremiah and me ...'

Burrel took her hand, the pressure of his fingers upon hers firm and reassuring. 'You have been kinder to me than you know, Rebecca. I shall not forget it. The greatest service you did was to make me look into myself and to see that bitterness and regret corrode the present, as they destroy the past. What has gone before cannot be altered. I must let it go. But now, and tomorrow, are in my control. I can make of them what I choose ...'

'And what do you choose?' she asked quietly.

'The only thing I know ... helping, as I helped Jeremiah.'

'Will you be allowed to do so? I mean after what has happened?'

'Prison, you mean?'

She nodded.

'Then do not be afraid to say it. There is much sickness in the towns. The cholera epidemic spreads each day, and there are so few to help. I do not think the victims will care too much, or enquire too deeply ...'

'But you are already sick, yourself. You are not yet truly recovered from your fever.' Rebecca protested. 'It would not be right to put yourself at risk!'

'I have little enough to lose.'

'Then I will come with you! I am used to hard work. I will do anything, however menial.'

'Oh Rebecca,' he said. 'What am I to do with you, for I believe you really mean it! No, my dear, it would not do at all! I have taken responsibility for things I did not choose, or do ... I would not now take responsibility for any living person, particularly the one person in life who means something to me.'

'He is right,' said Jeremiah, stoutly.

'You are young, Rebecca. You have the whole of life before you. There will be so many opportunities before you, places to see ... people to love ... so much to learn and give to others. Promise me that you will not throw it away untried, but make the most of every new experience which comes your way ...'

Rebecca said, 'I will try, I promise.'

'Perhaps you will write to me from time to time with news of yourself and Jeremiah. It would please me to know. It would help to make up for the other years.'

Jeremiah said, 'She has a good hand, sir, and can read like the best of scholars, as you well know, being one yourself. I can neither read nor write, for I was never taught ... but if you would like me to say things which Rebecca can set down on paper, then I will do it with good heart, and in gratitude for what you have done for me.'

Burrel grasped his hand and shook it solemnly.

'With two good friends, I am rich indeed,' he said. 'I will bid you both goodbye with the fervent hope that we will meet again before too long. Even if we do not, then I shall value having known you ... for I will not need your presence to remind me of your goodness. The remembrance of it will be with me every day.'

Rebecca kissed him, and threw her arms around him affectionately before he drew away. She walked with him to the front gate, insisting that he leave openly, by the proper way.

He walked some yards along the pathway to the village, then turned back to face her, gaunt, pallid, but with his eyes unnaturally bright.

'I had thought to take revenge, perhaps in a death,' he said gently. 'So you have given me two lives: another's and my own!'

When Rebecca and Joshua met again, after their disastrous visit to his father's farm, Jeremiah had expected to find that there was a coolness between them, a certain restraint. However, they greeted each other warmly and without reserve, and Joshua's attitude towards Jeremiah was no less affectionate. By tacit agreement, Dr Burrel's visits were not mentioned to the young constable and Rebecca hoped that it would never be necessary to reveal the part she had played in hiding him in the shepherd's hut, or her furious early morning ride to bring him to Jeremiah's bedside. Her justification was that Dr Burrel was innocent and had undoubtedly saved the old man's life. Some intuitive sense had told her that he was a man to be trusted. Hardly something of validity in law, or to Joshua, she knew. Sometimes she wondered uneasily what would have happened if she had been wrong, and how she could have lived for the rest of her life with the knowledge of it.

Now, however, Joshua had been summoned to Dr Mansel's house and told of the encounter with Burrel. He had returned to Rebecca's cottage immediately to discuss it with her and Jeremiah.

'It seems, after all, that Dr Burrel was innocent,' he explained, 'or so Dr Mansel believes.'

'What do you believe?' Rebecca asked, sharply.

'That what they suspect is very likely true. Mansel's wife might well be guilty.'

'What will happen to her, Joshua? If she is found, I mean.'

'Nothing. What could happen? It is all conjecture. There is not a shred of proof ... Besides, why should she admit it? Burrel would not testify against her. In any case, he has gone away and might never be traced.'

'It seems all wrong,' said Jeremiah, hotly, 'a decent man like Burrel losing everything ...'

'Met him, have you, Jeremiah?'

'It would hardly be likely that he would visit me!'

Joshua looked at him hard, and Rebecca, seeing the slow flush that crept up his face, said, 'Like you, we make our own judgements on what Dr Mansel says ...'

'Of course,' agreed Joshua, evenly. 'You would hardly have hidden him away, or befriended him, knowing him to be a killer.'

'No ... certainly not knowing him to be a killer,' repeated Jeremiah. 'Oh, damn it!' he cried angrily. 'Enough of this nonsense, he did come to see me! Rebecca fetched him in the middle of the night ...'

'The night you just happened to see the Crandles?'

'You knew!' she cried accusingly. 'You deliberately baited

me, and yet you knew all the time. What deceit! It is unforgiveable!'

'Hold hard!' he commanded, 'I do not think that either you or Jeremiah has anything to say about deceit ...'

'Go on, lecture us! Tell us that we were foolish, criminal even ... that we betrayed your friendship! You can no longer trust us ...'

'Is there any need?'

'Say what you will,' said Jeremiah, resignedly, 'I cannot deny that I have behaved badly, and I am ashamed of it and myself ... for you have been a true friend to me. Do not blame Rebecca, Joshua, for what she did was out of affection for an old friend ... and it saved my life.'

'Which is the only good thing to come out of this sorry business. I confess, Jeremiah, that I would very likely have done what Rebecca did, although I would have remembered my duty, afterwards! It has taught me the virtue of tolerance, keeping an open mind; I hope that you have learnt something equally salutary.'

'Oh yes,' said Rebecca fervently. 'First that you have missed your vocation as a preacher. Second, that the next time Jeremiah is at Death's door, I shall call at the "Crown" for the gaol-coach, for not only will I travel in comfort, but you can drive us directly to the cells!'

Joshua's mouth twitched. He turned to Jeremiah.

'Shall I tell you the greatest miracle any man will ever perform? Having the better of an argument with a woman!'

He stilled her exclamations with a kiss, which Rebecca thought absurdly unfair, although she made no protest.

Having ridden off, cheerfully, on the grey, Joshua went directly to the 'Crown' for a final word with the Widow Cleat and Rosa, who were putting the finishing touches to the coachhouse loft. Emily Randall was expected to arrive from the workhouse within the hour, the landlord having sent the hire-coach to fetch her, free of charge. Ossie had volunteered to drive her, and had been waiting all the morning in a lather of excitement and pleasure. He had set off, with the carriage and horses gleaming like newly minted sovereigns, and he, scrubbed and polished to match. In fact, his usual russet cheeks looked like rosy winesap apples, the skin so taut with scrubbing that a smile seemed likely to split them apart. Joshua was grateful to Rosa and the Widow Cleat for the selfless way they had worked to scour, furnish and equip the loft. It was clean, airy, and full of soft, pretty touches to make it welcoming. Rosa had brought with her a dainty blue and white transfer jug, bright with yellow marigolds, which she had placed on a small cricket table which Joshua's mother had supplied. Her elegant gowns, bonnets and gloves were prettily arranged in a corner of the room, behind a curtain, awaiting their new owner. Best of all, a tempting meal was cooking upon the fire and hob, newly installed by the landlord, who sent a note of welcome, bidding her use those facilities of the inn which might be of use to her. Her small cupboard-larder was filled with produce from the farm and some of the Widow Cleat's fresh brown eggs and Hannah's vegetables. What moved Joshua most was the genuine affection and goodwill felt by the two women to someone they did not even know, with no other claim to kinship than simple need.

When Ossie brought her in, Joshua could see that her pale composure had deserted her; her fine brown hair escaped in tendrils from the coil at her nape, her hands fidgeted restlessly with her gown. She came forward hesitantly, extending her hand to Joshua in greeting.

'Good day to you, Mr Stradling. It was kind of you to send the carriage.'

A small nerve fluttered beneath her eye as she spoke.

'Good day, Miss Randall. I hope that you will be happy in your new home. Rosa and Mistress Cleat have worked eagerly to prepare it for you.'

She looked about her carefully, taking in every detail, but saying nothing. Rosa and the Widow Cleat exchanged troubled glances. She was, they feared, very elegant and assured, perhaps it was not grand enough? Sudden tears softened her eyes, then spilled over, coursing down her cheeks and chin. They seemed to have nothing to do with the otherwise calm, poised woman, standing erect, and making no sound. She ran forward and clasped her arms around the

Widow Cleat, and then Rosa, and drew them close.

'I have always lived in other people's houses,' she said quietly, 'I have never before had a place of my own. A home... If I had been allowed to furnish it in any way I chose, it could never have been as perfect as this, there is not one single thing I would wish to add or change. I thank God for it, as I thank Him for delivering me from the life I would have led. Most of all, I thank Him for giving me friends such as you, for today, I feel truly blessed ...'

The Widow Cleat and Rosa, looking pink and pleased, hugged Emily Randall in return, and soon they were all three smiling, crying and talking together as if they had been inseparable from birth. They set out the tea cups, and offered refreshment to Joshua and Ossie, but they declined, promising themselves something stronger, while claiming to allow the good ladies time to become better acquainted.

'Women are strange creatures,' declared Ossie, over a tankard of ale. 'I cannot make head nor tail of them. They cry when they are happy, yet if they are really distressed, they pretend not to care a whit!' He shook his head in puzzlement. 'They are quite different from horses and men.'

'I had noticed,' said Joshua, gazing into his ale.

Rebecca, cutting pinks from the border in the small garden which fronted the house, buried her nose in their ragged-fringed petals. They smelled of cloves, and a softer, subtle fragrance all their own. Sometimes, after rain or a heavy dew, the scent of them seemed to drench the air itself, mingling with jasmine, rue, and the cool lemony smell of cypress.

The bull terrier, which condescended to accompany her into the garden now and again, gave a growl deep in its throat, hackles rising a warning. Before she even glimpsed the figure riding towards her, the dog had heard the thud of hooves on turf, as she now heard their rhythmic clopping upon the pathway. She grabbed the dog by his collar and, despite his protesting grumbles and snarls, bundled him safely inside, shouting a warning to Jeremiah to curb him.

She did not recognize the rider and wondered if, perhaps, he would take the track alongside the cottage and over the Warren to Merthyr Mawr and the river mouth.

Instead, he dismounted, took off his hat, bowing civilly, and enquiring, 'Miss Rebecca de Breos?'

'Yes, that is my name.'

'I have a letter for you, Mistress, I come here from your grandfather, Sir Matthew de Breos, of Southerndown Court.'

'I thank you for bringing it to me.' Rebecca took the letter, broke open the seal, and after reading the contents, replaced it carefully in the envelope.

'The gentleman who sends you is infirm perhaps?'

The messenger looked puzzled. 'No, Mistress, he is old, of course, but suffers no infirmities of the flesh.'

'He is sick, then? Perhaps he is afflicted with some fever, or pain?'

'No, Mistress.' The man fidgeted awkwardly with his hat. 'He is fit and well, thanks be to God! Save for those signs of aging which come to us all . . .' he added, wrily.

'I see.'

'There is a letter you wish to send him in return? A message, perhaps, which you would have me convey to Sir Matthew, my master?'

'Tell him, merely, that you have found me, as he required. If he wishes to see me, I am here. I will not come to him. He shall come to me . . . Good day to you, sir.'

'Good day, Miss de Breos.' He replaced his hat upon the straggling, grey hair, and remounted stiffly, clumsily. She watched him raise his hat courteously, then ride away.

A de Breos to her fingertips, the old servant was thinking in admiration, a woman of spirit and natural arrogance . . . pretty in face and speech. Her grandfather would be pleased with her, no doubt! But he would not have it easy. Oh no, he would not have it easy!

Chapter Twenty-One

To the people of the three hamlets, the sight of Illtyd, the little man, riding out upon his piebald pony, was a symbol of triumph; St George vanquishing his dragon could scarcely have experienced such rapture and acclaim. The Widow Cleat was much respected and Illtyd, for all his being a cripple, was gentle-natured and good. It would have been easy for him, they reasoned, to have sat in a corner, growing twisted and locked in mind, as in body. Instead, he had fought and won his spurs, become a man. It was doubtful if any one of them recognized that Illtyd's triumph was a victory over their own fears. Health, work, and a fierce determination were necessary to survive in a world which made no concessions, and showed little compassion to those too old, or weak, to make their own way. That Illtyd, the least of them, was a success, gave new spirit to them all.

If the vestrymen had any fears about the wisdom of appointing him as hayward, they were soon dispelled. Never had the common and downs been so trouble-free. The local flocks grew contented and fat, protected from thief and predatory bird. Those beasts which wandered by night from other parishes were swiftly impounded, and their owners warned. Persistent offenders risked a fine, or even confiscation of their stock. Those tempted to threaten or intimidate the little hayward into surrender were so abused by the villagers that they seldom returned. The few who did met the implacable obstacle of Doonan's fist. Everyone benefited from Illtyd's reign: the vestrymen were praised for their foresight in electing him; Joshua's standing and popularity grew with the gift of saddle and horse; Doonan earned respect as his protector, and the villagers relaxed, knowing that their animals and grazing rights were safe. As for Illtyd, what he lacked in physical stature, he now made up in new-found confidence.

Joshua, watching him from the sea-edge of Locks Common,

as he wove his way through the grazing animals on his piebald horse, wondered if the little man ever rested. He seemed to burn with restless vitality, as if his diminutive frame could not contain such energy. Joshua called out to him, and he came galloping across, smiling delightedly.

'Well, my friend,' asked Joshua, smiling in response, 'have you news for me of Doonan?'

'Yes. They have approached him, again. They will strike within the week, and have told him to hold himself ready for their command. He does not yet know the day or the hour he will be needed but, from the tides, he expects it to be between midnight and four of the clock.'

'How will they meet with him?'

'He is to be at the "Ship Aground" each night, and someone unknown to him will apprise him of their plans.'

'That should be no great inconvenience,' said Joshua, amused, 'for I swear he has worn a hole in the floor with his comings and goings.'

'He bids me say he will have no further talk with you, lest they suspect some involvement.' Illtyd's intelligent eyes were grave. 'I have begged him to take care, neither to talk nor drink too much, for already one man has died.'

'Wise advice, Illtyd. I commend it to you. You are sure that you desire to be part of this adventure?'

Illtyd looked at him intently, face inscrutable.

'I ask not because I doubt your courage, my dear friend, or your ability, simply because I would have you come to no harm. I have asked the same of Doonan, Ossie and Emrys.'

Illtyd nodded, satisfied. 'I would not miss it for the world. My blows may not bear the force of Doonan's, and I lack the experience of Ossie and Emrys in a fight, but I can ride through the narrowest gaps, or dart in and out to confuse them, or lure them after me, thinking me an easy target. Believe me, I will not be a hindrance to you, Joshua ...' he said earnestly.

Joshua put a hand upon Illtyd's shoulder, briefly touching the awkward curve of the bone.

'You are the finest man I know,' he said honestly, 'in spirit and in flesh. There is no one I would rather have beside me.'

Illtyd nodded and rode away, his remarkable eyes alert.

Joshua left him for a meeting he relished less, and of which he had no sanguine expectations. When Illtyd told him of Hannah's belief that Ezra the Box kept his 'earnings' in his own coffin, his friends had laughed. They believed poor Jeremiah to be afflicted with some feverish dream. Joshua was all too convinced of the reality of the claim, although he was at a loss to know how he could test it. Assuming that the wily Ezra had not already drunk the evidence, or removed it to some equally ingenious hiding place, he was sure to disclaim all knowledge of its source.

Joshua left the grey with Ossie at the 'Crown' and walked through the village to the carpenter's shop. He opened the street door and entered, savouring the smell of wood and the acrid pungency of the lotions and resins fused. Ezra came from the back of the shop, ingratiating as ever, wiping some slivers of wood from his shirt.

'Ah, Constable Stradling, an honour indeed.' He actually rubbed his hands together, as though washing away a stain. 'Well, sir, am I to be of service to you?'

'That is my hope,' said Joshua, wrily.

'A coffin, is it? For that poor unfortunate seaman? God rest his soul,' he said piously. 'Or will you be needing some furniture? A bed, perhaps ..?' he asked archly.

'A coffin ...'

Ezra looked discomfited. 'Have you something in mind?'

'Yes, I believe you could say that.'

'Pauper's plain would it be, then? Or something more fancy?'

'The fanciest you have!'

'Indeed?' Ezra's smile grew expansive, uncovering his small, pointed teeth. 'I am sure that I can accommodate you.'

'Not me,' confessed Joshua, straight-faced. 'I was thinking more of you.'

Ezra looked confused. 'Is it some joke you are making, Constable? I admit that I cannot, truthfully, see the point of it.' His little ferret face grew sharper.

Joshua made the mistake of glancing into the other room, where the ornately carved coffin was resting upon a cloth-draped bier. Before he had a chance to stride through to it,

Ezra was there before him, arms straddling the lid, holding it shut.

'It is not for sale!' he said, determinedly, 'It is my own. Nothing on earth would induce me to part with it . . . I have put my life into it!'

'And what else?' asked Joshua innocently, moving forward.

Ezra actually clambered upon the bier and seated himself upon the coffin lid, his pinched face unbecomingly flushed. Without a word, Joshua stretched his six-feet-three-inches of height, and lifted him to the floor.

'Come, little man,' he said, pleasantly, 'you are safer upon firm ground. I fear your temper might unbalance you, and topple you from your perch. It would be a pity to have use of the coffin too soon!' He lifted the heavy lid, while Ezra fumed and stamped a foot impotently upon the floor, scattering shavings.

'Well!' cried Joshua in mock amazement. 'What have we here?' He held up a bottle. 'Brandy, I declare, and what else? Tobacco ... Why, it is filled almost to the lid. There would scarcely be room for you, Mr Evans.'

'I can explain ...' cried Ezra, wildly. 'Let me explain.'

'No. Allow me to hazard a guess. You were following the lead of the Pharoahs: providing yourself with victuals and comfort for the after-life. Is that it?'

'Someone put it there.' Ezra blurted in desperation.

Joshua waited in silence.

'People are coming and going all the time . . . wanting things mended, or made. I cannot keep track of them.'

'Well, I had best remove the evidence, since it belongs to another ... but no, it might be better to call upon the exciseman. That is the only course open to me ... unless?'

'Unless what?' cried Ezra.

'Unless, of course, there is something you feel you have to confide?'

Ezra sat upon the edge of the bier, licking his dry lips. Joshua could see that his hands were trembling.

'As God is my judge ...'

'I think we may take that for granted.'

'Look ...' Ezra brushed away the film of sweat from his

upper lip, 'I am willing to make a bargain.'

'Oh, there is no urgency,' said Joshua expansively, 'I will give you twenty-four hours. When I return at the same time tomorrow, you will tell me who is behind this trade. I shall bring a friend with me who will be interested in some of your stock.'

'What stock?' demanded Ezra, hoarsely.

'That depends ... furniture, coffins, whatever you have to offer an exciseman.'

'Will you make me a promise?' Ezra's beady eyes blinked nervously.

'Yes ...' Joshua replied.

'You will?'

'That I will be back, Mr Evans.' He slammed the coffin lid shut. 'You may depend upon it. I will be back.'

When Joshua left the carpenter's shop and made his way back to his cottage, pausing to exchange courtesies, or pass the time of day with villagers and tradesmen, he was surprised to see a coach rounding the village green and continuing past the 'Ancient Briton'. He was further surprised to see that it was a town coach, driven by a liveried coachman, his colours of burgundy and gold reflecting those of the carriage, which bore a family coat of arms. As the pair of prettily matched horses passed by him, he stepped aside and glimpsed, through the window, a thin-featured elderly gentleman, sitting upright upon the seat, silk-hatted, the silver knob of his cane catching the light. It was certainly a nobleman's travelling carriage, elliptically sprung, extravagantly appointed. Joshua supposed that it belonged to some friend of the justice's, or the Knights at Nottage Court, who had been referred to the village for its sea-bathing. He half thought that the escutcheon seemed familiar, but seeing Rosa in the distance, he hurried towards her, and dismissed it from his mind.

Jeremiah was so greatly improved in health and stamina that he had been allowed to take an outing. Despite all his protestations of feeling 'as active as a mole in spring,' the landlord of the 'Crown' had insisted on sending Ossie for him, with the carriage.

He was to join Hannah, the Widow Cleat and Emily Randall at her coach loft to see what improvements had been made and to take tea with the ladies. It had needed much persuasion upon Rebecca's part to get him to agree upon the expedition, for, he grumbled, he would stand out like a cock-pheasant in a flock of chattering starlings. Finally, upon the assurance that Ossie would not desert him, he had been prevailed upon to go. Rebecca was to walk over later to join the party. She had watched him leave some quarter of an hour since, scrubbed to within an inch of his life and wearing the neatly gusseted shirt from Rebecca's father, and the coat provided by the Widow Cleat.

Rebecca completed the few tasks she had set herself in his absence and, dressed in her blue dress, cloak, shoes and bonnet, was about to set out to join him. She had settled the bull terrier comfortably in his outhouse in the yard and reached the living room, reticule in hand, when there was a heavy knocking upon the door.

The old gentleman who stood there was tall, attenuated, and standing severely erect. The splendid coach, with its liveried coachman, was drawn up some distance from the cottage.

'You are Rebecca de Breos?'

'I am, sir.'

'And I am your grandfather, Matthew de Breos. You will see that I have come to you, as commanded.'

'Requested, sir,' she corrected, smiling, 'if you will come inside.'

He followed her into the long, low-ceilinged room, where she bade him sit. He did so, resting both his hands upon his stick, his silk hat upon the floor beside him, nodding in approval at small pieces of furniture and porcelain and enamel boxes which he recognized, then he stood up and went to stand beside the drawing of her father, asking, 'May I?'

Rebecca nodded. She saw, then, the similarity between the two men. It rested mainly in the eyes: wide, intense, almost hypnotic in their vitality. Whereas the rest of her father's features had been subdued, so that they appeared delicate, feminine even, her grandfather's were strong, and uncompromisingly masculine. She wondered how much of her grandmother had been in her father's features and character.

'Yes,' said the old man, smiling, 'it is very like... Who drew it?'

'I did, Grandfather.' She hesitated before using the word.

He nodded. 'You had a tutor?'

'No. My father taught me what little I know. The drawing I learnt naturally.'

He looked at the titles of the books in the bookshelves and took one out, studying the bookplate intently.

'This is a book I gave Edward as a child.' He looked suddenly older, more careworn. 'He told you of me, of his family?' His voice was anxious.

'No, nothing.'

'It was a stupid disagreement. It could easily have been resolved, but we were too alike, stubborn, independent,' he gestured helplessly. 'I think it is a characteristic which you might well have inherited.'

She nodded.

'You have read some of these?' he asked, replacing the book upon the shelf.

'Every one. A dozen times and more. I could have wished my library a thousand times larger.'

'Then you must make use of mine.'

'I am not sure if I am ready,' she said, honestly.

'It would be a service to me. My eyes are less acute, perceptive, I am no longer able to read as I once did, and my books feel the neglect. I would not disturb you, hinder you at all. I would ask nothing of you, save that you come.'

'Then I will gladly do so, Grandfather.'

He came and stood beside her and tilted her face upwards, scrutinizing her carefully.

'You are a de Breos,' he said, satisfied. 'From what Dr Peate has told me, in character as well as flesh. He believes you to be a very remarkable woman.'

'I have done what I had to do to survive.'

'I am sorry that it was necessary, and it grieves me. It grieves me more that I did not know of your existence, Rebecca, so could not help you.'

'I do not think I would have changed my life, sir. No,' she said more firmly, 'I am sure that I would not. Despite its harshness it has brought me many good friends, and some happiness. My only regret is that my education is sparse. It ended when my father died. There is so much I would like to learn, to see.'

'It is not too late, if that is what you want. Dr Peate would willingly advise and help you. He is a kind man, a fine scholar,' he broke off awkwardly, 'but I see, my dear, that I move too fast, make you afraid.'

'No, I am simply confused. Life is changing too quickly . . . I am not ready.'

He nodded, and said compassionately, 'I understand. Believe me, Rebecca, I do understand. When you are old, time is so precious, every moment is an extra blessing. At eighteen, it is different. The future stretches before you endlessly; so many pathways. You must choose carefully, the one you wish to take.'

'Will you give me time, Grandfather?' she asked, anxiously.

'As long as you need.' He rose to his feet. 'I see that you are dressed for a visit. You must not let an old man detain you.'

'Not an old man,' she said, stretching upwards to kiss him, gently, 'a grandfather, and he has privileges, rights.'

'Rebecca,' he said, 'I want you to believe me when I say, truthfully, that I claim no rights over you. You are free to do whatsoever you choose. I make no conditions, expect nothing of you. I am only glad to have found you. There is money which I have been putting regularly in trust for your father, in the hope that one day we would meet. It is yours to do with as you wish.' As she moved to protest, 'No, hear me out, my dear. You may have it at any time. I will make the necessary arrangements.'

'I am grateful to you.'

'Again, I will be honest and say that, more than anything, I would have you make your home with me, but if you do, it must be because that is what you want, and not out of duty, or pity, you understand? If you would prefer never to see me at all, then I must accept that, too.'

'Now that I have found you,' she said earnestly, 'I shall see that you are always a part of my life. As for the rest . . . a little more time.'

He nodded, satisfied. 'Why is it,' he asked, puzzled, 'that you are not known hereabouts by your proper name? It has been difficult to find you.'

She said, wrily, 'They know me as Dabrosse. Or simply, the cockle maid.'

He nodded. 'Dr Peate has told me some of your history. Will you not now tell them that you are a de Breos? It is a good name, and one to be proud of.'

'But grandfather, a name is but an accident of birth. It is the people who bear it who make it a good name, and one to be proud of. I have always tried to be proud of myself, and to do what is right. Is that not enough?'

'It is all that is required,' he said, quietly.

When Rebecca had sat for a time, and composed herself after her grandfather's departure, she set out for the coach loft. As she walked, she thought of what her life had been until now, and what it might have been. She believed it was the truth when she had told her grandfather that she would not have changed her life, but since she had known no other, how could she be sure? If you have nothing to compare it with, even deprivation becomes bearable, since there is no escape. She had never before questioned her father's motives in keeping her ignorant of his family and past life. If he had sought to bury his past, then it was his own affair, but had he the moral right to carry hatred beyond the grave, and to let it spill over and erode the lives of others? She wished she knew what to do. She knew that the love she felt for Joshua was deep and sincere. He loved her, she could not doubt it, for he was pleased to accept her as she was. It was his parents who rejected her. If she refused her grandfather's offer, she would not only be limiting her own future, but alienating Joshua from his family. If she accepted, then his family would approve her for the wrong reasons and she might grow to despise herself, and them. Worse, in changing, she and Joshua might grow apart, as she might distance herself from Jeremiah and all the friends she had grown to love.

As she walked disconsolately under the archway to the 'Crown', Ossie came out of the stables and, seeing her, ran forward in greeting, his weatherbeaten face alight with pleasure. He guided her up the stone staircase to the coach loft, where her entrance provoked excited welcome and admiration for her pretty gown, and the becoming flush upon her cheeks, which brightened her fine eyes.

Rebecca was pleased to confide to Emily Randall that the village dressmaker had declared that she would welcome her help as a seamstress. If she chose, Emily might stitch the garments at home, a privilege which so delighted her that she kissed Rebecca impulsively, and hugged her for her aid. Jeremiah and Ossie, although more restrained, were warmed by the newcomer's good fortune, and Rebecca's part in it, and for a time she was able to forget her dilemma, secure in the company of friends.

It was Rosa, arriving late, who unwittingly precipitated a crisis.

'Oh! Such excitement and talk in the village,' she cried, taking off her straw bonnet. 'Did you not see that magnificent coach? It bore a crest, and there was a liveried coachman. I have never seen anything so grand and distinguished! Whoever could it be?'

There was a flurry of excited gossip and speculation, during which Rebecca grew increasingly embarrassed and distracted, finally blurting out clumsily, 'It was my grandfather, Sir Matthew de Breos.'

There was a burst of laughter and renewed chatter, until Jeremiah, seeing her tenseness and the whiteness of her face, silenced them, and went to stand beside her, putting an arm about her shoulders for comfort.

'It is true!' she said despairingly, 'I know you do not believe me but he *did* come. He came to take me home.'

There was an awkward, uncomfortable silence which seemed to last a very long time. Finally, it was Jeremiah who spoke, almost inaudibly.

'And will you go?'

'I do not know what I should do, I honestly do not know.' Each of them recognized the strain and uncertainty in her voice. It was a plea for their help, but they looked at each other, unable to give it. Even Jeremiah only patted her shoulder and shrugged helplessly.

'You must think about it very seriously, for there are many things to consider.'

'He is your kin,' said the Widow Cleat, gravely, 'there is a tie of blood.'

'Yes,' agreed Emily. 'It is a special relationship, deeper even than friendship.'

'We will all miss you,' Ossie offered, his walnut face seamed with concentration, 'but it is a fine thing to have a family, a great opportunity.'

Already, Rebecca thought, they have accepted that I will go.

'Does Joshua know? Have you told him?' Rosa asked, quietly.

'No.'

'He will be very distressed. It will be a shock for him, I am sure. I know that Cavan would break his heart if we were to be separated. But, of course, I would not go ... it would be too hurtful and selfish.'

Jeremiah hushed her into silence, saying that it was not her decision to make, and the Widow Cleat added severely that, far from being selfish, it would be extremely unselfish to give comfort to a lonely old man.

'Which, being the kind, unselfish girl that she is, she has already brought to me,' said Jeremiah, eyes soft with tears of weakness and affection.

Rebecca excused herself from the company, urging Ossie not to be too late in bringing the coach for Jeremiah, as he was still not recovered from the illness and must rest. Their goodbyes were subdued, for the weight of change and uncertainty had formed a constraint upon their high spirits.

Rebecca knew that she could expect no help from Joshua. She must make up her own mind. If only Dr Burrel were here to help her! But she knew what he would say.

'You are young, Rebecca. You have the whole of life before you. There will be so many opportunities for you, places to see, people to love; so much to learn and give to others. Promise me that you will not throw it away, untried, but make the most of every new experience which comes your way.'

But Dr Burrel was not Joshua, and could not know the hurt of it.

'Joshua, my dear love,' she cried inwardly, 'how could I bear to be parted from you? Without you, every day would be empty and meaningless, as it was before you came. You are my own spirit and warm flesh. It is the same blood which stirs our veins; the same passion which quickens our life and loving. To cut myself off from you would be to know the beginning of a death ... I do not know if I have the strength to face life without you, or the courage to stay ...' The tears of bewilderment and pain fell silently, and she tasted the salt bitterness of them in her mouth, as she walked. 'Oh, grandfather,' she thought, despairingly, 'why did you give me the freedom to choose? In releasing me, you have tied my bonds tighter. Whomsoever I choose, one of you will be hurt, and I, Rebecca, most of all.'

When Jeremiah had returned, tired by his outing, and emotion, Rebecca made him a spiced mull of ale, to warm and comfort him, and settled him in his bed, with the dog ensconced beside him. Then she harnessed up the cob to her cart and drove thoughtfully to Joshua's cottage.

They talked far into the night, speaking honestly of their deep affection for each other, keeping nothing back about their hurt over Joshua's parents, their fears, and their hopes for the future, together or apart.

'Oh, Rebecca!' Joshua had cried, his voice rough with fear that she might choose to reject him. 'I love you more than life itself! I cannot bear to think of being without you. When you are not near me, it is as if a part of me has been wrenched away; I feel the loss as a physical hurt ...' He had taken her in his arms and kissed her gently, tenderly at first, then angrily as if to show her the urgency of his need. She had responded to him with the same violence, her body quickened by his flesh, and the intensity of her despair. But she felt, too, a great tenderness and pity, as she cradled his head to her breast, and stroked him as if he were a child, murmuring endearments, and wiping away the tears from his lashes.

It was Joshua who broke away from the embrace.

'I cannot beg you to stay,' he said with dignity, 'for I love you enough to let you go, if that is truly what you want, Rebecca. I can offer you nothing but a love which will deepen and grow with the years, and a body which worships you. I have no riches, no great prospects, nothing but what I am.'

Rebecca wanted to cry aloud that it was all in life that she had ever wanted, and that she loved him with a passion and singlemindedness which matched his own, but she did not speak the words.

When, eventually, they drove the cob home, all that remained was for Rebecca to make up her mind and act upon it.

Joshua, walking back to his cottage by the pallid light of the moon, felt tired and dispirited. A barn owl swooped down before him, a ghostly blur of feathers, and rose with a mouse in its talons, then soared to the safety of a loft. Somewhere in the distance a dog barked, a thin staccato edge of sound, and the night air was alive with the movement and scent of unseen things. Yet he felt himself to be alone upon the earth.

Rebecca took out pen and paper and wrote to her grandfather. She wrote swiftly, without alteration, then, not reading it, sealed the letter and set it upon her desk. Tomorrow, she would rise early and take it to the 'Crown Inn', and ask the postboy to carry it, on horseback, to meet the mail coach at Pyle. It was done. There was no turning back.

Chapter Twenty-Two

Rebecca arrived at the 'Crown Inn' the following morning just as the church clock was striking nine of the hour. There were few villagers about, for the men were already at their labours and the women busy at their household tasks. Those she met upon her way greeted her courteously, usually adding some comment upon their hopes for the weather, which dominated the pattern of their day. An old woman in one of the cottages beside the church was struggling along the garden pathway, carrying a wooden bucket of chamber pot slops. Shoulders bowed with the weight and the concentrated effort of not spilling any, she poured it carefully into a large earthenware vessel sunk into the soil, alongside the wooden trough she used for washing her clothes. The urine would be used, Rebecca knew, as a cold water bleach, as sometimes dung was, to be followed by a lye of wood-ash, or the residue of burnt ferns. The woman glanced up as Rebecca passed her gate, smiling toothlessly, glad of distraction.

'Good morning to you, Mistress Dabrosse.' She glanced overhead. 'A fine day, but I fear we must pay for it later. There will be rain for sure. The sky is ribbed as a skeleton.'

'Yes, I fear you are right,' Rebecca agreed. 'It would not go well with your washing.'

'No,' the old woman cackled, delightedly, 'but some would say it would go better with me, and my old bones!' Still chuckling at her own joke, she hobbled back to her cottage, bucket in hand, and Rebecca went, smiling, upon her errand.

As she entered the yard of the 'Crown', she saw Ossie in the stable corner and called out to him. He left the bucket of bran mash he was carrying and came to greet her. She took the letter from her reticule and held it out to him, asking, 'Would you give this to the post boy before he leaves, Ossie, as I would like it to catch the morning mail coach?'

'He is here now, Rebecca. Within the inn. I shall call him out to you.' He disappeared into the kitchens and returned within minutes, bringing the post boy with him. 'Boy' was a travesty, for he was a man of middle age, tall, cadaverous, with the skin of his face leathery and deeply seamed from nose to mouth.

'Miss de Breos,' he beamed civilly, 'the ostler tells me that you have a letter to deliver into my keeping.'

'Yes, that is so.'

She handed it to him.

'And, I, Mistress, have in turn been entrusted with one for you. Will you take it now? It will save me a journey.'

The exchange made, Ossie returned to the stables, and the post boy to the inn. Rebecca took the letter to the village green, and sat upon a bench to read it. Her grandfather requested her to visit the attorney's office in Newton Village, where he had left instructions for the attorney to explain to her the details of a settlement he had made. If there were any other business matters, or requests of her own, to be attended to, she had only to give notice and they would be carried out.

She went without delay to the office of Mr William Thompson, attorney-at-law and notary, where she was received civilly by the gentleman himself, who dismissed his clerks to their desks, and conducted her reverently into his inner sanctum. This was a small oak-panelled room, with linenfold carving, thickly lined with bookcases, their contents overflowing on to floor and desk. The air was musty with the smell of old leather, ink and dank pages, plus a super-foetation of ancient dust. They were closeted together for over an hour, during which time discussion and suggestion flowed freely. Their business transacted to their mutual satisfaction, Mr Thompson escorted her to the door, reiterating that he would always be at her service. He was, thought Rebecca, a dry, desiccated little man, in keeping with his dusty surroundings, and all knees and elbows. When she thought of him in future, he always came into her mind as a chirpy, sharp-angled little cricket.

Once more in the fresh air, she breathed deeply. The money which her grandfather had originally settled upon her father had now been directed to her. It was a sum so incredible and unexpected in its enormity, that she was quite unable to comprehend it. It was hers, freely, and as an outright gift, the attorney had told her respectfully. There were no conditions attached to its use; she was free to dispose of it as she chose. However, that could be discussed between Sir Matthew and his granddaughter. He would, no doubt, be able to advise her as to investing it to the best advantage, if that was what she proposed to do.

When Rebecca returned to her cottage, Jeremiah was washed, dressed in his good clothes and seated upon one of the shield-backed chairs, with the bull terrier at his feet. By his air of restlessness and nervous anticipation, she knew that he was afraid of what she might tell him.

'Jeremiah,' she said, without preamble, 'I have something to confess.'

'I know,' he said, resignedly, 'I was sure yesterday that your mind was already made up. You are leaving? To be with your grandfather?'

'Yes, it is already arranged.'

'Yes, my dear, it is the only course open to you. If it is what you want, then I am glad for you both . . . although,' the sharp grey eyes clouded, 'I shall miss you more than I can say.'

'I am not travelling to the ends of the earth, Jeremiah! You will not be rid of me so easily.'

He shook his head. 'It will be farther than the ends of the earth, little maid. We will be set apart in different worlds. I fear I shall not be comfortable, or accepted, where you will go.'

'Oh, Jeremiah,' she hugged him impulsively. 'You are my dearest friend in all the world. Do you think I would let anything, or anyone, separate us? I had thought you knew me better.'

'I am a silly ignorant old man,' he said, penitently, 'with not a thought in my head but my own selfish needs . . . I should be rejoicing with you at your good fortune, and the adventure which lies ahead . . . No, I swear we will not be parted, for I would walk to London and back, and Charity with me, for a glimpse of your sweet face.'

'Do not say another word . . . for if you do, Jeremiah, I shall surely cry, and that would distress us both, and we shall end by weeping like babes. I shall make us both a good hot jug of elderberry wine, and then our noses shall drip and grow red, instead of our eyes.'

He laughed with her, but there was no mirth in either of them.

When they were settled, and feeling the glow of the heated wine, she said seriously, 'If I explain something to you, Jeremiah, will you promise not to grow angry with me, or displeased. You know I would not offend you for the world, or more.'

'I cannot imagine what you could say that would ever offend me, my maid, but perhaps you had best tell me,' he said, eyes twinkling.

'When I reached the "Crown Inn" with the letter for my grandfather, there was a letter awaiting me ...'

'From your grandfather?'

'Yes. I did not expect it, and had no inkling of what he would say. He asked me to visit the attorney. Oh, Jeremiah, he has given me so much money, more than I could use in all my lifetime ... even if I did nothing but spend it every minute of the day.'

'But how could that offend me, my child? I love you dearly and rejoice in your good fortune, for no one deserves it more.'

'It is not that, Jeremiah. I wanted those I loved best to share it with me. I have had the attorney draw up a deed that gives you the cottage and all it contains, save small personal mementos of my mother.'

'No!' He rose to his feet, crashing a great fist into his open palm, and making the dog shudder and leap to its feet. 'It cannot be done. I will accept no more from you than you have given! Your affection and care you have offered willingly and in the same spirit I have accepted them. I cannot take your money, it is not right.'

'Please listen, Jeremiah ... if you will live here in my house, and take it as your own, then I can always come back. There will be a place for me, a real home with a dear friend. If you will not do that, then I shall be cut off from everyone and everything I have known. I beg of you, do not refuse me.'

He stared at her for a long while, nodded, then sat down heavily on his chair, looking bewildered, and old.

'But what of my own cottage?'

'I had hoped that you would offer it to Rosa and Doonan. And whatever they wish to do to make it a family home, then I shall pay for it, if you can persuade them that I do it out of affection, and not charity.'

He nodded. 'Yes, I will do that.'

'For the Widow Cleat, I have asked for the sum of one hundred pounds to be set aside. I do so in case the day comes when Illtyd is no longer able to work, or she grows old or infirm, and has need of it.'

'Yes, that is kind and practical.'

'For Hannah and Emily Randall, I have arranged for the sum of fifty pounds to be paid, to do with as they wish, also to Emrys and Ossie . . . if you think that they will not be angry or humiliated, because I think myself some Lady Bountiful.'

'No, I am sure that any one of them would gladly do as much for you.'

'Good. I have set apart some money, too, to help Dr Burrel with his work with the poor, that he may buy instruments, food, blankets, whatever is needed . . . it will be sent as soon as there is news of him. I ask your help in these things, Jeremiah, because you are all the family I have known since my father's death. You have been dearer than a father to me, for you have always been ready to protect and care for me and would, I know, give me your life itself . . . it is only in you that I see what a father should be, for my own father was always a child, and it was I who needed to be strong.'

Jeremiah blinked rapidly, and pretended an absorption with the dog, who gazed at him questioningly with slanted intelligent eyes, head cocked in puzzlement.

Jeremiah looked up. 'There is one whom you have not mentioned, Rebecca.'

'No. I will see Joshua this day and tell him of my plans. I will not say choice, for I do not reject him for anyone, or anything . . . If he will agree to wait for me for just one year, and is still of the same mind, then I will come to him. My leaving will not mean that I love him the less. Do you not understand, Jeremiah?'

'I understand, Rebecca, but my love for you is the love of a father, not that of a man who would have you as his wife and cannot bear the physical separation.'

'But if I promise to return?'

'You will be two different people, Rebecca. If it were not so, then there would be no reason in life, or in what you choose to do. It would be a promise made by the girl you are now, at this moment. It would have no validity to the woman you will become, or to Joshua. He could not hold you to it. It could not be binding.'

'I will make it, nonetheless.'

As he walked up Clevis Hill to call upon Dr Mansel, Joshua's thoughts were upon Rebecca and the visit from her grandfather, Sir Matthew de Breos. It seemed that the simple research that he had asked Dr Peate to undertake had brought a result, the complexity of which he could never have imagined, both for Rebecca and himself. His object had been to give her 'roots', a feeling of stability. All he had done was to disrupt her life and, perhaps, to ruin his own. She was a very remarkable woman, but even someone of her intelligence and honesty would find it difficult to reconcile two completely alien lives. She would finally have to choose: life as a gentlewoman would enrich her, and extend her horizons, but she could never again be accepted in the life she had led; if she stayed, there would be regrets for what she had sacrificed, awkwardness, even with friends who had loved her, and the bleak prospect of being a village constable's wife. The nub of the matter was that whatever she decided, she was no longer Rebecca. She was a de Breos. She would argue, convincingly, that she was the same person she had always been, as she had done upon their abortive visit to the farm.

'Oh, damnation!' he cried, in anger and remorse, 'why ever did I let it begin?' Yet he knew that even if he lost her, he could not have denied her the chance to develop her independence, and grow.

Dr Mansel, who was busy at his roses, saw him enter the garden and thought how much he had changed since that first meeting over the dead body of Mary Devereaux; Stradling looked older, more responsible, but careworn too. There were few traces of the handsome callow youth, hiding his pink-cheeked innocence behind an imposing uniform, but with little authority. The authority was now his by right, but Mansel regretted the disillusion which must have gone into the making of it ...

'Good morning, Stradling,' he said quietly.

'Oh, good morning, sir. I fear I was miles away.'

'Somewhere as restful and renewing as a garden, I hope?'

Joshua merely smiled. 'I have come to ask you if you have any news of Mrs Mansel, sir.'

'No, none,' he said, resignedly. 'And you? How are you faring?'

'Little better than before ... there are so many threads ... I follow them, but they are separate, unravelled. They make no coherent pattern.'

'Perhaps some unexpected event will bring them together?'

'Perhaps,' Joshua said, unconvinced.

'Have you any news of Burrel, and what has become of him?'

'I believe that he is in London ... treating the cholera victims in any capacity he might serve.'

Mansel nodded, his opaque eyes troubled. 'I fear that his chances of survival are poor and grow less with each day ... it is a hellish scourge, Stradling!'

'No more, perhaps, than he has already been through.'

'He is a very sick man; the prognosis, as he must know, is poor. I cannot think he will survive many months.'

'Perhaps that is why he made his choice.'

'I do not know.' Mansel's voice was raw with regret. 'I only know that he is a good man. I misjudged him cruelly, Stradling. It is not something I am proud of ... it will be hard to live with.'

'I expect that he also feels distress for the way he misjudged you.'

'It might well be ...' Mansel recalled himself from his introspection with an effort. 'You have heard that the inquest on the drowned sailor has been postponed?'

'Yes.'

'The reason given was so that further enquiries could be

made. Have you any idea of the real truth?'

'Nobody has discussed it with me, sir,' replied Joshua, carefully.

Dr Mansel ran his fingers through the circle of pale fly-away hair. 'Well, I suppose Robert Knight has some knowledge denied to us. And then he asked abruptly, 'How is your mother, Charlotte?'

'She is very well, I am happy to say. I was to tell you, most earnestly, that she has not forgotten you, sir, and wishes you only well.'

Mansel nodded. 'If only her wishes had been shared by everybody, how different things would be.'

'Sir?'

'Leave me to my roses, Stradling. I am not fit company. Regret is a poor companion. It brings neither comfort nor solution. I wish you both in your quest, Constable.'

'Thank you, Dr Mansel. I bid you good day, sir.'

But Mansel had already returned to his roses.

As he walked out through the wrought iron gateway, Joshua wondered what had become of Mrs Mansel's beloved conservatory, with its exotic plants and ferns. Did Dr Mansel tend them fastidiously, although he had little love for them? A strong parallel, in a way, to the life they had endured together. The opposing forces of love and hate; like two antagonists pulling upon a rope, the ends stretching the fibres until they are farther and farther apart, yet, released, they may spring together. Love or hate, he thought, compassionately, I wonder which will prove the stronger? More and more he was beginning to believe that Mrs Mansel was alive. There was no news of her and a search of countryside and shore had revealed no traces, living or dead.

Well, now he had embarked upon another errand, and one involved, inevitably, with both. He must return to the carpenter's shop, and interview Ezra the Box; a prospect he little relished. He opened the door to the shop and entered, the resinous fragrance of pine and fir sweetly cloying in his nostrils. He saw Ezra the Box working in the room behind, and he came forward stiffly to greet Joshua.

'Good morning, Mr Evans,' said Joshua pleasantly, 'pray

do not disturb yourself on my account. This is a very brief visit, I assure you. I am on my way to see a friend, Peter Rawlings, the chief exciseman. I daresay you have had some dealings with him; in business, of course.'

Ezra's little ferret face grew more pinched.

'Not to my knowledge,' he replied, coldly, 'save over the accommodation of bodies, of course.'

'Of course, what else could you accommodate? I trust you have thought over the ultim ... I mean, suggestion, I gave you?'

'You had best be seated,' Evans said, ungraciously.

'I shall not be here long enough, but I thank you for your concern. Well?'

Ezra's small beady eyes blinked rapidly.

'I tell you straight, Constable, I am the innocent victim in this shameless conspiracy. I am a man of the highest moral principles, as every fairminded man will vouchsafe.'

'The name?' demanded Joshua, implacably.

'O damn it, man. Have a little pity! It would be more than my life is worth!'

'We will not haggle over its value,' said Joshua, smoothly, 'I believe that your friend, Packwood, is not altogether happy in his cell; some trouble with an arm. Not setting properly, I am told. You have heard from him, perhaps?'

'He is no friend of mine! Well, only in so far as we share the same trade.'

'Exactly.'

'Funerals, I had in mind.'

'So did I, Mr Evans. What foresight you had in preparing for your own. Providential, one might say ... the name, Mr Evans!'

Evans licked his dry lips. 'It is only hearsay, you understand. I have no proof. I hear little bits of gossip here and there in the course of my work.'

'And the gossip?'

Ezra looked around him desperately, as if seeking a way of escape, then said, defiantly, 'Crandle, father and son.'

'Thank you,' said Joshua, moving towards the door.

'Remember,' cautioned Ezra, a grimy finger to his mouth,

‘not a word has passed my lips.’

‘Then you are at one with your customers, Mr Evans. In future, you might do well to emulate them ... in their caution and inactivity, and if I were you ...’

‘Yes, Constable?’

‘I would reserve your coffins for the dead. They cause less trouble.’

Joshua returned to his cottage, pondering upon what Ezra had told him. He could not believe that the fellow, sly and furtive as he was, would deliberately lie about someone he considered to be of importance, like Hugo Crandle. No, it was all too likely to be true, confirming what both he and Rawlings had suspected. With what Doonan might be able to confide to him, through Illtyd, and what the exciseman could glean in addition, they could be well on the way to capturing the smugglers.

No sooner had Joshua set foot over his own threshold and removed his helmet, it seemed, than there was a rattling upon his door. When he opened it, he could not at first sight speak, so great was his astonishment at recognizing his visitor.

‘I am Roland Devereaux,’ said the young man of the locket miniature. ‘You do not know me, Constable, but I have come to seek your help.’

‘I do know you, sir, and you have come to the right place. I beg you, Mr Devereaux, to come inside, for I have long awaited this visit.’

After they had settled down, and explanations made on both sides, Joshua told him of his sister’s death and the manner of it, finding no way of softening the hurt of it in the telling. Devereaux, shocked and grieved, could not at first comprehend it, then he broke down and wept, with Joshua too pained and clumsy to offer him any words of comfort. When the man had finally composed himself, enough for the interview to continue, Joshua asked, ‘What brings you here, Mr Devereaux, to where Mary died?’

‘She wrote to me, after our great-aunt died. The old lady was a strange creature, and Mary’s life was not easy. I am very much older than she, an officer in the Merchant Navy for several years. I had hoped to earn enough to buy a house that Mary and I might live together ...' He stopped, unable to continue until he had recovered himself.

Joshua waited silently.

'When our great aunt died, what little money she had was gone. Mary wrote to me and said that a schoolfriend of hers had learnt of her plight and asked her to act as a companion-friend. She would live as one of the family, of course, but receive her keep and a small salary to enable her to live.'

Joshua nodded. 'But why have you left it so long before searching for her?'

'I had sailed for South America ... Valparaiso. The letter awaited me for several months at the office of my agents in Cardiff. I came as soon as I received it. I docked but twenty-four hours ago.'

'It is a tragedy I wish that I could have spared you,' said Joshua gravely, 'and I know that anything I say will be of little comfort, but I think that, later, it might help you to know that the justice, Mr Robert Knight, arranged for her burial and, as rector, conducted the service himself. It was a fine service, read with dignity and compassion, and well attended by the village people ...' He broke off awkwardly, then continued, 'It is not a pauper's grave and the cottagers see that it is never without flowers.'

'I thank you for your kindness, sir, and will certainly thank the rector for his, but I am at a loss to understand why the family she lived with did not arrange the burial?'

'We do not know who they are.'

'You do not? I merely came to you, sir, to ask the place where they lived, for Mary gave me no details, no address. She simply gave the name of her friend, Elizabeth Crandle.'

As soon as Joshua had taken Roland Devereaux to the coach loft to meet Mary's old nurse, Emily Randall, he booked a room and board for him at the 'Crown Inn', telling the landlord that he was not yet sure of the length of time his guest required to stay. Then, going out into the yard, he found Ossie and bade him saddle the grey, for he had business to attend to, urgently. The ostler watched him ride off under the archway, troubled at the strangeness in his friend's manner; he seemed nervous, abstracted, yet filled with unusual exhilaration. He supposed that the news of Rebecca's grandfather had unsettled Joshua and raked his usual calmness. Ossie would have been troubled more had he known the identity of Emily Randall's visitor, and that the young constable rode out to confront the Crandles alone.

This time, when Joshua arrived at Dan-y-Graig, a groom appeared from the stable yard behind the house and led the grey away. Joshua stood upon the steps to the house and pulled the brass bell-pull, looking around at the serenity of the lawns and shrubs and the background of grey rock and sheltering woodland. A maidservant answered the door instead of the surly footman he had encountered before, but when he began to enquire as to the whereabouts of Mr Hugo Crandle, he heard a commotion at the library door, and a young dark-haired woman emerged, looking dishevelled and breathless.

'You must excuse me, Constable,' she apologized, 'for my mother and I have but ten minutes ago arrived from Porlock. We are grubby and tired after a sea voyage. But will you not come into the library, for I heard you ask for my father, who is absent. If I am able to assist you in any way, then I shall be glad to do so.'

Joshua thanked her and followed her into the library.

An older woman, looking tired and pale, was seated at a small table, with a tray and silver teapot set out before her, and some dishes of bread and butter, conserve and cakes. The likeness between mother and son was noticeable only in the colour of their hair, but Mrs Crandle's was softened by age and incipient greyness to a blurred copper shade. Her skin was that delicate, luminous white which sometimes goes with red hair, her eyes startlingly blue against eyelashes so pale that, like her eyebrows, they seemed almost transparent. In fact, Joshua thought she was as unlike the fiery vitality of her son as moonlight to flame.

'Will you not be seated, Constable,' she invited, 'and take some tea with us? Then perhaps you will explain how we can help you.'

Joshua thanked her, but declined the offer of tea, saying that his visit concerned the whereabouts of a young woman, at which mother and daughter exchanged questioning glances.

'The young woman?'

'Perhaps you would like to see a drawing of her?' Joshua produced it, and Elizabeth Crandle took it from him to hand it to her mother.

'Why, it is Mary,' she said, smiling. 'Mary Devereaux, mother.' She turned to Joshua puzzled. 'But what is this all about? I do not understand.'

'She was to visit you, I believe.'

'Not visit,' corrected Mrs Crandle, 'live with us as a companion and friend to my daughter. She is a dear girl, and we have known her for many years ... since childhood, in fact.'

'She did not come?' Joshua persisted. 'She changed her mind perhaps, or some reason prevented her?'

'I am not sure,' admitted Elizabeth Crandle, 'for when we were in Porlock, I developed an illness, a slight fever ... the physician thought it wiser that I did not travel, but remain in the care of friends. It was then that Mary was due to arrive here.'

'And she did not?'

'No,' agreed Mrs Crandle. 'My husband sent a letter by one of the ships' officers to say that she would not now be making the journey, as she had been offered a home with a cousin who needed nursing care. I admit that I was surprised, for apart from her brother at sea, I believed that she had no family. But, please, Constable, tell me if there is anything wrong with the child, or any help we can give her?' she asked anxiously, 'for Elizabeth is very fond of her.'

'I am afraid, Mrs Crandle, that there is nothing anyone can do to help her,' said Joshua, gently. 'You see, Miss Devereaux is dead.'

There was a shocked silence, then Joshua was aware of the rattle of cup upon saucer as Mrs Crandle lowered it to the table.

'Oh, that poor child. How terrible!' she exclaimed, her voice rough with pity. 'How did it happen? Was it some terrible accident?'

'I am afraid that she was murdered.'

Joshua could see that the knuckles of Elizabeth Crandle's

clenched hands stood out like white bone, and from the anguish of her face, he knew that she realized why he had come.

'Your husband and son, Mrs Crandle, when are they due to return?'

'I do not know,' she said. 'Indeed, I find it difficult to think. I am so shocked and distressed by this . . . Elizabeth?'

'I believe that they will be away for three or four days.' Her voice was very low, almost inaudible. 'They take frequent journeys and are away at times for up to a week. It is to do with business . . . shipping, you understand?'

'Yes, I understand.'

'Is Mary . . .' she hesitated, unable to control her voice, then continuing more calmly, 'Has the body been buried?'

'Yes, it was all arranged by the justice, Mr Robert Knight, a week or so ago, when you were away.' He saw by her face that she was no longer in doubt.

'Mother, shall I see you to your room?' she gently offered. 'I know how fatigued you are by the long journey, and the shock of Mary.'

'No, my dear,' Mrs Crandle said, 'do not disturb yourself. Perhaps there is something else the constable needs to know . . . something you can help him with.' She rang for the maid, and gave her instructions to clear the tea-table, then left for her room.

After she had gone, Elizabeth Crandle said, hesitantly, 'Is there something you need to know, Constable?'

'Rather something I need to see, Miss Crandle.' Joshua was thinking of the room above the stables which the carrier had told him about. Young Crandle's hideaway.

She did not pretend to misunderstand. 'You mean Creighton's room in the yard?'

'Please, Miss Crandle.'

He followed her out through the front door and along the paths which skirted the lawns and borders and across the cobbled yard to the outhouses and stables. She preceded him up an external stone staircase and lifted the latch, then stood aside for him to enter first. He thought how calm and self-possessed she was, in total contrast to her brother. She had her father's dark colouring, but an air of tranquillity, an assurance which he found restful. He wished they had met under different circumstances, for he felt sure that she was intelligent and kind.

'Is there something in particular which you are seeking?'

'A piece of luggage . . . a portmanteau, the coachman would have me believe.'

'Then I will help you search.'

The room was set out as a bachelor retreat with cellarette, bookshelves, commode, shaving stand and the usual personal clutter attendant upon a solitary male. Its centre was dominated by a vast half-tester bed, with a bedcover of some unidentifiable animal's fur. Joshua was not sure if it was this, allied to the precise anatomical drawings of women set upon the walls, or the crudeness of colour, which gave it an aura of decadence and tastelessness, for the furniture itself was elegant enough.

Elizabeth Crandle, after a quick initial glance about her, began to search determinedly, face set and flushed. They worked in silence for a while, until she opened a small camphor-wood blanket chest at the foot of the bed.

'I believe that I have found what you are looking for,' she said tonelessly. Joshua lifted the portmanteau out, laid it on the closed lid of the chest and snapped open the locks. Inside was a tangle of nightwear and undergarments, tortoiseshell toilet articles and personal treasures, including a silver model of a pretty sailing ship, with sails full bellied in the wind. Elizabeth Crandle picked it up and examined it, her face drawn with sadness.

'I remember how she treasured this, it was a gift from her brother on her fifteenth birthday.' She replaced it carefully beside a delicate collar and cuffs of filigree lace, then closed the lid.

'You will want to take it with you, of course?'

'It would be better. I am sorry, Miss Crandle, for the grief and pain this has caused you, and the greater pain to come. Believe me, if I could have spared you by questioning your father and brother . . .'

'I know,' she acknowledged truthfully. 'Perhaps you think me hard and unnatural, but I feel nothing for my brother, neither pity nor regret. He is a cruel, selfish creature, with no thought for any save himself. My father over-indulged him and has never sought to check his wildest excesses. It is no surprise to me. He has long courted trouble, but I would never have imagined the hideousness of it.' She began to cry silently, not attempting to wipe away the tears, but letting them flow, unchecked.

'Please,' begged Joshua, helplessly, 'do not distress yourself. Please, Miss Crandle.' He handed her his large, white kerchief, but she shook her head and wiped the tears away with her palm.

'I am not crying for him, Constable, but for the grief it will bring to my mother, and for Mary's death. She was a shy and gentle girl, without malice or any kind of viciousness. I do not know how I can speak of it to my mother. I think it will break her heart. But that is not your affair, sir. You have worries enough of your own . . . I thank you for the honesty with which you have treated me.' She walked resolutely and with dignity to the door and waited while he unlatched it and saw her out. When they stood together on the wide stone platform atop the steps, he turned to her.

'Miss Crandle, I must ask you not to speak of this to your mother, or indeed anyone, until your brother and your father have been traced. You must not communicate with them in any way. I know that you will find it difficult not to warn them, and to bear the burden of this tragedy alone.'

'You need have no fear on either account,' she promised. 'I shall be grateful to keep it from my mother for as long as I can. For, once it is known, I fear that there will never be any peace of mind for either of us again. It is a nightmare from which, like Mary, I can never hope to awaken . . .' She touched his arm, lightly, and made her way down the staircase and across the yard to the house.

Bearing the portmanteau, Joshua went in search of the groom and his grey. His spirits were less sanguine than he had hoped.

Chapter Twenty-Three

When Joshua rode out of Dan-y-Graig House he hesitated at the lodge gate, wondering whether to return to the 'Crown Inn', or to go straight to Tythegston Court, to apprise the justice of his discovery. However, encumbered as he was with the evidence, Mary's portmanteau, he thought it more expedient to first ride to his cottage, and store it in safety.

This done, he called briefly at the coachhouse, where he spoke to Devereaux privately, and in confidence, telling him what had transpired. He begged him not to mention his sister's association with the Crandle family, but to keep his own counsel, for if news of his visit to Dan-y-Graig were to reach the men at Weare House, the consequences might be disastrous. Devereaux, distressed as he was by Joshua's revelations, willingly agreed, and it was arranged that they would meet upon the morrow, when Joshua would take him to his sister's graveside, and try to answer any questions which still ravaged his mind.

Then, easier in his own mind, Joshua re-mounted the grey and rode under the archway of the 'Crown', out of the village, and to the house of the justice, the Reverend Robert Knight.

Leyshon, looking infinitely more sprightly, and expansive, returned to the hall to inform Joshua that the justice would be pleased to receive him in the library. As he escorted him, he confided that a travelling bone-setter and tooth-puller he had occasioned upon while drinking at the 'Ancient Briton' had 'made a new man' of him. Joshua congratulated him, reasoning privately that it could only be an improvement upon the old.

The Reverend Robert Knight looked up expectantly as Joshua entered, brown eyes alert behind the gold-rimmed lenses.

'Well, Stradling? Not another death to report, I hope?'

'No sir, a murder resolved, I believe.'

'Mary Devereaux?'

'Yes sir.'

'I thank God to hear it! I have prayed, most earnestly, for an end to the matter. I wish no vengeance, for "Vengeance is mine, saith the Lord", and there is no greater or more terrible arbiter. I look, however, for justice on earth, you understand?'

'Perfectly sir.'

'You had best tell me what has occurred.'

He listened, in silence, as Joshua told him of the visit by Roland Devereaux, and his own visit to Dan-y-Graig, culminating in the discovery of the portmanteau.

'What a nest of vipers I have been nurturing!' He drummed his fingers angrily upon the desk. 'I can scarcely credit such infamy! You believe that both son and father are implicated in the murder, Stradling?'

'That I cannot say, sir, although it would be difficult to argue otherwise.'

'Hmmm ... Even if young Crandle alone killed her then his father is undoubtedly an accessory to the fact ...'

'Unless he was absent when his son took her to his stable-room, and he did not confide in him.'

'Surely the servants would have seen her?'

'I cannot be sure; the older Crandle claimed that he had dismissed them, all save his manservant, as his wife was absent ... I believe that the manservant was in his pay primarily as a smuggler, since, with the Crandles, he was missing today.'

'There is no risk of their discovering that you have found the evidence?'

'No, I think not, sir. The daughter of the house, Miss Elizabeth Crandle, is an intelligent, honest girl, with no respect or liking for her brother and his machinations ... She has sworn that she will not contact him, or inform her mother of what we suspect.'

'You believe her?'

'Implicitly.'

'Good, since we must rely upon her absolute discretion! And the man, Devereaux, you can trust him to keep his own counsel?'

'Undoubtedly, sir. He has given his word. He is grateful

beyond measure for your kindness in arranging his sister's burial, and would speak with you. It would have grieved him had she been buried in a pauper's grave, with stone or marking forbidden . . .'

'Yes. It is a sad enough custom, as if poverty renders a soul of no consequence, and denies him an identity in death.' He shook his head ruefully. "Blessed are the poor in spirit; for theirs is the kingdom of heaven . . ." I sometimes wonder if the poor in flesh, and spirit, might be more inspired by a small taste of it upon the earth.' He recalled himself abruptly. 'Well, Stradling, what do you propose to do about the Crandles?'

'I thought I would ride to Weare House and confront them with our knowledge of the murder, and the evidence.'

'Not wise, there is the other business of the smuggling.'

'But surely, sir, murder is the greater crime? The taking of life?'

'Agreed, but what of the drowned sailor? Was he, perhaps, murdered too, by being left to die? We do not know the circumstances.'

'You would have me wait?'

'I would have you charge the Crandles with one murder, and possibly both, also with control of the smuggling organization. We must make sure that when they are caught, and convicted, their sentences will be savagely appropriate.'

'I understand, sir . . . but if they escape?'

'They must not!' He smashed his fist upon the desk. 'It is your responsibility, Stradling!'

'Yes, sir.'

'You have someone who will insinuate himself into the ring, I believe . . . or so Rawlings informs me.'

'Yes, a man by the name of Doonan. A quarryman.'

The justice smiled involuntarily. 'Indeed? The bellicose Irishman . . . I am led to believe that he could subdue the three hamlets single-handed! Although I hear that Jeremiah Fleet got the better of him in the affair of the cockerels. Do not look so surprised, Stradling! I have my sources of information. I am not entirely ignorant of affairs here, or farther afield, in the Vale . . .' He looked at Joshua keenly, as if to proffer advice, but checked himself. 'You will see Rawlings, of course, and make arrangements with him, so that you may act in unison. If necessary, I can call upon the militia, although present circumstances do not warrant it. But have a care, Stradling, these men you are dealing with are dangerous. If cornered they will fight to kill, and to escape, for they have nothing to lose.'

'We will be well prepared, sir.'

'Good.' He stood up behind his desk, corpulent, dark-jowled, and offered Joshua his hand. 'God be with you, Stradling.'

'Thank you, sir, I shall keep you informed of what transpires.'

The justice's wide mouth expanded into a smile. Brown eyes gleamed from the pouches mischievously.

'I shall be there, Stradling! Offering my help! I would not miss it for all the tea in China, no, I correct myself, for all the cognac in France!'

As Joshua turned to leave, the justice called, 'Stay, Stradling, I had all but forgotten! There was another matter ...'

'Sir?'

'It will no longer be necessary to hunt for Dr Burrel.'

'No, sir. Dr Mansel has told me how the affair was ended.'

'Not ended! I have received word from my friend in the judiciary ... he who informed me of Burrel's release.'

'Burrel is not dead, sir?'

The justice shook his head. 'It seems that the friend of the murdered girl lied at the trial. The friend's own mother it was who wrought the butchery upon her, as upon so many other poor wretches before and since. It was only when she was apprehended for another such crime that she confessed all, hoping, no doubt, for leniency. Worse, it was Madeleine Mansel who assisted the abortionist, and contrived it, believing that with his child dead, Burrel would forsake that poor, bewildered girl and turn to her for comfort. There was no comfort for Ella Pearce ...' The justice continued, compassionately, 'She died believing that Burrel had no love for her, or the child within her ...'

The enormity of the injustice kept Joshua silent. He thought of Burrel trapped for twenty years in some sordid hell, knowing his innocence, bitterness and hopelessness eroding his spirit.

'I fancy the confession will bring him little comfort,' the justice said wearily. 'It has come too late. He will need more strength to bear this final irony, than for all his past deprivation ...'

'"God moves in a mysterious way ..."' ventured Joshua, awkwardly.

'Indeed, I sometimes find it obscure enough to follow, myself. Burrel must have long doubted whether He moves at all!'

As far as possible, Rebecca had set her affairs in order, she believed. It had not been easy. The parting from her friends had been the hardest and most sorrowful to bear, leaving her emotions lacerated and painful. Her protestations that she would not be far away, and that they could meet often, did not reassure them. It would not be Rebecca who returned, but some stranger, they were convinced. Someone removed from poverty and the unending struggle for survival that obsessed the villagers of the three hamlets. She could have no further interest in their lowly, trivial affairs. They did not blame her for it. It was as inevitable as the rising and setting of the sun, and unalterable. When she bade 'Goodbye' to them, it was as final and irrevocable as a death.

Rebecca had begged Jeremiah not to tell her friends of the money she had set aside for them, until she was well away from the village. Instead, she had visited them all, taking with her small, personal keepsakes which she knew they would accept; not for their intrinsic value, but for the memories they would evoke. To Jeremiah, she gave the care of her cob, and cart, saying that she knew he loved the patient animal, and would treat him with the affection he deserved. In addition, when Jeremiah had recovered, he would find it of use to transport him to the bay, and to take his catch to customers, or market, accompanied by his omnipresent dog. Despite his protests, she arranged with the attorney that a monthly sum should be paid to the corn and seed merchant to provide for the animal's needs, and for the upkeep of Jeremiah's vegetable plot. When she was settled in her grandfather's house, she determined that she would seek his advice about helping those most in need in the three hamlets, especially those out-paupers who were old and infirm, so no longer able to work. Perhaps there was some way in which workhouse paupers could be helped to regain their independence and self-respect, as Emily Randall had been helped by Joshua. Derelict cottages could be repaired, perhaps, by supplying materials and letting the men labour upon them themselves to make a home. And what of the lunatic parishioners, who, bewildered and afraid, were carted away to distant towns, losing all that was familiar and comforting to their disordered minds?

For the moment she must concentrate upon what could be done here and now. Her clothes and the few mementoes of her parents which she wished to keep were packed safely in a wooden trunk, ready for the morrow when her grandfather would send the coach to fetch her. Her goodbyes to Jeremiah had been said, amidst tears and many protestations of love and devotion on either side. She had worn his precious brooch as she had promised, and determined to do so, proudly, every day for the rest of her life. He had asked her, most earnestly, to write to him from time to time, with news of her life. 'For although I am not privileged to read or write, Joshua is clever and will relate to me what you say ... And remember, my maid, this is your home, and all that is in it. It is simply in my keeping until your return.' She had embraced him, begging him to allow her to go, alone, on the morrow, for another tearful leave-taking of her dear friend would break her heart.

It had grieved her most to bid farewell to Joshua. He declared that she was doing only what was right, that she must be given the opportunity to grow, and take her place at her grandfather's side ... any other course would be unthinkable. Yet, like a bewildered child, ruled by his emotions, he was alternately angry at her betrayal and cruelly indifferent to her pain. He accused her of leaving because she no longer loved or needed him. She replied that she loved him dearly, but had seen so little of life that her commitment would be all the greater if she returned freely, knowing that life without him could not offer enough. It seemed ironic that their positions were now reversed. In time, he accused, she would be unwilling to fit into the life of a lowly constable, unable to adapt to the ways of farmers and yeomen, whom she would consider loutish inferiors, not fitting to associate with.

'Joshua! It is I, Rebecca!' she wanted to cry out to him. 'Do you not know me? Can you believe that I will change so much?' Yet she said nothing, knowing that he spoke out of pain, and would feel regret and shame for doing so, after she had gone.

'I will write to you, often,' she promised, 'and you must come and visit me, and tell me of your life, and our friends. Then I shall have the best of both worlds.'

'You might end with neither!'

'Then that is the risk I take.'

'If you have decided to put me out of your life,' he insisted stubbornly, 'then it should be as you first suggested, for a year or more. I will not communicate with you in that time. You must be given a chance to live your new life unhindered . . . It would not do to be fettered by the past!'

'If that is what you honestly desire . . .'

So, to the sadness and regret of both, that was what was arranged. Rebecca was too hurt and resentful to make objection, or to plead with him, and Joshua too stubborn to recant. They parted affectionately enough, but the old, unforced intimacy was absent. Rebecca's last call was upon Emily Randall, to beg her to read to Jeremiah any letters which she might send, and to ask her to visit him, as would Hannah, Rosa, and the Widow Cleat, to see that he fared well in her absence.

There was nothing more to be done.

His interlude with Rebecca over, and with the thought of the long parting, which he had so foolishly insisted upon, lying heavily upon him, Joshua rode out to the 'Farmer's Arms' in Nottage. He had arranged to meet Illtyd to glean news of Doonan and the smugglers. It was thought that Illtyd would make the ideal intermediary, since no one could possibly suspect his involvement in the affair; they were, of course, wrong, and the knowledge gave him disproportionate pleasure.

When Joshua arrived and stabled his grey, he entered the inn to await his friend and informant. Illtyd was already settled in the chimney corner, talking to a sallow, etiolated fellow, who seemed to Joshua to have outgrown his strength, like those plants hidden from the sun, which stretch too far and too quickly to reach the light. When Illtyd saw Joshua, he arose at once, and came forward to meet him, explaining that he had been waylaid by the verger and clock-winder, who was incensed that the poor vegetable harvest had caused the vestry to cut his clock-winding salary from one guinea to but sixteen shillings a year. 'I suggested he set the clock to chime twelve every hour, quarter and half-hour through the night, until they relented,' said the little man, wickedly, 'but he was not amused!' Joshua and Illtyd watched some cottagers playing shuffleboard for a while, then moved away to occupy the tall settle beside the fire, where the landlord brought them tankards of ale.

'I saw you talking to the recruiter, Illtyd,' he ventured, his voice hearty. 'Trying to tempt you into taking the Queen's shilling?'

'Aye, I would have gone!' returned Illtyd, with a grin, 'but he wouldn't go higher than a sixpence!'

The landlord broke into laughter and went away to relate the story elsewhere.

'Is there news?' Joshua asked.

'Yes, Doonan met me today, upon the Common. He has been told it is tomorrow. He is to be at Weare House at seven of the clock, and will remain there until the early hours of the morning ...'

'That is definite?'

'Quite definite. There can be no mistake about it.'

'Good!' said Joshua. 'I shall contact the exciseman, Rawlings, and all will be arranged. I will tell you the hour and place to meet, as soon as I am able.'

Illtyd nodded, his head turned awkwardly to watch some geese in a treadmill, through the open door of the kitchen, as they strode on their endless task of spit-turning. 'Poor creatures,' he said, 'bred to labour unceasingly for others ... their only expectation to be plucked naked and put in a pot!'

'Indeed,' agreed Joshua, 'exchange the latter for a box, and our own expectations are not dissimilar!'

Illtyd laughed delightedly. 'I remember, once, they had a dog here, trained to the wheel, but he grew so wily that when he saw them grease the spit he would run away, and return when the meat was cooked . . .'

'If it were Jeremiah's dog, Charity,' said Joshua, 'it would be Jeremiah in the wheel, and the cur tasting the meat upon the spit, for flavour! I tell you, Illtyd, I have never seen a dog so cosseted and indulged!'

'I cannot understand it,' said Illtyd, seriously. 'Faith, my pony, has never been so treated!'

The next morning, when Rebecca was entering her grandfather's coach, with Jeremiah resolutely remaining inside the cottage, as he had promised, Joshua was about his business.

Rebecca, her luggage safely stowed away, looked about her for the last time, as mistress of the cottage, where she had spent all her growing days. She told herself that she was going to an exciting new life, a brave adventure. The endless treadmill of work and poverty was at an end. Why, then, was there this feeling not of rebirth, but the death of something loved and irrecoverable? Through the glass of the coach she saw a pale blur at the window of the cottage, which she knew to be Jeremiah, saying farewell.

'Are you ready, Mistress de Breos?' asked the coachman, fastening the door of the carriage.

'Yes, I am ready. All is finished here.' But it was not finished! Her love for Joshua was a vital, living thing; warm and quickening as the blood which flowed in her veins . . . He was part of her, so close, they shared one pulse, one common heartbeat. Without him she would be incomplete, bereft . . . 'Oh Joshua,' she cried silently. 'Understand, believe that I go not because I love you less. There is work that you must do; duty . . . it is part of your life, it is what makes you what you are. I would not ask you to forgo it. Can you not see, my love, that now I have a duty . . . to my grandfather, to myself and to others I do not even know? God help me to be strong enough to do what I must! I will come back to you, I swear, for I have no life without you ...'

The coachman, troubled by the sadness upon her young face, climbed upon the box and stirred the horses into life.

Inside the coach, Rebecca steadfastly held back her tears, and sat straight and tall. Inside the house, Jeremiah let his tears flow unashamedly for the loss of his little maid. The dog, feeling his grief, came and sat beside him, resting its head upon his knee, unable to bring him comfort.

Joshua, leaving the 'Crown', where he had been giving instruction for the night's vigil to Ossie, saw the de Breos coach turning, to drive up Clevis Hill. He glimpsed Rebecca, white-faced and erect against the cushions, looking to neither right nor left. He felt such a sense of desolation and rage that he swung from his stirrup and dismounted, unable to continue. Joshua heard the sound of Ossie's boots upon the cobbles behind him, and half-turned to speak but, regaining control, remounted and reined the grey away. Ossie, watching him, and hearing the distant rumble of the carriage as it breasted the hill, understood, and, shaking his head at the folly of men, returned to his horses.

Joshua rode off to the port, and entered the dockside, waiting beside the tramroad as a horse-drawn wagon went by, filled with shining lumps of rough-hewn coal, black as Whitby mourning jet; mountains of it ranged across the loading bays, narrow peaks catching the sun, bases thick with black dust. The prosperity of the Port depended upon it, and as much upon the men who laboured in the dark, below the surface of the earth. Like blind moles, thought Joshua, labouring ceaselessly in the blackness ... and wondered if the cost in human life and deprivation was worth it.

Rawlings, leaving the custom house, saw Joshua coming, and hailed him cheerfully. They walked towards the 'Ship Aground', speaking of generalities, until they reached a secluded corner of the docks where they could not be overheard.

'It is arranged for tonight, then?' Joshua asked.

'Yes, High Tide is at eleven, or thereabouts. My informant, Kingdon, is working with them and expects the loading to begin at a quarter to the hour ...'

'How many men have they?'

'Seven. No more ... and, of course, they can call upon the crew of the ship. It is the *Minehead Maiden*, due to dock at the quarter hour past eleven, which gives them but half an hour. It seems that they will have the ship's shore boats ready loaded.'

'What are your plans?'

'I shall have a cutter ready and waiting to intercept them at sea, and on the shore: six men, all armed, and Kingdon ready to renege upon them! And you, Stradling?'

'Doonan with the smugglers, and five on shore, unless you count the justice, which brings it to six.'

'I think we may safely suppose that he will do his part! Although, I grant you the privilege of including him in your watch. I fancy he is not used to taking orders ... excepting holy ones!'

'I doubt that there will be any confusion in his mind over who is setting them!' said Joshua drily. Laughing, and discussing their plans, they adjourned to the 'Ship Aground' to slake their thirst, and talk of other things.

At one quarter of the hour to eleven o'clock, Joshua's little band of men had broken rank, and slowly spread along the dunes edging the bay. They had crept forward inch upon inch, snaking upon their bellies for the final thrust, and were now concealed behind their hummocks of fine sand and marram grass, awaiting the exciseman's signal. Rawlings, himself, was hidden with two of his men on the rocky outcrop that jutted from sea to shore at the Newton side of Weare, the sea-carved stone and wide fissures giving them shelter. On the port side of the bay, three more excisemen waited, hunched awkwardly behind huge boulders thrown up by the tide, positions more exposed and vulnerable.

Two of the smuggler's band of seven were visible to Joshua, as they stood watch upon the access roads, one at the beach end of the carriage road from the 'Pyle Inn', the other guarding the bridle path from the heart of the Burrows. Neither man was known to Joshua, so it seemed that both Doonan and Rawlings' man were to be used for the unloading of the contraband. Joshua watched Hugo Crandle ride to the water's edge from the stables of Weare House, two men following him on foot, the latter holding a lanthorn carefully shrouded in cloth.

Joshua glanced around the hollows in the dunes to check upon his men. Next to him, upon his right hand, the justice, and beyond, sheltered in a sandy dip, Ossie. To Joshua's left, the crouched diminutive form of Illtyd, and further along, carefully concealed, Emrys. Behind the first ridge of dunes, in the grassy hollow of Plover's Plain, the ostler from Weare House waited with Joshua's grey, the justice's mount and Illtyd's small pony ... Joshua felt the tension rising inside him, and the dampness of sweat upon palms and lip; his shirt seemed fused to his flesh, his mouth dry and sour-tasting, making it difficult to swallow. Any command, he felt sure, would be, at best, an unrecognizable croak.

At the doorway to Weare House, Doonan was feeling equally tense and ill-at-ease as he stood alongside Creighton Crandle. He was not sure which of the smugglers was an exciseman, although he had heard, that day, from Illtyd, that he could count upon them for aid. He had purposely allied himself with Creighton Crandle and, in the several hours they had spent awaiting the tide, had drawn him into boasting and bragging, drinking little himself, but seeing that Crandle was well-served with wine from the cellar, despite his father's strictures before the unloading had begun. Crandle, when the evening had started, had been alternately amused and irritated by the big Irishman's obvious courting of his company. The man was palpably an inferior, lacking both manners and breeding, and ludicrously impressionable. He hung upon every word; Crandle was amazed at his naivety, yet flattered against his will. As the hours dragged on, and his father remained absent, closeted with the manager of Weare House, he became increasingly bored. Freed from parental restraint, his drinking increased, and with it his conceit and need of an audience ... Doonan was willing and waiting. Despite snubs and condescension he would not be shifted. His expression grew more rapt and admiring as he refilled Crandle's glass. Crandle, in turn, grew more boastful, his stories of conquests wilder and more extravagant.

'I hear that you are a great man for the ladies ...' Doonan

winked slyly at a man seated beside them, 'and those who are not ladies, too! I am sure that there is hardly a woman in the three hamlets able to resist you!'

'Hardly a woman?' smirked Crandle. 'No "hardly" about it! I tell you, truthfully, I have never, yet, failed to have my way ...'

Doonan refilled his glass, generously, and watched him drink.

'You are a man after my own heart!' applauded Doonan, 'But I tell you, in confidence, the women who send the blood hot in my veins are those fair, quiet ones ...' He winked knowingly, 'all hidden fire beneath the ice. There is an excitement about melting them, feeling them grow helpless ...'

Crandle smiled and said nothing.

'I have sometimes thought how simple it would be to subdue a woman like that,' mused Doonan, 'to slip my hands about her neck, force her to submit ...'

Something seemed to sharpen in Crandle's befuddled mind, but focussing upon Doonan's bland, ingenuous face, he relaxed, saying challengingly, 'Ah ... but have you ever killed a woman? Go on, man! Have you?'

Doonan shook his head regretfully. 'I doubt that I would have the courage. It needs a special kind of man: resolute, clever, afraid of nothing and no one. Where would you find a man like that? I ask you!'

'Here!' claimed Crandle, tugging at Doonan's arm, 'I have done it ... I swear to you upon oath! I can prove it ...'

'How?' asked Doonan, unimpressed.

'I have her clothes and belongings. There! You are beginning to believe me, to see the truth of it! I killed her upon the dunes ... just as you described it ... then dragged her to the sand, so that the tide would take her.'

'But what was she doing upon the Burrows?' persisted Doonan. 'And alone ..?'

'Not alone! She came with me, I told her that my sister was walking upon the shore, awaiting her, that we would take a boat, together, and row to the mouth of the Ogmore. A picnic, I said.' He started to laugh and splutter over his wine. 'Well?' he demanded, face flushed, and smiling still, as he thrust himself towards Doonan. 'Now do you believe me? Tell me... do you?'

'I believe you.' Doonan wanted to lift his fist and smash it into the stupefied, grinning face, with its glazed eyes, but his work was not yet done. 'And the sailor who was found upon the rocks? Was he one of us?'

Crandle tried hard to concentrate.

'Sailor?' he puzzled. 'Oh, yes. He was swept overboard from the ship. There was a swell, a high tide. The boats were filled with kegs to be taken ashore. Time was precious, and we might have been discovered. By the time we returned, with the boats emptied, he had already disappeared. It was a wild tide, and running high. He could not have long survived in that maelstrom, so near to the rocks ...'

'Creighton!' came his father's warning voice from the doorway, 'You have been drinking long enough. You will take no more! You, man, Doonan, is it? Get down to the cellar. Your help is needed with the barrels. They must be moved into the yard, to give us room.'

Joshua, lying in his sandy hollow in the dunes, thanked God for a clear, starlit night. The gibbous moon gave out a pale, gauzy light, soft with shadow, which helped concealment in the troughs and hills. Yet for those who stood watch upon the pathways and waited along the shore, its light was cruel, slashing them into silhouette. He studied the man who kept watch upon the coach-road, envying him as he paused and stretched his limbs. Joshua's own were cramped to numbness, yet he dare not risk a sound, or relax his guard.

Suddenly, along the sea-edge, there was movement and noise. The man with the lanthorn had uncovered the light. It hung for an instant, then Joshua saw Crandle bend in the saddle, and lift it high above his head, swinging it clearly from side to side to alert the crew of the *Minehead Maiden*. From the back of Weare House, he saw Creighton Crandle ride out of the stable yard, with the huge figure of Doonan running beside him, then falling back as Crandle spurred his horse to gallop the length of the shore. The moon had silvered the shallows, and Joshua saw the water break in luminous spray around the animal's hoofs. There was a confusion of noise and action as the men and horses took their positions. Then a brief silence, with the lanthorn held high and still to mark the way, and the rhythmic, unmistakable sound of oars upon water.

'Now!' thought Joshua, his heart thumping in his breast. He felt it pulsing in his veins and throat, and the sound of it filling his head, as he prepared to scramble to his feet.

The voice of Rawlings rang out clear. 'Excisemen! Halt in the name of the Queen!' He raised his pistol, and fired a shot into the air, crying out, 'Surrender or be shot!'

Joshua's men leapt from their hollows, staves raised high, yelling and screaming to divert the guards. From behind rocks and boulders the six excisemen erupted and converged upon the smugglers. Joshua sped after them, stumbling over grass and brambles, slithering in soft sand, then over the ridge of rock and pebble, determined that he would get to Creighton Crandle and drag him from his horse ... The battle moved to the water now, a clashing of sticks and bones, the thudding of blows, a confused tangle of flesh and falling bodies. One of the oarsmen from the ship already lay senseless upon the sand, feet in the shallows, as battle raged amidst the rolling, floating casks.

Joshua, seeing the towering figure of Doonan, ran to his side, only to see him try to wrench young Crandle from his mount. Crandle kicked out at him, the horse reared, hurling Doonan backwards upon the sand, and Crandle was away, spurring his horse across the bay. Doonan ran to where one of Rawling's men had unseated the elder Crandle, with a mighty blow of his stave. Doonan seemed to leap at the loose horse without putting a foot to the stirrup, and was off in pursuit across the bay.

Joshua, hearing his name shouted, turned to see Illtyd astride his pony and leading the grey. Within seconds they had joined with Doonan upon his chase. They followed the tracks of the two men along the edge of the sand towards Newton Bay, then through the soft sand into the dunes, between tufted marram grass. On and on they rode, never halting or slackening speed, the air cold upon their skin, faces pale and ghostly under the moon ... Ahead, Joshua saw the river, a silver thread, and as he neared, his mare's hoofs thundering upon the turf, he saw Crandle hurl himself into the water, urging his mount across, then dragging and cursing the animal as it slithered up the bank and on to dry land. Doonan hesitated only briefly, and flung himself after ... Joshua screamed back to Illtyd, whose pony was at his horse's heels, not to follow, the river was too deep, then launched himself off the bank into the fast-flowing race of the estuary. He felt the grey stiffen under the shock of its coldness, and the tug of the tide as the waters met ... then they were scrambling upon the mud of the bank and miraculously upon firm soil.

Now Crandle and Doonan were upon the highway, only fifty yards ahead, and Joshua called out to the grey, urging the good creature on, although its skin was lathered with foam and sweat, and its mouth flecked with saliva. Up on to the highway he followed, past the 'Pelican Inn', glancing across the river to see Illtyd safely dismounted upon the far bank. He then pointed his horse to the steep ridge on the left of the highway, its rocky outcrop making it sheer and hazardous, but the animal climbed, brave and sure-footed amidst fern and bracken, and startled sheep. Higher and higher they climbed, seeing below, the cliffs and the crumpled, silvery sea.

He did not know if Crandle and Doonan were tiring, or if fury and determination made him fleet, but he knew the gap between them was closing, and soon only twenty yards or so remained. They were reaching Dunraven now, and Joshua felt the thunder of hoofs beneath him, and the straining of the grey's muscles as it mounted the grass hillock to the top of the cliff. They skirted the castle and woodlands, galloping higher and higher upon the salt-washed turf. Doonan turned his head for an instant and Joshua, passing him, could have reached out a hand to touch Crandle as he drew abreast. For a split second it seemed that he and Doonan must head him off, forcing him to stop, then Crandle deliberately turned and looked hard into Joshua's eyes, his own triumphant, his mouth wide with laughter. Then he rode his mare straight to the edge of the cliff and over ... It seemed to Joshua that rider and mount hung suspended, black silhouettes in the moonlight, before they crashed to the rocks below.

Doonan dismounted, and without a word handed the reins of his horse to Joshua, walking to the cliff edge. He stood for a moment, unmoving, then shook his head. Joshua felt the sickness of gall burn in his throat, and did not know if the grey trembled beneath him, or if the tremor which shook his body was his own. Doonan remounted the elder Crandle's horse, and they rode slowly, and in silence, to the river where Illtyd waited upon the other shore.

When the three friends, tired and subdued in spirits, had returned to the bay, only the signs of struggle and turmoil remained; that, and the impatient, unmistakably rotund figure of the justice, the Reverend Robert Knight.

He listened in silence as Joshua related the drama of the chase, and Crandle's death.

'It was deliberate? A taking of his own life?' he asked, at length.

'Yes, I have no doubt of it.'

'May God rest his troubled spirit, and grant it peace . . .' The justice's voice was low, compassionate. 'What he did, and confessed to your man Doonan, the exciseman has already revealed. He was vicious, and pitiless.'

'A violent ending to a violent life . . .' said Joshua soberly.

'But perhaps easier for him to bear than death by another's hand . .?'

'Perhaps. Yet it is not something I will easily forget.' Joshua shook his head as if to rid himself of the memory of it. 'It seems to be burned into my mind . . . But you, sir, and the others, are unharmed? The capture went well?'

'As planned, Stradling. The cutter from the docks took the vessel in, and all the smugglers were detained. I fear that there will be a few broken skulls on both sides, and more work for the bonesetter!'

'Crandle? Was he captured?'

'Yes. Taken into custody by the excisemen, with his partner in business and crime, Stanton Gould, and Gwilliam and the others . . . Crandle will face a charge, too, concerning the girl's murder . . . but time enough for that.'

So it is all ended . . .' said Joshua, patting the grey, and feeling its coat damp beneath his hand, 'and nothing to surprise us.' He made to mount.

'Indeed there is, Stradling! The identity of the organizer ...'

'Crandle ...' said Joshua, perplexed. 'I thought you said Crandle?'

'He merely took orders; he confessed that he was financed and controlled by another.'

'Who?'

'Madeleine Mansel.'

'You have caught her, then?'

'No, she cheated us in this, as in all else.'

'So she has escaped? How, sir? By ship?'

The justice shook his head.

'I do not understand ...' confessed Joshua, bewildered.

'It was after you quitted the bay, there was a lull in the fighting. Yet all was confusion and sound, with the horses wild with the noise of the fray, and the smell of cordite upon the air ...' He stopped, unable to speak, reliving it.

'And Mrs Mansel, sir?'

'There was a sudden darkness ... the moon overshadowed by cloud. A cloaked figure rode out from the yard, brandishing a pistol, screaming aloud I know not what, possessed by some madness. It would have borne down upon Crandle, trampling him underfoot. As the horse reared above him, the exciseman, Rawlings, called out a warning to halt, or he must fire ...' He closed his eyes as if he might shut out hurt, then forced himself to continue.

'The shot rang out ... the horse, crazed with terror, veered away then ran into the waves, dragging the rider across the sand, a foot clasped tight in the stirrup. The wretched animal could not be checked, so wild was he with fear, save by the barrier of rock ... mutilating himself and her!'

'She is dead then?' Joshua's voice was low.

'I fear so ... yet, not at once. She was alive when I finally reached her, not knowing it to be a woman. Her hair had been hidden 'neath a beaver hat, but now hung loose, and she wore men's clothing. I did what little I could to bring her peace ... to grant her absolution from her sins.' His face was racked with the anguish of it.

'Did she not speak, sir?'

'She looked at me, and smiled, saying, "I admit no sins . . ." I had to bend low, for I scarce could hear her, so weak was she, but I swear she said "He is repaid . . ." Yes, that is what she said, Stradling. "He is repaid".'

'You have told Dr Mansel?' asked Joshua, wearily.

'No, I leave it to you. Her body lies here, at Weare House. I can do no more. But I shall ride, at once, to tell Crandle of the death of his son. It is not a mission I relish, or the breaking of it to his wife and daughter, but it must be told.'

He shook hands gravely with the three men, saying, 'I thank you for a night's work well done, although the tragedy and bitterness of it will linger, I fear . . .' He climbed into the saddle, looking sad and defeated.

Illtyd, Doonan, and Joshua watched him in silence as he rode away.

'I had thought it to be a great adventure,' said Doonan soberly. 'When Emrys told me, today, of Rosie and Crandle's fight at the pond . . . I thought I would kill him willingly, and with my bare fists.'

'We will go home, my friends,' said Illtyd, mounting his pony, 'and meet tomorrow, at the "Crown", for it has been a long night . . .'

Joshua, riding the grey back from Dr Mansel's house, felt a weariness of spirit, as well as body. It seemed to him that there had been three deaths that night. Crandle's, Madeleine Mansel's and, in all but flesh, that of the man she had rejected, despising his care as a weakness . . . Joshua had watched Mansel disintegrate before his eyes, hunched, formless face ravaged by weeping. He did not know whether the grief was for his wife, the manner of her dying, or for the wasteland of their past. He had neither love nor memory to sustain him.

'Did she speak, Stradling? Did she leave any word for me?'

'I know, sir, that the justice gave her absolution . . .' said Joshua carefully.

'She was at peace, then?'

'Yes, you may be assured of that, sir.'

'I am glad ... You are young, Stradling, but you will find that we are bound together by what is past, and shared. It does not matter what binds us: pity, duty, fear, even love ... We can never be free.'

As he descended the Clevis Hill, Joshua was thinking of Rebecca, and his longing for her, and his sense of loss was a physical ache within him. 'You are a damned, insensitive fool!' he berated himself. 'She wanted to return. She humbled herself ... told you of her love for you, and you rejected it, cruelly. Dear God! Why is it that the words we use are a shield to hide our feelings, and protect us from the wounds that others inflict upon us? If we had met honestly, without defences, I would have said, "I love you, Rebecca. I shall love you all the days of my life. Parting cannot alter or lessen it. I will wait ... I will gladly wait ... for without you I am nothing".'

As he approached his cottage, after stabling the grey, Jeremiah came out of the shadows, with Charity the dog.

'We have come to keep you company, if you will have us ...' he said, 'although you have but to say the word, and we will go away.'

'No, I am glad to see you.' Joshua opened the door and they went inside. 'It has been a long day, Jeremiah, and a longer night ... You saw Rebecca leave?'

'Aye. A good little maid ... a wise head on young shoulders.'

'She will not return.'

'I cannot believe that. It is hard for me to find the words to say what I feel, for I am not clever. It is like a wild bird, or coney ... or an abandoned cub. They have to learn to trust ... But you must never make them dependent upon you, for then you kill that which you admired most in them. Move slowly, and one day, when you least expect it, she will come to you trustingly, of her own free will ...'

'I do not know,' cried Joshua, helplessly. 'There are so many places to see, so many things to do, so many other men who will find her beautiful. Men eager to love her: richer, more articulate, with more to offer than a village constable. I do not know ...'

Jeremiah placed his hand firmly upon his friend's arm.

'Believe me, I know,' Jeremiah said stoutly, his voice emphatic, for in truth, like Joshua, he too was afraid.